By J. J. McAvoy

Standalone Novels
Sugar Baby Beautiful
That Thing Between Eli and Gwen
Malachi and I
Never Let Me Go

The Du Bells
Aphrodite and the Duke
Verity and the Forbidden Suitor

The Prince's Bride
The Prince's Bride: Part 1
The Prince's Bride: Part 2
*The Prince's Bride: Beginning
Forever*

Ruthless People
Ruthless People
The Untouchables
American Savages
A Bloody Kingdom
Prequel: Declan + Coraline

Children of Vice
Children of Vice
Children of Ambition
Children of Redemption
Vicious Minds

Black Rainbow
Black Rainbow
Rainbows Ever After

A Vampire's Romance
My Midnight Moonlight Valentine
My Sunrise Sunset Paramour

Child Star
Child Star: Part 1
Child Star: Part 2
Child Star: Part 3

Verity

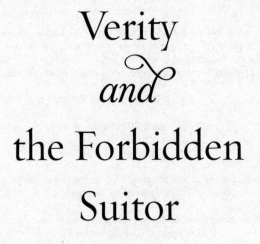

and

the Forbidden Suitor

A Novel

J. J. McAvoy

Dell | New York

A Dell Trade Paperback Original

Copyright © 2023 by J. J. McAvoy

Published in the United States by Dell, an imprint of Random House, a division of Penguin Random House LLC, New York.

DELL is a registered trademark and the D colophon is a trademark of Penguin Random House LLC.

LIBRARY OF CONGRESS CATALOGING-IN-PUBLICATION DATA

Names: McAvoy, J. J., author.
Title: Verity and the forbidden suitor: a novel / J. J. McAvoy.
Description: New York: Dell Books, [2023]
Identifiers: LCCN 2022041961 (print) | LCCN 2022041962 (ebook) | ISBN 9780593500064 (trade paperback) | ISBN 9780593500071 (ebook)
Classification: LCC PR9199.4.M386 V47 2022 (print) | LCC PR9199.4.M386 (ebook) | DDC 892.8—dc23/eng/20220909
LC record available at https://lccn.loc.gov/2022041961
LC ebook record available at https://lccn.loc.gov/2022041962

Printed in the United States of America on acid-free paper

randomhousebooks.com

2 4 6 8 9 7 5 3 1

Book design by Virginia Norey
Title and part-title art: mozZz/stock.adobe.com

Dedicated to
the people like me
who sometimes doubt
they are deserving of
a happily ever after.
You are.

Beloved Reader,

This is still *a Regency romance involving nobility and high society, in which there are Black people. This is fiction, and anything is possible here. I truly hope you enjoy it.*

Sincerely,
Your Author

PART ONE

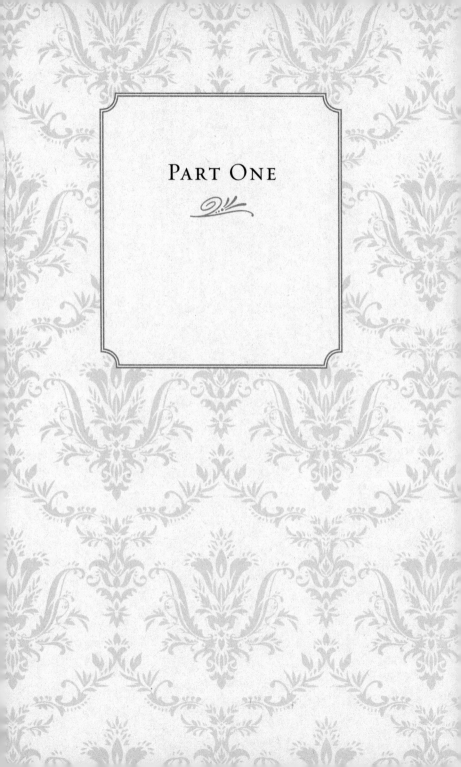

I

Verity

I am not a Du Bell.

But oh, how I longed to be. Not for title or wealth, nor even prestige and influence, as my family name, Eagleman, held all the same to even greater extents as a dukedom. With the exception of being a princess, there is no higher birth a girl could have than my own. And I was very much aware of the many who envied my life. Despite the many scandals of my household—my father's affairs and illegitimate son, my mother's misery and then death, followed by my father's wholly inappropriate marriage to my stepmother, a butcher's daughter; not to mention Evander, my elder brother, and his own marriage mishaps—there was no shortage of people asserting how fortunate I was to be born Lady Verity Eagleman. But given the choice, I would have preferred to be born Lady Verity Du Bell. To be born into a home filled with warmth, laughter, and teasing. A home filled to the brim with overwhelming love.

Instead, love seemed to always evade me. As though it had some personal vendetta against me. Evander was the godson of the Marchioness of Monthermer, Lady Deanna Du Bell, and as such was afforded many opportunities to experience such tender emotions with the family. I, on the other hand, was kept away from them and society at the behest of my father. By the time he passed, Evander had made a mess of our connection with the Du Bells, and, consequently, no other chances presented themselves.

Now, as I watched the candlelight of my brother's carriage fade into the darkness, taking him and his perfect new wife, Lady Aphrodite, to their long-awaited happily ever after, the opportunity had arrived, only I knew not how to stand before this family or society at all.

I was alone.

The name *Verity* means *truth*, and yet I felt as if I were nothing but a lie. In front of most people, I sought to appear confident, self-reliant, but the truth is I was afeard . . . of so much.

"I cannot believe it is done," said the marquess to his wife, whom he held openly within his arms, as we all stood before the gates of their London estate.

"After all these years, you still underestimate me, my dear?" the marchioness replied with her head held high, appearing pleased with herself.

The marquess was a man of white skin and golden hair that was nearly all gray now, with sharp blue eyes that always seemed focused upon either his family or a book. His wife was the opposite of him, with rich brown skin deeper in shading than my own and curly brown hair that she kept pinned up neatly. Rather than books, her brown eyes read people with frightening accuracy.

"Underestimate? Never. Stand in awe of your power? Always. Well done, my dear." He squeezed her arm slightly, making her laugh while their eldest son groaned.

Damon Du Bell, the Earl of Montagu, also stood beside his wife, Silva, whose face was a bit round with a nose a bit short, but her demeanor was pleasant. They were locked, arm in arm, very much a parallel set to his parents. The look on Damon's face showed he was not keen on the elder couple's public display of affection, even as he mimicked them.

"One would think that you would have some restraint at your ages," Damon said to them as though he were the parent.

"Dear," Silva muttered in apprehension.

"You should thank heaven we do not, or you would not exist," his father replied, making the marchioness's eyes widen.

"Charles!"

"Father!"

"What are you all talking about?" questioned the youngest Du Bell, Abena, her little face bunched in confusion. Alongside her were two of her sisters, Hathor and Devana, and her brother Hector.

"Nothing!" said the marchioness and her eldest son in unison.

"That does not seem like nothing," Abena pressed, frowning. "Are you keeping a secret?"

"Yes, they are," said Hathor, the second Du Bell daughter, causing Abena to look to her for an answer. "Mama and Papa were thinking of sending you off to a professional pot washer, seeing as how you've become so good at it of late."

Hector and Devana giggled and then laughed outright as Abena looked at her parents in horror.

"No, Papa!" Abena ran to her father, holding on to his waist for dear life, which made the marquess bend to her level and hug her.

"She is merely teasing you," he comforted her.

But at that moment, it was I who felt pain.

What must it have been like to hug one's father, one's own mother even?

I did not know.

I stood before one of the most prominent and amiable families in all the ton, one I had always wished to be a part of, yet now I desperately desired to escape their blissful company. The irony.

"Verity, my dear, are you well?" the marchioness asked, stepping away slightly from her husband toward me.

No, I am not well. How are you all so happy? These were my true thoughts. Instead of speaking them, I quickly presented my best smile and said, "I am afraid not, Marchioness, as your daughter has stolen away my brother."

Humor is always a good way to deflect from one's self.

"Ha! I beg to differ. For it is your brother who has stolen away our daughter!" the marquess declared with a hearty laugh, Abena still at his side.

"Father, someone cannot steal someone whom you have formally given away." Hathor rolled her eyes and pointed back to the house behind her. "Especially in such a grand fashion as this."

"Hathor, it is called a joke," Damon replied.

"Let us agree to call it the past, as in finished. As in, can we all retire for the evening so we may start afresh tomorrow? Hopefully with a new main character." Hathor didn't even wait, already turning to walk through the gate before anyone else.

"I pick Verity to go next!" Abena yelled, purposely running right by her sister's skirts, causing Hathor to nearly stumble.

"Abena!" Hathor hollered, steadying herself.

The small girl spun around, grinning. "She is much more handsome, and she's a duke's daughter! Everyone will be engaged this season before you!"

"To the pots with you!" Hathor dashed after her into the house.

"Only Mama can do that!" I heard her little voice yell back.

"Where do they find this energy?" The marquess snickered and then looked over to his wife. "Ah, never mind. I have found the source."

Damon, his wife, and the rest of his siblings all laughed. The marchioness managed only to shoot him a glare, detaching herself from his side entirely and walking over to me.

"Since you all wish to join your father in teasing me, I shall focus on this good child." She met my gaze and smiled from ear to ear, taking my hand. "Oh, how happy I am to finally have you stay with us, Verity."

"Thank you once again for having me, your ladyship—"

"Have I not told you that you may call me Godmother? I shall accept only that title. Now come, let me show you to your rooms," she said as she led me back into the house, where the splendor of my brother's wedding feast was slowly being dismantled by the servants.

"Ingrid," the marchioness called out, and immediately, a slender older woman with a white streak of hair amidst all her pinned-up dark hair arrived at her side, curtsying before her. I found it strange that a lady would ever call any servant by anything but their surname, but no one else seemed to be concerned. "Do tell the servants they may leave the cleaning up until the morning—"

"And they may have the last barrel of wine!" The marquess's voice boomed from behind us. Only now that we were inside could I see the redness of his cheeks more clearly. He was drunk. And I noticed that with a simple glance from the marchioness his valet was already beside him, leading him elsewhere.

"Ingrid, tell the servants they may take remainders of whatever they like," she spoke to the housekeeper. "They all did so splendidly. I shall come down and thank them personally later."

"Yes, madam." Ingrid curtsied again before going.

"You will thank the servants *personally*?" The question came from me before I even realized, but only because I was so surprised. The thought of the marchioness or any noble lady going to thank the servants in their quarters seemed . . . abnormal. My governess lectured me nearly to deafness over my many trips to the servants' hall or my escapes on my own throughout the grounds.

She glanced over at me, a bit saddened. "You do not think it is proper?"

"No, of course not. I mean, no, I do not think it is improper. My former governess would disagree, but she was very strict, though not unkind. I was very well taken care of. Just—oh, forgive me. I am a bit caper-witted all of a sudden." I had apparently lost all control of my speech. Who was I to judge the way a lady ran her household, least of all the woman renowned for having the best-run home in the ton?

I thought she might be cross, but she merely giggled as she walked up the stairs with me. "You need not be so nervous, my dear, nor do you need to be so rigid. This home is your home."

It very much was not my home. It was far too loud to be my home.

As if to prove my point, we both heard a loud crash above us.

"*Ouch!*" First came Hathor's voice, then came a blur of curly hair as Abena sought to run back down the stairs toward us.

The girl's small brown eyes widened in terror at the sight of her mother. "It was not my fault, Mama! Hathor is just cow-handed and you know it!"

"Who are you calling cow-handed?" Hathor's head poked out from over the rails, looking down at us.

"It seems you both desire nothing more than to cut up my peace, so shall I return the favor?" the marchioness asked calmly.

"Good night, Mama!" Hathor and Abena said in unison.

As Abena rushed back up the stairs, I couldn't help but giggle.

"Pay them both no mind. They are grieving." She smirked, shaking her head as we reached the hall.

"Grieving? What for?"

"The loss of their sister," the marchioness replied, opening the door to my room. "I should not say *loss* but the marriage of their sister. Hathor and Abena both love Aphrodite greatly and will miss her even more so. Since they cannot be sad at her marrying, they merely redirect their thoughts and energy."

"I can imagine that being the case for Abena given her age, but Hathor?" I thought it very obvious she envied her elder sister. It was at least something I found relatable.

"Do not let Hathor's sharp tongue and theatrics fool you. She is very much soft of heart," she replied as she moved to close the curtains, again something I thought strange for a lady to do. "Now, on to you. This was Aphrodite's room. The servants have already brought up most of your things. But should you need anything more, merely say it and I shall see it done."

"Your lady—Godmother," I corrected myself upon seeing the look on her face. "You have done more than enough for me already."

"I have barely even scratched the surface, my dear," she stated, frowning and leading me to the bench before the bed. "Verity . . . I tell you to call me Godmother, not simply because of your brother but because I am sure that is what your mother would have wanted."

Had my mother lived long enough to declare her such, she meant. But my mother did not even live five minutes after my birth, I was told. The thought of it all made my throat ache, but I did not want to look woeful before the marchioness, so I simply nodded.

She took my hands into hers.

"You may never have known her, Verity, but trust me when I tell you that she loved you ferociously. She wished you to be brought up kindly and protected at all costs. Watching over you and your brother were the only things she desired of me, and I fear I have failed you—"

"You have not," I replied. "You have saved me from much pain in the past. I am grateful. I am well now, and that is all that matters. You need not worry yourself over me, truly."

"You are well. But are you happy?" she asked suddenly and I paused, one part stunned the other part concerned about what she saw in me. I did not want her to perceive me to be the same pitiful little girl she had rescued all those years ago.

I quickly fixed my lips to give her a wide smile. "Of course! My brother has gotten married! And to the woman he's always loved, no less. Who would not be happy at such a blessed event?"

She opened her mouth to speak, then closed it once more and offered a gentle smile, placing her hand on my cheek before nodding. "I cannot wait to see whom it will be that stirs your heart as well."

I laughed. "I wouldn't give it much thought, Mar— Godmother."

"Oh dear, not one of you seeks to give me respite. First Aphrodite, now you." She sighed deeply. "Whatever do you all believe the purpose of presenting yourselves to society is for if not to secure an advantageous marriage?"

"Are you not tired of weddings, Godmother? You have had two within the year."

"Quite the opposite in fact, I am invigorated for both you and Hathor."

"Truly, there is no need!" I could feel my heart beginning to race at the thought.

"There is every need, my dear, *every need*, and I shall hear nothing more to the contrary. Now I shall leave you to rest. Sleep is a lady's secret weapon. Good night."

"Yes, Godmother. Good night."

She gave my hand a tender squeeze before rising and walking to the door, taking her leave.

I fell back onto the bed, stretching out and rolling onto my side to calm the panic in me. What on earth did she have mind to do?

It was true, securing a good marriage was the reason at the very core of the season. But it was not my purpose. I came merely to aid my brother.

Whom could I marry anyway? The thought of one of those stuffy and pretentious young lords as my husband reminded me of my father in the worst way.

No. I could not live my life in such a manner again.

Glancing at a trunk across the room, I realized none would have me anyway if they knew the truth. Pushing myself off the bed, I walked over and knelt before it as I opened the lid. I had to dig to the bottom before I finally came to the small jewelry box.

Just as I was about to open it, there was a knock at the door.

"My lady?"

Quickly, I placed the jewelry box back under my clothing, shut the trunk lid, and rose to my feet. "Yes, come in."

A young, freckle-faced maid with red hair and light skin entered with a wash basin and towel in hand, curtsying to me. Evander had told me to bring my own maid, but I'd refused, thinking he was being fussy over me as always. Now I regretted it.

"Good evening, my lady. I am to assist you while you are here," she said as she placed the water basin on the nightstand.

"It is not necessary. I can do well enough on my own to-night," I replied, walking to the bed.

"Are you sure, my lady? I could help you get your night-gown," she said, walking toward my trunk.

"*No!*" My voice was far too loud, and she jumped slightly before freezing. The look she gave me was one of panic. Quickly, I said, "I mean . . . it really is fine. I enjoy being self-reliant."

She only nodded. "And the candles, my lady? Her ladyship said I am to replace them with new ones to last the night."

I did my best not to bite my lip.

"Do the Du Bells normally keep candles burning through the night?"

"No, not in their rooms, my lady."

"Then neither shall I. Thank you. You may go."

She nodded once more and offered a curtsy before leaving the room. Only when the maid was gone did I let out the breath I was holding. It made me bitterly laugh at myself and how pitiful I was.

Holding the candle, I moved back to my trunk and took out both the jewelry box and my journal before walking to the desk to write.

May 9, 1813

Evander, my dear brother,
Is now with his lover.
It was a wonder to see
And yet the emotion was not meant for me.
There is a difference between him and me.
He a child of July, and I of December.
One raised by our mother and the other by our father.

The season began in the spring, and I am forever
in winter.
What heart could bear my freezing?
I dare not ponder.

Setting down my pen and closing my journal, I opened the small box, lifted the vial to my lips, and drank before blowing out all the candles.

2

Verity

"Verity."

"Verity!"

My eyes snapped open to see the marchioness staring down at me in panic. She sat at my bedside, still dressed in her white sleeping gown and a violet-colored robe with her initials embroidered on the chest, her hair still within her similarly colored silk bonnet.

"Are you well?" she asked me, placing her hand on my forehead. I was unsure what had happened but prayed it was not what I thought it could be. Sadly, those prayers were unanswered, as she went on to say, "You were crying out in your sleep, my dear. Did you have a night terror?"

Shame, frustration, and anger rushed through me as I sat up in bed. Why? Why did this happen? I had taken the tonic, a whole vial of it, in hopes of not causing a disturbance. What should I do? Smile and laugh it away? No, she would know something was amiss.

"Verity?" she called again gently. "Do—"

"Forgive me, Godmother. I did not mean to wake you. I haven't a clue what happened. I cannot remember," I replied, gripping my hands. It was not a complete and utter lie. I could never remember my dreams, and I did not care to. I merely sought to make it through the night without incident.

"It must be the new room," the marchioness said with certainty and then looked about the quarters as the morning rays of light began to peek through the curtains. "I instructed the maids to keep it well lit for you, but it seems they did not do so."

I did not wish anyone to be punished on my account.

"It is my error, Godmother, as I told them not to. My brother says it's quite unsafe to keep candles burning through the night. A tenant on our estate lost his house and nearly his wife one summer in Everely over a single candle. Can you imagine?" I forced out a nervous laugh, and again her brown eyes focused upon me. I felt like retreating under their weight. "Thank you for your care, but I am quite well. Forgive me again for startling you this morning."

"I am the mother of six children, so there is nothing short of the second coming of Christ that could startle me, my dear. I am pleased you are well," she replied as she rose from my bedside. "Breakfast shall be served in your rooms, I wish to give everyone enough time to recover from the festivities yesterday before we attend the private concert at the Rowleys' this evening."

"Thank you. I shall be ready." I nodded to her.

"I will call for Bernice to tend to you." She left me no room to refuse, as she was already at the door.

I waited until she was gone before falling back upon the bed, raising the sheets over my face. How mortifying and obnoxious, my first night here and I had already caused the marchioness concern!

Please, please, on all that is holy, I prayed that only she was aware of this. The last thing I wished was for my troubles to become an open secret among the house like it had in Everely. The more I thought of it, the more I groaned as I rolled on the bed.

"What in heaven's name are you doing?"

Immediately, I sat up and ripped the sheets from my head

to find Hathor at the door, still dressed in her nightgown with a lavender shawl draped around her, looking back at me.

"Nothing," I calmly replied as I released my grip upon the sheets. "May I ask why you've entered my room unannounced?"

"It is technically my room," she stated as she moved to the mahogany dressing table, the pulls of which were made of gold leaves to match the casing of the three golden mirrors—so one could see themselves at every angle. A quick moment of terror rushed through me as I remembered my journal and the box. But luckily, I had returned them both to the depths of my trunk.

"I thought this room belonged to Aphrodite," I said as I brought my feet down into my slippers and glanced back at the door she'd entered.

"It did. When she was merely my sister, but now she is the *Duchess of Everely* and has a great many other rooms she may call her own and, thus, can bequeath me this one. So, I would greatly appreciate it if you did not ruin the bedding."

I cautiously narrowed my eyes, as I was unsure if she sought conflict this morning. But it would not have surprised me. I knew few young noble ladies, but it was clear they did not like me. Not truly. Everyone told me it was envy, but still, it was tiring to negotiate between their pleasantries and their apparent venom.

"You are quite slow," she stated, frowning.

I scoffed in anger. "I beg your pardon?"

"Your responses. They leave much to be desired," she answered as she turned to look at the vanity, inspecting the creams there. "We Du Bells are a sharp-witted family. You must have a clever rejoinder for any perceived slight, or you shall make things uncomfortable."

"Sharp-witted or odd?" I spat out without thinking and immediately thought to apologize when I heard her giggle.

"Both," she replied as she began to sniff one of my creams. "Do not worry. You shall get used to it."

I was usually sharp-witted, at least with those I was close to, so mostly just Evander. "Will I also need to become accustomed to you entering my rooms in the morning?"

"Only if I come to like you. I have not yet decided."

"Then what brings you here now?"

"That reply was not nearly witty enough. You will need to work on that, I see," she replied, lifting another jar.

Again I scoffed. Who did she think I was?

"I did not realize it was my duty to keep you entertained."

"Much better." She smiled and glanced back over her shoulder at me. "And yes, it is both of our duties to keep each other entertained."

"Why?"

"Did you forget your purpose in coming to London?"

Again with this? Had her mother sent her?

Hathor sighed dramatically when I did not reply. "The season, Verity. We must find good husbands. There are still many weeks to go, which means you and I shall be spending a great deal of time together, and as such, I thought it only correct that you and I establish a footing this morning. Good conversation provides a good footing."

"You being here, in my rooms, at first light, is for us to plot how to secure a husband?"

Hathor frowned, her head tilting to the side. "What else is there for young ladies to plot?"

"I know not but hope our lives or, at the very least, our mornings do not revolve around such."

"What else are we meant to speak of? Sausage and eggs?"

I laughed. However, seeing her expression sour, I sought to compose myself.

"Fine. Forgive me for laughing. I rarely speak of such things as husbands or the like." Within the span of hours I had already had the conversation twice.

"Of course not. Your mama is not here to press you." She said it without thought, and I watched her eyes widen, but truly, I was not bothered, as she clearly meant it without malice. "I am—"

"That is the danger of being sharp-witted," I interrupted before she could apologize. "There is a tendency to speak without thought."

"I am sorry. That was impolite of me," she replied. For the first time, her whole body shrank back.

Rising, I moved to sit on the bench at the end of the bed, closer to her. "You are forgiven. Now, what is it you wish to plot?"

Immediately, she brightened, and I could see I would like her, as she so clearly wore her expressions and feelings for all to see.

"I have already spoken to my mama, and we will be going to every remaining event of the season, where you and I shall enchant the last two dukes left in town."

That was far too simple to be called a plot.

"How will we do that?"

"With our female charms."

She could not be serious. "Is that not what all young ladies do? What charms do we have that they do not?"

"Reputable family, title, wit, and beauty. The two of us together will surely gather attention, and many will also come to congratulate and inquire about the union of our siblings. I expect no less than an unyielding two weeks of everyone's full attention should we play our parts correctly. Along with my mother's efforts, that will leave us the toast of the ton."

"You do not think yourself a bit naïve in your efforts?"

"Not at all."

Such confidence . . . From where did all of their family find it? Feeling the need to tease her, I asked, "Are you not worried my beauty will outshine yours?"

"You're not half as pretty as Aphrodite. If I can withstand her, you are not of any concern. But thankfully, you are still above measure and, thus, will not hinder me either."

Was that an insult? I felt as though I had to keep a sword in one hand and a shield in the other just to endure a conversation with her. But it was much more engaging speaking to her than to the other ladies I had met. She was at the very least upfront with her thoughts and feelings. "Hathor, while this has been all very entertaining, I should tell you honestly that I have no desire to wed anyone, least of all a duke. I came to London for my brother's sake, and now—"

"And now, what? You shall languish in pretty gowns at the estates of others all your days?" she asked, eyebrow raised. "What do you desire if it is not to be wed?"

I did not know. "Surely ladies such as ourselves can aspire to something else."

"What is *else*? Your brother's life has been set, Verity. You must now see to yours. And there is no greater priority than securing a husband. Aphrodite, in a sense, is now all but the ruler of Everely, and while it will forever be your home, it is not your place. When you return, I doubt it will be the same as you left it. Which is why you must make a home for yourself." She looked upon me, baffled. "Have you truly put no thought into the trajectory of your life?"

"I have!" I sought to defend myself. I was quite unprepared for this but I would not back down. "Are you aware of what marriage truly is?"

She frowned, not understanding. "A union between two people—"

"No. It is a contract between a man and his property. We are the property. And I simply do not wish to be married off to some nobleman solely interested in me for my dowry and family connections."

"Very well, then marry a nobleman for love." She said it as though it were the simplest thing in the world.

I soured at her, now slightly annoyed. "You might not know this, given your family's abundant success in this matter, but love matches are rare for ladies like us, Hathor. How could they not be? We are presented to society and then over the course of a few introductions, balls, and walks are meant to trust we shall be loved? Noblemen will say anything to secure what they wish."

"And how do you know this? How many men have you known to make you such an expert?"

My hands tensed. Perhaps I did not, I did not know many men, but I had seen much of their ways through my father. "I merely mean that marriage can often be dangerous to women and you ought not see it as some fairy tale."

"Your view of men is rather villainous." She frowned as she looked me over. "But your view of me is rather unpleasant."

This may have been why other ladies disliked me, so I quickly added, "I do not mean to offend you—"

"You have not," she said calmly, which was rather perplexing coming from her. "I do not believe you are altogether wrong, Verity. I am not ignorant of the many women who have suffered in some way. However, my mama has always told me a *good* marriage is the greatest of all blessings. And I believe her, as she has proven it by example."

"Again, I do not doubt it. But how does one achieve it?"

"As with all things I can only assume it is through effort," she said. "If the idea of marriage alone does not inspire you to apply such effort then maybe you, like Aphrodite, can be moved by only one man."

"Who?"

"How am I supposed to know that? You only get that answer by accepting the introductions, balls, and walks." She grinned, rising to her feet as she clasped her hands together. "So, now our footing has been set. You and I will go to every possible event of the season to find our husbands."

Why did I feel as though I had walked in a circle?

"How is this any different from where you started the conversation?" I asked her.

"It is very different, how we both have greater direction going forward. You do not seem to care for title or status at all so you may look at whoever *makes your breath catch*, as Mama says. I shall do the same but with a duke. Our first opportunity comes this evening at the concert." She made not an ounce of sense but was clearly proud of this non-plotted plot.

I could only shake my head at her.

Knock. Knock.

"Enter," Hathor said before I could. The same freckle-faced maid from the night prior entered, basin of hot water in her hands and towels over her arm and another maid behind her with breakfast.

"Good morning, my ladies." Bernice and the other maid curtsied to us.

"Good morning, Bernice," Hathor said to her before she focused on me. "I shall leave. I must try on dresses for tonight. Please prepare yourself, for I shall not slow down for your sake."

With that, she left, with just as much ease as she came, leaving me a bit stunned as to what I had experienced.

"Is she always like that?" I asked the maid as she set the basin upon the vanity.

"Like what?"

That was answer enough.

"Lady Hathor, she is rather . . . unrelenting."

"Yes, my lady, she is," she said with a pleasant smile. I thought myself very good at reading people, and I had read Hathor to be rather spoiled, envious, and silly—like most young ladies. I did not think she had much depth to her. However, upon finally speaking to her like this, I realized she was a lot more . . . substantive than I had given her credit for.

"My lady?" Bernice called once more to get my attention.

Meeting her gaze, I nodded, moving to sit at the vanity. I wished to ask her more about not just Hathor but everyone in the family. I wished to know what they were truly like before I faced them for the day's events. But I remembered what my governess had taught me: Servants serve, not advise. So, I simply outstretched my hand for the towel she held and said nothing more.

Getting ready took much longer than I had expected because of my conversation with Hathor. It was not as if Evander had not brought up the topic of marriage once or twice before, but it was quite easy to deflect that conversation with him. A simple mention of his great love or a line of wit and his focus was elsewhere. That left me free to go about my day, which mainly consisted of watching over him and his daughter, Emeline, or writing letters to my younger half brother, Gabrien. However, as Hathor said, it was now Aphrodite's duty to see to my brother's affairs. And I could not possibly spend the rest of my life simply writing letters to Gabrien, who would eventually return home if only to beg me to cease.

So that left me with nothing else to do except to get married. But watching as Bernice brought out dresses for me to choose from, worrying if she'd reach my box or see my journal, I could not imagine such a life. Any efforts to do so made chills move up my arms and into my shoulders. Clearly, that was not a path for me. I doubted any man could change my mind simply by making my breath catch.

What did that mean anyway? That at the mere sight of *my one true love* I would forget to breathe? That was hardly a fairy tale. I thought back on all of the men I knew, unrelated to me of course, not one had ever stirred any emotion at all in me—

"You are keeping me, my lady."

I coughed as the tea I was drinking entered my throat wrong.

"Are you all right, my lady?" Bernice asked, turning back to me.

"Yes, fine, that dress, fine," I muttered, pointing randomly. Why had I thought that? *"You are keeping me, my lady."* It was what that physician . . . Dr. Darrington, had said to me before ever so rudely shutting the door in my face, within my own home, as he sought to treat my brother for an injury. A frown came to my lips as I thought of him.

I sat corrected: Most men stirred no emotion from me at all . . . with the exception of him. Most gentlemen were at least cordial, never mind their true intention, when in my presence. However, this doctor seemed almost distressed by me. How fortunate I had not seen him again or I would have remarked on his poor behavior.

"Shall we start on your hair, my lady?" Bernice asked me.

"Yes, please." I nodded, pushing him from my mind. I had more pressing things to worry about, like how I was going to survive this outing in society.

I did not care from whom it came, I would reject every advance made my way.

3

Verity

"Let us hope the poor girl has recovered," Hathor said, looking out the window of our carriage as it approached the brick townhouse covered in wisteria at the near end of the city.

"Which girl?" Damon questioned across from her. Beside him, as always, was his wife, Silva, both of them dressed in complementary burgundy and yellow colors. Although Silva seemed a bit concerned that the color was bright for her and drew too much attention, especially with the diamonds around her neck. But the marchioness had insisted she wear it. Everyone had to be done up as if we were going to the palace.

"Lady Clementina Rowley," Hathor replied, turning her attention back to us. "Her presentation to the queen was horrid and was all anyone could speak of."

My presentation had been immediately after hers, so I was just behind the doors and heard the queen question if the young lady had been stretched due to her long neck and considerable height. I also saw how the other young ladies behind me fought back fits of laughter. At the time, I was too concerned over my own issue, my stepmother, who had forced her way into being there, embarrassing me, to think of Lady Clementina.

"That was weeks ago," Silva said with a frown. "Surely, the talk of the ton has progressed."

"Of course the talk has progressed, as she has been absent from society since. She did not even come to our ball," Hathor reminded us.

"I am quite sure I saw Her Grace, the Duchess of Imbert, in attendance at your ball," I said, remembering the short but very proud woman wearing a sapphire tiara and matching gown with several bows at the bodice, whom the marchioness introduced to me that evening. "And she had her daughter with her."

"She brought only one daughter, Domenica. She is the one who married the Earl of Casterbridge a few years ago," Hathor answered, adjusting her dress as she turned to look at me. "Clementina was not there. This whole season, I've seen her only twice: once at the palace and then a few days later in the park, where she was still the topic of mockery. She left in tears, and since then, not a word about her."

"It is not like you to be so concerned about the problems of another," Damon replied, and even in the slight darkness, I could see his eyebrows rise. "If you are motivated to ask, you must fear for yourself somehow. Out with it."

Hathor rolled her eyes. "You believe me to be so self-centered?"

"Yes," Damon and I said in unison, causing her to scoff. Though I spoke in jest, Damon looked at me and nodded approvingly.

"Silva?" Hathor looked to the blonde woman across from me, hoping for an ally. Silva merely smiled back but did not answer, to her husband's amusement. "Very well, since you all have such little faith in me, I shall be the villain you wish and tell you I am concerned because I do not wish for tonight's attention to be focused on her absence."

"The truth at last." Damon snickered as he shook his head at her. "Sister, your mind sincerely amazes me."

Hathor quickly and childishly made a face at him, which reminded me in that moment of Abena, before turning back to the window as we arrived at the lavender-covered building. There were several other carriages already parked and being attended to. The one before our own held the marquess and marchioness. I watched as both Hathor and Silva readjusted their gloves, jewels, and dresses before the doors opened for us.

Damon exited first, placing his hat on before outstretching his hand to aid Silva to the ground, then Hathor, and finally myself. From the outside, it felt more like a ball than a mere concert, with the elaborately sculpted hedges, finely dressed coachmen marching about like royal guards, the hundreds of candles, and the large number of attendees.

"I am much obliged to your mother for insisting I dress so finely," Silva whispered to her husband as we took in the splendor. Even Damon looked a bit taken aback by it all, and we had yet to enter, as there was a queue.

"This is what is expected of a duchess," Hathor said to us all with her head held high, as though she were one. "Aphrodite should have waited a day so she could see her competition now."

"The Duchess of Imbert is far too old to be my daughter's competition," said the marchioness as they came to us. She was dressed in wine-colored silks while her husband had worn a simple black. "And you should be less concerned with your sister's rivals and more focused on your own. As you see, there are a great many ladies here this evening."

"They worry me not, Mama, as I am well aware of their capabilities." Hathor smiled, adding, *"If you know the enemy and know yourself, you need not fear the result of a hundred battles."*

"Sun Tzu?" Her father grinned, nodding. "Well done, my

girl. I did not know you had even begun the Eastern philoso-
phies."

"Everyone really ought to stop underestimating me." She
beamed with pride.

"She has barely even read the Greeks let alone the Far East.
It was Aphrodite who once said that to her," Damon interjected, making her turn to glare at her brother.

And just like that, they were all engaged in familial banter
once more. They slipped into conversations with such ease
and intimacy that even while in the room with them, I felt as
though I were nothing more than a secondary character
watching them live out their lives before me. I had never experienced a morning like I had today—the laughter, the teasing, and the open dialogue. Even the marquess was always
engaged, just pretending to be seriously preoccupied with his
paper.

I could not keep up then, and I felt myself slipping from
them even now. The feeling was exacerbated as we entered
the house. All around us, I heard people talking.

"Lord Monthermer. Lady Monthermer."

"Marquess. Marchioness."

"Good evening, Damon. My lady."

"Hello, Hathor!"

There was a choir of greetings from everyone and anyone
who saw them as we walked farther in. All the world was gracious and jubilant at the sight of the Du Bells, while I was
given courteous nods and ceremonial smiles. I was not unknown, and I was not out of place. This was my society. I was
simply distanced from it, as I had not been afforded the opportunities to intermingle with them throughout my life. Cre-
ating those opportunities was the task of a mother. This had
never bothered or upset me because I was never around them
as much before. And if I was, my brother was never more

than an arm's reach away. He was my shield. Without him here to distract me, I wished to leave—immediately. I glanced back at the entrance as it grew farther and farther away, and more people arrived.

But the night had only just begun. As if she could hear my thoughts, Hathor took hold of my arm and linked hers with mine.

"Mama, we shall go say hello to the other young ladies," she said to her mother, who nodded but gave her a sharp look, as well.

"Do manage to keep the air in your lungs so you do not faint, my dear."

Damon snickered, but I was not sure why.

"Of course." Hathor smiled at her and then pulled me away as her smile dropped slightly. "Have you seen anyone you like?"

"Like?" I repeated as we ambled about the room. "Hathor, we have only just arrived."

"There were at least a dozen eligible gentlemen between here and the entrance alone. You did not notice?"

"Not in the slightest."

She sighed heavily. "Effort, remember?"

"I am looking as intensely as I can and my breath still remains in my body," I jested in response.

"Hathor! Verity!"

We turned to see three young women, dressed in red, white, and a soft purple-blue, all with light-brown hair and green eyes. They had called my name, without title, as though we were close friends. However, I did not recall them.

"Oh no, not the garden sisters," Hathor muttered.

"Garden sisters?" I asked as we were already walking toward them.

"They aren't actually sisters, but cousins. However, that is not the point. The point is they will hold us in the most incommodious of conversations all night, so let us simply say hello and move on quickly," she directed, plastering a large smile on her face as we reached them. "Poppy, Lily, Iris, good evening. How are you?"

Poppy, Lily, Iris. I tried not to laugh as I understood now how they had gotten their collective nickname.

"As excellent as one can be. Congratulations to both of your families. The wedding was splendid. It was all my mama could talk about this morning," said the one dressed in red, who I assumed was Poppy.

"And mine," said Iris, I believe. Once again, I had no way of truly knowing, as they had not introduced themselves, which made me wonder if they had before and I had merely forgotten.

"They believed you would not make it tonight as you sought to recover from all the festivities. But I assured them there was no chance Hathor Du Bell would forfeit another opportunity to snag a duke this season." Lily giggled, and I looked to Hathor, waiting for her furious retort. However, to my great disappointment, she only nodded.

"I am glad you know me so well, Lily. Thank you for your congratulations. Now, if you will excuse us—"

"Hathor, we have barely made acquaintances with Verity," Poppy replied as she turned to me. "I feel as though I have heard of you all my life but barely have said two sentences to you. I am Poppy Perrin, Sir Grisham's daughter. These are my cousins, Lily and Iris."

I was correct. Their dresses matched their names, and I wondered if they did that often, and if so, for what purpose?

"Hello," I said to them as if I were unfamiliar with Sir Grisham. "It is a pleasure to make your acquaintance—"

"Oh, she is here!" Lily all but squealed, squeezing her cousins' arms.

When I turned to look, none other than Lady Clementina Rowley was coming down the stairs behind her mother and father. Her bright pink dress was nothing in comparison to the stunning rows upon rows of pearls around her tan neck. Never had I seen so much finery on anyone—beyond the queen and my stepmother.

"By heavens, she is like a walking chandelier," Iris whispered as she withheld her laughter.

"Truly, how does one get that tall?" Poppy whispered back.

"Stretching," Lily answered, and they started to snicker.

"The duchess truly spares no expense, does she not? To arrive at her home is always such an honor, though I do wonder about those to whom she extends invitations. I thought this concert was to be shared only among the nobility," Hathor said to me, reminding me very much of her own mother before kindly glancing back toward the others. "Do enjoy yourselves. I am sure such invitations *rarely* come to your households. And I so love your dresses. They look strikingly similar to the ones you wore at our ball."

There was the retort I was expecting. Proud of herself once more, Hathor took my arm captive and led me from the garden sisters toward another group of ladies. I was sure I knew these ones, as we all had been presented before the queen this year. However, even among ladies of our rank, they, too, mocked Clementina as she walked ever so slowly behind her parents, both of whom she was taller than, to greet guests. And even as Hathor redirected the conversations to topics of gentlemen, they eventually refocused on Clementina.

I found myself utterly bored by all of the gossip. So much so that, if I could have, I would have gone to sleep.

"Good evening," Lady Clementina said softly as she finally escaped her parents' clutches and found herself within our group.

"Clementina, how beautiful you look. Your skin is glowing."

"Your dress is magnificent."

"It is so long—"

"Lovely," Hathor interrupted the lady beside her.

I was not shocked by their words or actions, and neither was Clementina, who merely smiled back. However, before she could speak, the pianist made his way to his instrument, and more than a few candles were blown out while a series of them were lit around the pianoforte, drawing everyone's attention forward.

Hathor and I were about to return to where her family stood when suddenly, a long but slender hand reached into the space between us and grasped on to Hathor's arm. She nearly jumped out of her brown skin, looking up at Clementina, who was breathing heavily. Without the candlelight, it was clear she was not glowing but sweating, strands of her brown hair clinging to her.

"I . . . wish not to . . . cause a scene but . . . I must return to my rooms." Clementina struggled to get the words out. She truly was not well.

Hathor took hold of her hand and gave it to me. "Verity shall lead you, and should anyone notice, I shall distract them."

"Me?" I looked at Hathor, eyes wide.

"It is not as if anyone will notice your absence . . ."

"Shh," said the lady before us, causing Hathor to nod in apology before glaring at me with eyes wide.

"*Go!*" she mouthed.

Frowning, I took Clementina's arm and turned to navigate through the crowd of people before us. However, she dragged her feet as she walked and nearly fell upon me as we passed a table, her weight causing me to knock over a chair. Usually, it would not have been noticed, as gatherings were mostly loud, but a single chair was as thunderous as a cannon due to the silence.

"Oh!" A loud gasp echoed through the room, followed by an even greater commotion. I could not see what had caused it when I turned, but I was sure it was Hathor.

"You must walk," I whispered to Clementina, trying my best to pull her forward. However, she did not budge, her body sinking and taking me with her when, all of a sudden, I felt hands at my back, stilling me.

"Stay calm," a deep voice uttered directly behind me. "The maid shall help."

I did not understand what he meant until I realized Clementina did not feel as heavy; there was now support on the other side.

"Continue forward," the man ordered, and I did. It was not as though I had much choice, thanks to Hathor.

We made it from the ballroom into the hall without further incident, and there I saw two footmen as well as another maid at the ready; quickly they came to take her from me.

"Take her to her rooms and have the lady of the house notified immediately of my presence. I will need a basin of fresh water and towels."

With Clementina in their care, I finally turned, so surprised by who was before me, I stared at him in stunned silence. Dr. Darrington, dressed in a simple black tailcoat and white necktie, his skin a deep warm brown, hazel eyes, and short curly hair, stood a whole head and part of his shoulders taller than I.

"Lady Verity," he acknowledged me and then followed Clementina and the maids up the stairs.

It was only when he moved away from me that I realized I had been holding my breath.

Why had I not been able to speak?

I stood stunned at all that had transpired, unsure what to do next, when the duchess came out of the ballroom huffing angrily.

"I swear, that girl! It is as though she purposely chooses the most inopportune times to be an encumbrance! I—Lady Verity?" She stepped back, surprised at the sight of me.

I curtsied before her. "Your Grace."

Immediately, the expression on her face changed to one of politeness. "What in the good name are you doing out here, my dear?"

"Lady Verity helped the young miss out into the hall," the maid beside her whispered loudly. For a second, and only because I was observing the duchess's face, I was able to see her eyes widen in panic before relaxing.

"How nice of you, but Clementina is making far too much of a little cold. You need not worry about her. Luckily, Sir Grisham is attending to her—"

"It is another doctor," the maid whispered again, making the duchess whip her head to her.

"Another doctor! Who?"

"Dr. Darrington," I answered for her, finally able to speak his name. "I believe his name is Dr. Theodore Darrington, Your Grace. You need not worry. He's been in the service of my brother and . . . and the Earl of Montagu. He's quite skilled, I am told, as well as discreet. I am sure she is feeling much better already."

I was not sure if Dr. Darrington had ever treated Damon, but I could not simply give my brother as an only reference to the duchess, especially as he was not here. At the very least, Damon would be able to account for his presence when he had last come to our home.

"Oh." She calmed marginally. "Well, you should return inside, I would not wish for Deanna to wonder where you have disappeared to."

"Yes, Your Grace." I curtsied once more before doing as she asked.

As I reentered, hearing the pianist's hands glide upon the keys, I found myself reaching to touch my back where his hands had touched me.

Why were his hands so warm that I still felt heat there?

How strange.

4

Verity

I looked to the ballroom's door expectantly throughout the concert, waiting to see if he, the duchess, or Clementina would return. However, by the time the pianist finished his last concerto to a round of applause, none of them had reentered. And no one seemed to be the least bit aware of it.

The night continued as though all was well.

"Tell me now if you have lost your mind so I can make sure not to lose my own," the marchioness said to Hathor as we watched a few couples take to the dance floor now that the band had begun to entertain us for the rest of the evening. A place Hathor would much rather have been than held captive at her mother's side to be lectured. "Must you faint at every gathering?"

"That is a significant exaggeration, Mama. We had a massive gathering of our own just last night, and my legs did not even wobble as Father's did with all that wine." She giggled, causing her father to almost cough into his current glass of wine. Immediately, the marchioness's ire was on him, but before she could speak, another woman called her attention.

"You have thrown me to the wolf, your own father?" the marquess whispered to Hathor.

She smiled, nodding. "I must live to fight another day."

"Goldsmith would be dismayed at how you butchered his words." Damon snickered.

"Of all the novelists you would remember, it would be Goldsmith," his father responded. "And both of you should know the true originator of the phrase was none other than Sir John Mennes in 1641 . . ."

"Are you enjoying yourself?" Silva asked me gently, as the marquess went on with his lecture. When I did not answer, she leaned in, whispering, "They can be a bit overwhelming with all their familiarity, can they not?"

"Are you not part of them now?" I asked in turn.

"In a way, but I would be lying if I said I did not find myself often flustered by their antics. Sometimes it is as though a great play is unfolding before my very eyes, and all I can do is observe," she replied, allowing me into a conversation I could actually engage in. "Forgive them, they do not realize it can be overbearing."

I was glad I was not the only one who felt that way. I glanced around at the décor, wishing to find something to change the subject, when I saw the doors open, and in walked Dr. Darrington. His face, however, was now . . . grim, his jaw tensed and shoulders back. I had only made his acquaintance once before, due to my brother, and he had been rather terse and abrupt with me. However, he had never held that expression.

"Verity?" Silva called.

"Hmm?" I tore my eyes away to look at her.

She smiled as she raised her eyebrow. "Which gentleman has caught your eye?"

"No one!" I gasped almost too loudly, which only made her more suspicious. "Truly, no one. I have no plans whatsoever to engage in that . . ."

My voice trailed off as I saw him approach us, along with two men, one older and the other around his own age.

"Marquess, there you are!" said the older man with rather fierce-looking strips of hair grown on each side of his face despite the fact that he was balding at the center of his head. Hathor's, Damon's, and the marquess's demeanors changed as they reached us.

"Lord Fancot." The marquess nodded to him, and once more, I saw Dr. Darrington looking at me, but when our eyes met, he averted his gaze, focusing once more on Lord Monthermer.

"You remember my son, Henry." Lord Fancot stepped to the side to present his son, who was tall and burly, with thick, curly black hair, deep black skin, and a bright, charming smile. Lord Fancot glanced at Hathor as he spoke of his son.

"Yes, of course. Your father goes on and on about your many business exploits in the Americas last year," the marquess replied, shaking the younger man's hand before looking to his own son. "Damon, you recall he was your junior at Eton."

"Ah," Damon replied, clearly not at all recalling him. "I do hope you and all of your family are well."

"Very well, most well outside of a few missing hair strands." Lord Fancot chuckled, patting his own head. "And trying to marry this one off, of course. He never seems to wish to remain in one place. If you blink, he may very well be in India next, but a good wife would surely—"

"Dr. Darrington?" Damon interrupted, finally acknowledging the man standing quietly behind them both. "It has been a while. How are you?"

"Very well, my lord, and you?" Dr. Darrington replied, taking Damon's hand to shake. His voice was calm and flat. Not in the least bit moved at their presence.

"A friend of yours, Damon?" The marchioness had quickly found her place at her husband's side once more.

"Merely an acquaintance, your ladyship. Your son and I were fortunate to meet through the Duke of Everely."

At the mention of my brother, both the marchioness and

Hathor glanced at me. I did not know if I was meant to speak up, but luckily, Damon once again did.

"Yes, Mother, he all but saved Evander's life."

"By heavens!" the marchioness exclaimed, her eyes wide.

"My lord exaggerates. I merely—"

"I would not doubt it in the least!" Lord Fancot loudly interjected as he placed his hand on Dr. Darrington's shoulder. "Charles, this is the doctor I was speaking of. The genius of Oxford!"

"Genius," I spoke out, causing his hazel eyes to meet mine.

"You were the one admitted at the mere age of fifteen?" The marquess stepped forward with a grin on his face.

"Fifteen?" Damon gasped, then looked him up and down.

"Yes, however—"

"I tell you, he left all his professors dumbfounded," Lord Fancot interjected. "Arithmetic, science, all the classics, English, French, Dutch, German. He can even read Sanskrit. Where does one even begin to find Sanskrit to learn? I do not know, but he did!"

"Extraordinary. Absolutely extraordinary," the marquess replied as he looked upon Dr. Darrington. Even I was beyond stunned at this.

"What is your age at present?" The marchioness leaned her ear in to listen.

"Twenty-six, your ladyship."

"And your family, do I know of them? Is your mother here?" she pressed in the most obvious of manners, and for some reason, I could not help but feel a tad embarrassed.

"My mother has long since passed, and my father . . . my father is the Marquess of Whitmear."

There was silence. I was unsure why the marchioness's eyes widened and her shoulders dropped, but I did not like it.

"Oh well, he must be greatly pleased by your education."

She tried to recover and then took hold of Hathor's arm, ready to leave. Before the marchioness could speak, Lord Fancot interjected quickly.

"Henry, how rude of you not to ask Lady Hathor for a dance!"

Henry's eyes widened as he looked to his father. When the man nodded to Hathor, he was forced to look to her once more.

"Lady Hathor, would you honor with me a dance?" he asked, outstretching his hand to her.

"Only if Lady Verity takes to the floor as well." Hathor smiled brightly and shifted her gaze to me. It was now I whose eyes were in danger of falling out of my head. I glanced once to the doors, wishing to escape but knowing it was not possible, before glancing back to Hathor.

"Effort." She mouthed to me.

This . . . she . . . AH! I screamed on the inside.

Smiling back, I said, "I am without a partner, so—"

"That is not a problem at all, now, is it, Theodore?" Henry looked to him, and now like some sort of comedy act we all stood in a circle staring at one another under the heated gazes of our parents and guardians.

"Well? What are you all waiting for!" Lord Fancot pushed once more.

Hathor nodded, taking Henry's hand, and when Theodore's hand outstretched to me, I met his gaze.

"Lady Verity, may I?" he said gently.

I could not speak. I merely took his hand once more and it was so warm, though not uncomfortably so, nor was it sweaty, but like holding your hand up to the sun. Gently and quietly he led me to the center of the marble floor. So quietly that when I turned to face him again I felt my throat go dry, and I swallowed.

What on earth is the matter with me?

His hazel eyes peered into mine as we began to dance. I expected him to say something, make any sort of conversation, as one normally would in this situation. However, he did not, only stared at me unflinchingly . . . and with each turn, with each touch of our hands, it felt like pressure building within my chest. So much so, I felt slightly light-headed. Gradually, everything else faded away, the world around me distant, and I was just floating with this strange man to the sound of Bach—Prelude and Fugue in C Major.

Everything felt so . . . bright.

I was not sure how to explain it but when I finally found the air in my lungs to speak again, the movement was over and we had returned to our places across from each other. Theodore bowed his head and I curtsied slightly, but before I even rose fully he had walked away from me.

"I wish they had played something more joyful," Hathor said as she returned to my side, blocking my view of his retreating figure.

"What?" I asked her.

"For the dance?" She pressed glancing me over. "Are you all right? You seem rather short of breath. Do you not dance often?"

I was not short of breath from the dance, I was sure of it. But I did not want to attribute it to my partner, for that would mean twice my breath had caught because of him.

"I am fine," I lied to her.

"Good, see, a little effort does no harm." She huffed and walked back to her mother and father.

"Verity." I looked to Silva as she met us. "I've been instructed to tell you that you must accept a dance from a few other gentlemen this evening."

"What? Instructed by whom?"

She nodded her head back toward the marchioness, who offered me a smile and nod.

"I believe she is worried what talk there will be if you dance only with Dr. Darrington this evening. It would be rather . . . troublesome."

"Why? And what happened earlier? The mood changed so drastically before we went to dance."

"The Marquess of Whitmear has been married to Lady Charlotte for the last twenty-five years," she whispered back to me, taking my arm. But Dr. Darrington had said his mother had passed on.

"So his father remarried? Why would that be troubling?" Granted, a year later was relatively soon.

"The Marquess of Whitmear was never married before then," she answered, and when I still stared at her, unable, or maybe unwilling, to put the two together, she said it clearly. "He is the marquess's bastard."

The very first thought that came to mind was my now departed father and how his unfortunate choices had impacted all of our lives. The most public suffering was that of my brothers, of which I had three—Evander and Gabrien, who were considered legitimate, and then there was Fitzwilliam, the eldest and the bastard of Everely. I had rarely ever spoken to him, and it had been years since I had seen his face. I was not even sure if I would recognize him if he walked past me in town.

That is a lie. How could one forget their own brother, half or not, illegitimate or not?

The Eagleman family knew all too well what chaotic disarray came about from having a bastard in its ranks. The pain and trouble it caused were not worth the association, and as such, the marchioness was correct to remove us from his presence.

Yet. I glanced over my shoulder at their party to see the

marquess was still maintaining conversation with Dr. Darrington and Henry. My gaze was met by Dr. Darrington's and quickly I faced forward once more.

Although I was not sure why, for I was not doing anything wrong.

I glanced around, seeking to shift my thoughts, but I could not. That dance, it still went on in my mind.

"Lady Verity."

We both jumped, startled by the strange man who suddenly appeared before me.

"Would you do me the pleasure of this dance?" he asked, his hand outstretched directly before me.

"Forgive me, I'm a bit tired. Another time maybe," I said softly, nodding goodbye to him as I pulled Silva with me to escape.

She tried to remind me, "Verity, you are to dance with—"

"Later." I had not yet recovered from this first dance enough to think of taking any other.

Theodore

From the very first moment I laid eyes on her, I knew Lady Verity Eagleman was simply, purely, rather unfairly the most stunning creature I had ever beheld, and the mere sight of her would forever enchant me. That dance would forever repeat in my mind.

To think she of all people would have danced with me, a . . .

"Must you start every introduction with, 'Hello, I am a bastard,'" Henry moaned as we left the company of Lord Monthermer and his son. "Such things must be said with tact or preferably not at all."

"It is not I who starts the conversations as such but them."
I lifted my hand at the so-called nobility that surrounded us.
Without fail, each and every time I wandered into this circle
of people, I was asked within the first five questions to state
my background and lineage. "Would you prefer I lied?"

"Yes, I would, in fact. Lie, Theodore. Lie. It would not kill
you." Henry sighed and took two glasses of wine from a footman's tray, moving to give me one, but I held up my hand in
protest. "Please, do not continue to be aggravating and take the
damn drink."

I had met Henry Parwens at Oxford; however, when he
entered I had long since graduated and was assisting other professors with research when our paths crossed. I thought he
would do as everyone else did, either seek to use me for my
intelligence or avoid me due to my background. He did neither, and instead sought to be my friend. Years later, I was
unsure what he had gotten from this exchange other than free
medical advice.

He was strange but had become my only friend, though he
tested the limits of that friendship sometimes.

"*I* am aggravating? Was it not you who forced me into a
dance?" I snapped back at him. Was he mad? He had to be
fully mad.

"You wanted me to take to the floor alone!"

"Yes! For why on earth must I accompany you in that?"

"It was because of your conversation that the mood was
ruined and my father sought to remedy the situation by forcing me to dance with the Lady Hathor. If I must suffer, you
must suffer as well!"

He was such a child sometimes. "Henry, the conversation
soured as it dawned on the marchioness that she did not wish
the ladies under her care to be associated with me. You then
forced me to ingratiate myself even further. That does not

help ease the tension. It was quite obvious Lady Verity was not pleased to be forced either." She had said not one word to me and stared at me as though she were confused as to why she had accepted at all.

I knew to expect as much from a lady of her standing but still . . . it was not pleasant to accept.

"I—"

"Oh, how harsh," came a male voice from the right of us.

"He's left to look the fool."

"He is the fool for going to her at all."

Henry and I followed their gazes across the ballroom to where another man stood alone while others around him snickered.

"What show have we missed?" Henry asked, already among them as though they were the best of acquaintances.

That was the gift of Henry. In university, they called him the chameleon, since he could easily insert himself among any type of people. It did not hurt his cause that he was considered to be the ideal gentleman in looks and status.

"Anderkins over there sought to engage the Lady Verity in a dance and was utterly rejected," one of the men answered, trying not to laugh as Anderkins, as he had called him, puffed up his chest and sought to walk away as though no one had witnessed the ordeal.

I tried not to, but I found myself looking for her, and with little effort, I saw her, standing near the window, dressed in blue, the candle's light perfectly hitting her cheek. It was as though it shimmered.

Our first meeting was after I had been called to her home to tend to her brother. Immediately I had been a bit taken at the sight of her. I was not sure if it was her beautiful heart-shaped face, her big brown eyes, or her demeanor. It was then

I realized, I was not merely astounded by but smitten with her. However, instead of expressing that, I found myself quickly seeking to sever any further interaction as promptly as possible.

"It serves him right. Is he not the son of a baron?" one of them asked. "He reaches a bit too high with his standing for her."

And this was why. She was the daughter of a duke, and whether he was dead or not did not change the fact that she was at the very highest tier of all society and I . . . at the very lowest. To even have any sort of fondness for her was imprudent on my part.

I watched as once more she glanced to the entrance, like she had done before the suggestion of our dance. Was she waiting on someone? A suitor perhaps?

"Did you not see the Lady Verity danced with my friend here, Dr. Darrington," Henry said to them, head lifted as if there was some pride to be had in this.

"Yes, and it was quite clear she was forced." One of them laughed. "We saw she did not utter a word to you."

I nodded. "She did not, and Henry here was the one who forced her by asking under everyone's gaze."

They snickered among themselves.

"I knew it."

"Henry, you are cruel, poor girl was terrified."

"I do not know what you mean, she seemed quite taken with him," Henry said in jest. I nearly punched him, as she was not a lady he could jest about. We all knew how easily even the slightest rumor could ruin a young lady. One word of her enjoying the company of a bastard would leave her open to ridicule.

However, the way they rolled their eyes as if it was not even a possibility in their mind was not lost on me.

"Lady Verity was not amused. But gracious," I replied sternly. "Let us hope she is free to dance with someone of her own choosing next time."

"One would have to be a mighty lord indeed," one said, looking her over lustfully. I bit the inside of my cheek and clenched my fist but said not a word.

Henry, the ever-hopeful fool, would not let it rest.

"The woman Lady Verity stands beside . . . was she not once the daughter of a lowly nearly ruined baron? Now she is the Countess of Montagu and the future Marchioness of Monthermer. Anything and everything is within reach, gentlemen, so long as you have the bravery to outstretch your hand. I drink to the young Anderkins and to you, Dr. Darrington," Henry exclaimed, lifting his glass before all and then pouring it down the back of his throat.

They snickered, mimicking his actions and drinking as well. He made it sound so easy. Simply outstretch one's hand? I glanced down at my own. I could do a great many things with these hands of mine. I had managed to save lives even.

But . . . I glanced up at the young lady in blue, remembering how she felt in my hands, how I desperately wished to pull her closer to me. To think I at least managed to dance with her. It very well might have been the last time I would come close to touching a woman of her stature unless she needed medical attention.

"Gentlemen." Henry nodded to them, returning to my side so we could walk through the hall. He took the drink I had not tasted out of my hand. "So, will you tell me now about the young lady you are interested in?"

"I am not interested in anyone," I lied.

"You rarely ever come to such functions as these—"

"That is because I do not receive invitations to such functions as these." To be here tonight, I had come with his father, the viscount, and I did not find that man as amicable as his son.

"That is because no one knows who Dr. Darrington is."

"I'd rather be an unknown doctor than the bastard son of Whitmear. Did you not say to avoid mentioning it if at all possible?"

"Do not use my words against me." He sulked, then drank before speaking again. "Be brave at the very least, and ask for a dance or something."

I had already gotten that. But I couldn't be too angry at him, for even if he had done it unknowingly, it was still a gift to me.

"It is best to forget such things altogether," I said, taking another glass of wine as a footman passed by. "Innocent infatuations are part of life and need not always be acted upon. I am content."

"What a load of horseshit," he remarked as I gave in and drank this time. "You surely cannot have come all this way just to look upon her from afar."

I had, actually. Now that her brother was married, she would be leaving for Everely, and I was not sure our paths would ever cross again. I had rarely seen her in London over the last few weeks, so I thought to put an end to this silly infatuation of mine.

"Dr. Darrington!" the maid all but shouted as she rushed up to me, her face flushed red and eyes wide. "The duchess requires your assistance immediately! Lady Clementina is dying!"

All other thoughts fell out of my mind.

"My medical bag is in your carriage. Have it brought to me at once!" I shouted to Henry as I shoved the glass into his hands and began to run.

5

Verity

"Lady Clementina is dying!" The words spread throughout the ballroom like a fire in trees. People, like leaves, drifted off into other groups to spread the news, and before long, even the music came to a stop.

The first person I looked for was Dr. Darrington, catching him just as he dashed through the doors with the maid in tow. I could only imagine what sight he would be met with.

"Silva, Verity," Damon called as he reached our side and took his wife's hand. "We are leaving. My father is already leading my mother and sister out."

"Yes, it is hardly appropriate for us to stay," Silva replied, gripping on tightly.

"Do you both have all your things?" he asked, looking to me.

I nodded, not sure what to say. I could not believe it was true. Lady Clementina? A girl of her age dying? Her mother had said it was nothing but a cold. And while she had clearly looked ill—far too ill even to walk—beside me moments earlier, it still had not occurred to me that her matter would be so grave. All the splendor of the Rowley home seemed to have vanished by the time we reached the outside. Instead, the air was quite grim and silent as everyone walked to their carriages. Ours had just approached when, like thunder ripping through the skies, we heard a scream that sent chills down my spine.

"*Clementina!*"

I stared back at the house in motionless horror.

"Quickly, into the carriage," Damon ordered, taking my hand and helping me inside. Even within my seat, I could not look away from the windows. I was unsure from which the scream hailed, but for some reason, I stared in hopes that I would be able to . . . to . . . well, I did not know what I hoped to accomplish. Only when our carriage had driven so far that I could no longer see even the slightest hint of the wisteria flowers did I sit back. Before me, Damon and Silva sat quietly, their hands locked so tightly that I could not tell whose grip was firmer.

"We must think all will be well with her, and all shall," Silva said gently into the darkness, and Damon nodded in agreement.

I wished to say that there would be no such thing as cemeteries if it were that simple. But I held my tongue, and the ride back to the Du Bell house was silent and strangely quick, as if all of society had sought not to be out upon the streets, as though death were contagious.

"Welcome back, my lord," said the butler at the door to Damon once he'd exited the carriage. "Your father has just arrived and wishes to see you in his study."

"And my mother?" Damon questioned.

"In the drawing room with Lady Hathor. She's called for tea."

"You go see your father, my dear. Verity and I will go to your mother," Silva said to him before looking at me. I nodded and handed my gloves to the maid before following Silva, when Hathor stepped from the room.

"Verity and I will go straight to bed," Hathor proclaimed, taking my arm faster than I could blink.

"But what of the tea?" Silva called after us.

"No, thank you," she responded, already on the stairs and moving so quickly I had to lift my skirts.

"Hathor, slowly, or I shall fall!" I called after her as we went. She did not slow until we were back in my room. It was then that she spun around to look at me, her honey-colored eyes wide.

"What happened?" she demanded, and I stared back at her, my head still practically left downstairs. "Well?"

"Well, what?"

"Clementina! What happened when you left the room? Did you see anything? I saw when you both nearly fell over and knocked into the chair. But then I had to cause a distraction, of course, which left me surrounded and unable to see what occurred next. I tried to exit as well, but Mama held on to me as though I were a prisoner until you returned. Was she all right? Well, obviously, she was not all right considering the news that came after. But surely, she could not be dying? Though who would suggest someone was dying if they are not dying!"

Throughout her blustering, I had managed to take a seat on my bed and take off my shoes.

"Hathor, I do believe you should breathe," I said as she stared off, lost in deep thought.

"She looked horridly ill, did she not?" she asked instead. "Maybe it is fever? But people do not die of mere fever—do they?"

"As I am not a doctor, I do not know," I replied. "And yes, she was pale. Her mother came out soon after we had and said it was a cold—"

"People do not die of colds!" She huffed and then took a seat beside me, kicking her foot. She took a deep breath and met my gaze. "I have never once seen my mama look as she did when we heard that scream. And I believe she even meant to go back inside. Whatever for, I do not know. But . . . but the look upon her face. It was dreadful."

"Is that why you wished not to stay downstairs for tea?" I asked her.

She shook her head. "There is no point in sitting with her now. I swear this house transforms her somehow. The moment we entered, it was like nothing at all was wrong, and she calmly asked for tea. She would merely deflect from the matter and treat us as though we were children. I do not think I can uphold insincere colloquies at this moment."

Sighing, she lay back on the bed, and I did the same beside her. We both lay there, looking up at the drapery of the bed in silence for a moment before she asked, "At the very least, did anyone catch your eye?"

"Even in this state, you do not yield in your quest for a husband?"

"I just wished for something good to have happened tonight. Something to take my mind off Clementina," she replied softly. "So, any news?"

Strangely, my mind went to Dr. Darrington.

"No. None in the least," I lied. I was lying often now but I was not sure how to put into words what I was feeling. I had no one to ask, and since Hathor seemed to think on these things more, I felt the need to press. "Though I do wonder what you meant by someone making one's breath catch? Did you mean you stop breathing? But that can happen for any reason, can't it?"

She looked to me and then shrugged. "I am not sure. That is merely how my mama described it. She said the moment you are smitten with someone it feels like your chest is heavy and your mind becomes silly and you believe you are walking on air."

"Walking on air?" I repeated slowly.

"Yes, it does not make much sense to me either. So I asked Aphrodite how she knew she loved your brother and she said when she was near him all the rest of the world disappeared. Which also made no sense to me. How does a world disappear? Each person I speak to about it has some odd analogy or description I can barely understand." She sighed tiredly and then shifted closer to me. "Do you know what Damon said?"

"You even asked your brother of such things?"

"Yes. Papa too, as one should have good references for all things, should they not?" she replied. "Anyway, Damon said, 'She made me infuriatingly livid and yet joyous at the same time.' And Papa said he found the greatest peace in *teasing* Mama. It all sounds like the loveliest bit of gibberish to me but I look forward to my own turn one day." She giggled.

She was right, it was all gibberish and yet I found small traces of sense, all of which led me back to Dr. Darrington. But surely it could not be love. I did not know him. I had barely spoken to him. This was . . . something but . . . ugh.

Groaning, I lay back, placing my hand on my head.

"What is the matter with you now?" Hathor questioned.

"Nothing, Clementina merely came to my mind again." Once more a lie. Lies, to cover lies. What a tribute to my name I made.

"Now I am worried once more," she said, sitting up again, her shoulders slumped. "I shall leave you to change and rest. Should I call for the maid?"

"No, I shall manage the night. Thank you."

"Very well. See you in the morning."

I nodded and watched her go without additional comment, wondering how I had managed to further make a mess of my mind. Rising once more, I went to my trunk and dug inside for my journal and jewelry box. I sat staring at my journal not sure what to write of myself, and so I wrote of another having a much harder time than I.

May 10, 1813

The air this night is grim.
As a lady's life hangs upon a limb.
She, too, is a duke's daughter presented this season,
she too far unreasoned.
Even stricken ill, she was adorned with diamonds
    and pearls,
seeking to dance like the other girls,
the only chance for romance or a change in
    circumstance.
My lady, triumph to you in this fight,
Wisdom upon your knight,
For mightier you are in the sunlight.

Closing the book, I opened my jewelry box, lifted a vial to my lips, and drank it all. I was confident that this time, there would be no disturbance; I was already so exhausted. I barely managed to change, put my things away, and enter my bed before sleep carried me off.

Theodore

It took all my strength not to yell as the rage poured into me from every direction. I held the brown glass vial in my left hand and the prescribed order in my right one, a list of ingredients including everything from mercury and laudanum to onion juice, among a host of other nonsense, all with the purpose of treating . . . height?

"How much of this has she taken?" I asked Her Grace, the Duchess of Imbert, who was still covered in diamonds as she sat beside her weakened daughter, her husband on the opposite side of the bed on his knees. That is how dire this situation was.

"I do not recall but it cannot be more than three weeks now, once at night and then every other morning with fruit, as she detests the taste," she said.

"Give me all of it," I snapped at the maid before snatching the box that was filled with more vials. I marched to the open window and tossed it from the room to shatter across the ground below.

"What on earth are you doing?" the duke hollered, rising to his feet.

"One could ask you both the same, since you have been feeding your daughter poison." I bit my tongue for a moment to calm down.

"Poison!" The duchess arose from her chair. "We have done nothing of the sort, how dare you accuse us of such a thing! As I explained to you, this was to help—"

"Your Grace, there is no cure for one's height," I said and lifted the list for her to see. "Consuming mercury on its own daily is enough to kill someone, let alone mixed with everything else here. It is by God's grace alone she did not succumb weeks ago."

"I do not understand this at all. And I will not have you blame my wife," the duke snapped as he marched over to me. "We were prescribed this by a most reputable doctor, which cannot be said of you. Who are you anyway to—"

"Clementina? Clementina? She's not breathing!" The duchess screamed once, grabbing on to her daughter who did not move.

"What are you doing? For God's sake treat her!" the duke hollered at me as I listened to her chest. "Forget this madman, someone call for Sir Grisham at once. It is his medicine, he will surely—"

"With all due respect, Your Grace, I ask for you to be silent!" I hollered at him before listening again. "She is breathing, but barely. The laudanum in the medicine she took is slowing her heart."

Rising, I moved to the basin of vinegar, peppermint, and herb-soaked napkins I had been working on before they showed me the prescription. I turned down her sheets and lifted her arm.

"What are you doing?" the duchess asked, staring at me with tears in her eyes. It reminded me once more why I ought to calm down. She was a mother who had made a mistake.

"The antidote I have is working. This is merely to help ease the toxins through the pores of her skin." I took the clear jar from the maid. "It will need to be changed every hour. I shall stay and do so."

"Or the best case would be leeches." An older gentleman stood at the door, stern-faced and grim-looking, wearing a short gray wig that was pulled into a ponytail at the back, and dressed in a deep violet overcoat. With one hand he held on to a black cane and with the other his professional bag. He bowed his head to the duke and duchess. "Forgive me, Your Graces, I had only just arrived this evening into town after seeing to another patient when I received word."

His blue eyes shifted to me. "And who may this be?"

"Ah, Sir Grisham, this is Dr. Darrington," the duke replied. "He was the first to see Clementina, since he attended the concert."

"And whatever are you doing to my patient, Dr. Darrington?" he all but sneered at me.

"Your tonic caused great harm, sir, so I am saving her life," I replied, wrapping her arm carefully.

"By making her a mummy?" he questioned. "I thank you, but as I am here there is no more need for your services. I can assure you that it must have been something else, maybe she ate food disagreeable to her."

"What do you believe she could have eaten?" The duke quickly looked to him. "This doctor has gone on and on about poison. I knew it could not be so. Clementina can be a bit of a glutton sometimes and will eat whatever looks the sweetest. She used to have stomachaches all the time as child."

The instant deference and respect the duke gave to Sir Grisham did not go unnoticed. I waited for him to ask me to step away from his daughter, but instead it was his wife who spoke.

"I wish for Dr. Darrington to stay," she said sternly.

"But dear, Sir Grisham—"

She turned to them both, her head high as she held on to her daughter's arm. "I know my daughter. I know what it looks like when she has a stomachache and this is not that. She told me many times she felt ill after taking your tonic, Sir Grisham, but I trusted your wisdom to be greater than hers. Now see where we are."

"Your Graces, I assure you—"

"Thank you for coming all this way, Sir Grisham, do please take care on your journey home!" She squeezed her daughter's hand even tighter and turned back to me. "Dr. Darrington, I shall have no excuses from you later either."

"Yes, Your Grace." I nodded and did not look back at the duke or Sir Grisham.

What a night this was.

Verity

"My lady?

"My lady!"

"Ugh!" I gasped out, all of me shivering as my eyes snapped open.

"My lady?"

It took me a moment, because all the world felt as though it were spinning, but as my vision steadied, I looked at the freckled face of Bernice, who knelt beside my bed, watching me with wide eyes.

"Are you all right, my lady?" she asked as I slowly began to sit up.

"I—" I jumped at the flash of lightning and sound of rippling thunder that quaked outside the window. It only added to the splitting ache that spread through my head.

"I shall tell her ladyship—"

"No!" I grabbed her arm desperately. Seeing her startled expression, I sought to calm myself, releasing her and taking in a deep breath. "It is nothing, truly. I believe I might have gotten a bit foxed last night. I surely do not wish her ladyship's concern over it."

I tried to smile, but my head still hurt, so I quickly rose from the bed. Bernice lifted a robe for me to step into. Typically, the medicine prescribed by Dr. Cunningham, our family's physician in Everely, worked perfectly. Yet two nights in a row, I had awoken to cold sweats and worried glances.

"I will draw water for you, my lady," Bernice said.

I merely nodded as I sat by the window. I had no clue what to do if the medicine did not work. It was not as though I could call for Dr. Cunningham. I thought of writing to Evander, but I doubted he'd even be able to read it for days, if not weeks, while he tended to his new wife. Also, it would be in poor taste for me to be writing to him now. He'd think me a bother—well, maybe not, but he would be concerned, and the last thing I wished to do now was disturb his peace.

"My lady, what would you like to wear?" Bernice asked me.

"Anything is fine. I doubt we shall be going out in this weather."

"Yes, the rains have been terrible this season."

I knew that to be a fact. Upon coming to London, the wheel of our carriage had gotten stuck in a rut, and part of me believed it was a sign for us to turn back. But coincidentally, at that very same time, a carriage belonging to the Du Bells drove past, and Evander had stared at it as though it had wings. It made me wonder at the time if there were always two forces at work, one willing us to go forward and one trying to keep us stuck in place.

"My lady, is this all right?"

I glanced back at Bernice to see the simple lavender dress she held up for me. I nodded and rose to my feet again.

It took us about thirty minutes for me to get ready, and in the process, I heard the rest of the family rise. It was like one moment there was utter silence, and then the next, a rumbling of feet and voices in the hall.

"*Abena!*" I heard someone—Hathor—yell as soon as I opened my door. I glanced down over the railing to see the little girl run from one room into another, a box of ribbons and a single shoe in her hands.

"She truly loves to drive her sister mad." I smiled as I walked down alongside Bernice. "Is she not worried her mama will be angry at her?"

"Lady Abena seems to forget about consequences while in the act of having her fun," she replied just as Hathor opened her door, still in her nightdress and nightcap . . . and her cheeks excessively painted with rouge.

I bit my lip to keep from laughing.

She glanced at me, her eyes wide. "Which room did the little bug run to!"

It took all my strength not to laugh. "I did not see."

"Very well. I know how to deal with her." Hathor huffed, marching back into her room and slamming the door.

"We should continue on, my lady, for things shall get *louder*," Bernice added. "Rainy days are never short of . . . Abena."

I wished to see what she meant but took her advice. We were just before the doors to the dining room when I heard the marchioness's voice.

"Truly? You mean it? Clementina is all right?" she exclaimed, and I moved closer to hear without being seen.

"How many times must I tell you yes?"

"How is it that you know such news before I?"

"The coachman went to retrieve my pocket watch in the early morning hours and saw all the servants were in much brighter spirits. He heard it himself that the young lady was well."

"They made it seem as though she were minutes away from being read rites. Did you not hear the way her mother screamed? Such sounds are made only when—"

"Apparently, the girl truly was upon her last breaths. But that doctor, the one we were introduced to, all but brought her back to life with his bare hands. Evidently, he stayed till past dawn."

"The bastard?"

"Deanna."

"What? Is that not what he all but proclaimed to us?"

"You asked about his parents, and he told you the truth. But that is neither here nor there. The man has saved the duke's daughter. Such a thing, *such a brain*! I tell you, my dear, truly what makes a man is his mind."

The marchioness giggled. "You are merely excited at the prospect of speaking to someone who knows all of your great books and philosophers."

There were muffled sounds from the marquess before he said, "Mark my words, this Dr. Theodore Darrington shall no doubt become well-renowned one day. I have an eye for these things."

I had never heard the marquess speak so much and so freely.

"Yes, dear. It is still a pity, though," the marchioness added.

I frowned, not sure why I was a bit annoyed at her tone, but I ignored that feeling for a better one. One of relief . . .

Dr. Darrington had saved her.

"What has you smiling so early this morning?"

I turned to see Bernice had gone, and now Silva and Damon stood at the stairs. *Smiling? Was I smiling?*

"Damon, leave her alone." Silva nudged him.

"What?"

"Clementina is going to be all right," I said, since that was why I was smiling . . . wasn't it?

6

Verity

It had been three days since the concert at the Rowleys', and since then, neither the rain nor the ton's interest in the newly famed Dr. Darrington had subsided. Even in the downpour, women still came to visit the marchioness in order to share what information they had managed to gather or to describe the way in which he had either miraculously healed them or someone they knew.

"Your ladyship, Mrs. Marie Loquac is here for you," Ingrid announced to the marchioness as she entered where we all sat in the drawing room.

"It seems not even the rain could stop her either." Hathor giggled from behind her easel. "I wonder what sort of news she brings with her this time."

"Hathor." The marchioness gave her a stern look as she placed her cake down and rose to her feet. "Do see her in, Ingrid, and have tea sent."

Hathor quickly moved from her painting to sit beside me at the window. I had not known of her talent for art until I saw her sketches, many of which were of her family.

"Mrs. Marie Loquac? She is the favored modiste, correct?" I asked Hathor, sure I had heard that name recommended to me by one of the other ladies in town.

"Yes, she is the *granddaughter of an earl* and never wishes anyone to forget. But I much prefer to call her the ton spy," she mused. However, before she could say another word, the doors opened once more for a rather short, plump woman with rosy dimpled cheeks, green eyes, and wavy brown hair that she had pinned up with a green feather, though her dress was a soft pink. Behind her were two plain young ladies, one holding books and the other a measuring tape and hat. Their hems were soaked in mud, though Mrs. Loquac's was not.

"Your ladyship." She curtsied to the marchioness and then once more to Hathor and me both. "How lovely you all look today."

"We must not take credit for that, as your dresses seem to make us radiant even on a gloomy day such as this," the marchioness said as she outstretched her arm to gesture for Mrs. Loquac to sit. "I see you've brought more designs to part us with our pocketbooks."

"I do believe that with or without my dresses, you and your girls would be the envy of the ton. Many inquired about the silk used in your daughter's wedding gown, and even upon trying it themselves, they still could not match half her beauty," Mrs. Loquac exclaimed, and I heard Hathor take in some air beside me. But to my surprise, she did not speak. Instead, she held out her hand for Mrs. Loquac's assistant to give her the book.

"Verity, I do not believe you have been introduced. This is Mrs. Marie Loquac. She is quite the dressmaker," the marchioness said to me as Ingrid came with the tea. "Mrs. Marie Loquac, I am sure you know of my goddaughter, Lady Verity Eagleman. She shall be staying with us for some time and will need a few more dresses as soon as possible."

"Godmother, you need not—"

"I wish to, and I shall," she interrupted with a smile. "You do not have nearly enough, my dear, and before he left your brother all but begged me to see to your needs."

"Does he really think me so lacking?" I'd thought he worried I spent too much on clothing. I did do my best to keep up with the fashions of the ton but felt them ever-changing.

"He does not but merely wishes you to have all your heart's desire."

"Correct me if I am mistaken, but isn't Damon his closest friend? Why has he not inherited such a trait? I see no such concern for my needs," Hathor stated as she flipped through the book.

"Unlike Evander, I have far too many sisters for me to be concerned with their wardrobes, and your needs, in particular, are never-ending, Hathor," Damon spoke from the door as he adjusted his sleeves. "Do excuse me for the intrusion, ladies. Mother, I shall be off."

"Oh, I thought you had already left to meet your father at the club?" The marchioness looked up from the book before her.

"Silva was not feeling well, and I wished to stay with her until she rested."

"Really? Why did you not say? I would have come. She looked well during breakfast. Whatever could be wrong?"

"She wished not to worry you and claims it is merely a headache."

"Pardon my intrusion," Mrs. Loquac spoke up, "but it would be best if you called for Dr. Darrington."

"I do not believe a mere headache calls for a doctor, ma'am. Thank you." Damon nodded to her before looking at his mother to speak once more when Mrs. Loquac added, "You can never be too sure, and now that we have such a great doctor in town, it would be a waste not to use his services. It was he who cured Lady Clementina. She had—"

"Yes, we have already heard," Damon replied shortly before speaking to his mother. "I am off. Good day to you, ladies."

"Do watch the roads!" the marchioness called after him, but he was gone with such speed that I looked to see if he was not already within his carriage.

"Do forgive him, for he is never one for conversation," the marchioness said to Mrs. Loquac. Even though Damon always seemed to be conversing, at least with his family, I had noticed he was rather short-tempered with the rest of the world. "What is this you heard of Lady Clementina? She is altogether fine now, is she not?"

"Finally, more information," Hathor muttered under her breath without looking away from her book. Due to the rain, all we had managed to gather was that she was recovering but not much beyond that.

"Yes. Apparently, she is in much better spirits," Mrs. Loquac said as she lifted a biscuit for her tea.

"Thank heavens she is well. It was such a fright." The marchioness was clearly not at all interested in any of the designs despite her frequent gaze upon them.

"To think it was her own mother's doing." Mrs. Loquac scoffed.

"What?"

Everyone's head rose to look back at the modiste.

"You have not heard?" Mrs. Loquac sat up on the edge of her seat. "Evidently, what preceded her misfortune was that the duchess noticed Lady Clementina had grown another half-inch taller. She requested the help of another doctor to stop the poor girl from growing. He prescribed her a tonic."

"Is that what made her ill?" I asked, while, in my mind, I thought of my very own tonic.

"Ill? That poison nearly killed her!" Mrs. Loquac exclaimed before taking a bite of biscuit. She shook her head and let out a breath. "They say that upon discovering the source, Dr. Darrington threw it out the window."

"My heaven." The marchioness frowned, closing the book in her hand. "Who prescribed the tonic? Surely they cannot be a true physician."

"That is what is so shocking, your ladyship, as it was prescribed by none other than Sir Grisham."

"Truly?"

I looked to Hathor, remembering my introduction to the "garden sisters," one of whom had been his daughter. She nodded as though she could read my thoughts.

"Maybe it was a mistake with the apothecary who took the prescription?" the marchioness said gently. "After all, Sir Grisham was knighted due to his proficiency and dedication over the years. I have never called upon him before, but his reputation has not been called into question."

Once more, Mrs. Loquac leaned in, so Hathor and I leaned in as well.

"Do not take it from me, your ladyship, but I have it on good authority that he hadn't a sixpence to scratch with after acquiring the title. It is rumored that his prescriptions are no more than a scheme to line his own pockets." She huffed, taking a rather large gulp of her tea. "They rarely ever work. Lord Fancot claims the man has been treating him to his satisfaction, but his wife complains she has seen no improvement with his so-called tonics."

My mind went again to the vials within my trunk. Dr. Cunningham had treated our family for several years; Evander trusted him greatly. But for some reason, I was no longer seeing improvements myself. Not a day went by that I did not wake up in a fit of terror. I was fortunate in that the rain had so far shielded my problem from the rest of the house, but it couldn't rain forever.

"Surely, he could not be cruel-hearted enough to take advantage of the ill," the marchioness replied.

"Let us hope. But as my mama once told me, there is never a shortage of people looking to take advantage of others." Mrs. Loquac huffed and took another biscuit into her mouth as she sat back in her chair. "That is why the best doctors are those like Darrington . . . while his lineage may be questionable, he is clearly not motivated to maintain such a profession for wealth. After all, he is clearly well backed."

"What do you mean?" I asked.

"My dear," she spoke to me as though I were a pet cat. "Such an education as his does not come cheap. It is believed that the Marquess of Whitmear has not only provided for his son's every expense throughout the years but continues to send him a small fortune. What a shame he is illegitimate, for I would have happily offered my daughter, Catherine, but as you know, I am the granddaughter of an earl, and I'm sure the mere thought of it would make Grandpapa spin in his grave."

"He died before she was even born, and her daughter is a spinster," Hathor whispered to me, shaking her head. How she managed to remember everyone's family history was a wonder to me.

"Well, how intriguing. We must make haste, for I am expecting visitors later this evening," the marchioness calmly spoke as she lifted the book up for one of the young ladies to take from her. "Verity, please stand so they may take your measurements."

"Yes, Godmother," I replied, moving where they directed while my mind was a mess of thoughts.

What was I to do now? Keep taking the tonics? Should I have them checked? To do that, I would have to tell the marchioness, but I could not.

Also, who would check them? Dr. Darrington? Surely not.

Though it would provide me a chance to talk to him. But why did I wish to talk to him?

"Verity, Verity?"

"Hm?" I glanced at the women in the room.

"Are you all right, my dear?" the marchioness asked me.

"Yes, of course." I smiled and put my arms down as they finished.

"You have such a fine shape, neither small nor big. Are we sure you are not a Du Bell? You nearly match Hathor's measurements," Mrs. Loquac teased as she looked over her shoulder.

"No, she is very much her mother's daughter. They have very similar eyes," the marchioness replied before setting her tea down. "Thank you for coming. The blue and the lavender dresses will work best for her."

"Mama, what of me?" Hathor gasped.

"You have four dresses, two hats, a pair of silk gloves, and new shoes on order already. Do you wish me to cancel them for you to make new choices?" her mother asked as she rose to walk to the door.

"Never mind, I am quite satisfied," Hathor said as she moved back to her painting, and I tried not to laugh but failed, causing her to glare at me. "Will you please sit so I can finish my drawing?"

"Of course. May I ask why you need *four* new dresses?" I asked her.

"Yes. The answer is because I liked them. Now, chin down," she ordered.

I did as she ordered while Mrs. Loquac, along with her assistants, took their leave. I watched through the window as the driver of her rather beaten cabriolet rushed to bring an umbrella out for her. But what made the scene nonsensical was the way in which her assistants, one on either side of her, hoisted up the bottom of her dress so it would not be stained.

"Mrs. Loquac acts as though she is a renowned countess," I said to Hathor.

"Only in her dreams, as her mother married quite low—a dressmaker, of all people. Can you imagine the uproar it caused? Her father disinherited her. She was all but exiled from the ton, and her husband soon lost all his clients and became destitute."

"How then did she come to live with such finery now? Is she truly so great a modiste?"

"Mama said that before his death, the earl found it in his heart to leave his poor daughter a small sum of two thousand, two hundred pounds, and it was from that they re-erected their shop. It does help that she truly is a good modiste. But had her mother chosen correctly, I doubt she'd ever have been subjected to such work at all."

"How is it that you always know so much of the lives of others?"

"I listen," Hathor said as if it were the most obvious thing in the world. "Just as she comes to speak of others, others come to speak of her. Either way, Mama says she is a lesson on why we must take care to plan our lives, not that we would ever be so foolish as her mother."

I watched the cabriolet leave, and her assistants were forced to walk together in the rain, as there was no space for them within it.

I could not help but wonder—how deeply her mother must have loved her father that she cared not what any would say or what she would lose.

"Mama, who is it you are expecting for dinner?" Hathor asked when the marchioness returned.

"Your father has invited some members of his club, and, I believe, Dr. Darrington."

A chill went through me as I ripped my gaze from the window to her, not sure what I was feeling but suddenly aware that I could no longer think.

Theodore

"I must ask if you secretly despise me for some untold reason?" I asked the smirking man across from me in the carriage.

"On the contrary, Theodore. I think of you as a brother."

"Then tell me, *brother*, why do you drag me from bed this evening, knowing the events of late, the storm, and my request?"

"First, this is hardly a storm, merely a drizzle. If we were all to stay home due to rain, we'd never leave our houses in this country. Besides you enjoy the rain," Henry replied, his smile spreading across his face from ear to ear. "Secondly, I am ignoring your request *because* of recent events. I cannot allow you to squander this moment."

"What is this moment?"

"Theodore, you have become an overnight sensation with how you saved that young lady. The talk of the ton. Now is not the time to sleep. You must capitalize on this and expand your enterprise—"

"I am a physician, not a bank, Henry. You do realize that capitalizing on this moment, as you say, will require more sick patients, and that is not my goal."

"Well, the sick will be sick either way, and you shall be their first choice, provided you present yourself as amiable. So, do keep the scowl off your face. It is not as if I am dragging you to a ball."

"Where are you dragging me to exactly?"

I truly would rather have been sleeping. The sun was high in the sky by the time I'd felt as though Lady Clementina did not require my further assistance and I left the Rowley home. I had closed my eyes for only an hour when I began to receive requests from other notable persons throughout town. I felt like I had been walking from one lavish house to another every waking moment since. Not even an hour ago, I'd returned home only to find Henry at my door, demanding I change and follow him with no clear reason as to why. However, my answer soon came as we entered a familiar row of grand townhouses.

"Henry, where are we going?"

"Do not worry. You are not being called for a patient," he replied.

"What other reason would I be here for?"

"Dinner."

"I beg your pardon? Dinner? With whom?"

"The Marquess of Monthermer."

I stared back at him dumbstruck while, in my mind, the vision of *her* flashed like lightning.

"Before you accuse me of merely dragging you along to deflect from my father's scheme to acquaint me with the Lady Hathor, do know the marquess especially requested an invitation be extended to you. I was worried your pride would compel you to ignore it, so I brought you without your input."

I inhaled to calm my rapidly increasing heartbeat, forcing myself to stare out into the street, fearful he would somehow notice.

"So, your father is set to engage you with the Lady Hathor? Does that mean she will be in attendance?" If she were, then surely Lady Verity would be, as well.

"Yes, of course. As if he would lose such a chance. He's even brought along my mother and sister to ensure it. We shall meet them there."

Will you calm yourself, you fool? I tugged slightly at my necktie.

"Are you all right?" he asked me.

"Perfectly well," I stated without hesitation. "When will you simply tell your parents that you are in love with another woman?"

"When she finally drops all pretense and accepts me." The smile on his face spread, and he even seemed to sit up straighter, nothing but determination in his eyes. "When that day comes, I will surely run through the streets singing and praising."

I couldn't help but chuckle. "How are you so certain she is the one—"

"The very first moment I saw her, all of me quaked. I could not sleep or eat without the thought of her, and I did not even know her name. Such a feeling is never to be doubted."

The way Henry navigated the world was like none other I had ever seen. All I could do was shake my head at his madness.

"Do not pretend as if I have forgotten your mystery woman, as well," he stated as the carriage came to a stop before the iron gates of the Du Bell home.

"No such person exists."

"You must keep your story straight. Either you do not believe she is attainable, or she does not exist. Please make up your mind so I may discover the creature who has managed to enrapture you," Henry replied as the door opened and the footmen held umbrellas above us.

I was not sure if I was comforted or disturbed by the other carriages I saw. In some sense, it provided cover—the more people, the more freely I could . . . I could maybe speak with her. But at the same time, how could I do so under their gazes?

Would it not look improper of me to speak with anyone else but the host who extended the invitation to me?

"Gentlemen, his lordship awaits in the drawing room," the butler said when we entered, already leading us. There was a single knock before the door opened, and I heard the man say, "Sir, Mr. Parwens and Dr. Darrington have arrived."

When he stepped aside, it seemed as though all the world had vanished but her. She sat by the pianoforte, dressed in yellow, the smallest of smiles upon her sweet face, and, as Henry had described, I trembled.

Like thunder in the clouds and the greatest of tempests, I trembled.

7

Theodore

I had heard much of the Marquess of Monthermer. It was consistently said that he was a learned man with great fortune, luck, and family, that not one ill word could be spoken of him, and that he valued the intelligence of even the poorest of men to the company of princes. And if that were not enough, he and his children, especially his eldest son, Damon, shared a relationship more likened to a matured friendship than simply father and child. He was so highly regarded that, as the son of a marquess myself, I found it hard to believe such talk could be altogether true. I believed it an exaggeration of those seeking to get within his good graces for their own elevation.

However, in the short twenty minutes or so that I had been granted this opportunity to converse in their drawing room, I discovered I would likely speak of him with such fondness, as well. Never had I met a lord so . . . gentle and scholarly. But it was not just him. The whole Du Bell family seemed to radiate a warmth I had witnessed only in families with little else to cling to in life. Despite my status, he spoke to me as though I were of equal value with all the other lords before him. I would have greatly enjoyed his company if it had been in any other setting and only us males. But that was not the case.

Like an applied heat upon my back, I could feel her presence mere steps behind me. I did not know how such a phenomenon was possible, but it was. She was so close that my lungs felt as if they were compressed, yet at the very same time, she was so far that I could not even utter a word to her. When I looked, she had glanced toward the doors, as though she were waiting for someone. But whom?

Before I could find courage to speak, her eyes shifted to mine just as the door opened, and the butler, dressed in red, walked in, his shoulders back and his face forward. "My lord, your ladyship, dinner is served."

"We will have to finish this discussion afterward, gentlemen." The marquess gestured for us to go before him, and everyone waited for the women, of which there were the marchioness, Henry's rather taciturn mother, Lady Fancot, and his equally reserved sister, Miss Amity Parwens, both of whom had red hair. There was also Lady Montagu, Damon's wife, the Lady Hathor, and, of course, Lady Verity, who met my gaze for the briefest of seconds before she followed the party out.

I did not expect any chance to speak to her, though I had to admit I did wish to. As we walked into the dining room, I thought myself merely satisfied with being able to look upon her. However, my heart skipped when I noticed the only chair left for me was next to her. I stared, waiting for someone else to claim it and punish me for daring to aspire to it.

"What are you doing?" Henry whispered from ahead of me when I did not move.

Not replying, I walked to the chair the footman pulled out for me. It was only when the marquess sat at the head of the table that we all took our own seats. I said nothing, staring down at the silverware, seeking to ignore the slight smell of jasmine that could only be coming from her.

"Do you believe me unsuitable for making conversation with, Dr. Darrington?"

Immediately, I looked up to find her brown eyes peering

directly into me. Only when I noticed her slight frown did I find the mind to speak. "No, I do not."

"Then why are you failing to do so? Even your companion has already begun," she said, and I noticed Henry and Hathor were speaking, as they also sat side by side.

"I lack my companion's ability to converse so freely with your sex."

"What is it about my sex that makes us so hard to converse with freely? Surely, it is no different if the topic is appropriate."

"That is the problem in and of itself, to maintain propriety, but what man can do so when faced with the charms of a beautiful woman?" The words poured out of me before I could even think. My eyes widened as I stared back at her.

"So, your answer then is you cannot maintain a proper conversation with my sex because you find us all beautiful? Is that why you did not speak during our dance as well, you were distracted by all the young ladies there?"

"No, of course not, you mistake me. I did not speak during our dance because . . ." *I was so deeply in awe of you?* I could not say that but I did not know what else to say either.

The frown upon her brow deepened, and she turned away from me as the first-course soup was brought out.

Fuck.

I knew nothing else to say and thought to spare myself from further idiocy. But when else would I be afforded a chance to speak to her like this? Desperately, I searched for anything to salvage this situation, but nothing came to mind.

"Dr. Darrington?" the marchioness called out to me.

"Yes, your ladyship?" I said, immediately looking at her, grateful to be saved.

"Are you staying in town with Lord Fancot, or do you have family here?"

"I do have family in town, relatives of my mother, but their home is rather full, so I have taken up lodging at the Crown Inn."

"It must be quite lonely without the comfort of family," she replied as the footmen brought out the next dish, which looked to be lamb.

"Or tranquil," Damon muttered behind his glass, earning him a glare from both his mother and wife and a chuckle from all the other males in attendance.

"Worry not, your ladyship," Henry spoke up. "Theodore is like my brother and, thus, I take it upon myself to disturb his peace whenever possible."

I fought the urge to roll my eyes.

"I find myself at the inn only to sleep and, thus, more than enough," I said.

"For now it may be enough, but it cannot possibly be when you take a wife," Lady Fancot spoke up.

"I do not have a mind to take a wife, my lady," I replied to the horror of the whole table, including, it seemed, Lady Verity, who stared at me, eyebrow raised.

"Why ever not?" the marchioness replied, aghast. "Do you find the young women of London so disagreeable?"

"No, on the contrary, I hold women in the highest possible regard. Especially the ladies of the ton, for they handle their harsh fates with grace and dignity that is far superior to any man."

"Whatever could you mean, *harsh* fates?" Lord Hardinge laughed, lifting his glass. "I am quite sure nothing so severe could happen within a drawing room."

I was not surprised by his reply.

"If you, sir, were forced to remain in a room where you were taught skills you had little interest in, would you not find that cruel?" I asked, and he paused with the rim of his glass barely at his lips. "That is the reality for young ladies of the ton. They are kept in drawing rooms, taught etiquette, literature, how to play an instrument, then the arts, as well as needlework. Whether they care for these things is irrelevant."

"What else could they possibly care for?" Lord Bolen huffed, a deep frown upon his lips.

"One would have to ask them, my lord, but no one does," I answered, frowning. "They are simply told their place and forced to remain there. Their only freedom to venture outside is when they are deemed mature enough to be married, and once married, they are sent to another drawing room."

"You speak as if the women in here have no choices. My dear, tell him, could you see yourself doing anything else?" Lord Fancot looked to his wife, who jumped slightly, as she was not expecting to speak. "Do you so greatly dislike your drawing room, my dear?"

"I much prefer it to a workhouse or farm, for certain." Lady Fancot laughed, brushing her red hair behind her ears.

"See." Lord Fancot nodded proudly. "You advocate for a position none desire—"

"I dislike drawing rooms."

Verity's comment brought silence as she ate a bite of lamb. Everyone's attention was now on her.

"I do enjoy reading, but I must admit the sole purpose of my study of the pianoforte, arts, and embroidery was to be proficient enough that my governess would leave me be."

"My dear girl, whatever else could you wish for?" Lady Fancot asked.

"I . . . I think I would have liked to go to university," she answered.

"University? To study what?" Hathor asked her.

Verity smiled slightly. "Writing."

"To write you must learn to read. That can be achieved within your own home," Lord Hardinge spoke again.

"If so, why do men attend university?" She glanced to him and he did not have an answer. None of them did. I tried my best not to smile.

Not sure what to say in return, they looked to the marquess, who had not said a word. Neither had his wife, strangely.

"Charles, do you hear this?" Lord Hardinge questioned.

The marquess nodded his gray head. "I do, and sit amused at how the doctor has deflected the initial topic regarding his lack of desire to marry."

Damn. I had hoped they would have moved on.

"Ah yes," the marchioness spoke up. "For I do not understand why your reasoning would interfere with obtaining a wife."

I did not wish to dwell on this matter, so I smiled and said, "I fear I have no drawing room."

Verity giggled beside me, as well as Hathor and even Silva. But still the elders would not let me free.

"Of course, she certainly will not be a grand lady expecting a sizable estate to manage, but she will at least seek a small home of her own to live in. A small foyer could even do," Lady Fancot stated.

"Mother, not all of us must marry." Henry tried to ease the interest off me.

"All of you most certainly must," said the marchioness finally, lifting her spoon. "Amiable young men such as yourselves are surely in need of a wife, and thus a wife is out there in need of you all. You ought not disappoint them. The sooner you find your wives, the better."

"Mother, I am one year Darrington's senior and did not wed till this very year," Damon replied, trying to help as well.

"Do you take that as a thing of pride? Had you come to

your senses earlier would that not have made life easier for Silva? Right, my dear?" she pressed back, and looked to the young blonde in question.

Silva's eyes widened as she looked between her husband and mother-in-law. "Yes, it would have, your ladyship."

Damon could only sigh.

"See? And besides, Damon, you were not in nearly the same situation as the doctor, as not only do you have multiple homes but a great many people to watch over you. Dr. Darrington dedicates his life to those in need. A wife would do him good and would watch over him, for we do more than languish in fine rooms," the marchioness stated.

"That comes in time," Lord Bolen stated before looking down toward me. "You ought to think wisely, for marriage is a serious commitment."

"Has Lord Bolen not been engaged twice and never married?" Hathor said so softly that I thought I misheard it. However, the look on Henry's and Verity's faces said I had not.

"A commitment we must all make. And I shall see it done, for I am marriage's very own advocate." The marchioness drew our attention once more. "I could very well introduce you to Mrs. Frinton-Smith's niece Edwina. She is quite lovely."

"Those are the bakers on West Elm?" Lady Fancot questioned.

"They also own several inns in the countryside. I hear they are acquiring a copper mine in Cornwall as well."

Beside me, I noticed Verity's grip on her fork tighten, but I was not sure why.

"Thank you, your ladyship, but I believe your efforts are better served on Henry," I replied, my final attempt to save myself. Henry looked to me wide-eyed, his nose flaring.

Better you than I, I thought as they began to hound him while the butlers brought out the next course on sliver trays.

"You seem well able to converse now," Verity whispered, glancing up to me. "Or is it because they are married women?"

"They simply are not you." The words flew from my mouth without a thought.

"I knew it." She frowned heavily. "But what have I done to offend you, sir?"

"Nothing," I replied quickly. How had I so badly caused this misunderstanding!

"Then what makes me different?"

I fixed my lips to answer but there was nothing . . . nothing at all I could say but the truth. And the truth frightened me to admit.

"I see. Very well, I will not force you." She turned her face from me and the sheer movement alone caused me to fear hurting her feelings.

The truth would hurt me and my silence would offend her.

How maddening it was that her feelings already took greater precedence to me than my own.

I exhaled softly and simply said, "I did not speak during our dance because I was nervous. Currently I am still nervous and to avoid embarrassing myself I chose silence. But that has given way to misunderstanding between us."

When she finally met my gaze, I knew what she would ask so I braced for it.

"Why on earth would you be nervous? I did not think myself to be so unnerving."

"The fault lies with me, for being so greatly enamored with you," I said softly and when she once again looked to me I dared not look away. "I was and am nervous due to my feelings for you, Lady Verity. That is what makes you different to me. I beg your forgiveness."

Her gaze was unflinching and I could not at all read her

expression. My courage now gone, I quickly made conversation elsewhere with Henry.

Damn me!

Damn this racing heart of mine.

Verity

The dinner had ended with the promise of another dinner later in the week at Lord and Lady Fancot's home. It was quite obviously a plot designed to bring Henry and Hathor together. However, I could not help but think it would also bring Dr. Darrington and me together once more.

His words . . . they left my head spinning.

The fault lies with me, for being so greatly enamored with you, he had said. I was certain I had misheard, or at the very least misunderstood his meaning. But since he wished to leave no doubt, he stated he had feelings for me.

How could he have feelings for me? We hardly knew each other.

And what . . . what was this sensation? I reached to touch my chest, rubbing over my heart as if I were trying to keep it from jumping up and down.

So strange.

"Are you awake?"

I glanced to the door to see Hathor's brown face poking in. The moment she saw me sitting up in bed she smiled, rushing in and closing the door behind her. Since I was still dressed for the evening, she hopped onto my bed.

"Did Aphrodite let you do this often?" I asked her.

"Yes. Why?"

I shook my head. "Very well, I concede. Now, what brings you here? Oh, what else but the topic of marriage?"

"Ah right, you much prefer the halls of Oxford or Cambridge?" she mocked me in return.

"Is that so strange?"

"Yes, and that Dr. Darrington is even stranger," she shot back to my annoyance, but just as I was about to speak she added, "I have never heard a man advocate for us ladies in such a manner before. It is surprising, is it not? I have never minded drawing rooms, I love drawing and I enjoyed playing the pianoforte, I only stopped because I feel so inferior to Devana's talents. Not once did I find myself forced, but he made me wonder what other young ladies feel. Then you go and boldly claim you are one of those other young ladies. Do you truly hate it?"

"Not every day," I replied, pulling my knees to my chest and resting my head on my knees. "Sometimes it is relaxing. But I do think of other things. Like seeing other countries and peoples."

"Marry Dr. Darrington and you might get your chance." She laughed at me.

"Hathor!" I snapped as now the idea filled my head. "Me and Dr. Darrington? That—"

"Relax, I speak in jest. Obviously, that would never work."

"Because he wishes not to marry?"

"No, Verity, because he is illegitimate," she reminded, as I had in fact forgotten. "What a shame, though, for if he were not he'd be quite the catch for most young ladies. Handsome, young, skilled, and interested in a woman's mind."

How easily she could just say that, was she not embarrassed to admit it? Wait, why would she be? Why was I?

My mind was a mess; all I could see was his face.

"Should your focus not be on Henry?" I questioned, seeking to not speak of the doctor anymore.

"No." She frowned, her brown eyes now gazing up at the top of the bed. "He is not the one for me."

"How do you know?"

"He told me." She sighed. "Right as the third course came he confessed that his heart was already with another and thus his parents' efforts were for naught."

That gained my attention and I lay beside her. "He seeks to marry someone else?"

"Apparently he cannot marry her."

"Why?"

"He did not say. He told me so I would not have expectations of him and I am quite grateful for his honesty." She smiled brightly. "His character is charming enough that I might have gotten distracted from my true goal of a duke."

I rolled my eyes and laughed at her steadfastness, then paused, wondering. "What would have happened if he confessed to caring for you?"

"What could happen but either I reciprocate or reject him?"

"How would you know to do either?"

She looked at me strangely. "Would it not be by how his words made me feel? If he liked me and that brought me joy, I would reciprocate. Why do you seem so lost?"

Was that the sensation I felt? Joy?

"Why are you so certain of these things?" I asked back. "You have no greater experience than I and yet this whole process, selecting a husband, liking or not liking, feels as foreign to me as the depths of the sea."

"You do not make sense to me." She sighed. "Why would your own feelings on these matters be foreign? You like orange juice, do you not? I have seen you happily drink it each morning this week."

"And?"

"You are capable of knowing you like things. So the same would apply to people, no? You can like a person for being handsome, or well established or anything at all. This knowledge is not the depths of the sea, it is the depths of you. That should not be foreign at all," she replied, rising from the bed. "You are strange, Verity. But I like you as a person, another strange sister of sorts. Good night."

"Are you not going to ask if I like you?"

"You apparently have no clue what you like. Besides, who could rightfully dislike me anyway?" She smiled brightly and skipped to the door.

I chuckled then laughed.

She was just as strange as I was.

But as the laughter faded and I thought of Dr. Darrington, my heart once more began to flip.

And the depths of me feared she may have been right.

8

Verity

"What are you doing here?" my father questioned, glaring up at me from behind his desk. He looked almost exactly like Evander—tall, sand-brown skin with short curly hair and deep brown eyes, but unlike my brother's his were cold, angry.

"Papa—"

"How many times must I tell you that you are not to call me that?" he snapped at me.

I hugged my doll, the one Evander had given me before leaving. "I'm sorry, Your Grace—"

"No, it is I who is sorry, sorry I could not send you off to school with your foolish brother." He grumbled, lifting another paper to read. "This is why daughters are such a terrible inconvenience. I can rid myself of you only by paying a lofty dowry."

"I'm sorry . . ."

"Is that all you know how to say? You are no better than your mother, always sorry but never changing! If she was going to die she should have had the good sense to do it while producing a son."

"Is everything all right?" Datura, his new wife, whose skin was pure white and hair golden, came to stand behind me. She was dressed in bright red and wore rubies around her neck.

"No!" he yelled at her. "I knew it was going to be beyond

your lowly capabilities to keep the house in order, but I did think you would at least know how to manage a child. Yet here she is, roaming about."

"Worry not, I shall take her now." Datura smiled at him but when she reached for me I immediately stepped to the side, hugging my doll as tightly as possible.

No!

Please, no.

"No, Papa—"

She closed the door to his study, the smile on her face dropping as she glared down at me angrily.

"What did I tell you about leaving your room?" Datura sneered as she reached for me, grabbing my arm tightly. I pulled away, but her grip only tightened more.

"Papa!" I screamed but she placed one hand over my mouth and yanked me away. Please, *please*. I didn't want to go.

"Come!" Datura dug her nails into my arm. "Must you always be such a nuisance?"

"No!" I tried to dig my heels in but it was no use, they just slid upon the marble. She was so much bigger than I; there was no escaping. I bit her arm and tried to run, but she pulled on my hair, dragging me to her. I reached up to her hand, trying to free my hair, but I was met with a smack, then another, and another.

"You are nothing but a pest," Datura snapped as we reached the room. "A useless bother to everyone."

"Please, no!" I cried against her hand when I saw the wardrobe. I tried to push, but she hit harder and harder on my sides . . . everything hurt.

Please, someone help!

But no one came. No one was here.

"Don't you see this is the only place for you? No one wants you. All you do is ruin everyone's day with your horrid little face," she said as she lifted me up off my feet and threw me inside, slamming the cabinet doors shut behind me.

I banged my fists against the doors.

"I'm sorry! I'm sorry! Please let me out!"

"Be quiet!" She slammed her fist on the other side of the door. "I swear, it would have been better for us all if you had died with your damned mother, you spoiled little terror."

"Please," I whispered, closing my eyes as total darkness now surrounded me. *Please don't leave me in the dark!*

I'll be good.

I promise.

Hugging myself, my doll now gone, I started to cry.

But no one could hear. No one ever heard.

Please!

"Verity! VERITY!"

"No!" I screamed loudly as my eyes opened and turned up to the canopy of the bed. I felt arms around me as I cried and gasped.

"It is all right. You are safe. I promise, my dear, you are safe."

It took a few moments, as the nightmare of my memories faded, for me to realize I was in the arms of the marchioness herself. She hugged me tightly, rocking slowly back and forth.

"It is all right. You are all right," she whispered, kissing the top of my head as I calmed down.

But with the calm came my shame. How loudly had I been screaming? Who else had heard? What was I to say?

"Verity, my dear girl, what is wrong?" she asked me gently.

"Nothing," I whispered, slowly lifting myself from her arms to look at her. Her face looked so terribly . . . grief-stricken as she stared at me in what I knew to be pity. "Just a bad dream, Godmother."

"Verity . . ." She let out a deep sigh as though she did not know what more to say.

"Truly I am fine now, forgive me for the disturbance."

"Do you want to rest a bit longer? You need not come with us to the royal menagerie," she said as she reached up and brushed the curls that had fallen out of my bonnet away from my face.

"But I so wish to go, Godmother," I replied earnestly. The royal menagerie at the Tower of London was meant to show all the animals given to the royal family from across the world. "I promise you I am quite all right now."

"Very well," she replied as she rose from the bed. "I shall leave you to ready yourself for the day."

I nodded, rising as well. "Thank you."

"Not at all." She offered one smile to me before taking her leave. I placed my hands upon my face.

When will this end?

When can I sleep and wake like everyone else?

It had been years, and still my past haunted me. I wished to forget altogether, but I could not. Now, once more, the whole house would know that I was . . . that I was not right. And then soon I would become a nuisance again, I knew it.

"Good morning, my lady. Did you sleep well?" Bernice asked as she entered, as though she had no idea what had occurred . . . Maybe she did not? Maybe only the marchioness had heard me somehow?

"I did," I lied, and she nodded to me.

"Shall we prepare, my lady?"

I remained quiet, allowing her to help me clean and ready myself. All the while, other maids entered and went—no one mentioned or even seemed to know of my incident. By the time I walked down the stairs for breakfast I was truly confident that none had heard, and then I heard the small voice of Abena.

"Why can I not ask if she is all right at least?" the smallest of the trio at the bottom of the stairs asked her brother Hector and sister Devana.

"Mama said not to, Abena," Hector hushed her. "We are to pretend as if it did not happen at all. So if you ask Verity if she is all right that defeats the purpose. Do you understand?"

They were speaking of me. They all knew, and I had not yet been here a week.

"No. I do not understand at all." Abena crossed her arms. "Why is everyone acting like this is so bad? It's just a nightmare. I get those sometimes too. I want people to ask me if I am all right."

"She is not you, Abena," her sister said. "And that is all you need to know. Besides, do you wish to go against Mama? She will not allow you to come to the royal menagerie."

"Fine!" She sighed and marched from them.

I stepped away from the stairs, not wishing to go down now, but after insisting, I had no choice.

What sort of misery was this?

Theodore

This was the very worst kind of misery.

The royal menagerie was meant to show all of the ton how greatly beloved the prince regent was by showcasing the numerous animals gifted to him by rulers and peoples of the world.

"This is a lion too?" Miss Parwens gasped, the greatest of the expressions I had seen from her, as she stared up at the creature within its tiny cell. "Why does it not have a large mane like Edward there?"

She pointed to the other lion in its cage beside it.

"A lioness, a female lion, does not have a mane, Miss Parwens," I answered, as her brother was far too busy looking over at the gathered nobility. Searching for whom, I knew not; I could only guess it was his beloved.

"And that beast there, why does it have black spots? I was not aware lions could look as such. Is it a different breed?" she pressed, pointing once more.

"No, Miss Parwens, that is a leopard," I replied, staring as it roared and banged its head against the bars only for the guards to beat it away with clubs to the jeering amusement of the gathered crowd.

"It is quite ferocious. I thought the lions were the greatest of all beasts. Yet all these ones do is lie here." She giggled, looking back at the lions before us. "They are nothing but big cats, like Miss Peggy, is that not right, Henry?"

"Yes, exactly. Only those in there could eat you whole, Amity. But other than that, surely there is no difference." Henry scoffed, still searching.

"Excuse me for a moment," I said to them both, already walking away before Henry could question why.

As I did, I could not help but watch the people more than the animals. How much joy this brought to them and how excited the children were as they built the courage to approach the animals, only to run back giggling at the slightest roar or rumble. Everyone was having such a splendid time, and I did not wish to be the one to turn it sour. However, as I walked by, I could not help but see an elephant; its keepers threw fruits at it to pick up with its long nose. And the thought came to me once again.

"This is horrid."

But it was not I who said it. I turned to the voice beside me to see none other than . . .

"Lady Verity?" I gasped out in surprise. She was dressed in a soft lavender dress with a matching hat that had white flowers on the side, a pair of short gloves covering her hands.

She tore her gaze from the elephant and looked at me, her brown eyes widening in surprise.

"Dr. Darrington, you have ventured out into the wild as well?" the marquess questioned from behind her, and there I saw the entire Du Bell clan in attendance. They truly did move as one organism.

"Yes, good day to you, your lordship," I replied, bowing my head to him. "Henry and his sister extended the invitation, as Lord Fancot and his wife could not be in attendance."

"I am not surprised. Lady Fancot cannot even stand the sight of a parrot," the marchioness said as she stepped forward.

"And it is only by God's grace my sister's cat has lived so long," Henry said as he and his sister somehow managed to find us. There were hundreds of people here and yet somehow, I managed to run into the one creature I feared the most.

My eyes shifted to hers once more only to see the intensity of her gaze still upon me. Clearly, she had not forgotten what I had said to her. How could she? It had been but a handful of hours ago.

"Well, since you are all here, there is no harm in joining us as we venture." The marchioness smiled and then looked to her daughter Hathor.

The plots of mothers. I expected Henry to seek his method of retreat so I might go as well, but instead the blasted fool agreed with her.

"Lady Hathor, how are you enjoying the exhibition?" he asked as he moved to her side.

What on earth?

Just like that, we all began to walk again, and once more I was left beside . . . Lady Verity. She stared back up at the animals with a deep frown upon her lips.

I kept my arms tucked behind me and sought not to distract or annoy her in any fashion whatsoever. If she had asked me to grow wings and fly away from her, I think I could have managed it.

"I thought I was going to enjoy this?" she said softly, and I was not sure if she was speaking to me or herself so I said nothing. However, when she turned to me, her eyes sober, I found myself speaking.

"Are you not?"

She frowned. "It would be normal to do so, would it not? After all, everyone here seems quite entertained."

"Not everyone," I said.

She glanced around. "Who else is not?"

"Me."

"You?"

I nodded, looking to the monkeys as they too called out. "These poor creatures, plucked from their vast forests and nature, stuffed into cages for our amusement. It is rather sad. I must admit I did not think of it when I decided to attend. It was only upon seeing their—"

"Their eyes," she finished for me, and once more my attention was on her. "They are not happy, you see it too."

I nodded, not sure why I was smiling. "Yes, I do, but apparently many others do not. They are far too transfixed by the wonder of them existing at all."

"That is because none of them know what it is to be in a cage," she muttered.

"I beg your pardon?" I was not sure of her meaning.

Her eyebrows furrowed as she glanced back up at me. "Are you truly as kindhearted as you seem, Dr. Darrington?"

"I do not think myself a vicious person, but I do not pretend to be angelic either."

"So you are so kindhearted. For only those kind in nature deny being called such."

"I am not sure of that logic, my lady." I smiled. "For the cruel will deny being cruel as well. I believe it is best to judge a person by their words and actions."

"What words or actions of mine have led you to judge me as a person worthy of your affection?" She questioned so calmly, yet all of me shattered into chaos.

I stared back at her. Each time I met her, she stripped me of all reason and ability. I swear I was quite intelligent, but never could I show it beside her. I merely became a fool.

"You have no response? Am I to take it you were struck utterly by my appearance?" she questioned, her head tilted to the side.

"We ought to keep pace," I said, seeing the gap between ourselves and our party growing and taking a small step forward. When she joined me, I focused on the cobblestones at my feet. "I will not deny that when I first made your acquaintance it was your appearance that so utterly awed me."

"Is that why you slammed a door in my face?"

"I did no such thing."

"Well, it was not a slam, but it was very . . . abrupt . . . and in my face."

I recalled that moment before I'd had to tend to her brother. And it was true I was abrupt. "Forgive me, I . . . I did not know what else to do then but run."

She giggled, and glanced up at me. "Are you always so honest?"

"About myself? No. I'm rather guarded and temperamental so others will leave me be. But . . ."

"But?"

"Papa, can we see the birds?" the second-youngest Du Bell girl, the one with blonde hair, Devana, called out as she pointed to the aviary.

"You wish to come all this way for birds?" The youngest girl, Abena, frowned. "There are birds in England. I wish to see the other animals."

"You both have come to an impasse, what are we to do?" the marquess asked, glancing between them.

"We call a vote," said Devana.

"We can be kind and listen to the youngest." Abena grinned, causing her papa and mama to laugh and her siblings to grumble.

"She abuses her status as the youngest far too often, Mama." Hathor shook her head beside Henry and Miss Parwens. "She is spoiled."

"As were you at her age," her mama replied, and then glanced to where Verity and I were standing, looking between us. I felt an urge to take a step away immediately, unsure of what she thought.

"Verity, my dear, what would you like to see? You are our guest and thus you choose."

They all looked back to her, and she glanced around at the cages before looking over at the aviary. I watched as she took in the sheer size of it and the birds that flew around at the top.

"I do believe I would prefer to see the birds as well," she said gently.

"The birds it is then." The marquess nodded, taking his youngest daughter's hand as her face fell but she walked on.

I waited for us all to begin again before speaking to her. "Did you choose birds because their cage is biggest, thus it will feel least like a cage?"

"Was it that obvious?"

"Maybe to me alone," I replied, and then remembered another thing that lured me to her every other time I had set eyes on her. "And if I was correct, I do have another question."

"Yes?"

"Oftentimes at balls or when I arrived at your home or at dinner, I noticed you looking toward the entrance. At first, I thought you were waiting for someone. But could it be you were looking to escape?"

Immediately she glanced up at me, eyes wide just as we entered the aviary. Her mouth was agape, astounded by me while everyone else was astounded by the trees and the colorful little creatures that flew around them.

She frowned, gripping her own hands. "You have observed me to such an extent?"

"Forgive me, I—"

She turned from me, walking inside farther. I meant to follow, but Henry once more was beside me, letting out a deep sigh.

"I need to see . . . someone. How long would it take you to forgive me if I were to abandon you with them and go?" he asked, his body already pointed toward the door.

"Several hundred years," I snapped at him. "Are you mad? Forget me, what of your sister?"

"Can you not watch over her—"

"No. For she is not *my* sister. Close as you and I are, her reputation could be harmed," I reminded him. He bit his lip, turning back to his sister, clearly fighting the urge to run off . . . most likely to this woman of his. "Henry, you have a responsibility to her—"

"Is everything all right?" The marquess turned to us as the rest of the ladies went onward.

"Your lordship, please forgive me; a matter of grave importance has arisen that I must see to. Would your wife kindly watch over my sister till I return?" Henry asked, and I clenched my fist to stop myself from smacking him over the head.

"Yes, of course." The Marquess nodded to him.

"Thank you, your lordship," Henry replied, and not a second later he had run off as fast as his feet could carry him, the damn fool.

"And which young lady is of such grave importance to him?" The marquess chuckled as he came to stand beside me.

I stared back at him, shocked, but quickly said, "Your lordship, I doubt—"

"Come now, there is no need to cover for him, it is obvious. What else could be so grave for a gentleman but a lady? He has been rather distracted throughout our short time here," he replied and then let out a deep breath. "Anyway, I wished to resume our conversation from last night on the works of Descartes."

I wanted to resume my conversation with Verity but nodded to him instead. "Ah yes, your lordship, on which text? We spoke of both *Meditations on First Philosophy* and *The Passions of the Soul*."

His eyes lit up with joy as he began to ramble off. I listened and responded, following him as he walked, but my mind wandered. I couldn't help but think this was another one of the great differences between Henry and me.

When his heart told him to run . . . he ran.

I, on the other hand, hovered like these birds, allowed to fly only so high.

9

Verity

I was lost.

Well, I had purposely chosen to hide. But if anyone was to ask, I would simply say I was lost. I sat behind a bush, far away from where everyone else had gathered. I sought to breathe but my chest was tight.

Was it my corset? No. It was his words.

Could it be you were looking to escape? They reentered my mind. How long had I looked to exit the room that he had noticed? Had everyone else noticed as well? Were they all simply pretending, as they did with my nightmares? Why were all my secrets and flaws spilling out before the world?

Oh, if I could just return to Everely. I wanted to walk the grounds alone once more. Worry for no one and nothing. But it was still much too soon, I couldn't return now, not without being a bother to my brother and his wife. I did not want that. So, I was stuck here. Stuck hiding. First from the Du Bells, now from this Dr. Darrington.

"I now know for sure: I do not like him, he is quite rude," I grumbled at the orange-headed yet green-bodied bird that sat before me on the tree branch. "Why would he ask me that? If I am looking to escape what does it matter to him? Do people become so meddlesome when they are infatuated?"

Its head turned to the left and then it flew off, going right by the body of . . .

"Dr. Darrington?" I sat up quickly, surprised that he had found me, but he did not meet my gaze. *Had he heard me?*

"Her ladyship will notice your absence soon. You should return quickly; she is on the other side of that tree to the left." He pointed to it and then made a move to leave.

"I apologize!" I called out quickly.

He turned to me, frowning. "Whatever for?"

"You heard me, did you not?" I glanced down at my gloves, pulling at them.

"It is I who should apologize for being meddlesome. Now you ought to go—"

"You are not meddlesome," I said before he could leave once more. Taking a deep breath, I glanced up at him. "And I do not dislike you. I am merely embarrassed. I did not think anyone would notice my apprehension."

"Your apprehension?" His body moved toward mine and I noticed again how beautiful his hazel eyes were as they stared down at me. "At what?"

"Gatherings. Society. London." I threw my hands up slightly. "All of it. All of them. The people, everyone is so much . . . all the time. And I do not feel like I fit in amongst them. But I am supposed to fit in nevertheless. As a young lady of society, I ought to be amiable, full of wit, charm, and grace. It took all my energy to manage for my brother's sake so he would not worry for me. Now that he is gone and I am alone here, all I wish to do is run and hide. So yes, I am looking to escape. Because I wish to escape!"

"Can I tell you a secret?" he asked gently, and I was surprised by the question.

"Yes?"

"The only people who do not wish to run away are the people who cannot belong," he replied and frowned.

"Are you a philosopher or a doctor?"

"Which are you in need of?"

"Neither." I sulked.

He laughed at me and it sounded . . . nice. His whole face lit up and it made him look quite handsome.

"Then I shall simply be a person, and say, it is all right, Lady Verity. There are a great deal of lords and ladies who never venture into society, nor request that society come to them. They live their days quietly on their estates with no care for anything else."

"How do I do that?"

"You marry a lord with a fine estate, I believe."

I groaned, my shoulders drooping in a rather unladylike manner. "Why do people say that as if it were easy? Marriage is . . . forever. And the person one marries has the power to turn the greatest estate into the greatest of miseries. Believe me, I know."

"Have you been married before?"

I gasped, eyes wide. "Of course not!"

He laughed at me again. "Then how can you speak with such certainty?"

"I—I . . . Are you not against the institution as well? Also, is it not odd for you to be so after confessing your feelings for me?"

"No, I think not, as I do not have the mind to marry," he said, glancing up at the colorful bird that came to him, perching upon his hand.

"Are you admitting to being a rogue?"

"No, I admit I am a bastard," he replied as he stroked the bird gently. "Nothing can ever come of my feelings, I am aware. So I have no thoughts beyond their existence."

I frowned, not liking that at all. "If that were true you would not have told me."

"It was you who pressed for an answer at dinner."

"You cannot lie?"

"You seem keenly able to discern the truth from me. Besides I was far too unsettled to think of a believable lie."

I laughed at the childish pout and frustrated brow on his face. "Are you not meant to be a genius, Dr. Darrington? I heard you and the marquess speak endlessly on ancient works."

"They are not so ancient, and while I am not a fool I am no genius, especially not when I am faced with . . ."

"Young ladies seeking to run away from society?" I grinned.

"You. Exactly." He smiled back.

"Nevertheless, you ought to do better."

"How so?"

"In your confessions, it is hardly romantic to say such a thing over a ragout of beef."

"Understood. I shall say it over the roasted beef next time."

I giggled so hard I snorted, and quickly covered my mouth. "Pardon me!"

"Whatever for? You are magnificent," he said and I froze. The look on his face, the gentleness of his smile, I had never seen it directed toward me before.

The longer I stared the more I heard my heart thumping away in my chest. I knew not what to say. Suddenly another bird, similar in size to the one on his hand but colored all blue, flew right by my face. I jumped back, startled as I watched the two birds fly around each other.

"Are they fighting?" I asked, staring as they moved up to the tree. I watched as they pushed against each other over and over.

"No," he replied, watching them as well. "They are hugging each other."

"Birds do that?"

"These ones do, especially when they are in love."

"What?" I glanced back at the pair. They did seem unable to separate, just like . . . just like lovers. "They are in love?"

"This species of parrot is known for their devotion. So much so they are called lovebirds," he explained with a soft amusement on his face. "They are monogamous birds, and once they court each other they remain together their whole lives. If one of them dies or gets separated from the other, they grow very distressed and can even die of misery."

"Truly?" I gasped, stunned as I looked. "They grieve more even than people."

"Some people, for sure," he responded.

"Where have they come from?"

"They are native to the lands south of the Sahara Desert and to Madagascar."

I frowned as I sat back down. "So these are the lucky ones."

"What do you mean?" He turned to face me, confused.

"Either they were already mated or began their courtship here," I explained. "Imagine the birds that were separated from their mates or the ones that shall now never find them. Those ones will grieve as you explained, will they not?"

He stared at me and I sat rather uncomfortably under the intensity of his eyes. "You are correct. These are the lucky ones."

I nodded. "Well, at least there is some bright spot in this whole exhibit."

"You are quite compassionate, Lady Verity," he said to me suddenly.

"Me? How so?" I asked.

"You came to London for the sake of your brother, attempting to help him earn the hand of his now wife."

"How did you know?"

He smiled. "How was one not to know when all the young

ladies of the ton complained that whenever they sought to engage your brother in a dance, you would interrupt either by engaging their company or demanding your brother dance with you . . . despite etiquette."

I opened my mouth to speak then closed it. I was guilty of what he said. I had done my best to keep the other ladies and mamas away from my brother as a way to ensure no misunderstandings or obstacles arose. Which often meant dancing with Evander, which was not altogether proper, but who would say anything to us on the matter?

"Yes, I did do that, and the young ladies of the ton would hardly say that was an act of compassion," I finally managed to say.

"True, but your brother would say otherwise."

"He is my brother, so it is not so odd to be kind to him."

"And to Lady Clementina?" he mused. "Did you not seek to help her in her time of distress?"

"The greater credit lies with Hathor, for she was the one who not only noticed but threw herself upon the floor." I chuckled thinking about how dramatic she was.

He glanced at me. "Why do you seek to avoid praise, my lady?"

"I merely believe myself undeserving of it."

"What do you believe yourself deserving of?" he asked, then smiled, adding, "Other than a grand confession of love."

"I am not!" I tried not to smile back. "And how can you say such things with ease? Are you not embarrassed?"

"I am greatly embarrassed, however, words said can never be unsaid, and thus I must go forward undeterred."

"You are stubborn and strange, Dr. Darrington."

"Yes, forgive me."

I laughed but before I could say more I heard Hathor calling out, "Verity? Verity?"

Quickly I rose at the same time that Dr. Darrington stepped behind the bush beside me. His eyes looked around, but his body was so close to mine I could take in the scent of him: warm honey and apples. Once more I felt his heat upon my skin even through my clothes.

"Verity?" Amity called as well but her voice was rather far off.

Dr. Darrington glanced around. "You ought to go quickly, Verity, before a scene is caused."

"Verity?" I repeated, looking up at him. His eyes, however, were still focused elsewhere. "Does that mean I may call you Theodore?"

His whole neck snapped as he looked back at me, his face full of shock. I grinned.

"I shall go now, *Theodore*, thank you," I whispered to him, and ran behind him back toward the main path.

"There you are!" Hathor said as she rushed to me, Amity alongside her. "Mama was nearly in a panic when she realized you must have gotten separated from us. We all began to search. Where on earth did you vanish to?"

"Forgive me, I was mesmerized by the lovebirds," I lied with a smile.

"What? Are those truly birds?" Amity's eyebrows rose.

"Later. We ought to return to my mother before she calls for the London guard," Hathor replied, linking arms with me. "I swear, Verity, sometimes it feels like you are seconds from drifting away."

"I am not sure I know what you mean," I replied, glancing back over my shoulder to the bushes Theodore was surely still hiding behind.

All of a sudden, my day was much brighter.

And just like that, I realized I liked him . . . Now what was I supposed to do next?

Theodore

The smile on my face, the joy that coursed through me . . . came with a sense of dread and frustration.

What purpose did I have for doing this? For speaking to her this way? I told myself confessing my feelings would put an end to them. But it did not. I assured myself that the only reason I had come to her now was that I did not wish for her to be lost or for the marchioness to worry for her. However, I knew it was not true. As the marquess and I spoke I could not help but glance at her, watching her every step as if she were the wonder brought from across the far ends of the globe. When her strides purposely slowed and she moved farther and farther away . . . I took the chance myself. I lied to the marquess, saying there were patients in need of my care, just so I could go to her, so I could speak to her.

Now that I had done so I found myself asking once more . . . what was the purpose? No good could come from her and me being near each other. Had anyone seen us, I could have easily stained her reputation.

"Enough, I must keep my distance from her," I whispered as I made my way through the crowd. It was for the best.

"Pardon me, sir," I said as I slightly bumped into a frail blond-haired man with skin so pale, I could see the blue of his veins underneath. I was not at all a small person, but I was not so large as to knock him off his feet at the mere colliding of our shoulders. However, the man screamed as if all the world were attacking at once. He collapsed into my arms, gripping his head.

"Alistair!" A woman dressed in periwinkle with white gloves dashed to his side, her brown eyes wide with fear as the man once more struggled to stand on his own.

Nevertheless, he reached out for her white hand through gritted teeth. "It . . . I . . . sorry."

"My lord, you must breathe," I said, checking his pulse. It was dangerously slow. I looked to whom I could only assume was his wife. "My lady, we must get him home at once, he is—"

"Brother?"

Within mere seconds another man, slightly taller than myself, with blond hair similar to the man in my arms, rushed to our side.

"What is the matter? Yumiko, what happened?" he immediately asked the woman beside us.

"I do not know! He wished to leave, as he was feeling a slight fever, and next he was falling and screaming—"

"Tristian . . . It . . . AHH! AHH!" From the name of his wife and brother, I was sure he was none other than the first son of Lord Wyndham, Lord Alistair Yves, the Viscount of Tregaron. And it was far too late to be worried about a scene. Everyone within hearing distance had now turned to look at the spectacle.

"My lord, I am a doctor, and we must get him home at once!" I said, regaining their attention as they seemed to have all but forgotten I was here.

"I shall help you move him," his brother replied, already on the other side of him and placing his arm around his shoulders.

"I can walk . . . on . . . my own."

"My lord, you can barely breathe on your own!" I said as we quickly moved toward the exit.

"Make way! MAKE WAY!" his brother yelled at any and everyone, with clear panic and fear in his voice as we rushed.

It took us nearly eight minutes to reach his carriage, and when we did, he was all but unconscious.

"Brother!" Tristian yelled as we laid him on the back seat.

"ALISTAIR!" his wife screamed. I understood but neither was helpful.

"Sir, I need you to go to the carriage of Lord Fancot; there you will find my medical bag!" I said directly to Tristian and he was off running a second later, leaving me with his wife, who had also entered the carriage, gripping her husband's hand.

"Alistair? My love, open your eyes, please open your eyes, please!"

I thought it foolish, not in the realm of possibilities, for he was so clearly ill, and yet somehow his eyes opened, and he glanced up to her and smiled. How? I was not sure, but soon they closed once more and immediately I reached for his neck. He was so weak. I had heard the rumors that Lord Wyndham's heir was nearly upon his death bed so . . .

"What on earth was he doing on his feet?" I asked, mostly to myself as I undid his ascot and his shirt in order to make sure neither restricted his breathing.

"It is my fault!" the woman cried beside me. "He knew I wished to see the exhibit, so he pushed himself to come with me."

Before I could say anything, his brother returned with my bag. "I have it and I have sent a man ahead to alert the house. You all go now, I will ride behind," he said, shutting the door and ordering the coachmen to make haste.

Reaching inside the bag, I pulled out my mixture of lungwort, peppermint, and featherfew, tilting his mouth open to help pour it down. It was not much in the way of treatment but it would keep his airway free and open and soothe his heart.

"What are you giving him? And I have not even gotten your name. Who are you?"

"I am Dr. Theodore Darrington, and I need you to tell me everything about his condition thus far. Everything."

And she did.

For six months, the Viscount of Tregaron had suffered from the gravest headaches, loss of balance, overall weakness, and rapid weight loss. There were even times when blood came from his nose and ears. No doctor, physician, or scholar consulted could diagnose the reason for his condition, and even worse no one knew a method to help him either . . . no one other than Sir Grisham, who had offered him a tonic that seemed to have helped him to venture out today.

"Thank heavens we are here!" his wife called out as we finally reached the iron gates of their white townhouse, where Lord Wyndham, who stood tall for someone so short, along with his wife and nearly all of their servants, was already waiting. The doors were ripped open and the footmen were there to carry him as if he were Christ out of the tomb.

"Take him to his room at once! The baths must be prepared as Sir Grisham instructed!" Lord Wyndham commanded from the top of the stone stairs. His wife along with Alistair's followed quickly into the house.

"My lord, I do not believe a bath will do him much good right now!" I called out as I exited the carriage last.

"And who are you?" He sneered down at me.

Introductions did not seem pertinent but nevertheless I said, "I am Dr. Darrington—"

"I thank you for your efforts, Dr. Darrington, but my son is under the care of Sir Grisham. You may go," he declared, turning his back on me.

"MY LORD! Your son needs—"

"The rider my son Tristian sent has gone to alert Sir Grisham. He shall be here shortly," he said.

"If that is what you prefer, but at least allow me to see to his care in the meantime," I offered.

"Father, there is no harm in letting him stay. I've heard of him among the ton, he is the one who helped Lady Clementina," Tristian said as he was halfway up the stairs to his father.

"If the Duke of Imbert wishes to leave his daughter's care to a bastard that is his choice. I, however, will not subject your brother to such a dishonor," was his reply before he turned and marched into his home.

"I beg your pardon, Dr. Darrington." Tristian frowned as he looked at me. "And thank you for your assistance. Would you like our coachmen to take you back . . . ?"

"No need. Should you require my services, I am to be found at the Crown Inn. My best wishes to your brother," I replied calmly, bowing my head to him before turning back. This was a much-needed reminder for me.

Nothing I could do or be would ever change the status of my birth for those like Lord Wyndham. A bastard, whether he saved the life of one noblewoman or a thousand . . . was still a bastard.

I felt a bitterness rising within me as I began to walk, a curse rising in the back of my throat, and as the words nearly left my lips, I felt a drop of water from the skies above fall upon my nose. Another drop fell, then two, then rain suddenly drowned the whole earth. I glanced up, allowing it to wash away my ire, standing there like a madman, with a smile upon my face, taking in the rain.

Finally, reason got the better of me and I began walking. I walked until the day faded and the night rose, until the lavish open streets of the west were replaced with the crowded cobblestone streets of the east side of town, where drunkards and gamblers alike made their way to ale houses in order to squander their meager earnings. They were cheerful, laughing, and skipping through the rain. After all, the night had just begun and they had yet to lose anything. I walked to the third house on the moss-covered cobblestone street, the only one with a small iron gate. I glanced up at the dark bricks. Sometimes it felt like this home was held together by God's will alone. The door barely closed and had a small rat-sized hole in the corner; the windows were so dirty I could barely see the faintest light coming from inside. However, no one here would notice these things, for only one family shared this house, and so it was already considered to be quite luxurious.

I did not bother going to the front door. Instead I walked the narrow path around back until I came upon the stairs and a familiar stench filled the air.

"You ought to keep this door closed, Grandfather," I said as I entered, cleaning the rain from my nose.

"You look awful," was the first thing he said to me when I entered the kitchen, even though his attention was upon the small pot on the fire.

"You could at least look at me before you give your assessment, Grandfather," I said, placing my bag upon the only clear spot at the table. As always, it was covered in an array of plants, fruits, roots, and miscellaneous other treatments. He had everything from echinacea, ginseng, elderberry, and valerian to laudanum, leeches, and cream of tartar. Growing up he used to tell me all the world was located here in his kitchen just east of all the ton's greatest society, which made him the richest man in England . . . except for the king of course.

"There is no need to look, you only come back here when you are feeling awful," he replied and turned around to look me over. His hair was gone in the middle but gray on the sides; his back was slightly hunched, possibly from decades of stooping over books and pots; and his eyes, like mine, were hazel in color. "See . . . as I thought, awful. What happened?"

"Nothing. Can I not simply visit my family?" I asked, rolling up my sleeves to investigate what he was brewing.

"You are in dire straits then?"

"Grandfather!"

He chuckled and knocked my arm. "Very well, since you shall not share your life, share your medicine. What ails the great lords of the *ton* now?"

"Gout, greed, and gluttony," said my uncle Hamish as he marched into the kitchen dressed in the same tattered waist-coat he'd worn for the last ten years. The evidence of its service were the multiple patched holes and seams throughout. We Darringtons were not a poor family, but we were by no means affluent either; my grandfather's abilities as an apothecary and my uncle Hamish's work as an ironworker afforded us just enough to never be in fear of starving. However, my uncle, whose faith was stronger than a clergyman's, was known never to spend even a pence on any "finery" . . . it was unsightly to God, he proclaimed. He would wear a sock with several holes in it until his whole foot was able to go through it. Which made him often unrecognizable from the poorest of men in town on most days.

"I do believe greed and gluttony are similar in meaning, Uncle," I said to him. "And not only the lords of our society are suffering from it."

"Only they can afford to suffer from it, for everyone else is suffering from hunger," he huffed at me, and before I could say another word he turned to my grandfather. "How many times must I tell your grandfather to stop brewing these horrid potions in the kitchen during dinner?"

I could feel myself growing irritated. "These are medicines, Uncle, not potions. He is not a witch."

"The only true medicine in this world is the word of God. Or have you forgotten that while you run around the feet of *those* people?" he snapped at me bitterly, so disgusted his face bunched. "I have not seen you come to church in quite some time. Do you even go to church at all anymore or have you found a golden calf?"

"Hamish, enough! He has only just returned home," my grandfather yelled at him, and I felt the urge to tell him to relax and not worry himself. I had long since become accustomed to this. It was why I preferred the inn.

"I believe church should edify the soul not condemn it," I said to him.

"Like always you wish to be told sweet words, Theodore, and believe in the good of this world," he grumbled, shaking his head at me. "While your great and noble friends feast on lavish banquets over on their side of town, children cry out in the streets on this side. They are all greedy, foul, devilish—"

"Judgment is for the lord," I voiced loudly, looking at him with a smile. "Is it not, Uncle? You do not know them all as they do not know you. With that, I bid you both a good evening."

I glanced back over to my grandfather, whose shoulders were low and his face grim. He was old, he did not wish to fight, he did not wish to argue, he simply wished to study medicines and eat pie with a side of ale. Walking over to him, I placed my hand on his shoulder.

"I shall visit again—"

"You are soaking wet. At the very least stay and change, have supper," he said to me, but I'd much rather suffer the bitter cold of my clothes and risk fever than remain with my uncle.

"Grandfather, I—"

"If he wants to go let him go!" my uncle snapped. "Maybe you can try seeing if any of your so-called medicine works out there. For those people . . . our people."

I clenched my jaw but said nothing more, taking my things before heading to the door, slamming it behind me. I stood there for a long moment before exhaling and marching back up the stairs . . .

It was strange. No matter where I was, whether on the west side or the east, my presence was still not welcome.

10

Verity

I did not have a nightmare, as I had not slept. Instead, I found myself pondering over birds . . . and him: Dr. Theodore Darrington. Maybe it was this lack of sleep and the stillness of the night that brought forth such clarity. I had asked myself over and over again why my mind was stuck on him. Why did thinking of him leave such a strange feeling coursing through my chest? Why did I wish to see him even now? I simply had to imagine it was someone else asking me these questions. My brother, Hathor even. And in doing so came my answer.

I liked him.

Had my brother or Hathor told me of these very same thoughts, I would have simply told them they were caused by the affection they were feeling. But why was that so hard for me to accept? Why did admitting that leave me feeling as though I were going to roll into a hole in my floor and land directly in the drawing room?

"I like . . ." I whispered the word and then covered my face with my hands. I couldn't say it.

"Is everything all right, my lady?"

I rolled over onto my side to look at Bernice, who had entered the room and was watching me with basin in hand. I stared at her freckled face. No, everything was not all right. It was absolutely the opposite of all right. I was enamored of the very worst option of suitors for me. Evander would sooner let me marry a pig farmer than . . . someone like him. Someone like our Fitzwilliam. The very mention of it would . . . oh . . . I could not even dare to think it.

"No, I am not all right at all," I whispered. It was best for me to forget him altogether . . . and yet I remembered how he'd smiled at me yesterday and that made me smile.

"Are you ill, my lady?" Bernice put the basin down and reached over and placed her hand on my head.

"My lady, you are a bit warm," she said in a panic.

"Am I?" I reached up to touch my own forehead, but I felt no fever. "I believe—"

"Wait one moment, I shall call her ladyship!" She was already rushing to the door.

"Surely it is not so bad," I called out to stop her, but she was already gone, leaving her panic with me. I was not ill, nor did I wish to cause a fuss, I merely wished to . . . to wallow in my emotions.

Knowing the marchioness, now the whole house would be galvanized.

But if they thought I was ill, would they be calling on *him*? Again I smiled but then frowned, sitting up quickly, not wishing for him to see me look such a mess.

"Verity!" The marchioness rushed into the room, eyes wide, along with one other maid, pressing her hand to my head. "You are ill. I know it was from the rains yesterday. I told you and Hathor to rush to the carriage but instead you were playing!"

"I am not ill," I said. And I had not been playing in the rain yesterday. I was just enjoying the cool water upon my skin, along with the sight of all the others running for cover.

"Mary, have the kitchen send up lemon tea with honey as well as carrot ginger soup. Bernice, have a hot bath brought in, the trick is to fight back early!" she ordered them, clearly ignoring me. They all but ran out of the room.

"You are not calling a doctor?" I asked her, already relieved.

"For a cold? Hogwash." She smiled, helping me lie back down. "If I called a doctor each time one of my children caught a cold people would think my home was diseased. No need for all that drama. You shall be given the Du Bell family remedies and be back on your feet by tomorrow."

"Who catches a cold in the spring?" Hathor said from the door as she finished braiding her hair at the side of the head. "And from a little rain no less."

"If you are not going to offer her comfort, Hathor, it is best you go downstairs so you do not fall ill as well . . . from a hand on your backside!"

I giggled, settling into the pillow.

"I am not a child anymore, Mama, you cannot discipline me so."

"Would you care to wager on it?"

They stared each other down before Hathor stepped from the door. "Ladies do not gamble, so I shall go draw . . . since someone so inconveniently decided to fall ill, preventing us from going on our walk—"

"Go with your father, Hathor."

"Lord Hardinge will be visiting Papa and thus I will be stuck listening to them speak on Descartes the whole way." She sighed dramatically and looked to me. "You've been little help so far."

"HATHOR!"

"Going!" she said as she left quickly.

"Forgive her," the marchioness whispered, petting my head slowly. "For some reason, she never wishes people to know she cares."

I wished to tell her again that I was not ill. But on the other hand, I was struck by the way in which the marchioness tended to her family. She was far more attentive than I expected a lady of her status to be.

"Why do you go so far?" I asked her softly.

"What?"

"Evander said it is because you and my mama were the very closest of friends. But it has been more than eighteen years since her passing. How could such a friendship last even when one person is now departed?"

She chuckled. "It is because she is gone that it lasts, my dear. I can no longer remember any of the bad things that rock a friendship nor am I able to let go of the good things. I owe your mother a great deal, everything I have now is because of her."

"I do not understand."

"It is far too complicated and painful to explain. All I can say is that your mother . . . was love's biggest advocate."

Then why did love disappoint her so horribly? was what I wanted to ask, when a knock came at the door. I watched as the footmen brought in a copper bathtub, and a stream of maids brought in kettles of water to fill it with . . . they were certainly fast here.

"Mary, Bernice, help her up," the marchioness said to them, and I did not protest.

My mind was but a fog and I knew the cause not to be a fever, but my own thoughts. I was not so weak as to be brought down by rain, not as often as I had found myself walking through it. No, I was sure the cause of my present condition was that man and my confusion over what I was now supposed to do.

Was this how he felt upon discovering his attraction to me? What mess of himself did he make pondering such emotions?

I wished to ask him . . . I had so much I wished to ask him.

But there was no way for us to speak, not like we had done yesterday, in the aviary. I could do nothing but wait and hope for another series of events to bring us together again. But surely if that were to happen it would be called fate.

Fate.

Very well, I would leave it to that power, and if he somehow managed to appear today as well, I would not question . . . these feelings, but dare to explore where they would lead me.

After all, it should be impossible for us to meet again so soon. He was a doctor. He had patients . . . before recently I had seen him only twice, and briefly, on my brother's account. The Du Bells would have no engagements outside today. The only possible explanation would be the will of God.

It was that simple.

Theodore

"Tell me, Doctor, what is the matter with her? She's already lost two of her teeth and gone limp!" the older woman begged beside me as she held one babe on her left hip and the other small child clung to her apron.

I had decided to listen to my uncle and visit a few patients on the east side of town, and somehow found myself seeing more than two dozen children within the same home. At least five families were sharing the house I was in now. I'd gradually gone up the stairs, door by door, examining children no older than seven, who were unable to get out of their beds.

"I'm telling you it was Amanda's boy, on the second floor . . . he got the rest of them sick. His disease is going to kill my baby!" the woman hollered at me and her husband, who stood at the door, arms crossed. Both his shirt and his arms were covered in ink and sweat.

"Rebecca, calm down and the let doctor work, you are scaring them. It's a few teeth—"

"She is a girl, Tim! Who is going to marry a girl with no teeth?"

"She is six years old! Her teeth were going to come out anyway."

"And the bruises on her body?"

"She is a child, she bumps into things, that's what children do. They were all playing rough—"

"I know my daughter, Tim, and I know she is sick! That rotten little boy made her sick, made them all sick, and now . . . and now . . . she's going to die!"

"She needs oranges," I finally spoke, glancing from the little blonde girl back to her parents. They looked at me as if I were mad.

"I beg your pardon, Doctor?" Tim frowned, glaring at me. "Oranges?"

"Strawberries will do too. Even tomatoes. Not just her, but Mrs. Miller's son on the second floor also. They have scurvy . . . the remedy is fresh fruit and vegetables." It was a disease most common among sailors from my studies . . . it should not have been affecting so many children. "After a few fruits she should start feeling better in two days, continue for two weeks and she shall make a full recovery."

They were silent, which in my short time here I noticed was not common. Rebecca said nothing, holding on to the two children beside her tightly. Finally, Tim spoke up, his voice a bit softer.

"You don't have something else that will work?"

I stared at him. "No, unfortunately."

"There isn't much in the way of fruits on the market these days," Tim said to me.

"I saw a stand of fruits not a minute's walk up from here—"

"Andy's shop?" Rebecca huffed, lifting the baby again on her hips. "I'd need to sell this one just to afford two or three of his rotten supply."

"Rotten?"

"He buys off any leftover from the other side of town and brings them here to sell to us for nearly half a day's wage."

"Surely the man would want to have customers for his enterprise. He cannot be so overpriced." What good was it to sell food no one could afford to buy? "Will it not go to waste if he does not sell?"

"He does not care. The price is the price, he says," Rebecca replied. "We barely have enough for grain and lodgings here."

"Don't worry, I'll get it," Tim said sharply.

"How?" Rebecca snapped at him. "We don't have enough—"

"I said I will do it and I will do it."

The tone of his voice . . . gave me a bad feeling.

"If that's everything, Doctor . . ." He held out his hand to give me three pence. Since this was the last child in the building, I had dealt with enough fathers today to know I could not reject his payment. Wealthy or not, a man's pride was a man's pride.

"Thank you. I'll return in two days," I said, accepting the payment and offering a small nod to them before moving to the door. The moment I stepped out a drop of water fell from the roof of the house onto my head. I ignored it, squeezing past the kids on the stairs as I made my way down. It was not the only thing I had to ignore: the stench, the crying, the . . . exhaustion of every adult within.

"Gout, greed, and gluttony. Only they can afford to suffer from it, for everyone else is suffering from hunger." My uncle's words returned to my mind as I made my way to meet this Andy. But when I got there, neither he nor his overpriced fruits were anywhere to be seen.

I sought two other vendors, but they had only grain, potatoes, and port for the day. It was utterly baffling to me. How was it possible that an enclave like this, filled with hundreds of people, was left unable to get basic foods . . . and yet no more than a short walk away, as I crossed what seemed to be an invisible line dividing the west and east sides of London, I was able to see every fruit under the sun in the market square. Even the scent in the air had changed over here.

"What tickles your fancy, Dr. Darrington?" The fruit seller lifted a whole rack of peaches onto the table. "These beauties just arrived today."

I paused, eyeing them all, sure the cost would greatly affect me later; however, the thought of those children stuck in my mind, and the determination on the face of that girl's father . . . I knew the look of a man who was ready to do what should not be done. I could prevent it.

"If I were to purchase all you had on sale here today, when could it be delivered?" I asked him as I brought out the last of my money to give him.

"All of it?" he gasped, a wide grin spreading across his tan face, his hands already outstretched. "I . . . I could have my boys deliver them by tonight. Where to, sir?"

"There are apartments on Langley Cross. I will write the address . . ."

"Langley Cross?" the man repeated, his smile now fading. "On the east side?"

"Would that be a problem?" I asked.

"I can't have my boys deliver over there."

"Why?"

"It is not the safest."

"I managed to walk from that very place just now unscathed. I'm sure your boys—"

"Forgive me, Doctor, you didn't have goods with you. A

load like this, those savages would rob my boys five minutes into walking into that hellhole. We cannot risk it." He was already handing my coin pouch back to me, his nose turned up so high you'd think he was the lord of fruits.

"I—"

"Pack them up, my footmen will deliver it."

I turned back to see none other than Henry, his clothes slightly disheveled and a clear smug grin upon his lips. He leaned over and grabbed an apple from the stand.

"Trying to be a hero all on your own again, my friend?"

"Why is it that you are always appearing when I wish for your presence the least?"

"The same could be said about you," he replied, taking a bite of the apple before nodding to the man and his fruits. "My men will be here within the hour to retrieve the order. Do package them nicely, even savages wouldn't want mushed peaches."

"You do not have to do this, Henry, it's fine. I'll—"

"Carry them on your back across the city yourself?" He gave me a look, shaking his head. "You've already given them all your coin. At the very least keep your health."

I ignored him, walking away from the stand, when I realized . . . I would barely have the funds to pay for my lodging at the inn tonight. So either I returned to my grandfather or . . . Henry. Both thoughts left me rather frustrated with myself.

"Have you realized you will need more of my assistance yet?" Henry chuckled, still eating his apple as he came up beside me once more.

"You are not exhausted from your other affairs?" I questioned, nodding to the rogue stain at the neck of his blouse.

"Let us focus on why you have decided to buy a month's worth of fruit at the expense of yourself." He changed the subject, adjusted his shirt, using his coat to better cover the stain. "You cannot keep doing this."

"Doing what?"

"Squandering any money you earn on the downtrodden. You've been doing it for years. You alone will not be able to save them. I do not know why you carry such guilt. It was not you who caused their present circumstances."

Henry was a good man, a kind man. Far better than many I had the misfortune of meeting. He went out of his way to aid when needed. However, at the end of the day, he was still a nobleman, and therefore unable to fully understand the lack of fairness in this life. And I never pushed to change his views because there was nothing that could.

Life was unfair. It would always be unfair. And thus, the greatest anyone could hope for was a person to be as good as they could be.

"It is not squandering if it helps someone in need," I replied as we walked across the street.

"Charity is always a fine endeavor, but you often do so at your own expense my friend. You have given them food today, what shall happen tomorrow or next week? You are not rich enough to be such a benefactor—"

"Has anyone told you that you are starting to sound like your parents?"

He paused and looked at me aghast, placing his hand on his chest. "That was a harsh blow. Must you be so cruel?"

"I must. For you—"

"Mr. Parwens? Dr. Darrington?"

We both turned to see Lady Hathor, dressed in light blue, a matching parasol above her, her hand holding that of her youngest sister. Not so far off in the distance was her father and Lord Hardinge in some deep conversation, the topic of which was sure to be philosophy.

"Lady Hathor, how nice it is to see you," Henry said.

"I am here too." The little girl beside her pouted, making him laugh before nodding to her.

"My apologies, Lady Abena."

She smiled, nodding. "You can just call me Abena. I'm not a very good lady."

"Abena!" Hathor snapped down at her.

"What?"

"Excuse her, she is . . . young," Hathor said with a very tight smile on her face, making Henry beside me smile.

"What brings you ladies out today? Are you in need of ribbons?" Henry questioned while I glanced to see if Verity was close by, as they were normally always together. But she was nowhere in sight.

"We planned on a family walk, but that changed this morning and now we are on a quest for anything sweet one could have while sick with a cold," she replied.

"Are you ill, my lady?" I asked.

"Not her," Lady Abena spoke. "Verity is sick, and we wished to get her something to make her feel better. I said chocolates but *someone* does not agree."

It was like the earth shook underneath me.

Hathor shook her head. "Chocolates, when you are unwell, make you worse, Abena—"

"Lady Verity is ill? What are her symptoms? Does she have a fever? Has a doctor been called already? Is she—"

"One question at a time, Doctor, or how will they answer!" Henry placed his hand on my shoulder and gave me a stern look. It was only then I saw the looks of both the girls before me. "Forgive my friend here, when it comes to medicine, he often loses his mind."

"Oh, I get like that with food!" Abena grinned, causing her sister to sigh.

"If I were a smarter person, I'd be home with Devana," Hathor muttered under her breath, looking to us. "Thank you for your concern, Dr. Darrington. I believe she is fine and in no need of a doctor. Our mama has defeated many a cold before. We only sought to get her something while we were out on our walk. We ought to be going now."

She turned to leave when I stepped forward again. "Laoshan tea!"

"I beg your pardon?" She turned back to me.

"Laoshan tea with a bit of sugar. It's very sweet and tastes a bit like chocolate. It's also very good for health," I said softly, trying to calm myself, but I knew I would not be able to until I saw her. However, what could be wrong? She had seemed perfectly well yesterday.

"A tea that tastes like chocolate?" Abena gasped.

Before I could reply, I heard the voice of their father calling out, "Benjamin!"

His voice was so loud that everyone within hearing distance paused and turned to watch as the marquess grabbed on to his friend, who was clutching his chest struggling to breathe.

Again?

Had this not just happened yesterday? I did not need another repeat performance. Nevertheless I rushed toward him, helping the marquess carry the weight of the man nearly keeling over before us. Henry came over to help ease the burden off the marquess.

"What happened?" I asked, reaching to touch Lord Hardinge's pale white neck.

"I am not sure. He was well one moment, and then the next began a fit of coughs he could not shake."

"Can you hear me, my lord? Stay calm, breathe slowly," I instructed, looking into his panicked eyes. The man nodded but still was breathing quite irregularly. I looked at the marquess as well as the gathering crowd. "I cannot examine him here, we must take him home—"

"My home is closer. You will tend to him there!" Lord Monthermer said before calling for his carriage, and I glanced back up at him.

You will tend to him.

The five words refused to me yesterday were given freely today. I always wished for the best with all of my patients, that did not change, but I could not deny there was a greater spark of . . . determination in me.

And also . . . hope that I'd be able to see her.

11

Verity

May 15, 1813

What is it to like or to love?
Who is it that measures the portions of either?
Is it akin to a tether, bound hereinabove?
Like lovebirds who found themselves in
   a strange world?
Afraid, taken from their heaven.
But such the only thoroughfare to their beloved.

"Should you not be resting?"

I closed my journal immediately, turning back to the only person who ever entered without warning or permission.

"If I rest any longer, Hathor, the bed and I shall become one," I replied as she outstretched her hands to give me a cup of tea. "Thank you. May I ask why *you* brought tea instead of a maid?"

"I was forced to do so because apparently there is a plague." She huffed as she sat on my bed.

"A plague? In London? Yes, I do see why the maids are pre-occupied." I chuckled, blowing on my tea as she let out an even deeper sigh, which was why I was sure she was being dramatic and there was no actual cause for concern. Besides, no one had mentioned anything when my supper was brought up.

"There is no other explanation for why everyone is suddenly turning up ill left and right. How are we supposed to enjoy the season if everyone is collapsing?" she grumbled.

"I was merely tired this morning, Hathor, no need for you to—"

"Not just you! First Clementina. Silva has been rather unwell and unable to accompany me as of late. Yesterday Lord Wyndham's son collapsed in the middle of the royal menagerie. Then you—"

"Once again, I am perfectly well," I interrupted before taking another sip of the tea. It was much sweeter than the ones prepared this morning.

"And as if that were not enough Lord Hardinge collapsed during our walk this afternoon."

"Truly? Is he all right? What was the matter?"

"We do not know, and he has yet to recover even still." She let out another sigh and fell back on the bed. "Thank goodness Mr. Parwens and Dr. Darrington were nearby or father would have injured himself trying to bring Lord Hardinge back home with us. Now the whole house is running to aid Dr. Darrington."

I coughed against my teacup. "I beg your pardon?"

"Father insisted that Lord Hardinge be brought back here for Dr. Darrington to treat him. Mama of course sent me off but I—"

"Is he here? In the house? At this very moment?"

"Who? Lord Hardinge? Yes. Are you not listening to me? Dr. Darrington is tending to him in the guest room downstairs."

I could not believe the words coming out of her mouth. Just this morning, on the very bed she now lay upon airing out her grievances, I had made . . . a bet? An oath? I was not sure, but I clearly stated in my mind that if Dr. Darrington somehow managed to arrive this very day, I would not . . . I would not deny my feelings. And this evening he was here.

How was it possible for him to be here?

This could not be. Such things said in jest did not happen in truth. Never had I ever requested anything and had it appear before me within hours. I was so stunned that I was not sure what to say. But as Hathor explained the events that had led to this moment my eyes drifted to the floor beneath my feet.

He was here.

Just a few steps below me, he was here.

My heart began to pound fast, so much so that the room felt as though it were no longer steady. Carefully I placed the tea on the desk behind me before rising and throwing myself upon the bed.

"Are you all right?" Hathor asked from beside me.

"I am unsure."

"Was it the tea?"

"No."

"Then should I call Dr. Darrington—"

"Certainly not." For that would make me feel far worse.

"What has come over everyone lately?" She shook her head at me as she rose from the bed. "Soon, I'll end up being some sort of nurse."

"Wouldn't the logical outcome be you unwell, rather than becoming a nurse?" I asked.

"I do not get ill, as sickness does not look good on me. Now please hurry up and gather your senses so tomorrow you will be of more use. I shall come to check on you once more should you need anything. Mama will be preoccupied with our other guests."

I smiled, as she truly did not need to do this, and I was sure no one was forcing her either. She merely could not help herself, even though she complained. "Hathor, truly I am fine, worry not. Tomorrow we may go wherever your heart desires."

"I shall hold you to it!" She nodded before going to the door. "Good evening."

When she left, I rolled onto my back and covered my face with the pillows because . . . because . . . what in heavens name was I supposed to do now?

He was here!

Theodore

"He is barely breathing," said the marquess from the foot of the bed as I examined Lord Hardinge. His face was dangerously pale, and his breath shallow, with a faint odor. On top of this, he was sweaty due to his fever. He was drenched, as though he'd fallen into a fountain and not the road. I had seen this before. "Is it a stroke?"

"I do not believe so, for these are not the signs of such. However, I will not be able to rule it out until he wakes up. Word should be sent to his wife that he cannot return home this evening in this condition," I replied as I moved back from the bed to where the footman had brought my bag.

"His dear wife passed last summer," said the marchioness from the door, as her husband would not allow her to enter the room, rightly so. Still, she insisted on staying close. "They have one son, but the boy is no older than twelve. He has no other relatives. You must save him, Dr. Darrington, or the child will become an orphan. It is Benjamin's greatest fear."

"He shall do everything he can, my dear." The marquess turned back to him, still speaking to the marchioness. "You should allow him space to work. Go see the children. Hathor and Abena were there as well and must be worried."

She sighed, nodding, then looked at me once more. "Dr. Darrington, this is our housekeeper, Mrs. Ingrid Collins. Should you need anything more, instruct her, and she shall see to it. I assume you shall be staying as well to tend to him?"

I nodded. "Forgive me for the imposition."

"Not at all. We are grateful you are here." She let out a deep sigh, her eyes shifting to Lord Hardinge once more before taking her leave.

"I shall need boiling water, a cup with no more than a tablespoon of ginger and sugar, and a spoon, as well as an empty basin and towels, if you can, Mrs. Collins." I moved back to Lord Hardinge to check his teeth and gums. She nodded, leaving quietly and closing the door behind her.

"I doubt you need those items for tea. What is it?" questioned the marquess. "Now that the women are gone, you may speak freely."

"I do not want to speculate and cause panic," I replied, opening the man's mouth wider to look down his throat.

"By not providing answers, you create exactly that. Fear and panic are the by-products of ignorance," the marquess said, sounding like a professor. Even now, the fact that he stood at his friend's bedside instead of shrinking away in fear himself said a great deal about his character.

"Are you not worried you shall catch whatever may be ailing him?" I questioned in return. "Most others would be speaking to me behind a door or, at the very least, with a handkerchief covering their nose and mouth."

He chuckled, shaking his head. "I trust in your skills enough to know that if the situation were so dire, you would have asked me to refrain from entering and taken precautions to protect yourself. Plus, the relaxed nature of this conversation seems to imply you are not that worried."

"You are, as they say, my lord, a man of reason," I replied as I stood up straighter and looked at the patient before me.

"And one of curiosity. So, do tell me of my old friend here," he pressed once more.

Usually, I never spoke of my patients to a person not of their family, but as Lord Hardinge had no one else, I had little choice.

"Has Lord Hardinge been in the care of Sir Grisham?" I asked, looking at the marquess, who frowned and shook his head.

"I am not sure. Why?"

"His case is presenting similarly to that of Lady Clementina Rowley," I said.

"What? But did she not take a tonic of some sort? I could not imagine Benjamin desiring to become shorter."

Neither could I. "Yes, and it was highly toxic, which is why I intend to have him expel the contents of his stomach, just in case, to clear it from his system."

Just then, there was a knock at the door.

"Enter," said the marquess.

Mrs. Collins arrived with a tray of all I had requested, two other maids beside her, one with the water and the other with an empty basin.

"I shall need two footmen to help lift him toward the basin once he consumes this," I replied, taking the ipecac from my bag and carefully putting the smallest drop of it into the cup for him to drink.

I turned back to the patient, and saw that the marquess had removed his jacket to help the footman beside him lift Lord Hardinge.

It startled me, but I pushed the thought from my mind as I prepared to work. Taking the spoon, I carefully poured some into Lord Hardinge's mouth.

In the back of my mind, though, I was still wondering when . . . or if I could see Verity.

Verity

I tried to journal the evening away, and at one point I even began needlework to distract my mind. However, nothing could sway my thoughts from the man downstairs. I found myself moving to the door to see if I could hear his voice, or catch anything of his presence. Bernice later came to check once more that I was all right. Instead, all I did was press her about Lord Hardinge so I could hear of Dr. Darrington. I had rested so much during the day that as the night came and everyone else had gone to sleep, I was wide awake . . . My thoughts were full of . . . of Theodore. I thought of the ease with which we had spoken to each other just the day before, how he sheepishly smiled . . . I also thought of his feelings, the ones he confessed to me, and all of me shook with excitement once more.

I wish we could have spoken more, I thought, reaching into the box for a vial, and feeling my shoulders drop as I thought of what he would think if he knew I took this or the reasons why. Would he still feel the same?

I pondered over that question again until the urge to end my torment finally grew to the most extreme levels. Gripping the vial in my hands I rose to my feet.

He was still in the house, and I knew what room he was in, as Bernice had said he refused to leave Lord Hardinge's bedside.

I could go.

"I should not, though," I said to myself in the mirror. I could only imagine the consequences should I be caught. To think of it was insanity. For what reason would I be in the dark seeking him out? Merely to speak for a few more minutes? It was ridiculous. And yet I found a devious plot brewing in my mind. Evander would not have been surprised. It was only because I was under the marchioness's care that I sought to be on my best behavior. If this was Everely, I would have already done what I wished.

"I shall go," I said, turning toward the door only to immediately sit down. Perhaps he was sleeping as well.

If that is the case, I will merely say I went down for milk, I thought, taking my robe. The last thing I took was the vial. I would be honest, as he was with me, and then I would learn if these feelings were real.

I opened the door slightly, sticking my head out to see nothing but the slight glow of a candle coming from the bottom of the stairs. Tiptoeing out, I sought to see if it was a maid, but instead, at the very next landing was none other than the man in question. He had only removed his coat and was staring intensely at something in his hand, even sniffing it, and when his face wrenched up into a foul look, I couldn't help giggling.

Immediately, he turned to look, and I ducked as if I were a child. What in the heavens was the matter with me?

"Hello?"

"Shh!" I shot up quickly, fearful someone would hear him.

"Lady Verity?" He still spoke as if we were in a ball.

"Shh!" Slowly, I walked down the stairs, my heart pounding with each step. Maybe that is why I lost my footing on the last stair, tripping over my hem. All the blood rushed from my legs to my heart. I tried to catch myself, fearful of the noise I would create, but instead of hitting the floor, the wall, or the railing, my chest collided . . . with his, and his arms wrapped around me tightly.

His face was so close to mine that I could see even the finest lines around his eyes, which widened as he stared down at me.

"Are . . . are you all right?"

I could not speak, so I merely nodded.

He nodded as well before shaking his head and stepping back, helping me to stand on my own.

"What are you doing out so late?" I finally managed to ask him.

"The same could be said of you."

"I asked first." I felt embarrassed to say I had not expected to actually see him so suddenly.

He chuckled. "That you did."

"So?"

He lifted an empty vial for me to see. "I was investigating."

"What is it?"

He opened his mouth to speak, then glanced around the landing where we stood. "We ought not to be here."

I nodded, going farther down the stairs, but he did not follow. "Are you not coming?"

"Lady Verity—"

"Did we not agree to call each other by our first names in the aviary, Theodore?"

I saw his chest rise and fall before he spoke again. "Should anyone discover—"

"They very well will if we stay here," I replied before going down the stairs to the drawing room. Reluctantly, he followed.

"Lady Verity—"

"Just Verity." I turned back to see the great distance he had put between us. He stood at the doors, and I stood by the fireplace.

"Neither that nor any of this is appropriate. Should the marchioness, or anyone for that matter, know you were alone in the company of a man—"

"I shall say not a man but a doctor," I replied, walking toward him. He stiffened, but he did not move. I stopped when there was but a foot between us and lifted the vial for him to see. "Should anyone come, I will tell them I sought your care due to an ailment."

He reached out to take the vial from me, but I held it back. "What did you discover in your investigation?"

"I do not speak of my patients to others."

I frowned. "Then why did you bother to tell me at all?"

"I appear to be having an extreme lack of judgment this evening," he muttered and exhaled. "Lady Verity—"

"You—"

"Verity," he finally said, and I smiled, nodding.

"Yes."

"What in heaven's name are you doing?"

"I'm not entirely sure."

12

Theodore

From the second I saw her face over the edge of the railing, I was as sure as the day was long that this was a temptation from on high. The rational, reasonable, and cautious parts of my mind had disappeared at the sight of her. Now I tried to convince myself to flee. She had taken a seat beside the fireplace, staring back at me as I stared at her.

She was haunting yet breathtaking in only the dim light of my candle. When else would I see her so . . . unperturbed? In a housedress and robe, no less.

"Please say something," I begged, not strong enough to withstand this.

"I feel as though I can breathe for the first time since coming here."

"Ironically, I seem to be having the exact opposite experience." I had never been able to breathe less.

"Forgive me. I did not mean to impose—"

"You are not imposing. This is just—"

"Inappropriate. Yes, I know, you have said so twice now."

"Because I am at a loss for what to do or what you seek. A lady in your position should—"

"Be strictly managed by her mama until she is given to a husband to then be strictly managed by him." She frowned, and so did I.

"Hopefully, that will not be your case."

"You are not disagreeing?"

"Why would I? You speak the truth."

She looked genuinely surprised, then smiled. "Are you aware I have no mama?"

"We all have a mother. Yours is merely not here any longer," I replied, leaning against the wall.

"As I do not have even one memory of her, it would make no difference if you told me I fell from the sky to Everely. Do you remember your mother?"

"Yes."

"How old were you when she passed?"

"We are back to the personal questions," I said, and her shoulders dropped. I could not bear to see that. "She died when I was two weeks from my seventh birthday."

"I am sorry."

"As am I for you."

She was silent for a moment, glancing around the room as though she were searching for something to make conversation about. When her eyes finally met mine, she frowned.

"Verity, I must ask you again what is it that brought you here—"

"You."

"I beg your pardon?"

She took a deep breath before repeating herself. "You. You being here brought me here, Theodore, as you have plagued my thoughts since . . . I do not know when. So I wished to see you. Though now that I have, I am unsure of what to say or do."

She inhaled and it was as if she were stealing my breath from my body. I stared, uncertain if I were dreaming or losing my sanity. How had I ended up in this situation?

"I . . . You . . . Forgive me but can you be clearer with your thoughts?" I finally managed to say.

"I would if I could think clearly." She smiled gently. "All I have figured out is that I think I have come to like you as well, though I do not understand how, as we are barely acquainted. Is this normal?"

I laughed but it was like a breath of relief and a surge of joy as I looked into her brown eyes. My mind was a mess of things. "I am unsure of what normal is anymore."

"That is unhelpful," she said. "How am I to make sense of these feelings when no other has made me act this way or say as much as I am now?"

"Stop." I reached out to grab her arms. "For if you say any more, I shall think I am dreaming."

"I cannot stop, that is the problem. I keep wondering how? How does one come to like someone so suddenly? Is it possible that maybe your soul and mine recognized something within each other before our minds did, thus reason cannot apply?"

I knew that this moment with her would be one I would never forget. However, I could not allow myself to let my feelings overcome me.

Taking her hands, I felt the thundering in my heart grow louder as my voice grew quieter. "I am delighted by the fact you hold any sort of feeling for me, Verity. These words are like medicine to my soul. But I must be honest, had I known there was even the slightest possibility you would care for me, I never would have spoken my true feelings."

"I do not understand . . . why?"

"Because nothing can come from this but pain, Verity. You are a lady, I am an illegitimate son of a nobleman. Such a match would never be accepted. And thus, it is better not to mention it."

"Better for whom?"

"You."

"Should I not be the judge of that?"

I shook my head. "Society judges, and you do not know how vicious it can be to those that go against it."

"Do not think me so naïve on that front, I am quite aware. My family has had a great number of scandals—"

"Titled men can weather the storm of scandals, while women are crushed upon the waves. Your father and brother are not the same."

The frown on her face was heavy, and her eyes clearly confused. "Are you . . . rejecting me?"

"I am begging you to reject me." I hung my head for I wished . . . oh, how I wished. But I would not have her hurt because of me.

"No."

At that, I glanced up to her, confused. "No?"

"Yes. As in no, I will not reject you based on your birth, and I ask you to show me the same courtesy, for it is ridiculous—"

"Verity."

"If you wish a reason to reject me let it be this." She held up the vial for me to see and I felt she was desperately trying to change the subject to keep me from saying the truth. "It is a tonic I drink, as I have suffered from nightmares for years. Sometimes, I find that I cannot move. Other times, I awaken in a cold sweat or tears."

Immediately, I remembered her brother speaking to me of this very condition. I thought he had been referring to himself, even when he denied it, as most men of his status would not admit to such an affliction. Never had it occurred to me he had been talking about her.

"The only people I have spoken to about this are my brother and Dr. Cunningham. The latter, of course, prescribed me this. It worked for a time but has stopped being effective recently."

It was only then that I found the power within myself to go

toward her. Taking the vial from her soft hands, I uncorked it and sniffed.

"Do you know the contents of it?"

She shook her head. "Is it dangerous?"

"I am not sure. But I would not think so if you've had no other symptoms. It is not unusual for medicines to lose effectiveness over time. How long have you used this one?" I looked down at her, and I should not have because once again, my thoughts were scattered to the winds. The shameful look upon her face . . . I wished to reach out and touch her. "There is nothing for you to be ashamed of. At some point in time, every last person, from the strongest to the richest, or wisest, will seek some sort of aid."

"Five years," she whispered. "Dr. Cunningham has given me various others throughout that time. You say at some point, we will all need aid, but for me, it feels as though it has always been so. I've come to accept it, and this was my remedy."

"When your brother spoke to me of this, he made it seem as though no medicine had yet been prescribed—"

"My brother told you?" She looked mortified, as if she had not just told me as well.

"Yes. However, he did not say it was you. I thought he was speaking for himself."

She relaxed. "Oh, and what did you say?"

"I told him that nightmares are often rooted in other issues and feelings. This medicine is most likely to help ease your body and mind. However, the more you take it, the more you shall need, as your body has become resistant to it."

"Are you telling me I ought to stop taking it?"

"No. I am saying it is never going to be a true remedy."

"What . . . what else am I to do then? Let the whole house hear me? Let all of the ton talk of me? Laugh at me?" She hung her head, the grip on her dress tightening.

"Verity."

She glanced up at me, her eyes shining but not a single tear shed. "Do you find it disturbing?"

"Find what?"

"That the woman you like is . . . ill, like this."

I frowned. "Did you not hear me? Almost everyone has some ailment. Why would I find this disturbing?"

Her chest rose and fell as she let out a deep breath . . . this was dangerous. "Verity, you ought to return to your rooms now."

"Theodore." She said my name, and again I had to press down my feelings . . . the pangs of lust were rushing to the surface. She did not know how tempting even the simplest words from her lips were.

"I beg of you, please go," I truly begged, for too much had been said already between us.

"I cannot."

"Verity, our conversation goes beyond—"

"Decency, yes I know, but so does this moment," she whispered and my heart quaked. "Since we are already beyond that I will say it: I wish to understand your feelings and more of mine."

Once more my mind told me this could not be real . . . and yet. I could see the determination in her eyes.

"It is not something I could ever explain in words, Verity . . ."

"Then by action?" she questioned. "If so, show me."

And I had to keep myself from groaning. Dante clearly forgot to mention this level of hell, or was this purgatory?

"Verity."

"Show me."

Fine, if I was to be damned, I might as well not hold back.

I placed my hand on her cheek and . . . and I leaned in,

pressing my lips against hers quickly. It was so short but the moment her lips touched mine I felt myself . . . harden. She stared up at me wide-eyed.

Fuck.

"Forgive me—"

She leaned in and pressed her lips tentatively to mine for only a few seconds before sitting back.

"You ought not have done that." I shook my head.

"I felt a sensation and I wished to see if it would happen twice."

"Did it?"

"Yes."

Dear God, forgive me, I thought and pulled her up into my arms, kissing her gently at first, allowing her to get comfortable with my lips upon hers. When her hands rested on my chest I deepened our kiss, my tongue sliding into her mouth, one hand cradling her neck the other on her ass. All too soon she copied me, and her tongue rolled over mine as well. With every second I felt myself growing harder. My hands moved underneath her robe to lift up her nightgown.

Theodore, stop! You fool, you must stop! sanity screamed in my mind but I could not bear to. I wanted more. I needed more. I needed her.

STOP! Immediately upon touching her bare thighs I did.

I broke away from her slowly. She stared at me with lustful eyes, her luscious lips just barely parted, her chest rising and falling as she desperately drew air into her lungs.

Only then, staring at her, did I . . . quickly let go completely, taking three steps back and placing my hands over my eyes.

"Fuck." I wanted to scream curses into the air. However, I could never allow anyone to know of this.

"Theodore—"

"Return to your room now," I snapped at her. "Verity, go.

Make sure no one sees you. I have made a terrible mistake. Go."

"But, Theodore—"

"I cannot speak to you right now."

She said not another word before taking her leave. It was only when she was gone that I placed my hands on my head and sank down to the floor.

How could I have done this? How could I have crossed this line? In another's home no less, for all the damned hells!

I was a fool, a fiend, and a villain.

And my desire to do even worse was still raging within.

Verity

I had wished to stay with him but the look on his face, as though he were holding back out of fear he would devour me whole, compelled me to leave more than his words did. My body . . . tingled. It had started from my lips, where we kissed, and spread all over me like fire. A fire that did not burn, but brought warmth . . . and I . . . wished for more. Even now, being separated felt as though I had been tossed out the door into the cold. My mind felt as if it were in the sky, each step I took back up the stairs felt as though I were floating.

"What were you doing?" said Hathor from the doorway, managing to both whisper and yell at me.

I stared at her wide-eyed. "Why were you in my room?"

She glanced around to make sure no others were awake before taking my arm and leading me inside.

"I came to see if you were all right, but you were not here. What were you doing?"

"At this time?"

"Obviously my timing was impeccable, as you were awake,

merely downstairs . . . with the doctor." Her face was very serious, akin to her mama's, and instantly fear rushed through me. I did not know what to say or what she knew and so she went on. "When I could not find you, I went downstairs and saw you enter the drawing room with Dr. Darrington . . . alone. Verity, what—"

"It is not as you think!" I said quickly, turning to her.

"What else could I think? What else could anyone think? You were alone with a man—"

"A doctor," I said, holding the vial for her to see. So much for my secret. It appeared that I was just freely speaking to anyone about it now. Fortunately, Hathor's shoulders relaxed and her honey eyes gentled.

"Is this for your nightmares?"

"Yes." To think I would admit it not once but twice tonight. I had told Theodore . . . because I truly wished to see if the look in his eyes would change once I told him. Would he use that as an excuse to reject me? Instead, his eyes had been unchanged. Everyone always looked to me with shame or pity; even Hathor's expression had softened sorrowfully at the vial in my hands. But not him.

"I shall not press, but you ought to be careful. Misunderstandings come about quite easily," she said as she sat upon the bed. I was starting to wonder how often her sister Aphrodite had been subjected to this behavior.

"Yes, I know," I replied, moving to lie next to her . . . at least knowing she'd distract me from . . . the feelings I had.

"Lord Hardinge is a kind man," Hathor said suddenly, lying back and staring up to the ceiling.

"I do not know him, but he seems to be a jolly fellow."

"Yes, but not just that. Years ago, when he first met his wife, Lady Jane, it is said that he fell madly in love with her at first sight. But he was not sure she had taken a liking to him. He knew she liked gardenia flowers, so he had some sent secretly to her house with poems."

"He is a poet?"

"Papa says he badly wished he was, but he does not have the skill. Instead, he searched our library and copied all the world's greatest poetry to send to her. That's how he and Papa became such good friends. When he ran out of the poems he knew of, he came to Papa, asking for any other books. And nothing excites my papa more than a quest for literature. Papa had the best books from India, Asia, and the whole continent of Africa."

"How many languages does your father know?"

"Eight, I think, but he did not translate them himself. He sought other scholars, and then Lord Bolen soon joined in to help."

"Wait"—I turned to look at her—"how long did he send her poems?"

"A year." A smile spread across Hathor's face. "Three hundred and sixty-five poems and flowers. It would have continued had it not been for Mama."

"What did she do?"

"She spoke to Lady Jane."

"Why?" I frowned. "It was not her secret to tell."

"The only person who seemed to believe it was unknown was Lord Hardinge. No secret can be kept in the ton for long, especially with the parade of flowers and letters arriving at Lady Jane's door."

"So, Lady Jane already knew?"

"Yes, and she liked him but could not bring herself to say anything in return."

"Why?"

"Because years prior, she was in a riding accident, one many said she had been lucky to survive, but her injuries meant that she might not have children. Lord Hardinge had no other relatives but a distant aunt."

Now I understood. "She thought it cruel to marry him and, thus, end his family line."

"Yes, which is why Mama went to speak with her. She told her that it was cruel to let him continue on as he was and that, at the very least, she should tell him the truth," Hathor said. "So, Lady Jane did, and guess what Lord Hardinge said to her in return."

"I assume he asked her to marry him, seeing as how she became his wife."

"He told her, 'You, as you are, no more, no less, is all I have ever dreamed of.' They wed not even a month later."

"And later, they were able to have a child." For a brief moment, I was pleased knowing they had gotten their own happily ever after. But no sooner had I thought it than I remembered Lady Jane had passed, and Lord Hardinge was profoundly ill in bed within this very house.

"Yes. He was heartbroken when she died, in utter misery when he came here, sobbing as I had never seen a grown man sob, and . . . And I knew it was wrong, but when I saw him weeping that day, I remember thinking, 'I hope my husband loves me exactly like this.' "

Hathor was silent for a moment, so I reached out and touched her hand. "I am sure he will."

"I like to think so too, but not everyone is fortunate to have a loving marriage. Sometimes I wonder if there is a finite amount of love. And if there is, how much is left? My parents, Lord Hardinge, Aphrodite, Damon . . . what if they have all taken the greatest of it?"

I was surprised she would think this way given she seemed so determined to be wed.

"What will you do if there is?" I questioned. "What if there is only so much love out there to be found?"

"Defy the odds and ensure my own."

I smiled because, as simple as that, Hathor returned. "Such confidence."

"Papa says if we dwell on our fears, they defeat us. I will simply tell myself I shall become a duchess until I become one."

"A viscountess is not bad either. You very well could win Henry's heart."

"I wish not to be in competition, and this is not my point in telling you all this."

"What is your point then?"

"Sometimes, my fears keep me up too."

Oh, she was speaking of my nightmares . . . she was seeking to comfort me once again.

"Your mother is right, you are rather soft on the inside."

"Oh, hush, you!" She shoved me and I could not help but giggle.

We spoke a little while longer until she fell asleep alongside me. I had never thought much about having a sister, yet Hathor seemed determined to make me one. I smiled . . . but soon my expression shifted as I thought of the very same thing I had pondered earlier that evening.

Hathor was right, there was a plague amongst us.

It was love.

For it must have been on the minds of every adult within this home, maybe within all of London. Love did not care if we were wed or not. Alive or not.

Love was at the root of it all.

13

Theodore

"Dr. Darrington? Dr. Darrington?"

I opened my eyes to see Mrs. Collins, the Du Bell housekeeper, before me. Confused, I sat up, my back aching from the chair I had fallen asleep in. It was then that I recalled returning to Lord Hardinge's room after Verity had gone . . . I prayed it had just been a dream. That I had not crossed such lines.

"Forgive me for waking you, Dr. Darrington, but his lordship sent me to have you reminded of breakfast."

"Breakfast?" My mind was still disheveled, and the pain in my breeches was considerable, as still I found my thoughts on her lips, on her body pressed against mine.

"Yes, the family are gathering now."

Rubbing my eyes, I rolled my shoulders, trying to calm myself before I moved to Lord Hardinge's bedside to check him over.

"His lordship had some clothes and fresh water brought for you to freshen up."

"Do thank the marquess for me, but I shall eat here in the room—"

"Father will not be pleased to hear that," Damon said, appearing at the door. Mrs. Collins curtsied to him before stepping aside. "And it would be deplorable for us to keep you here all night and not offer you a decent breakfast."

"Dining with his lordship once was already beyond me—"

"Would it be better if it came not in the form of an invitation but an order?" he asked as he reached me. "My father requests you join us for breakfast, and you could not possibly deny him, could you?"

I frowned. "I must stay with my patient."

"Mrs. Collins will sit with him while we eat. And despite how she looks, she's a swift runner. She often chased my sisters down on our estate." He chuckled, and the woman behind him smiled slightly. When I moved to speak, he put his hand on my shoulder. "Lord Hardinge is my godfather, and you saved him, so the very least we can do is give you a meal. Please do not be difficult, or I shall be forced to be difficult in return."

"Very well," I said, not because I truly wanted to but because my mind wished to piece together what was real and what was in my dreams last night. "I shall be done in a moment."

He nodded and let go of me before facing Lord Hardinge. He patted the man's leg once before turning and taking his leave. Mrs. Collins also stepped out, allowing me space to clean up. She had done more than simply bring fresh water but also a new shirt, scented oils, and face towels.

I sniffed my own shirt and cringed, then panicked. Surely, I had not smelled like this last night . . . Verity would not have been able to kiss a man who reeked as I did.

Verity? Had I already settled into calling her that now?

Pushing all the thoughts from my mind, I cleaned and changed quickly before stepping out once more to see Mrs. Collins and one other maid beside her.

"This is Bernice. She shall lead you to the dining room while I wait here."

I nodded. "Should he begin to cough or show any signs of waking, summon me immediately."

"Yes, sir."

"This way, sir," said the second maid, gesturing for me to follow.

I did so, but the closer we got, the less I needed her for direction because I could clearly hear their voices.

"Abena, enough, or I shall see to it that you do not eat again until tomorrow!"

"Mama, that is murder!"

I smiled at the chorus of laughter that seemed to echo like music throughout the whole house.

"You—"

"Dr. Darrington, my lord, my lady," the maid said and stepped aside for me.

When she did, I was able to see a whole feast spread upon a long table, and around it was all the Du Bell clan, at the head of it Lord Monthermer. They all glanced up at me curiously, especially the youngest ones. However, the pair of brown eyes I sought most, those of Verity, were not there.

"Dr. Darrington, welcome. Please sit," Lord Monthermer said, extending his hand toward an empty chair beside Hathor.

"Thank you, my lord. Good morning, my lady." I bowed my head to the marchioness.

"I do hope you are hungry, Dr. Darrington. Our cook seems to be feeding an army this morning," the marchioness said to me as I took my seat.

"I hope I am worthy of it," I replied, glancing at it all.

"Why would you not be worthy of food?" asked the youngest Du Bell child, her head tilted to the side and a bit of jelly on her upper lip.

"It is an expression, Abena," said her sister, the one with golden curls, from across the table.

"Oh," Abena replied, taking another large bite. "You should have the eggs and sausage. It is the best. But Mama won't let me have more."

"Abena, last warning!" the marchioness called out to her. "Do forgive my youngest. She sometimes likes to act as though she were raised by wolves."

I did my best not to laugh and reached for the eggs and sausage. But I nearly dropped my utensil as Hathor bumped into me. When I looked at her, she was nearly nodding off.

"Hathor!" her mother called to her, making Hathor sit up quickly and look around.

"Here."

All the family except her mother began to laugh.

"I was wondering how you made it down to breakfast today so early, and I see now it is because you left your mind upstairs," Damon teased her as he drank his tea.

"Silva, I must ask once again, of all the men in the ton, was he truly the best you could do?" Hathor snapped, glaring at her elder brother.

"Unfortunately, yes," Silva replied with a smile.

"Unfortunately?" Damon turned to her, eyebrow raised.

"Dr. Darrington, please excuse my family. We are normally much more . . . behaved at breakfast," the marchioness said to me as I quietly, and quite happily, ate my eggs. The child was right; it was very good.

"I know not what you mean, your ladyship. I have never seen a family better behaved," I replied, and it was the truth. What a joy it was to have a morning like this. I did not even experience this at Henry's home.

"Wise man indeed." The marquess chuckled as he folded the newspaper. He opened his mouth to speak when Silva, not noticing, spoke up.

"Where is Verity? Has she not awakened? Is she still unwell?"

"Apparently, she and Hathor stayed up talking last night. I am allowing her to rest," the marchioness replied, and instantly, I felt . . . alarmed. Had it been a dream? When had Hathor gone to her rooms?

"Mama, I must ask you again, did you find me under a tree? Why was I not allowed to rest?" Hathor asked.

Her mother merely glared back. "Because it was you who went to disturb her."

"She was already awake—"

"I was."

I turned at the sound of her voice. She stood dressed in soft pink, her curls down, and when her eyes met mine, she stared for a moment before looking back to the marchioness. "Good morning. Please forgive me for being late."

"Of course, please come and sit, my dear."

The only chair for her to do so was once again right beside me. I felt the need to hold my breath, almost as if I were bracing for a punch.

"Dr. Darrington, good morning." She nodded to me, and just as I was to conclude that last night had in fact all been a dream, our eyes met once more and she pressed her lips closed . . . I inhaled as I just knew.

I truly had taken advantage of her.

"Good morning," I managed and once more faced my food. I wished to ignore her, ignore my own mind, when the second Du Bell son spoke my thoughts.

"You look pretty this morning, Verity," he said so effortlessly that I was jealous of him.

"Thank you, Hector." She smiled from ear to ear.

"Careful, Hector," Damon called out to his brother. "If you are not vigilant, Mother will have you engaged to her."

"Damon! Do not be ridiculous." The marchioness frowned. "Unfortunately, he is far too young."

"See, it had crossed her mind, if but once," Damon teased as he ate his toast. "I foiled her grand plans."

"What?" Hathor gasped, looking between Verity and Damon, then at her mother. "Mama, you could not have thought it. You wished to give up both Aphrodite and Damon to the Eaglemans?"

"I see you all wish to torment me this morning. Damon, are you still foxed from last night? Why would you say such a thing? Can you not see you are embarrassing Silva?"

The woman in question looked up, almost confused as to why she had been called. She quickly put her spoon down and said, "I am quite fine. Damon has shared a great many things—"

"Yes, well, a conversation between a husband and wife should remain between a husband and wife," the marchioness interrupted.

"Rightly so, but this was a conversation between my brother and me," Damon shot back, not at all ashamed. "Hector, be careful showing any interest in a young lady, or Mama will move the earth to see you married to her before sunset."

"I would not—"

"If that is the case, Mama, may I marry Lord Darvish's daughter?" Hector leaned over to ask, and it was as if the room was filled with pigs the way all the women squealed.

I could barely keep up as they pressed him on how someone as young as he knew whom it was he wished to marry. The whole atmosphere was so thoroughly different from the dinner I'd had with them days prior that I was amazed.

"Do you feel yourself disappearing?" Verity's soft voice whispered beside me. I glanced over to see how she watched them. "They are like this every morning: rays of sunshine, bouncing off one another to further radiate light. Leaving little room for anyone else to come close or interject a thought. We are reduced to mere spectators."

"Why not simply bask in that warmth?" I whispered back.

"The world is full of so much bitterness. Is this not a welcome reprieve?"

"Is not realizing the familial happiness in another home while lacking it yourself cause for further bitterness?" She glanced up at me, frowning. "Do you not find it difficult to be around them like this?"

As someone who did not have even half as much—no, a quarter as much happiness as this in my own home, I understood what she meant. "Yes, I am greatly jealous of them, but at the same time, seeing such a bond exist is inspiring and gives hope."

The sulk on her face did not leave. Instead, she faced the table. "And yet you sought to reject me last night."

Without thinking I replied, "Because I do not think it is possible for us to have this."

I had not meant to be so harsh, and though she did not speak, I felt as though I had harmed her with my words.

"This is not possible for me . . . but you . . . should you meet—"

"I have only just settled on wanting you. I do not believe I could withstand the thought of any other . . . could you?"

We looked at each other. And the loudness that came from the table before us seemed to vanish, as if she and I were the only ones there. It was far too early for these conversations.

"You push me and give me no room to walk," I whispered.

"It was you who pushed first," she replied softly and she was right. Had I never said anything . . . had I not tried so desperately to gain her attention for even the slightest moment, we would not have reached this point.

"Verity, are you all right?" the marchioness asked.

"Yes, of course," she replied and neither of us said another word. To not draw any further attention to ourselves, I turned to Hathor and her brother, speaking to them as Verity spoke to Abena.

I felt it torturous to have her so close and not be able to speak and yet speaking was even more painful. When breakfast had finally come to an end, Lord Monthermer stood and called out to me.

"Dr. Darrington, please."

Nodding, I rose from the table and followed him out into the foyer. The moment the door to the dining room closed, he turned to me, his demeanor stern, not at all the relaxed one he held with his family.

"Benjamin? How is he?"

"He is in a much better condition, sir, but I will need to speak to him more on his illness when he is conscious."

As if the man could hear me himself, Mrs. Collins appeared at the top of the stairs.

"Doctor, Lord Hardinge is awake!"

The one thing everyone in the ton had was not wealth but pride.

"Benjamin, do not be foolish," the marquess said to Lord Hardinge as he put on his gloves. "Stay and rest a bit longer."

"It truly would be no imposition," the marchioness quickly added.

"I thank you both for your tremendous hospitality, but I simply could not. Honestly, I feel as fit . . . as . . . a fiddle . . ." His words were broken up by a fit of coughing.

"That is not the cough of a man who is fit, is it, Dr. Darrington?" the marquess asked.

I frowned but did not answer. Instead, I looked at my patient, who was clearly struggling to stand on his two feet, even with the aid of a footman. He was still sweating, his face pale and his breathing haggard, but his pride would not allow him to rest another day with them. And I had no other choice but to help him quickly back to his own home. "Worry not, my lord," I said to the marquess. "I will accompany him home and stay if need be."

"Surely to bleed me dry. If not with leeches, then of coin," Lord Hardinge grumbled as his carriage approached.

"Whatever the cost, you must bear it. He's already saved your life once," replied the marquess, following us to the carriage.

"Yes . . . yes . . ." Once more, Lord Hardinge was taken over by his cough as he climbed in.

I waited for him to settle inside before moving to join him, when the marquess sought my attention.

"Dr. Darrington."

I turned back, and his face was grave. He turned slightly so Lord Hardinge would not see before speaking again. "Should anything happen, send for me immediately. Do not simply take his word on the severity of his condition."

"My lord, I will give him my utmost care as I do all my patients. I understand you."

He looked me over, then nodded and allowed me to enter the carriage as well. The look on his face changed as he glanced back at Lord Hardinge. "Do not give him a hard time. I shall come to visit you."

As they spoke, I caught sight of Verity in the window. The way her eyes widened, as if she had not expected to be seen while sitting so close to the window, made the corners of my lips turn up. What I did not anticipate was for her to smile in return. How I wished to be next to her, and how very many things kept that from ever being so.

"Charles, you have several children and a wife to concern

yourself with if you wish not to go any grayer. Good day to you, and thank you again!" Lord Hardinge huffed and knocked once on the side of his carriage. "Driver!"

I watched as her figure grew smaller as the carriage pulled away. It was only then I could look to Lord Hardinge. He managed to keep his head up, body straight, and face void of all emotion. It looked as though he did not even take a full breath until we were finally through their gates and on the road. When he did, his body hunched over, and I immediately held the basin I'd asked the maid to put in the carriage out in front of him. He hurled into it for a good minute before falling back upon the seat, taking a deep breath.

"You did well to hold it all this time," I said, placing the basin on the carriage floor and taking his hand to check his pulse. "That should be the last of it out of your system for now."

"What wretched concoction did you give me?" He dabbed his mouth and forehead with his handkerchief.

"It is unpleasant, yes, but it was the only way I could be sure you would remove all of whatever it was you had consumed. Now, what is it that you were taking?" This morning, his only concern had been to leave the Du Bell residence, and he would not properly answer me until I had helped him in that matter first.

He exhaled slowly. "I thought to give up smoking. Sir Grisham said it would be in my best interest that I do so."

"That is wise." I nodded for him to go on.

"However, in doing so, I felt myself altogether worse— headaches, nausea, dizziness, not to mention the dry mouth. Sir Grisham said this was the effects of long-term tobacco use, and the only remedy was for me to purge the bad blood from my system."

I almost hung my head, as I knew what he would say next.

I had examined his body enough to have a clear idea. "And in what way did he suggest you purge?"

"The common practice, of course—bleeding, leeches, a few mustard baths, and the tonic for any stubborn remnants."

"And how many times did you undergo this treatment?"

"Two or three times."

I did my best to remain composed. "Two or three times a week?"

"A week? Sir Grisham said it would be most effective to do a treatment once or twice a day."

Dear God on high.

"My lord." My composure left the carriage altogether. "You have put yourself at tremendous risk! Any one of those treatments once a month alone would be dangerous."

"Sir Grisham assured me—"

"Sir Grisham is"—I bit my lip to calm myself—"*very* much mistaken on his course of treatment. You are quite fortunate to have survived. But as you can see, your body nearly fell victim to them last night. You took his tonic again?"

"Yes." He frowned, and once more, I had to remind myself that he was the victim of a poor physician and not deserving of my temper. "I was feeling rather ill again, and Sir Grisham told me that should it happen while I was not in his care or able to call upon him, I should light a pipe but not smoke and inhale the aroma as I drank his tonic."

He might as well have told him to cast a spell while he was at it.

"My lord, you do not know me well, and I cannot guarantee you will be cured of all ailments, but I can assure you that my treatments will do you better and will not require bloodletting or leeches, nor will I have you perform whatever other rituals Sir Grisham prescribed."

He looked me over, his eyebrow arched. "Should one as

young as you be so confident in your own abilities? You should have some humility and deference toward your elders. I am not as easily swayed as the newer faces of the ton. Sir Grisham is quite renowned and has been dedicated to—"

"Have you noticed you have stopped coughing, sir?" I interrupted to ask.

He paused, his eyes widening as he just realized. He placed his hand on his neck and took a deep breath, once, then twice, and then once again. "What in heavens have you done?"

"Allow me to treat you for a period of time, and if you do not feel better, you may continue with Sir Grisham's practices."

Again, he rubbed his neck before nodding. "Very well. I shall try your methods, but you are not to speak a word to Lord Monthermer. I am already greatly indebted to that family, and I do not wish to be any further burden."

"Very well. Though it did not seem as if Lord Monthermer or his wife believed you to be a burden."

"Of course not. They are too good people to think so, which only succeeds in making me feel worse for . . ." He paused as if he only just realized he was speaking so personally.

"Nothing you say of your health and well-being shall be shared with anyone," I replied, but he still was a bit stiff and unconvinced. "As a bastard, I am a child of discretion, after all."

He chuckled. "If that were the case, no one would know of your parentage."

"If that weren't the case, I could have caused far greater havoc too, for which I would be infamous. And yet all of the ton is probing stalwartly for more specifics of my background."

"So, you are aware."

"Always. This is why I assure you that, as my patient, I value your privacy."

This time, he smiled and nodded. "I am starting to see what Charles meant about you."

I did not know what he meant by that, but the guilt returned as I thought of the trust I breached during my time with Verity. I ignored the feeling, since the carriage had come to a stop outside his home, ending any further conversation on the subject.

I spent another two hours at his home before I finally felt comfortable enough to return to my own. I usually would not have taken his carriage but since I had arrived at the Du Bell estate with Henry and not my own horse, I had no other option. I could have walked, but I felt far too exhausted to exert myself further. However, I immediately regretted my decision upon arriving at the Crown Inn and seeing the looks of everyone outside as I stepped out of a lord's private carriage.

"Well, tare an' hounds! Now, who be this well-inlaid gent at my door?" was the first thing the innkeeper exclaimed, with a broad crooked smile, as I entered. "Movin' up in the world, are we, Dr. Darrington? I have been hearing your name more than any trollop, gull-groper, or bounder of late."

"Good afternoon to you too, Mrs. Howard," I said politely. "Is there any mail for me?"

"In your room already, *milord*," she teased as she curtsied low for me.

"Leave the man alone, you old hag, before he finds finer establishments to rest his dainty doctor head," her husband called out from behind her, causing a few others to laugh.

"I shall remember that, Mr. Howard, should you need any further care for that rash," I said loudly despite having never treated him for such an ailment. However, it thoroughly got his wife's attention.

"What is he talking about?"

I quickly made my escape, going up the stairs two by two. Only when I was in my small room did I finally allow myself to breathe. I then fell onto the bed. My mind was a mess—one part thinking of medicine, another part thinking of her, and the last part thinking about my life.

I needed to slow down, at the very least to prevent further talk of me from spreading. The last thing I should do was appear to be climbing my way within society. I did not wish for that. What did I wish for? Weeks ago, I would have said a simple, upright, and happy life. Now, when I pondered the question, a face appeared in my mind. It felt as though every day I was becoming more and more . . . enraptured. And these feelings left me utterly wary.

"What am I to do?" Logically, I ought to stay away from her, but I did not wish to.

Exhaling, I sat up and moved to my desk to see the letters. There were no requests for my services, but there were several wax seals from different members of the ton. And the first thing that came to mind was not their care but how such patients would further ingratiate me with society and allow me greater access to her.

The thought disgusted me, as I did not wish to be that type of man.

Collecting them all, I placed them into a drawer and, instead, took out my notes on my other patients over the course of my time here in London. I had neglected them enough.

I needed to avoid Verity for now.

Give her time to forget these feelings.

Verity

May 16, 1813

So far, my stay in London has involved me with a whole cast of characters and personalities, all of whom

have left me to further inspect myself. And upon this in-
spection, I find my most pressing thought to be: "Why?"
Why is everything this way? And why do I have no
power to control or change it to my liking?

I glanced up from my journal and out of the window to
where Theodore had stood beside Lord Hardinge in front of
the marquess and marchioness. I could not hear what they
were saying, but it did not matter much. I stayed watching . . .
him, remembering our conversation over breakfast. I had been
shocked to see him sitting there but quickly felt glad of his
presence. Another outsider to ally with me. But to my surprise, he'd seemed rather comfortable, happy even.

Did not all illegitimate children have a sordid past that left
them embittered and acrimonious? I knew that to be the case
within my own family. The thought of Fitzwilliam ever happily sitting at a table as Theodore had seemed so far beyond
reality in my mind. And yet, Theodore managed to blend in,
something that I, myself, struggled with. Was it just me? No,
Silva said she had struggled as well. So maybe it was because
he was a man? Did that give him some further advantage I did
not know of? Either way, his words to me had made me . . .
sad. The idea that a family would be denied to him simply
because of his birth . . . no, not a family . . . a family with me
because of our statuses. I had never even truly given a thought
to having my own family before, but the feeling of him outright denying the possibility of it . . . hurt. I understood his
reasoning but the injustice also frustrated me.

"What am I to do, Theodore?" I whispered down to his figure, and as if he had heard me, he looked up. I do not know
what expression I made, but I could clearly see the slight smile
on his face, and in return, I felt myself smile as well.

All too suddenly, he and the carriage were gone.

"What are you looking at?"

I turned to see Abena in my room. Clearly, knocking before entering was foreign here.

"Nothing, just writing," I said, closing my journal. "Is everything all right?"

She stepped closer. "When do you go back home?"

"Do you not like me here?"

She shook her head. "No, not that. Mama said that I can't go see Odite until after you had been home for at least three weeks."

I had not known there was such a rule. But it was clear what she meant. "You miss your sister?"

She made a face and skipped over to me. "Don't you miss your brother? Aren't you writing to him?"

I had not actually thought to write to him because I assumed he would be far too preoccupied with his own happiness, and I did not wish to remind him to worry over me.

"No, I was writing to myself."

"Yourself? Why? You are with you all the time."

I chuckled. "Yes, I am. That is the problem sometimes. I have so many thoughts and want to order them, so I put them down in a book."

"What do you do once they are ordered?"

"I try to learn from them. I'm not actually sure, but it does make me feel better."

"Okay." She lost interest and then once more asked, "So, when do you go back to Everely?"

"Sadly, it shall not be for another few weeks at least."

Her eyes grew. "That? Plus, another three weeks? That is so far away."

"I am sorry."

Her cheeks puffed up. "I hope no one else gets married."

"Do not curse us!" Hathor barged in.

"You especially!" Abena shot back and then tried to run. But Hathor grabbed her and held on to her tightly. "Let go!"

"I will not till you take it back."

"I shall not!"

"You shall," Hathor demanded and began to tickle her. Abena squealed, and her legs kicked up as she sought to escape. "Take it back!"

"No! Haha!"

"Take it back this very moment."

"*Ha!*" Abena laughed.

"Is everything all right?" Silva questioned, looking inside with Devana beside her. One by one, they all seemed to gather, as if this were another drawing room.

But I said nothing and, instead, smiled as I thought of what my own family would or could possibly look like one day.

And the person I wished to see it with was Theodore.

I said I would not fight these feelings and was not, but Theodore clearly wished to fight his.

So, what could I do but make him stop doing that as well?

I would not allow him to push me away.

14

Verity

He was avoiding me.

I was sure of it.

Four times now over the last three days, I had come across Theodore, and each time he avoided my gaze or presence altogether. He did so on purpose, and I felt my temper slowly rising at the foolishness of it all.

At the foolishness of him! Part of me wished to ignore him in return but I could not manage, and instead found myself straining my neck each and every time we wandered outside in hopes of catching a glimpse of him.

I too had clearly become a bit foolish, but I would lay the blame at his feet.

"Verity, are you ready?" Hathor asked, adjusting her hat as she entered my room.

"I am, though I shall not compare with you in such an outfit," I replied as I gathered my hat and gloves.

"That is altogether the point." She grinned, turning for me to once again take in her fine burgundy dress trimmed in gold, with matching gloves, a feathered jeweled hat, and, of course, a coat. "Are you sure you wish to wear that?"

"This is already quite more than I normally wear for a simple ride in the park," I said as I followed her out into the hall.

"It is not a modest ride. Everyone shall be there today."

"How do you know?" And by everyone whom did she mean?

"It is the third Wednesday of the month," she said as we reached the bottom of the stairs, as if that should mean something to me.

"You both look splendid, but I doubt you can ride to the park dressed that way," her father said when we reached the door, where the marchioness was adjusting Abena's dress.

"Ride?" His wife immediately looked up at him as if he were mad. "On horseback *to* the park?"

"Did you not request that the servants bring the horses?" he questioned. "Whatever for if they are not meant to ride?"

Hathor giggled. "Papa, they are for us to ride *at* the park. We shall take the carriages there first. If we were to ride there now, our dresses would be ruined, and everything would be for naught."

"Will they not be ruined once we ride in the park anyway?" I questioned. I actually had thought we were riding to the park, as I had done so many times in the past.

"My thoughts exactly," the marquess replied.

"If they ride slow and gracefully, that shall not be a problem until much later, after everyone has already looked upon them," his wife explained, earning a proud nod from Hathor.

The marquess glanced down at Abena, placing his hand on her head. "Feel free to do whatever you like today."

"Thank you, Papa!" Abena exclaimed as she exited through the doors.

"Charles!" his wife nearly screamed, and he merely laughed at her.

"Let her have her fun before she grows up and is forced into this ludicrous plotting," he replied.

"Should she make a jester of herself today, I shall leave you to handle it." The marchioness angrily pulled up her gloves. "Girls, let us go."

"Are you regretting it yet, Papa?" Hathor asked him as she walked forward.

"Slightly, but I shall remain resolute. After all, how much trouble can Abena cause?" he said before chuckling. "You shall come to my aid?"

"And make an enemy of Mama? Never. Verity is much better suited."

"Why is that?" I asked.

"Because Mama will not lose her temper with you," she replied and stepped out. I followed, and though I knew she did not mean it as an affront, I could not help but take her words poorly.

Once more, she had painted me as the outcast. Her mama felt free to yell, lecture, or punish her and her sisters because they were her daughters. They were her family, and no matter what, that could not change. I, on the other hand, was not her child, and in her effort to take care of me, she treated me as if at any moment, given the slightest pressure, I would break.

"What good weather finally," the marchioness said when we were inside the carriage. I had only just noticed she had banished her husband to the other carriage to sit with Devana, Hector, and Abena. "The park shall be lovely."

"Mama, is the Duke of Alfonce still in town?"

"Hathor." She gave her a stern look.

"What?"

I looked at Hathor. "Is that who has caught your eye?"

"He is quite dashing, very tall, and—"

"And has shown zero interest and has actually avoided you, I do believe," her mother replied, making Hathor's shoulders drop. "This is a lesson for you as well, Verity. Ladies of your stature can never be seen as too eager or, heaven forbid, desperate. Suitors are meant to call on you, and not the other way around—ever."

"But we should at least hint that we are open to—"

"A simple smile," she interrupted her daughter, "a short conversation, and multiple dances at a ball are more than enough to establish willingness. Should he be a man with even half a brain, he would understand clearly and waste no further time beginning a courtship. You need not exert any further pressure or effort. That is beneath you. Am I understood?"

"Yes, Mama," Hathor grumbled.

The marchioness glanced over to me as well, and I was taken aback but quickly said, "Yes, Godmother."

"Good." She exhaled and glanced out of the carriage window. "Which reminds me, Hathor, Lady Fancot has expressed interest in seeing you attached to her son, Henry. I do not think it a poor possibility."

"On the contrary, I do. Mama, even if you do not see me with a duke, do you not believe you are aiming rather low?"

"Do not be so obviously materialistic, Hathor."

Hathor huffed. "Oh, well then, in that case, let me just marry Dr. Darrington."

"Do not be ridiculous either!"

She was determined to stress her mother and so turned to me smiling. "Well, Verity, I must admit Dr. Darrington is quite handsome, intelligent, and pleasant, do you not think so?"

"I do," I admitted. While Hathor giggled at her mother's deep sigh, I found that I actually did think all of those things. He was rather handsome.

"I know you speak in jest, but you ought not to," her mother replied. "There is no need to make a mockery of him. While he may be a wholly inappropriate suitor, I have heard he has done a great deal of good, so he still deserves some modicum of respect."

"Yes, Mama," Hathor replied, though her attention was greatly occupied by the view outside.

I looked as well, but my mind was on her words, *wholly inappropriate suitor*. Yes, in the days since he had taken to avoiding me he had become an even greater topic of conversation. This was because he had rejected a great many calls for his services from other lords and gentlemen in order to take care of the poor. Even the marquess was baffled to hear his invitation earlier in the week had been left unanswered. Instead of being affronted, however, it seemed to make the ton even more curious about him. I was sure he did care for those in need, but also sure he sought to keep himself from me.

"Finally, we are here," Hathor said joyfully as the carriage came to a stop. She once more adjusted her hat as her mother stepped out first.

As I exited, I noticed the whole park was filled to the brim with people.

"Why are the third Wednesdays of the month so popular?" I asked as the coachmen moved to bring our horses.

"Parliament, of course."

It was not Hathor who answered but Henry Parwens, who stood behind us in a coat of light blue and gray, with a white horse beside him. At that moment, I found myself quickly looking around him. If Henry was here, he would not have come alone. Sure enough, coming up behind him with a dark horse of his own was Theodore.

I noticed Theodore's eyes widen and jaw tense at the sight of me.

"Ladies." Henry bowed his head to us.

"I sense a plot brewing," Hathor whispered beside me, her attention glued to her mother speaking to Lady Fancot.

"Do you ladies also plan on riding?" Henry asked just as our coachmen brought the reins of our horses forward. "Do you mind if we join you?"

"Will both of you be joining?" I asked, looking to Theodore.

"Yes—"

"Forgive me, ladies, I have other patients—"

"I am sure they can wait, Theodore." Henry grabbed the reins of his horse, giving Theodore a stern glare.

"The ill should never be forced to wait," Theodore grumbled back.

"If that were the case, doctors would be akin to slaves, or do you simply not desire our company?" I asked him directly.

His lips tightened into a thin line.

He said nothing more as the coachmen aided us onto our saddles rather gracefully. Though upon seeing Hathor seated as though she were a princess, a part of me slightly regretted not applying greater effort.

"As I was saying, Lady Verity, the third Wednesday of the month is so popular due to Parliament," Henry continued as we began our ride—Hathor and himself in front with Theodore and me following behind.

"Are members of Parliament only given freedom on the third Wednesday?" I tried to jest, looking at Theodore, but he did not say a word, his eyes focused ahead.

"No, of course not," Hathor replied. "They normally have sessions late in the afternoon on Mondays, Tuesdays, Thursdays, and Fridays. Votes can take such a long time—into the evening if truly contested. By the third week, most are exhausted from debates and find themselves here."

"You are quite knowledgeable, my lady." Henry looked at her, surprised.

"Do not give me credit but my father. He stays so informed that I am also informed, not by my choice." She snickered.

They spoke back and forth, allowing me to focus on Theodore, who was still paying me no mind.

"Have I offended you, Dr. Darrington?" I asked softly.

It was only then that he looked at me, eyebrow raised. "Not that I am aware of."

"Then you truly seek to avoid me."

"Forgive me, my lady. I am merely tired."

"That feels like a lie," I replied and he frowned.

"What do you wish me to say to you?"

"The truth."

"You know I cannot."

"No, I do not know anything of the sort."

He let out a sigh, as though I were being the difficult party. And so, we rode in silence. Well, Hathor and Henry spoke. Theodore refused to say anything unless addressed by either of them directly, but even then, it felt like his replies were not as cold as they were to me.

How had he gone from kissing me to . . . this?

Was I mistaken?

Why was speaking so . . . difficult now?

The more the silence lingered, the more frustrated and upset I became.

"Theodore," I muttered only loud enough for him to hear. He looked at me with his eyes wide. "Oh, good. You are aware I am beside you. I thought you had forgotten."

"My lady, you ought not to call me so—"

"What shall you do about it? Ignore me?"

He opened his mouth to speak when a voice called out.

"Dr. Darrington!"

He turned to see none other than Lady Clementina, also upon horseback, dressed rather finely in deep purple and, strangely, wearing a top hat.

"Lady Clementina." He nodded to her. "How are you?"

"Finally, you have inquired about my health. I had come to believe you no longer cared after you cured me." She smiled and then glanced over to Hathor and me. "Hathor, Verity, forgive me for not seeking you out earlier. I owe you both a great many thanks as well."

"I am quite pleased to see you out today looking in much better health." Hathor grinned widely.

"How shall I thank all of you? I do not know," Lady Clementina replied.

"Singing our praises to all the world may very well be the place to start," Henry interjected, causing us all to glance at him.

"And what did you do to deserve praise?" Theodore questioned.

Henry gaped dramatically. "Ladies, I will have you know he has all but made me his henchman. It is I whom he orders to dash toward the carriages to fetch his bag. Lady Clementina, as you are aware, there are a great many stairs in your home, and I am the one who ran up them all to deliver what he requested."

Theodore rolled his eyes, but Lady Clementina giggled. "I thank you, sir, for telling me. I would not wish to ignore any of my gallant heroes. I shall sing your praises as you requested."

"That is much appreciated." Henry nodded.

"Lady Clementina, do you mind if we speak separately?" Theodore asked her and thus found his escape.

"Of course not. I shall see you later, Hathor. You as well, Verity," she said, pulling on the reins of her horse in order to go in the opposite direction and, in so doing, taking Theodore with her. As I watched them go, I found myself even more upset.

"Whatever did I do to deserve the company of two great ladies today?" Henry said, drawing my attention.

"I do believe our mothers might have something to do with that," Hathor replied, sighing as she looked at me. "Which begs the question: When are you to tell your family you desire another?"

"Hathor?" I hushed her, sure he did not wish to have his affairs spoken of so publicly.

"I see you were unable to keep my secret to yourself," he said as we began our ride once again.

"I have told only her, and that doesn't count, as she does not speak to anyone but her journal," she teased me, causing me to give her a stern glare. "Anyway you must either come to terms with the fact that this woman is clearly inappropriate for you or state your intention publicly so as to avoid further confusion."

"Hathor! His choices are none of your concern," I snapped at her. "Forgive her, Mr. Parwens. She is rather blunt."

"Yes, I have noticed. But do not worry. It is why I felt inclined to tell her. She is not wrong," he said in reply. "Also, please just call me Henry."

Hathor nodded. "Well, Henry, have you not picked a path?"

I wished to reach over and smack her arm. But I quickly looked at him. "You need not answer her."

"He cannot just give us part of the story," Hathor replied.

"He need not give us *any* story," I muttered back. Talking about it might very well be painful for him . . . as I was currently undergoing the same ordeal.

"The answer you seek is simple. I cannot make such a choice on my own. For both parties must be in agreement on such matters."

"She is not in agreement? Why?" Hathor asked.

Did she not see she was basically demanding he bare his soul to her?

"It is complicated." He sighed heavily. "Everything about love is complicated, ladies. For it brings out the worst and best in us. One moment you are joyful, as if nothing in the world could injure you, and the next you are left covered in nothing but wounds."

"That sounds rather exhausting." Hathor exhaled as if she were already tired from listening. I wondered how she would get the love she craved when she seemed so hostile to it.

He laughed. "Believe me, it is. But we cannot choose whom we desire. Right now, she seems satisfied by watching from afar. How she or Theodore manages to do that is beyond me."

"Theodore?" I asked, surprised.

His eyes widened, and a look of guilt shot across his face. "Ladies, please forget I said that—"

"Impossible. What of Dr. Darrington?" I asked, my tone surprising even me.

He sighed. "Should this become gossip, I shall know it has come from you both—"

"Oh, out with it, what of him?" Hathor pressed.

He glanced over his shoulder as though he feared the man in question would appear behind me. "Apparently, he is rather smitten with a lady of the ton."

"Who?" Hathor gasped while once more my heart was shaken.

"I know not, for he shall not tell. But it is the first time I have seen him like this in all my years of knowing him."

"And he cannot say anything because he is the inappropriate one." Hathor nodded, understanding.

"There is nothing unsuitable about him," Henry said defensively.

"I do not mean his character. I mean his background," Hathor replied softly. "If she is a lady of the ton as you say, who shall allow their daughter to marry a . . ."

"Bastard," I finished for her.

Henry frowned, clearly upset. "It is a great injustice that a good man's life is derailed and stunted by the choices of his father. Had he been born with a title, all of London would be at his feet. He would not need to forcibly humble himself before every person he meets."

"Humble himself? What do you mean?" I asked.

"Whenever he receives attention, whether now or back in school, he shrinks from it. Why? Because he fears people will think he is devious in some manner. That he wishes to plot a way into our society."

"Why would anyone's first thought be that he is calculating and not intelligent as he proves himself to be?" I frowned, now feeling rather angry myself.

"In school, when the other boys mocked him behind his back, I knew it was clearly jealousy. After all, their fathers looked upon him and wished that he were their son so they could boast about him, of course. Though Darrington and I were not classmates, he is so near to us in age that it was hard for us to see him as an educator. As we grew older, I thought others would behave with more maturity, but they did not. Instead, I find that those who stand out in any manner are ridiculed much more harshly."

"As was the case with my sister," Hathor replied, frowning. "The great beauty of London, yet she was forced to leave for some time to avoid their talk of her."

"At the very least, your sister had the protection of her family in society," Henry replied. "Theodore has none, nor can he hide. He must have some sort of occupation, so he does his best to dampen his own greatness."

"That is incredibly . . . infuriating," I muttered, gripping my reins tightly.

"That it is."

I glanced back over my shoulder, as if I could still see him from this distance, but I could not. Nor should I have been so distracted, for one moment my horse was steady, and the next, I found it bolting forward.

"Verity!"

Theodore

"Any headaches? Do you find yourself short of breath in any way?" I asked Lady Clementina as we rode toward where her family was by the pond.

"None whatsoever. I truly feel much better," she answered with a smile. They all did this—ladies of their upbringing— always smiled despite their thoughts, feelings, or condition. Verity also said she was fine when I could clearly see she was not.

"Even if so, it is not the best idea for you to be out riding so soon." I frowned and glanced over to where her mother talked amongst her friends, cheerfully chatting away, looking like a pink bird in her clothing. "I can only assume it was your mama's idea."

"I do not wish you to think harshly of her, Dr. Darrington," she said softly as she, too, looked at her mother. "Everything she does is for the securement of my future."

The woman fed her poison. Yes, she had not known it was toxic or would cause so much harm. But nevertheless, her mother had forced her to take medicine for a condition that did not exist.

"Your height is not a detriment to your future, my lady" was all I could bring myself to say without being rude.

"If only that were so." She frowned and glanced toward me. "I know you do not wish to offend me, but the truth of the matter is I am a giant in comparison to my peers. Even among gentlemen, I often stand a whole head, sometimes even shoulders, above them. Who will want such a wife—"

"If you believe that to be true, I shall not argue with you, but I will ask: Do you believe yourself to be the only one of your kind?"

"What?"

"If you are a giant, you cannot be the sole giant in the land. There shall be a match for you whether he be a giant or not. There is someone for everyone. You merely have to believe it."

She laughed. "I did not think you such an idealist, Dr. Darrington."

"I am not, but I still do not wish for you to harm yourself or allow harm to come to you for mere matrimony."

"It is merely matrimony to you, a man, but everything to us ladies," she reminded me, and she was not wrong. The proof of it was the sheer number of people in the park around us. "Nevertheless, I shall heed your warning, and so shall my mama. I do not believe anyone has ever admonished her for her actions as you did. She feels a great deal of regret. She even told me I need not come and should rest. It was I who pushed to show the world I was well."

"Very well, but should you feel ill in the slightest, you must call for me."

"Shall you come?" Her eyebrows rose. "The talk of the ton is that you have snubbed us for those less fortunate."

I sighed—these people and their *talk*. "I have slighted no one. I merely wish to be fair in my treatment. And as you are a former patient, I shall always be of service."

She opened her mouth to speak but was interrupted by the voice behind us. "Dr. Darrington!"

I turned to see a much older man. He was slender, tall, and graying, with age spots around his nose, holding on to his sleek cane and dressed in the finest velvet suit, with a group of men behind him.

"Sir Grisham?" Lady Clementina said.

"Lady Clementina, how are you?" he questioned. "I do hope this . . . person is not bringing you greater confusion."

"No." She glanced at me. "What could I be perplexed about?"

"Lady Clementina, I believe it best you return to your mother," I said as I got off my horse.

"Gentlemen." She nodded to them before quickly taking her leave.

I glanced over them all. I could only assume they were doctors as well. Why else would they ally themselves behind Sir Grisham? "How may I help you, sirs?"

"You may return to where every bastard originally stems from!" Sir Grisham snapped at me.

"As my mother is dead, I do not believe that a possibility, sir."

He took another step toward me. "Do you believe this to be a matter of jest, boy? Who the hell do you believe yourself to be to ruin my reputation? Long before your ill-begotten conception, I had been called a doctor. And now you think to slander my practices and steal my patients? They say your kind has no honor, but at the very least, you should have sense."

My hand clenched into a fist, and fury rose up like fire within me. How badly I wished to show him how much sense he lacked.

"Apologies, sir, if I have offended you," I forced out instead. No good would come from fighting with him. Even if I were to win in an argument or fistfight, at the end of the day, all anyone would hear was that the bastard son of Whitmear was causing trouble in London society.

"You have greatly offended me, and you shall now remedy it by returning all my patients and retracting your accusations about my treatment."

"I shall not, for my diagnoses are sound, sir. You are free to meet with these patients again and explain yourself to them. But I will not go against my own word."

"I will not tell you again, boy—"

"What shall you do if I do not agree? Beat me here in the park?" I felt my resolve breaking under the weight of my annoyance. "Your remedies caused greater illness. That is a fact."

"I can make your life very difficult, *Dr.* Darrington."

I chuckled, because no, he could not. "Sir, my life has always been difficult, so I do not think I will notice."

"You—"

"Theodore!" I turned to see Henry rushing to me, his clothing a mess, and his eyes panicked. "Quickly! Lady Verity was thrown from her horse!"

It was as if the rest of the world fell away, and my heart contracted to the point of agony. Within the blink of an eye, I found myself once more on my horse, riding faster than I ever thought possible.

15

Verity

I did not feel so bad, but there was blood, and as such, all the world descended to where the Du Bell family had settled by the pond, and where I had been brought after my fall.

"The bleeding is not stopping, my lord," Bernice said as she held a cloth to my head.

"Where is the bloody doctor!" the marchioness demanded as she held my shoulders. It was the first time I had heard her use such language. You would think I was dying. Was I dying?

There were so many people around me, rushing from left to right, calling out one thing or another. It had all happened so fast. I was upon my horse, calm one moment, and the next it was galloping toward the trees and bushes, and I flew through the air before landing in the dirt. I glanced down at my hands to see my gloves had been torn. The skin underneath was cut and dirty from bracing my fall.

"Make way!" I heard the marquess holler, but still, I looked at my hands.

"Lady Verity?" This voice was not panicked or loud, so I looked up to see the warm eyes of Theodore looking back down at me.

"Dr. Darrington?"

"Good, you still know who I am." He smiled gently. "What hurts the most?"

"Can you not see she is bleeding from her head!" the marchioness snapped, but her voice shook to the point I thought she was crying.

"My dear, allow him to do his work," the marquess said, coming to guide her from my side, though she stayed not even a few inches away.

"Lady Verity?" Theodore called to me again, this time reaching his hand up to take the cloth from my head. I flinched at the feeling of air upon the wound. "So is it your head that hurts the most?"

"Honestly, I cannot feel anything right now," I finally spoke.

"Oh God, what does that mean?" the marchioness questioned from above me.

"She might very well still be in shock," he answered her but never looked away from me. Reaching over, he pinched my arm as hard as he could.

"*Ow!*" I gasped, my eyes wide as I touched my arm. "Whatever was that for?"

"One . . . two . . ."

I did not know why he was counting, but I cried out in pain when he pressed the wound on my head.

"You are hurting her!" the marchioness exclaimed, and he was.

"Pain is sometimes good. I can only treat what I know is injured," he answered, then looked back at me.

"What hurts?" he asked me again.

"My head, hands, and now my arm, thanks to you," I pouted.

"What of your legs and back?" he questioned as he focused on my head. "Did you hit those anywhere?"

"I cannot remember, but they do not hurt."

"Move your foot for me," he said, and I did so. "Very good. Lord Monthermer, have the carriage brought immediately. I shall treat her further at your home. The cut is deep but not life-threatening. You did well to have pressure applied to it."

"I do not wish to go home, I feel as though I have been trapped indoors all week," I muttered.

"Verity, you are bleeding, my dear! We must get you home at once," the marchioness said.

"The carriage is already here," the marquess replied.

"Brilliant. I will lift her," Theodore said, and my eyes widened.

I gasped. "I can walk—"

"Verity, enough! Do not be ridiculous right now! You are injured," the marchioness insisted. "Dr. Darrington, please do whatever is necessary."

He did not wait for further instruction, and I felt his arms reach around my waist and underneath my thighs. When I glanced up at him, it was as if the sun had been reflected into my eyes. He seemed to shine as a knight did in armor.

"Hold on," he whispered down to me, making me shiver strangely. Quickly, I looked away, not at all sure why I was reacting as I was.

Those before us parted, making way for him. With so many eyes watching, however, I closed my eyes. Was this not embarrassing? Honestly, I did not feel all that unwell, yet suddenly, it was as though I were a princess.

"Has the pain increased?" His voice was directly in my ear.

When I opened my eyes once more, I found myself staring into his eyes, which were far closer than earlier.

"No . . ." I whispered as he laid me on the bench in the carriage, kneeling before me.

He nodded, then glanced up to Bernice as he spoke. "Tell the driver to move as gently as possible and make sure someone goes ahead to alert the house staff to have dressings ready for me."

"Yes, sir," she said quickly, and stepped out of the carriage.

"Why are you now pretending to care?" I snapped at him when we were alone inside.

"You believe me to be pretending?"

"I do not know what to think! One moment you proclaim you are enamored of me, you are always around, you kiss me, and the next you treat me as though I were insignificant and ignore me—" Before I could finish my complaint, he kissed my lips gently . . . too quickly.

"I thank God you were not injured any worse . . . the sight of you like this is already far too much for my heart to bear," he whispered down to me.

I frowned, glaring up at him . . . wishing he'd kiss me once more. "You've been avoiding me."

"Yes."

"Stop that at once for it hurts worse than this."

"Verity . . . you and I cannot—"

"Let us try anyway."

"In what manner? Verity, I am trying to—"

"Dr. Darrington!" Bernice interrupted at the door of the carriage. "Everything is ready. May we go now?"

He nodded to her, and still I was within his arms. My heart beat so fiercely I was sure he could feel it against his chest. It was strange how nice it was to be held like this. How secure I felt. As if he alone would be able to shield me from all the world. Resting my head against him, I took a deep breath and instantly took in the warm smell of him. He smelled nice, like a garden.

Never had I been so glad to be injured, for no one would question me or make him release me.

"Drink this, it will ease your pain," he whispered to me with the liquid already at my lips. When I stared up at him he was staring back down at me. I slightly parted my lips and yet it was he who seemed to swallow a lump in his throat.

Whatever spell was between us in that moment broke only as the bitterness of whatever he gave me touched my tongue, making my whole face grimace in protest.

"Ugh," I grumbled, turning my face, not desiring any more.

"You must finish it, my lady."

I wished to protest his refusal to say my name but I knew he could not do so, as Bernice was right beside us both, concern on her face as she watched.

I nodded, finishing, and whatever was in it was potent, for within a matter of moments I found myself so exhausted.

I looked upon Theodore's face once more before I found myself staring into the stern eyes of my own father.

Must you always be such a nuisance?

I tried to speak but the words would not come out. I tried to scream but I could hear nothing . . . and then I could see nothing as everywhere was filled with darkness.

No.

No. Not again!

NO!

"Lady Verity! Lady Verity!"

Opening my eyes, there above me and gripping me tightly was—"Theodore?"

Only when I felt his hand on my forehead did I realize this was not a dream. He was real. *This* was real. But why could I not stop shaking? I was awake now, so why did I still feel scared? So much so that I felt like a child again and could not speak. He tried to move, but I would not let go.

"Verity, it's okay," he whispered. "You are okay, I promise."

I glanced around, remembering only the carriage. Somehow, I was now in my rooms. How many hours had passed since the park? I was unsure, but it had to have been many, as it was now dark outside. Had he been there the whole time? What had he seen of me?

"Lie back," he whispered, carefully forcing me to lie once more on the pillows.

"How long have I been asleep?"

"A few hours."

"You have been here the whole time?"

He nodded, brushing my hair from my face gently. "The marchioness was adamant I stay until you woke."

I frowned. "Is that the only reason you stayed?"

"You know it is not," he whispered, his hand in mine. "My heart would not let me leave even if ordered."

"You are beginning to confuse me, Theodore." I smiled, squeezing his hand. "Do you wish to stay with me or do you wish to run from me?"

"Both." He smiled. "My mind tells me to run. My heart tells me to stay. I am a man at war with himself."

"If I say I wish you to stay, would that help turn the tide in favor of your heart?"

"Everything you do is in favor of my heart," he replied, lifting my hand and kissing it. "Verity, you know not how much I wish to be beside you. But . . ."

"I do not care what your status is. Whether you are titled or not, have estates and drawing rooms or not," I whispered back. "I merely wish . . . I merely wish to be beside someone who makes me not search for the exits."

"You are far too bold for a lady," he muttered, shifting closer to me. "Your boldness only inspires my recklessness and that will only cause trouble. What we are doing right now is . . ."

"Fun." I smiled.

"You being thrown from a horse is hardly what anyone would call fun."

My smile widened. "No. But being tended to by such a fine doctor is."

Slowly a smile spread across his face. "What am I to do with you?"

"What is it you wish to do?"

"Such things cannot be said aloud."

"Then write them down?" I asked, and he gave me a rather annoyed look, though still the smile persisted.

"You jest about my fears." He chuckled, shaking his head. He was about to speak, but the door opened suddenly, causing him to release my hands as in came the marchioness.

"Verity!" She rushed to me, panic clear upon her face. When she reached me, she pulled me into her arms as if I were a child, hugging me. "Oh, thank heavens you are awake. I could not sleep for worry of you, my dear. Are you all right?"

"Yes, I feel well enough now. Forgive me for the trouble," I replied, watching from her arms as Theodore moved back to the corner of the room where his medical bag and things were.

"Your ladyship?" he spoke up. "She is well, but I shall come back tomorrow afternoon to check on her."

He was leaving again? Running from me again? We had only barely begun to really speak.

"Are you sure?" asked the marchioness, her grip on me tightening. "I believe she may need something for the night."

"No," I replied, seeking to sit up on my own. "I do not wish to sleep again, Godmother."

"Verity, you need your rest, is that not so, Doctor?"

He nodded. "Yes, I have given instructions to the maid for a remedy. It is a simple soup, but it shall make it easier for you to relax."

"Soup?" the marchioness questioned.

"Yes. It is best for her not to take much else today. After her fall, I gave her a tonic to ease her. The soup shall help, as I believe she is still tired and under the effects of it," he stated, but the way he spoke sounded almost indifferent. He looked to Bernice, who stood off in the corner behind the marchioness. "Have it brought for Lady Verity now, please."

I wanted to tell him not to go but . . . I could not say a word, not with so many people between us. There were always so many people between us and our chances to speak with each other were like the passing wind.

"Good night, your ladyship, my lady. I shall see you both tomorrow."

"Yes, thank you, Dr. Darrington. Truly, we have called upon you much of late," the marchioness replied.

"It is nothing." He bowed his head to us before taking his leave, and I felt myself . . . dejected once more.

"Verity?" the marchioness called, returning my attention to her. "Are you in need of anything?"

"I am fine," I said without hesitation, but that seemed only to displease her.

"I cannot do this for a moment longer. It is not my nature." She sighed heavily, throwing up her hands.

"I do not understand. You cannot do what?"

"Wait for you, my dear, Hathor is quite right. You simply will not move until pushed." She spoke in a way I did not understand. "I know of your nightmares. As well as the medicine you take for this condition. I have waited and waited for you to feel comfortable enough to confide in me. Instead, you look to me and say you are fine when you so clearly are not."

"Godmother . . ." I hung my head and clasped my hands together as I did not know what to say. However, she lifted my chin up.

"Verity, I cannot help you if you do not talk to me."

"What am I to say, Godmother?" I whispered. "Tell you about the horrors of my past that you already know of? And forgive me, but if a doctor cannot cure me, what is it that you or anyone can do should I speak anyway?"

"There is a solution to everything, and two minds are greater than one, so surely we can figure something out."

I gripped my hands tighter. As if it were so simple. This was what frustrated me about their family—the way they thought everything would just happen because they desired it to.

"Verity, do not simply tell me you are fine—"

"I do not wish to speak of it because you will not understand, your ladyship," I snapped, only to see her face fall and her body pull away from me. Immediately, I regretted it. "Forgive me. I am tired."

I lay back down and turned onto my side. It was not right for me to lash out at her. All she wished to do was care for me. I knew that. But at the same time, I just felt aggravated.

"I shall leave. Bernice shall sit with you should you need anything." She gently placed her hand on my shoulder before I felt the bed shift as she rose.

When the door closed, I rolled onto my back and looked above me. I truly wanted to go home. I wanted to sleep in my own bed and be where people would leave me in the darkness of my mind.

Knock. Knock.

"My lady."

See, this was what I meant.

"Enter," I said, sitting up as Bernice brought a tray with a single bowl and spoon on it and placed it before me. I stared at the light-yellow chicken, carrot, and pea soup.

"This is it?" I asked her. For some reason, I was expecting more.

"Yes, my lady," she replied, lifting the spoon for me. I took it from her and leaned over to taste a bit of it, and shockingly, it was so sweet and warm.

I grinned. "It is good."

"I am glad. I was worried when Dr. Darrington said he would cook it."

"What? He made it?"

"The cook had already retired for the evening. I'd planned to go retrieve him, but Dr. Darrington suddenly said he would prepare it himself."

"And he did not make a mess of the place?"

"No, my lady. He seemed well adept. I merely brought the ingredients he sought."

I stared down at the soup. I had learned something new. Not only was he a scholar and a gifted doctor, but also a cook.

I could not help but giggle. Just when I felt like succumbing to my misery, he somehow lifted my spirits.

"My lady?"

"Nothing." I smiled, thinking of how he must have looked, as I took another bite.

It truly was delicious.

Theodore

I had surely lost my mind, for why else would I be in their kitchen? I had forced myself to leave when the marchioness had entered Verity's room, as I could not bear to be beside Verity and not hold her. Yet I could not bear to leave either. As soon as I had made it to the doors, it was as if I were taken over by some greater force, and I searched for any other reason to stay. Even though I knew it was not possible, part of me wished for her to ask me to remain with her.

"This is maddening," I muttered to myself as I cleaned off my hands and moved to get my bag from the kitchen counter.

I had to leave.

"Dr. Darrington!" called out a familiar voice from the servants' exit. None other than Damon Du Bell was at the stairs. He was dressed simply but not yet for bed, despite the lateness of the hour.

"My lord?" I said to him.

He glanced around and down the hall before nodding for me to follow him upstairs. "If I could have a moment more of your time?"

By God, can I not free myself from this place! I thought but, nevertheless, followed him. It was only at the top of the stairs that he spoke but lowly.

"I do not wish to alert the house. However, is it possible for you to examine my wife?"

"What is the matter with her?" I asked, now following him down the hall.

"Lately, she has been plagued with a horrid nausea that sometimes results in vomiting both day and night. It leaves her greatly fatigued. Each time she claims it is merely the food that disagrees with her. But I am beginning to worry it is more than that," he said as we reached the door to his room.

"Any other complaint?"

"Not that she tells me," he replied. He opened his mouth to speak, only to stop himself.

"My lord?"

He shook his head. "Nothing. I believe it might be my imagination. However . . ."

"However?"

Again, he paused. "It is best you see her yourself."

I waited for him to go in before I entered. She was sitting up in bed, reading a book, and upon seeing me, her eyes widened immediately.

"Dr. Darrington? Damon? What is going on?"

"Sweetheart, I cannot bear that you are unwell, so I have brought him to find the cause—"

"Damon! I told you I did not wish to cause a fuss. I am perfectly well."

"Mere moments ago, you looked as though you were ready to empty the contents of your stomach upon our bed," he replied and then looked at me. "I beg of you, look to her. She would rather suffer in silence than have my mother think her ill."

I nodded, stepping forward, when she rose from the bed angrily, holding her arms over herself.

"I do not wish to be looked to. I am fine."

"Silva, please do not be difficult—"

"Difficult?" She tilted her head, and I wished for escape, as I did not desire to be a witness to a murder. "Dr. Darrington."

"Yes, my lady."

"I thank you for your dedication today. We have greatly monopolized your time. However, I assure you, it is much too early for a doctor, months too early," she said, giving me a look that I read clearer than any book.

"Ah, I understand. I shall take my leave—"

"Wait!" Damon held his hand out to me. "What do you mean months too early? So you are aware of your ailment and wish to delay treatment? In what way does that make sense? You are being illogical, and I am quite surprised by your agreement, Dr. Darrington."

I hung my head as if to pray for the fool.

"If this child grows to be illogical, it will be a trait inherited from you."

In the silence, I glanced up to see his face at the implication behind her words. He stared dumbstruck, mouth agape, eyes wide, and his wife did her best not to break out in a fit of giggles. It was then he turned to me, and never had I seen Damon Du Bell so blissfully happy.

"I shall leave you both. Good evening, and congratulations." I showed myself out, closing the door behind me, as neither of them could speak.

It was only in my absence that they began to laugh on the other side. It brought a small smile to my face and a hint of jealousy as I walked down the stairs. How marvelous his life was, how simple, how life ought to have been for everyone. To find a mate they desired, wed, and have a child, to worry not of status or wealth or name.

Upon reaching the exit, I glanced around their home once more and found myself finally able to leave. I was not destined for this, and staying only brought further misery to myself.

Reaching beyond oneself and one's place in the world led only to tragedy.

16

Verity

I waited until noon, then all day, but he did not come.

Instead, he sent a letter saying he had been held up with another patient in dire need. He left directions for Bernice to call for him should I feel any significant discomfort. And it was quite childish of me to be so very . . . upset by it. There very well could have been an emergency, since those seemed to plague him wherever he went. Nevertheless, I still thought— I still wanted him to come to me. I told myself that surely he would visit, but he did not, and my anger turned to hurt. Once again he was running from me.

I sat in the garden, as the marchioness believed it would do me good to take in the fresh air. She was another person I worried over. She had not said a word about my behavior but was clearly more reserved in my presence. Sighing, I opened my journal to write.

May 20, 1813

I feel myself to be a bush with a single rose surrounded by thorns. I wish to produce more flowers, yet I create only briar instead. How many roses are required of a plant before it is considered a rose bush and not a thorn one?

What good is it to be wellborn
But under the throes of shadows?

Composed in daylight, overwrought at moonlight.
A horror . . .

"My lady," Bernice called from behind me as I wrote. "Dr. Darrington is here to see you."

Immediately, I stood up and turned around. There he was, standing in a dark-blue waistcoat, bag in hand, his face a bit flushed, as if he had run here. He stared at me calmly regardless.

"Lady Verity—"

"Dr. Darrington—"

We both spoke at the same time. He nodded for me to go first as I nodded for him to do the same. Now we both looked at each other.

He took a step forward. "Lady Verity, forgive me for the intrusion. How are you?"

How was I?

"I feel rather neglected by my physician of late," I replied sternly.

"Forgive me, there was a fever that spread amongst some families at Langley Cross. I did not seek to be neglectful," he replied and I watched him for a moment before nodding.

"Were you able to cure this fever?"

"I did my best . . . but not all have recovered," he replied and the sorrow upon his face made me feel a bit guilty for my earlier lamenting. "Your head, how is it? Please sit so I may see."

I immediately sat and, in so doing, remembered my journal. When I moved to close it quickly, I spilled the ink not only upon the table but also my dress.

Why!

"My lady!" Bernice rushed to aid me, though there was nothing to clean it with, so she merely pulled the table away so as not to get further ink on my dress. "Come, my lady, we shall get you changed."

It dawned on me then that this could be to my advantage.

"Let us not fuss," I said to her. "It is merely a dress, Bernice. I should not take much more of Dr. Darrington's time, as he has other patients. If you could please get someone to clear this and have a new dress brought out for me as I speak to him, then we may go change."

"Of course, my lady." She curtsied and rushed back into the house, allowing us a few moments alone.

"I thought you had forgotten me, Theodore," I found the courage to say as I turned to him.

He seemed taken aback. "Did you spill the ink on purpose?"

"My brother says I can be a bit calculating, but this was just an accident I seek to take advantage of."

"Take advantage?" he asked, still at a distance from me, making me frown.

"How do you plan to examine me from so far away?"

"It is best I do not touch you while you are unaccompanied . . . I do not wish to be tempted any further."

I did not like how formal he was being. We did not have much time to speak freely. "I cannot bear the short times we have to speak. So tell me plainly: If you care for me and I for you, what is to be done?"

"That is the problem, there is nothing we can do—"

"I do not believe that. Why do you?"

He frowned and then proceeded to look to the wound upon my head. "How is your head? Do you have any other pain?"

"My head is fine. I barely even noticed the stitches. Thank you for hiding them so well. I am a bit sore but nothing altogether too unpleasant." I answered each of his questions, before again asking, "Why are you so certain there is no way?"

"Because I myself am a product of two people who believed they could defy society."

"What?"

"How else are bastards born if not by two people who should not have been together daring to hope they could anyway?"

I opened my mouth but heard Bernice speaking with someone from inside. Once again our time was coming to a close far too quickly. It would take me years to know him truly at this rate. "I will find a way we can speak more *privately* to each other."

He stared at me but said not a word as Bernice returned.

"Is everything all right, my lady?" she questioned.

"Yes, *Dr. Darrington* was waiting for you before he tended to me further. You wished to see my head, correct?"

He nodded. "Yes, *my lady*."

I was unsure what he was thinking, but I desperately wished to know, so I thought to see if I could create another distraction or cause another mess to force Bernice to leave us once more. We needed to speak . . . to freely speak for longer than a few minutes.

But the question was how?

Theodore

I was sure she did not know what she had asked for. A woman or man only asked to see each other privately so they could do private things to each other. She was far too naïve to know, yet the thought of it came to my mind and excited me nevertheless. The things I would do to her if I could, and if she knew, she would brand me a scoundrel several times over. I planned to push it from my mind altogether, but once more she had managed to distract her maid with some other task and whispered to me.

"Is my request possible?"

"It is not." I finally found my voice to speak.

"Why?"

Verity and her bloody *whys*. Why? Because she was who she was, and I was who I was. Why? Because I lacked the self-control to remain within my bounds. Why? Because I loved her. Did she not realize how hard the truth was to speak?

"Do you not wish to see me?" she infuriatingly asked instead.

"Of course I do," I muttered, unable to stop myself.

"Then do so."

What hellish temptation this was. I could bear it no longer.

"You know not what you speak, for if you did, you would realize you open yourself to ruin. Should anyone find out—"

"Let no one find out." She did not avert her gaze as I attended to the wound on her head. "You are one of the very few people I truly enjoy being with, Theodore."

She was too close, whispering exactly what I wished to hear.

Oh, how . . . how desperately I wished to kiss her, to listen to her whisper a thousand questions in my ear, to hold her. How desperately I wanted to fulfill her request. But even if I wished to, it was impossible.

Exhaling, I leaned away, trying to prevent the blood in my veins from rushing to places it ought not to in a lady's presence.

"Verity, London allows for no such privacy," I replied, and as if to prove my point, the marchioness herself met us outside.

"Well, Dr. Darrington, how is she?" she asked me.

"Apparently, I have irritated the wound while tossing in my sleep, Godmother," she lied, for I had said no such thing. "I have asked him to make a new tonic, but he insists he must observe me first."

"Well, if that is the case, Dr. Darrington, please do so," the marchioness replied.

"Godmother, I do not wish to be under observation." She frowned, her eyes forlorn, fully dedicating herself to whatever play she had concocted in her mind. "And how shall it look if anyone were to find out. It is not as though he can come here every night, or people will think I am dying."

"God forbid." She gasped and then looked at me. "No one shall speak of it because Dr. Darrington shall come to converse with the marquess."

"Your ladyship, I could not—"

"Go and change, my dear, for we are expecting a guest later this evening." The marchioness interrupted my protest to speak to Verity, offering a slight smile.

After she had retreated inside, the marchioness faced me once more, her expression heavy.

"That young lady means a great deal to me, Dr. Darrington," she stated. "However, she pushes away any attempt I make to truly speak to her. She would rather recite a script, line by line, than speak about what troubles her. I fear she believes all the world would think poorly of her if they knew what happened."

I paused, all the lust within me gone and replaced by genuine concern. "What happened?"

"I tell you this in the hopes you will be able to treat her, but you must never repeat it," she said, and I nodded. "Many years ago, as a child, she was greatly neglected by her father . . . and harmed by . . . the evil woman daring to call herself her stepmother."

"Harmed?" I repeated, feeling my hands tense. "In what manner?"

"Even I, to this day, do not know the true extent. But . . .

she was nearly starved and imprisoned in the smallest of cabinets or rooms."

I could barely withstand the rage that coursed through me. My mouth opened, but I felt as though I wished to breathe fire instead of speak.

"How dare they." The words finally formed. "And this woman, this beast, still walks among us?"

This woman—that woman, who had harmed her, had the audacity to stand beside her as she was presented to the queen. That woman lived within this very city. How was she meant to sleep at night when saddled with such misery?

"Trust that if I could remove Datura from all of our lives, I would in an instant," she said to me, nearly as angry as I was. And I said *nearly* because it was clear she had considered throwing the woman into a dark hole in the earth herself. "This is why I need your help. I wish to free her from these pains. My husband has great faith in your abilities, and I desperately need him to be right."

I did not deserve that faith, for I did not care to help her merely as a doctor to a patient. My intentions were altogether not pure. Nevertheless, I could not bring myself to walk away, not after hearing this. My desire to stay with her grew even greater.

"I am not sure what I will be able to do to cure her. Or if anything can be done, but I shall desperately try even still."

Once more, I had tried to run from her only to find myself running toward her.

17

Verity

I had not truly believed that my plan would work. Where the idea came from, I did not know. Maybe it was birthed from my sheer stubbornness. I desired his company and did not wish to be denied. So I had used what I believed to be my only available option: my condition. I sought not to seem too eager for his aid, feigning despair at the thought of having to be "observed." Despite all of that, I had not honestly thought the marchioness would afford us the proximity and privacy to speak.

Now that he stood before me in the marquess's study, I felt a bit of guilt. It was just us—yes, the door was open, and I was aware of both Ingrid and Bernice as they walked by, but even so. The marchioness must have been worried about me to allow this. I was taking advantage of that kindness, but at the same time I was so happy that we could finally speak.

"I am surprised this method worked but nevertheless so glad," I said happily, moving to take a seat in one of the chairs by the desk.

Whatever joy I was feeling was not matched by the expression on his face.

"I do not wish to lie to you," he stated simply.

"Thank you. I do not wish to be lied to. So?"

"Her ladyship told me of . . . of what happened to you as a child. What your stepmother did."

It was as though I had been slapped. Had anything been in my arms, I would have dropped it. Had I been standing, I would have fallen to the floor. Nothing could have stripped the joy from me faster. It was as if I had been dragged once more into that room, and I could not speak or see. Everything was dark, and I was scared, and all I could do was suffer.

Why?

Why had the marchioness gone that far?

Was that not my past to tell or to keep secret?

I wanted to go home.

Please . . .

"Verity!"

Blinking, I looked to see him before me now.

"Ver—"

"I am tired. I think we should speak some other time—"

"Now it is you who is running away?" he asked. "After your great effort to create this time for us?"

I frowned. "I am not."

"I know what it looks like to run away, for I do it often," he said, pulling a chair in front of me. "I am expert at running from my past as well. What I began to say in the garden I wish to finish now."

"What do you mean?" I asked.

"As I now know some of your past, I shall share my own," he whispered as he took a seat across from me.

"So, you tell me not because you want to but because you feel guilty for prying into mine?" I did not want that to be the reason.

"I did not pry—well, I did, but I do not feel guilty. Do you not want to know more of me?"

I said nothing, looking away from him to see Ingrid peering into the room again.

"Now that I am to start, I do not know where to begin." He

chuckled, gripping his hands. It was only now that I saw his nervousness. "As you know, I am illegitimate, the bastard of the Marquess of Whitmear. My mother was named Sarah Darrington, and she was the daughter of a doctor. Actually, she wanted to be a doctor as well."

"A female physician?" I grinned, for I had never heard of such a thing. "Not a midwife or an aide?"

"No, specifically a physician. My grandfather says she was clear on it. She practiced alongside him as an aide, despite his best efforts to deter her, and she always complained about not furthering her studies. She told him she would not marry if he did not teach her himself."

"I quite like her." I giggled. Hathor would have fainted. "Is your grandfather still alive?"

He nodded. "Yes, as is my uncle, my mother's younger brother. He is an ironsmith and has forsaken medicine."

"Why?"

"It is a long story that also involves my mother," he said with a deep frown. "You see, my mother loved medicine, she believed in it, and she loved to see people recover from whatever ailed them. She thought it a miracle each time she saw someone she had once tended look as though they had never been ill. It also allowed her a great deal of freedom."

"Just hearing it makes me wish to become a physician myself."

He smiled, but it was half sullen. "I believe it was truly the happiest she was, and I wish I could have seen her so, for that was not how I remember her. She changed after meeting my father. A meeting of sheer luck. She and my grandfather had been called to attend to one of his friends while in London, and from every account, my mother and father fell madly in love at first sight. I never thought such a thing was possible until I myself became victim."

I smiled. "So, your heart is similar to those of your parents?"

"It would seem so. Which is why I wish to run from you, for their love was a tragedy," he replied, nearly whispering. "They were in love with each other, but she was simply a doctor's daughter, and he was the future Marquess of Whitmear. A great many responsibilities were before him. Nevertheless, he could not deny himself with my mother. There are rumors he planned to elope with her despite his parents' wishes."

I gasped. "Elope? Gretna Green?"

"What do you know of Gretna Green?"

"I may not know much but I am not so naïve either. I have seen plenty in my freedom at Everely. Well . . . I have seen enough." Young lovers who were denied permission would flee to this place in Scotland to take their vows. "Let us not be distracted from what happened next—I mean, from what happened to your mother."

It was not just a story in a book. It had been his mama.

"What always happens. Gossip among the ton spread like fire, and of course, it burned the weaker of the two parties, my mother," he whispered and leaned back in his chair. "My father's family could weather a scandal. It was embarrassing, yes, but it would not ruin them. For my mother's family, that was not the case. Everyone severed ties and accounts with my grandfather once the talk began. My grandfather was not a poor man, but he nonetheless needed income and standing. My father said not to worry, that once they were married, he would see things made right. He promised to return the first night of summer for my mother."

"Did he break his promise?"

"No . . . it was my mother who did not meet him."

"What?" That did not make sense. "Why would she fail to meet him? She loved him, did she not?"

"Deeply, but she also loved her brother, my uncle. My father was betrothed to Lady Charlotte Griffinham, and their family was adamant he would marry her. So much so, they threatened my mother with her brother. One day, when my uncle crawled back home beaten to within an inch of his life, she broke the engagement without telling my father why."

"Wait. They attacked her brother? Your uncle?" Did such things truly happen?

"And instead of invoking further scandal, my mother lied to my father, saying she wished not to marry but to dedicate her life to her patients. She refused to speak to him, and he returned to his family heartbroken. She was not aware she was pregnant till later. She suffered melancholy before my birth and even more so afterward, but no one noticed, as she smiled regardless. She did her best to care for me despite the abuse she received from others until one day . . ." He became very quiet, his eyes no longer on me. It was as if he had turned to stone.

"Theodore?"

Blinking, he glanced at me as if only just then remembering I was here. "Forgive me. I have not spoken of this in many years."

"No, it is fine. You have already shared so much."

"None of that matters if I do not tell you how she died," he whispered. "No matter what happened, my mother would always smile at me. She always told me she was fine. It was the last thing she told me before she put me to bed, went to her room, drank hemlock, and never woke up again. I was the first to find her."

My hands covered my mouth to keep the shock down. "Theodore, I am so sorry."

"It has been twenty years, and there are times I still have

nightmares of that day. Times when I wonder if I had seen she was not all right."

"You were a child. You had no control over what could have happened."

"So were you," he reminded me gently, and my shoulders slumped. "We can tell ourselves it is not our fault over and over again, but that does not always work, does it?"

"It does not." I knew that all too well. "What of your father?"

"My father, upon hearing the news of my mother, broke down in grief, grief that plagues him to this very day I am told. And I cannot bring myself to be around him. I have not seen him in many years," he answered.

"You were not raised with him? Or did your stepmother not allow it?" I asked. "I, too, have an illegitimate brother. His name is Fitzwilliam, and after my mother's death, he came to live on the estate, though I rarely saw him. He and Evander cannot stand being in the same room for more than a minute without coming to blows."

"I have heard rumors of your family, but I try not to listen. I try not to follow the lives or families of other illegitimate children. I fear I'd end up comparing my life with theirs, good and bad. In my case, my father wished to raise me on the estate. However, I refused to go."

"Why? People always seem to be dreaming of life on a grand estate." Little did they know of the pains within.

"After my mother passed, I realized very quickly that home was not a place; it was people," he said very softly. "If I did not like the people, I would not stay. As I grew older, I found no place ever felt like home to me, not even my grandfather's, as they, too, suffered from the loss of her. My uncle's pain and anger over the years has caused him to hate those in high society. In all their faces he sees the same people who attacked him, who caused his sister's death. I thought faith would help him. But it has not. So I could not bear to stay in my grandfather's house. However, I refused to live with my father as I . . . I am angry at him even still."

"As one who understands anger toward fathers, can I say that so far, I do not think yours the worst?" I said gently. "Mine . . . I do not believe he ever wanted me. And I do not know why. In all my memories, he is cross with me. Annoyed that I exist at all. I used to think it was because I killed my mother—"

"You did not kill your mother," he snapped at me. "Some sickness or ailment hindered her birthing and that killed her. You are blameless."

"Nevertheless, that is what I thought. Do you know that my family home here in London is where I was born? So, it is where she passed as well. I realized my father cared for neither her nor I when Evander once had to remind him of this fact. He cared so little he did not even wish to remember that. Therefore, hearing that your father at least sought your attention . . . makes him far better than mine."

"You are right." He hung his head. "He is not the worst. I know this and I have tried to move on. But my anger remains. And I cannot bring myself to see him. Part of me wishes, at the very least, to see my younger brother, Alexander. He is but eleven, and I am curious about him sometimes."

"Then get to know him. Surely, your relationship with your father should not hinder yours with him."

"It is best not to complicate our lives further."

I thought of Fitzwilliam once more and how he did not care in the least if he complicated our lives. Theodore was so much kinder.

"May I ask the root of your anger toward him?"

"In my mind, I thought he should have stayed away. He should have understood it was not possible, should not have given my mother hope." The grimace on his face seemed to grow as he stared at me. "Now I fear I might understand why he found it so hard to do so."

"So, does that mean you shall make peace with him?"

His jaw clenched and his expression soured.

"It seems your pride will not allow you, Theodore . . ."

"I told you this, Verity, not for you to help reunite me with my father," he replied, releasing the tension in his mouth as he looked to me sternly. "I told you so you could see . . ." He took another deep breath before lowering his voice. "Despite the joy you bring me, I cannot allow us to continue on as we have. If the fault were only on me, or the blame on me, I would not care. I would not run. But you? If your reputation or life was harmed as my mother's was . . . I could never forgive myself. Ever. That is why I beg you to cast me aside."

I understood him so much more now, and it gave me strength.

Which is why I smiled and said, "No. I will not cast you anywhere from me."

He groaned. "Do you not see that this will be to your detriment?"

"I have been harmed much by many other people and things beyond my control. If this is to be my downfall then at least I choose it myself."

"Never have I met a woman as stubborn as you," he grumbled.

"I shall take that as a compliment."

"Verity—"

"We go hand in hand to our demise, *Dr. Darrington*, or . . ."

"Or?"

"I may make a greater fool of myself in hopes of seeking your attention."

He stared at me for a long time. "I fear I must join you to stop you from plotting anything else, *my lady*."

I grinned . . . for the first time I truly looked forward to my time here in London.

18

Theodore

Like everything in my life of late, I was compelled to action because of none other than Lady Verity Eagleman.

For years, I had done my best to stay on the outskirts of the ton, neither drawing attention nor vanishing completely. Now I found myself in the center of it. Late in the afternoon, I was not in my lodgings, reading over notes on patients or books, but instead, at one of the most respected and exclusive gentlemen's clubs in London. This invitation was extended to me, not by Henry and his family, but by the great-grandson of a founding member, the Marquess of Monthermer himself.

Why?

Well, partially to solidify the story of me going to his home to converse with him and his son, not the Lady Verity. But also because he simply wished me here, and it was not even the highlight of the evening. Everyone was to meet later at the theater with their respective families. I also was expected to attend.

I was greeted left and right as I walked farther inside.

A month ago, not one of them knew my name or cared to. And usually, upon finding out my background, their interest in me dissipated. Now everyone was rather pleasant. What had changed? Did they accept me now because they knew of my skill? I did not think so. I believed their respect was merely by extension and truly toward my benefactors.

I was not sure if I liked that much better.

So why come?

Verity.

The better these men knew me, then maybe . . . maybe—

I could not even bring myself to think it.

"Ahh, Dr. Darrington." Damon Du Bell left his companions and came to me.

"My lord." I bowed my head.

"I believe us far too well acquainted now for titles. Simply Damon shall suffice," he replied, motioning for a drink to be brought to me.

"Then, of course, you may call me Theodore, as well," I replied, taking the drink.

"Right, about the other night . . . my wife?" He stepped closer, turning his back to where his father sat at the tables. "Nothing is to be said to my parents or family as of yet. Silva will tell them when things calm down."

"It never crossed my mind to say anything," I assured him. "How is her health otherwise?"

"She says fine. And it is a mystery for me to figure out when that is true."

"I do not understand."

"Ah, yes, you do not have sisters or a wife." He seemed partly jealous. "Sometimes 'fine' means they are upset and wish you to keep probing until either you figure it out or they get annoyed with your incompetence and tell you. Then other times, they truly mean what they say. But rarely is there a clue as to which is which."

I chuckled. "Is it not a fifty-fifty chance?"

"There comes the twist. Should you ask them if they are fine, thinking they are not, and they are actually *fine*, they will become annoyed at you and no longer be fine."

"I see why your father's hair is so white."

"I fear I am not that far off." He laughed, looking back to the man who, in return, waved us over. "I believe you're being summoned."

"How do you know it is I and not yourself?"

"He'd merely yell my name across the room," he stated, and as if to prove his point, his father called.

"Damon!"

"Parents are rather predictable people. How much do you wish to bet he simply wants us to be spectators over their game?"

"I am not a betting man."

"Stay here long enough, and you shall be," he said, turning to walk to his father, and I followed behind.

I had heard much of Black's Gentlemen's Club and it was as everyone had described—a highly esteemed gathering of the most educated lords, surrounded by books, drinks, and cards. However, the openness with which they seemed to speak of one another's own personal affairs one moment and philosophy the next had me taken aback. Within my first five minutes here, I heard at least three men speak of their mistresses in one corner of the room, while in the other were discussions of Aristotle's six works on logic in *The Organon*.

"Have you lost our fortune, Father?" Damon asked as he stepped beside him.

"I would sooner lose your head." The marquess laughed casually. "Welcome to Black's, Dr. Darrington."

"Thank you for the invitation, my lord," I replied.

"Not at all. You are coming to the theater tonight, correct? There is plenty of space in our box," he stated, examining his hand.

"And should you wish not to be run over by the company of women, you may join the rest of us in mine," Lord Hardinge said and snickered.

"Quite the generous benefactors you have here, Dr. Darrington." Lord Bolen shook his head. "It seems you all have thrown your lot in with him. Do you not think yourself disloyal to Sir Grisham, Benjamin?"

"What is loyalty to good health?" Lord Hardinge replied. "I feel as though I can finally breathe again, thanks to Dr. Darrington's treatments. I prefer a doctor that cures my ailment, not adds new ones. That man damn near bled me to death. Unlike yourself, I have a young charge who still needs me."

"You wound me." Lord Bolen held his hand over his heart before laughing as he looked at Lord Monthermer. "And what is your excuse, Charles? I did not think you ill enough to judge who is the better of them."

"It is a mere feeling . . . an instinct," the marquess replied as he casually tossed one hundred pounds into the center of the table. His eyes shifted to me, and he gave a slight nod. I nodded in return, though I was not sure why. "And so far, it has been the advantageous choice, which is more than I can say about your decision to play this game."

"Treacherous fiends," Lord Bolen grumbled, folding his cards and waving over another drink before looking at me. "Forgive me, Dr. Darrington. It is nothing personal. I simply do not ascribe to the notion that the young should replace the old before their time. You have all but stolen the man's patients. Is there no honor among doctors?"

"There is between good ones," I replied, causing a chorus of chuckles and snickers. I really ought to put the drink down before I let myself say anything more.

"Is that so? And you believe yourself good?"

Fuck.

Inhaling, I turned around to, once more, find myself in front of Sir Grisham. He stood gripping his cane so tightly that the veins in his hands protruded from his skin. "Tell me,

Dr. Darrington, what gives you your expertise at such a tender age?"

"I will not deny my youth or limited experience, sir, but I can assure you, both will change with time. That said, as I told you before, your methods and tonics do no one good." I sought to sound resolute but not insulting.

"And you would know of bad tonics, since that is how your mother took her own life, correct?" he proclaimed loudly to all the room, and it was as if everything and everyone had gone silent.

My hands balled into fists, and I wished for nothing more than to beat his face, but that was clearly what he wanted, to have me branded uncivilized and unworthy to be here—just like in school. The boys did not become better with age; they just became cruel men.

"Yes, sir, that is how she passed, which is why I have an aversion to your treatments. Is there anything else you wish to announce to the room? Is there anyone here who is ignorant of my background?" I asked, glancing around. They looked at me but said nothing. "As I thought. Sir Grisham, your methods of humiliation are even more archaic than your methods of medical practice. The boys of my school have you beat by over a decade, at least, with this."

Damon snorted beside me and had to look away as Sir Grisham stepped closer to my face. However, he did not speak to me but to the man behind me.

"Lord Monthermer, I believe this is a *gentlemen*'s club. One should think wisely on whom he invites inside."

"Noted, Sir Grisham," he calmly replied as he rechecked his cards.

Sir Grisham turned from me and took his leave. I could not even relax because everyone was still quiet and watching.

"What is the production tonight?" Damon asked me.

"*Hamlet*."

"Is that not the same play Drury Lane Company had in production that caused the fire a year ago? The theater only reopened a few months back, and they are tempting fate again?" He looked to his father.

"Are we never to hear *Hamlet* again because of that? Surely a thing will not happen twice, for I have heard they have taken a great many precautions," his father answered, and just like that, everyone returned to their conversations, and the altercation seemed to fade into the background . . . for now, at least.

I was sure it would produce more speculation about me.

I wished to leave, and a part of me thought I ought not to have come, but when the marquess rose to go, he reminded me I was to sit in his box, and her face came to mind.

I would be able to sit beside her, and that alone was worth the world.

Verity

May 24, 1813

By his mere gaze my soul is left asunder.
One part aching,
The other soothing.
Some nights filled with terrors,
Dark rooms without exits.
Tongues that curse above me.
But
Some nights are filled with delight.
Rooms where he and I exist alone.
Kisses that reach the depths of me.
Wary am I . . .

Truly I was wary. All of me could not rest, for either I was overtaken by my nightmares or thoughts of Theodore. Each moment I was away from him made me more impatient at the chance of seeing him.

"*Oh, God!*"

The scream was so loud I sat up and turned to the door.

When I heard even more screams, I closed my journal and rushed downstairs into the drawing room, where everyone was dressed and ready for the theater, only to see Hathor jumping and hugging Silva tightly. Beside her were Abena and Devana as well.

"What is happening?" I asked, watching them all radiate with joy.

"Verity." Silva turned to me, placed her hand on her stomach. "I'm—"

"Having a baby!" Hathor said. "I'm going to be an aunt!"

"Hathor, calm yourself, and take a step back before you do damage," Damon ordered and nearly pushed her. Hector had to steady her so that she did not fall over.

"Damon!" Silva gasped. "I am not that fragile."

"We are all so delighted by this news," said the marchioness from beside her husband, rather calmly by comparison, which could mean only that she already knew.

"Congratulations," I said to them.

"How does the baby get in there?" Abena questioned loudly as she stared at Silva's stomach, causing them all to pause.

The expressions on her parents' and Damon's and Silva's faces looked to be of panic.

"What a silly question!" Hathor said, gathering her shawl. "A child is a gift from God. He puts it there for married couples."

I bit my lip so as not to laugh.

"Yes, exactly," her mother said, apparently the source of that lie.

"But"—Hathor frowned, thinking now—"if that is the case, then how are there illegitimate children?"

"We are very late!" the marchioness snapped, hands up. "Ladies, we must be going. Sweethearts, be good. We shall see you soon."

The marchioness kissed Devana, Hector, and Abena before walking quickly over to me. Hathor followed but seemed to still be pondering. Meanwhile, her father and brother were part panicked and part amused.

"Do you like *Hamlet*?" Hathor asked.

"Yes, actually. It is comforting to see another dysfunctional family," I joked, forgetting to whom I was speaking.

She looked at me strangely as we got into the carriage. "I have heard many things said of the play but never 'comforting.'"

"I mean entertaining," I lied, smiling. I felt that if I had said as much to Theodore, he would have understood.

She seemed to accept the answer and relaxed back as Damon and Silva entered.

They made conversation, and as always, Damon mocked his sister. But it was clear he was so happy that even his insults to her were affectionate in nature. It was all so sweet that I truly could not wait to watch a tragedy, if only for balance.

"Oh, that reminds me," Damon said. "Do strike up a conversation with Dr. Darrington should he be alone."

"Why?" I asked, though I was looking forward to seeing him more than I was looking forward to the play.

"There was some trouble at the club today, so there is sure to be talk about him tonight. He is our guest in the box, and I wish to dispel as much embarrassment as possible."

"Since when are you so nice to strangers?" Hathor questioned.

"He is hardly a stranger at this point," Silva reminded her.

"Besides, he is this family's . . . what shall we call him? We are not all his patients, but he is—"

"A friend," I said, causing them to look at me. "Our friend."

"It is not becoming of a lady to have male friends," Silva replied, which caused me to frown. "So we will say he is Damon's friend. Or your brother's friend, Verity."

I could only nod, but then I asked, "Should he not have met us at the house?"

"He had some affairs to clear up but shall meet us there," Damon answered me as we neared the opera house.

"I do hope it is the actress I like for Ophelia. The new one they employed recently has the most terrible facial expressions," Hathor said once we pulled to a stop before the theater.

I believed she was still speaking. However, I did not pay any mind, as right outside the door was Theodore, waiting and dressed in his best.

My heart began to race further.

It felt like years went by, waiting for him to finish speaking to Lord and Lady Monthermer, then greeting Damon and Silva, followed by Hathor, then finally me.

"Lady Verity," he said with a slight uptick in his smile.

"Dr. Darrington." I finally exhaled. "I do hope you are fond of *Hamlet*."

"Yes. I sometimes, odd as it may seem, find Shakespeare's tragedies comforting," he replied, and I found myself unable to look from him, nor could he look from me.

"How strange. Verity, only moments ago, said the same thing." Hathor pulled my attention. "I came to cry beautifully, not to be comforted."

"You cry beautifully?" Damon tilted his head to the side. "Never in this world. I have seen a corgi weep more prettily."

"I hope you have a daughter that relentlessly mocks you," she snapped.

"Hathor!" He groaned, looking around.

Her eyes widened, and she clasped her hand over her mouth and looked at Dr. Darrington.

"Luckily, he knows, but will you please not inform the whole ton tonight?" Damon shook his head, leading his wife away.

"My apologies!" she said as she went after them.

"So, they are always like this?" Theodore whispered to me.

"Always," I whispered back.

"How amusing for you," he said.

We were escorted to Lord Monthermer's box by the staff, and it was only when we were seated next to each other that I could whisper back.

"Sometimes, it is amusing, while other times, I feel as though I am a fury in a room with angels."

"You are far too beautiful to be a fury," he said.

I looked at him, but he was looking over the crowd below. He did peek at me from the corner of his eye briefly. And somehow, maybe it was just timing, or maybe it was by his wish or mine, but somehow our hands touched, and it filled my heart with air.

His fingers brushed past mine once more and though I looked upon the play, my thoughts were only of him. It felt like the air was becoming thicker and thicker, to the point that breathing became more difficult to maintain. It did not help that when I glanced to him his gaze was upon me and the look in his eyes, even in this darkness, did not help matters at all. Gently I felt his touch drift slowly up my arm. So gently it reminded me of that night . . . in the drawing room, when we kissed.

I longed for another.

"Silva, are you well?"

I turned to see Damon looking over his wife's flushed face.

"Forgive me, I feel a bit warm," Silva whispered, trying to smile and defuse the attention upon her. It was only then that Theodore's touch left me as he stood to aid them both. Slowly they helped her from the booth.

"Do not be so concerned, my dears, such things are to be expected in her condition," the marchioness said to Hathor and me as we watched them go. Though I believed only Hathor was truly concerned, for I was only saddened to see Theodore go. I had not realized how selfish and uncaring I could be. It was not that I did not worry for Silva. I just felt . . . more for myself? Her husband was beside her, could hug and tend to her whenever she pleased. It was I who . . . wished for the same.

To not be alone.

I sat there, the minutes going by, desperately wishing for him to return and take my hand in the darkness once more. However, after ten minutes, I found my patience no longer able to hold.

"Godmother, may I step out for some air?" I whispered to her.

She looked my face over. "I shall accompany you—"

"Please, I do not wish to interrupt. I shall return with Damon and Silva."

She nodded and carefully I stepped around the chairs and through the curtains to the back room. Just as I reached the door, it opened and Theodore appeared before me, his eyes as wide as mine were. Stepping forward, the space between our bodies caused that similar heaviness of breath to return. He closed the door behind me and I noticed no one else in the small room.

"Damon and Silva?" I whispered up to him.

"They sought to retire for the evening," he whispered back down to me.

"So, we are alone?"

"We are very much not alone," he stated as the Du Bells were just behind the door. "But we are alone enough."

"Enough for what?"

"Folly," he stated, and then with no other warning his lips were upon mine. All of my body leaned toward him, as though awakening for him. His tongue dipped deep into my mouth as his strong hands gripped my waist first and then traveled up and down the length of my body until one hand had cupped my breast and the other lifted my thigh. He did not stop there, his kiss moving from my lips to the side of my face . . . down to my neck. I shivered and a sound I'd never heard escaped from my lips.

This feeling . . . never had I felt this before.

"If you knew what I wished to do to you in this moment you would think me a monster," he whispered into my ear before kissing it.

"I could never," I replied gently when his head rose and his eyes slowly met mine again. "Tell me."

"You would not understand even if I did."

"Then explain."

"Words cannot do so." And again he kissed my lips, but this time gently and only once before stepping back from me.

He inhaled deeply through his nose, closing his eyes for a moment.

"Theodore."

"Go back inside, Verity," he said when he opened his eyes again.

"Why do you always tell me to go after you kiss me?"

"To prevent myself from doing more than kissing you."

"What could be more?"

"So much. There is so much more."

"Show me."

"I cannot."

"Why?"

"It is the duty of your husband to do so."

"I shall have no one else but you, so it is your duty."

Again he inhaled deeply and moved closer to me, and this time he lifted my chin. "This mouth of yours will get you into trouble, *my lady*."

I smiled. "How lucky I am you are a doctor then, sir, for is not your duty also to aid me?"

"You leave me incapable of mounting any defense." He kissed my forehead. "So now I must beg you, go inside. For both our sakes."

I frowned and he kissed the side of my face.

"Worry not, I doubt this shall be the last time we end up like this. Now adjust yourself and return."

I nodded, allowing him to step away again before I turned back to the door. I took a deep breath seeking to calm myself. It took a moment and I could not look back at him or all my efforts would be undone. When I did finally go back inside and take my seat I found myself counting the seconds until we would be able to hold each other again.

19

Verity

"What is it that you are always writing in your journal?" he asked as we walked. "You are quite secretive with it."

We were once more at the park, and Henry's family had arranged for him to speak with Hathor.

"I am not being secretive."

"Any time someone is near, you rush to close it, as if you fear someone will read it," he teased, his eyebrow rising along with the corner of his mouth.

"So, you shall not tell me? Fine." He pretended to pout.

"It is not that. It is just . . ."

"Just?"

"My brother Evander gave me my first blank book many years ago and told me to record whatever made me upset. Over time, I started to write poems or stories. One day, my governess read one of them and told me to stop."

"Why?"

"Apparently, it sounded like witchcraft."

He paused and turned to look at me and actually laughed. "Witchcraft? Now I must read it."

"Never," I replied, head high.

"It makes sense."

"What does?"

"Why I am so fond of you," he whispered, his face serious,

but the glance he gave me was softer. "You have bewitched me."

I scoffed, stumbling over my words.

"What is so amusing?" Hathor turned to ask us, twirling the parasol she had in her hands.

"Your charade," I lied quickly, looking at her and Henry, who was watching Theodore curiously. "Did you not say you cared for someone else?"

"Henry says I will attract more interest if I am unattainable, and he hopes to make his love jealous with my company," she replied without shame.

"If you two continue on like this, people will think you truly are to be engaged," Theodore said to them.

Hathor and Henry looked to each other. "His point has merit. You should consider speaking to other young ladies, as well."

"To then be seen as a rake? Or worse, desperate? Never. Besides, she would then know I only sought to make her envious." He nearly cringed at the mention of it, and Hathor nodded as if she understood the absurdity.

"Do you not worry that you may come to fall in love with each other with all this proximity?" I asked.

They both looked at me as if I were mad.

"Verity, do not be ridiculous. This is real life, not a play." Hathor huffed, turning her back to me and continuing on, her parasol twirling as she went.

I glanced at Theodore, and he merely shook his head at the sight of them before saying, "I do not know who is behaving more ridiculously, them or us."

"It is most certainly them."

"You are biased in our favor."

"I quite like the words *us* and *our*." I smiled, closing the gap that had formed between us and Henry and Hathor. Theodore was never out of step with me. He said not a word in return, which I had learned over the last few days meant he agreed with me but would not dare say it aloud.

We had spoken much over the past few days . . . and found ourselves kissing much more as well. I tried not to think of those moments, all of me flushing with warmth at the thought of his hands as they gripped me . . . as they cupped my breasts . . . how soft his lips were.

. . . *No.*

I pushed those memories out of my mind so I could think of the other things we spoke about. Like how I had learned of his time in university and his trips across the country in search of different doctors to learn from. And I shared about my time riding horses and walking in Everely. My world was much smaller than his, it seemed, but he listened as though I had traveled to some foreign land filled with intrigue. The thing I liked the most was his honesty. No matter what I asked, he was always sincere, pushing me to ask even more. I was determined to know more of him than anyone else in this world.

I glanced up at him in our silence only to see he was looking at me. I looked away so as not to smile.

"What are you thinking of?" he asked.

"Nothing."

"That is surely not true. Tell me."

I looked to the pond, not wanting to say it to his face. "I was thinking how I wished to know you better than anyone else in the world."

Silence again.

I knew what it meant, but still, I turned to look at him when he did not respond. However, he was looking not at me but at a dark-haired woman dressed in soft yellow in the far distance. She stood among a group of women speaking, though her eyes did wander to him as well.

"Do you know her?" I asked, but Henry was right beside him before I could even blink, turning him around playfully.

"I feel as though we have dragged these poor young ladies far enough, my friend. Why don't we return?" He pretended to laugh as he took Theodore away from me.

"What has happened?" I looked to Hathor, as she was now at my side.

"The Marchioness of Whitmear is here," she whispered despite our distance from the woman in yellow she was clearly motioning to.

Theodore's stepmother. She was rather youthful and petite, with a round face and dark hair.

"How horribly awkward," Hathor said as we began to walk behind them. "It might be best if he simply leaves."

I frowned. "Why would he leave? It is not as though she owns the park."

"Of course. However, with both of them here, there is sure to be even greater talk."

"There shall be talk either way. Should he run, it would seem like he has done something shameful. Last I checked, being born illegitimate is not a sin of his making."

"Why are you getting so upset?" Hathor frowned. "I am not the one who made the rules."

I tried to calm myself. "I know. But it all seems . . . so unfair. I dislike it."

"Yes, well, there is nothing we can do except never find ourselves in such a situation." She shuddered at the thought. But then her mood brightened, and I thought it was because she had found some solution. "Should we take a boat out on the water?"

I was not in the mood for that. "With our luck, someone may very well fall in this season and need to be rescued."

"How awful to say!" She giggled, going on without a care. I

glanced at Theodore to see Henry speaking animatedly to him despite the fact that he was indifferent.

Was he all right?

Theodore

My mind had stopped for a moment upon seeing her. She and my father rarely left the estate, so for her to be in London now . . . I did not know what to make of it. Did that mean my father was here as well?

"Theodore. Theodore!"

"What?" I faced Henry.

He sighed. "Did you hear a word I said?"

"Not at all."

"I knew it." He chuckled and picked up a few rocks to skip across the pond. "Well, what are you to do? Will you go say hello?"

"Are you mad?"

"Then you plan to run away from them?"

"I see no reason for me to do anything. They live their lives, and I live mine," I replied, then remembered Verity. I turned to find where the Du Bells had picnicked only to see Henry's mother heading straight for us. "And you need not worry over me, I believe you have your own affairs to attend to. Your mother is coming."

He looked to the sky as if to pray. "Why will she not leave me be?"

"What do you expect as her only son?" I tried to step back to escape when he pushed me forward.

"Do not leave!"

"Do not be ridiculous. This does not concern me."

"Where is your loyalty? I helped you."

"I did not require your help."

"Yes, you were—"

"Henry!" her voice cut in, and we both immediately ended our nonsense and faced her seriously.

"Mother!" he exclaimed in the same high pitch and I merely nodded to her.

"I saw you walking with Hathor once again. Is she not lovely? A true treasure to find one as mature as she, yet lively and full of wit," she said, the largest grin on her face, and she then shifted her gaze to me. "Do you not agree, Theodore?"

"You are correct, my lady. She is splendid." I nodded, and Henry punched me in the back. I did not care, for I would not fight his mother on his behalf.

"Of course, I am. Well, Henry?"

"She is a nice girl, yes, and I am glad to have met such a *friend*." His stress on the word was clear, as was the change in her face. I desperately wished to leave.

"Henry."

"Mother."

She clenched her mouth closed, inhaled through her nose, and glanced at me once more. "Theodore, would you excuse us? I would like to speak to my son privately."

"Of course," I said, already stepping away from them. Henry glared, but I shrugged in return, trying not to laugh. I walked on and glanced up at the sky. It was a rare sunny day, and I had no appointments to tend to. All I wished was to sit by the pond as other families did—with Verity.

Again, I looked over at the Du Bells, but strangely, she was not there.

"Who are you looking for?"

I spun around, and there she stood before me, alone.

"You," I muttered, a bit stunned. Was she really here, or was I dreaming?

"Well, you need not search any longer." She smiled.

"Where is your chaperone?"

She grimaced. "I have only just escaped them."

"Escaped?" I chuckled. "Why?"

"Why else but to see you? It is hard enough with God-mother always near. Nothing moves in their home without her attention, and I am quite unsettled by it."

"She has many ladies under her care, and thus, she must be vigilant. Come, I will walk you back."

"If we were in Everely, I could be gone all day and no one would notice," she replied as she walked in the opposite direction.

"I would hope someone would, as that is dangerous. And the Du Bells, I believe, would notice."

"I know." She grinned as she continued to walk away from them. "Are you worried for me?"

"Yes." I worried deeply for her and myself as I followed.

"Then am I free to be worried about you?" When she asked me these questions so directly, I found myself unable to answer. I was partly stunned and then far too delighted by the words to reply immediately.

"There is nothing for you to fret about over me," I finally replied, "other than maybe tainting your reputation."

"I care not about that—"

"Yes, from our time together thus far, I'm quite aware. But—"

"Let us not go any further? We are breaking all rules of decency?" she mocked and then giggled. "You have said this to me numerous times and yet nevertheless when I embrace you, you embrace me."

I had no rebuttal, for she was right.

I protested and yet at the slightest chance crossed the line over and over again. So long as she kept reaching out for me, I knew I would follow her to the farthest ends of the world.

"Since you are unable to deny it, I shall change the subject and ask . . . are you all right?"

"Of course, why would I not be?"

"Your stepmother." Her eyebrow rose. "You looked . . . unlike yourself at the sight of her. Are you on bad terms?"

"I do not think it possible for us to be on good terms. However, neither of us has harmed the other. So I do not think of us as great enemies."

"Then why did you turn?"

"I do not know." I honestly did not. I was simply used to not being near her.

"I often wish to turn away," she softly replied as she glanced up at the sky. "Especially from the Du Bells, as you know. It is because they are always good-natured, kind, and happy. I feel . . . smaller near them. I like them, but at the same time, I am deeply jealous I cannot have a happy family, as well."

"You believed yourself not part of one?"

"Do you not know my story?"

"I know your past. But that is not your present or future," I replied. "Verity, you are part of a happy family. You are part of the Du Bells—"

"I am not."

"You are, for is not your brother their in-law? Will not your future nephew or niece be their grandchild or relation, as well? You are family. If not by blood, by connection. And I know better than anyone that even the thinnest connections matter." I was connected to my father's wife, even though she had never spoken to me.

She pouted. "Were we not supposed to be talking about your life? How did we again return to mine?"

I tried to withhold my amusement. "I believe it was you."

"Well, I shall change the subject back then."

"*Lady* Verity, we very much should return," I said when I noticed two women whispering as they watched us.

"I—" She paused at the rumbling of thunder.

The once beautiful clear sky morphed into an outright downpour in the briefest of seconds, sending everyone around us into a sprint for cover.

"Theodore!" She grabbed my hand, and I stood stunned at the contact. As the water soaked her face, she grinned wildly. "Run with me!"

Enchanted, truly bewitched, I held on tightly and did as she requested.

We ran away together.

And for a brief moment, it felt as if everyone else in the world had fallen away. I was not sure how far or how long we ran, but I wished so desperately to continue running with her forever. My heart leapt with joy when I was with her. I felt such freedom and openness with her.

"Oh!" She gasped with a hand over her chest, seeking to catch her breath when we reached a hidden pathway under a small bridge. All of her—from her light blue dress to her hat and even the curls underneath—was drenched. Nevertheless, she stared back at me with the largest and purest smile. "I have not run like that in ages."

I was frustrated by how I could not better describe my feelings for her.

"Theodore—"

"I am so very much in love with you." The words spilled from my lips like the rain from the sky. "I do not know when or how but you have become my greatest joy. I have nothing to propose to you with, and I know I am not worthy, but even still, I wish more than anything for you to be my wife."

She stepped closer and before she could speak I reached into my pocket, taking out a necklace made of blue silk with a floral pendant and a tiny pearl at the end. Until now it had been kept buried away in a small jewelry box with my things. "It is not much, but it is the only inheritance left to me by my mother."

She stared at it and then back at me. "You are giving it to me?"

"If you shall accept."

"How could I not?" Slowly, she turned her back to me. "Shall you help me wear it?"

Brushing her curls to the side, I did as she asked, but my hands could not help but linger upon the skin of her neck. Even the slightest touch of her warmed me, and when she faced me once more, her beautiful brown eyes held me captive. Lifting her chin up I could feel her breath upon my lips. She leaned forward, her eyes closed; however, before we kissed a thunderous voice called out.

"Theodore!"

Verity jumped from me, placing distance between us as we turned to see there, at the entrance of the path, was the woman in yellow, my stepmother, and beside her was a coachman, holding an umbrella. She stood, eyes wide, looking between us.

"I . . . we . . . Lady Whitmear—" Verity stumbled over her words.

"The rain has eased, Lady Verity. I shall walk you to your carriage. Come stand beside me," she snapped harshly, though her glare did not leave me . . . and I was too shocked to speak, too shocked to think.

Fuck.

Oh fuck!

Verity

I knew not what to say, so I did as ordered, moving to her side. Then we began to walk. When I turned back, Theodore was just standing there, his head down, fists clenched . . . I could not see his expression but I knew with each step I took farther away from him, this did not bode well, not at all.

Dammit!

What was I to do?

Would she speak of this to anyone?

Or, worse, would she use it to hurt Theodore?

The fear rose in me until she spoke.

"Has he taken advantage of you?" she asked lowly. "You must tell me honestly. I cannot save you if you do not."

Save me? "I need no saving from him."

"You may not—"

"He has done nothing except help me, be kind to me, and care for me. Nothing beyond what you saw has taken place."

"What I saw was already far too much. How could he—"

I stopped and glared at her. "You do not know him. He's warned me a great many times that I ought to be careful, and he always tries to distance himself. It was I who took his hand and asked him to come with me. Please do not cause any trouble. Please."

She looked at me with surprise.

"Verity!"

I turned to see Damon and his valet calling out to me. Again, I looked at her and begged, "Please."

"Verity, are you all right? We lost sight of you before the rain," Damon exclaimed as he reached me.

"Yes, I do believe that was my fault. I wished to speak with her, and then we were caught in the rain." Lady Whitmear smiled as she looked at him. "Do tell your mother I apologize for any fear her absence may have caused."

"Thank you for seeing to her, Lady . . ." his voice trailed off, as he clearly did not know her.

"Lady Whitmear," she said, and his eyes widened.

"Of course, forgive me." He bowed his head and then looked at me and offered his arm. "Thank you, once more."

"Thank you, your ladyship." I curtsied, only now remembering my manners.

"Do take care, Lady Verity," she said, and it only made the dread in my heart increase. Theodore had not followed us, and I could only imagine what his feelings were. If someone had caused my stepmother to have unimpeachable evidence against me, I would want to fall into a hole and never return.

Verity, you idiot!

20

Theodore

"What happened?" Henry asked, coming up beside me. "Nothing I need to—"

"Bullshit," he snapped, getting in front of me. "I saw—it's Lady Verity? Is she the one you—"

I grabbed his arm tightly. "You followed us in the rain?"

"I was not following you," he replied as he yanked back. "I was following Sir Grisham, who was following you."

"Fuck!" I hollered. Had all the world come to witness this moment?

"Calm yourself. I stopped him," Henry said. "He did not see. I only went to fetch you both before anyone else did. However, by the time I reached where I thought you had gone, I saw Lady Whitmear with her instead."

It brought little relief to me. She had seen too much . . . for we had done and gone too far. I had known it was only a matter of time before we were caught. And yet even still I had not stopped myself.

"What will you do?"

"I do not know yet, but I have to speak to Lady Whitmear." More like I had to grovel as if my life depended on it because Verity's life did.

"I shall meet you at the inn later."

I said not a word and walked to her carriage. I knew the one, as it had my father's family crest upon it. I did not know what to feel, but I was not thinking of myself. Whatever she wanted of me, I would do it. I would do anything so long as she did not damage Verity's reputation in any way. That was my biggest fear. She was not at all to blame. She was merely reveling in her newfound feelings. I was the older party, so I was the one who should have known better. This was my fault.

"Theodore."

I glanced up to see Lady Whitmear as she arrived before bowing my head once again. "Your ladyship."

"Ride with me," she said as her coachman moved to open the door.

I waited for her to enter before following. It was only when the doors closed again that the words all but spilled out of me.

"I beg of you, say nothing of it to anyone. Not for my sake, but hers. I cannot have her reputation—"

"Clearly you knew the risks, and still, you did not stop?" she snapped at me. "Have I been mistaken in your character this whole time? Are you so devious as to plot to ruin this young woman?"

"It was no plot!"

"Then what could ever make you think to act this way? To . . . to embrace in a public manner, during the day, no less. Any number of people could have seen you both! You could have destroyed that girl's whole future in an instant. What were you thinking of if not to ruin her?"

"I was not thinking!" I snapped in return. "I can hardly ever think around her. You are right. I knew the risk. I wished to abide by propriety, and yet I find myself before her always! For once, I wanted . . ."

"Well, do not stop now. You wanted what? To pretend as if you are a lord? The heir of Whitmear?"

Of course, that is what she would think. How typical. "No. For once, I wanted to be freely happy."

She was silent, and with how we spoke, one would have thought us familiar. To think this would be the nature of our first conversation together.

"She begged me not to blame you," she finally spoke, though her gaze was fixed outside the carriage. "She did not care at all for her own reputation. For a young lady in her position, that means she cares for you deeply. I will assume you care for her as well?"

"Yes," I admitted, hanging my head.

"Then you must end it," she replied. "If you truly care for her, dare I say even love her, you must not do this to her, Theodore."

I looked up to see her gazing at me with sympathy. "She does not know what it is like to be the center of gossip and mockery; whatever talk of her family, those sins were not her own. As such she has never not been highly regarded. For her to fall from such a height in society will harm her greatly."

I already knew this.

I had told myself all of this.

Yet I never truly accepted it.

Now I had no choice.

I had to leave her.

"I do not know how to be without her," I whispered. "I do not wish to be without her."

"Then you shall see her ruined?"

I did not answer.

"I shall help you," she said.

"Why?" I frowned. "Is there something you want in return?"

"Yes . . . I wish for you to go visit your father."

Of all the things I thought she would request that had never come to my mind, so I was not sure how to respond.

"No."

"Theodore—"

"With all due respect, your ladyship, my answer is no. I have no desire to see that man." Even less so now in light of present circumstances. "Surely there must be something else you would require—?"

"What could I require of you? You have nothing to offer me or any other lady of the ton. My desire is simple. Your presence at Wentwood House."

"To what end? I have no business with the man nor him with me—"

"Your father is ill," she said and paused. I met her gaze clearly for the first time. "He wishes to see you before it is too late. That is why I have come."

"What is his illness?"

"No one knows. We have called many doctors, none have been able to cure him. As you yourself have become so renowned the very least you can do is visit him, is it not?"

"That is all you wish for?" I asked carefully. "You shall not speak a word of—"

"Lady Verity's reputation is risked by you alone," she replied, causing me to once more wish to fall into the earth. Instead the carriage came to a stop at the Crown Inn. I moved to open the doors myself when she spoke once more.

"Theodore, just because life is often unfair does not mean you are free to rebel against it."

I snickered in that moment as bitterness and anger filled me. "Said the great and noble woman who became so on the bones of someone else. Do not fret, your ladyship, I am well versed in this, good day!"

I could not bother to spare her or the carriage another look. Marching inside the inn, I did not even hear the voices of the innkeeper nor the patrons inside. My ears were ringing from anger.

Entering the room, I ripped off my jacket, throwing it to the floor and slamming my fist against the wall beside me.

I folded under the weight of the rage I felt but could not express, falling to the floor where I sat, wishing, praying, begging for some . . . reprieve. But none would come. None ever came. It felt like hours had gone by, because hours had, the day outside turning to night. It was only then that I rose to my feet and moved to the trunk at the end of the bed.

Knock. Knock.

"Theodore?"

I exhaled at the sound of his voice. Of all the people I did not wish to see now, he was at the top of the list.

"Theodore?" The door opened as Henry entered.

I said nothing, moving to my vanity to collect my paperwork.

"What has happened? I came to see—"

"Go home, Henry," I muttered.

"Like hell I will! What did your stepmother say? Does she mean to threaten you? Pay her no heed. No one will believe her or they will simply think she means to destroy your character—"

"Henry, go home," I said again.

"What are you doing? There is no reason for you to run—"

"HENRY!" I hollered angrily. "For the love of God himself, LEAVE ME BE!"

"Theodore, I just wish to help you—"

"There is nothing you can do or say to help! You do not even have the capacity to understand. How could you? You are the only son of Lord Fancot, the future viscount. The greatest of futures has been assigned to you since birth, every door open to you, and even still you reject it. You bemoan your circumstances and begrudge your parents who live and breathe to secure your happiness with the most amiable ladies in society. How could you even begin to help me? Shall you make me legitimate? Shall you give me the hand of the woman I desire? No. You can do nothing, so all I ask is for you to LEAVE ME BE!" I took a deep breath, hanging my head. "You have no idea what it is like to be a bastard, Henry."

"I shall give you space" was all he said as he turned around, closing the door gently. It was then I tossed the papers in my hand.

I cared about nothing . . . nothing but her, which was why this hurt so badly.

Verity

I had not slept or eaten as I waited in torture to hear of any gossip of me amongst the ton the next day. I half expected Mrs. Loquac to come knocking at the door to investigate further on behalf of her other clients. Thankfully, there was none. Instead, everyone spoke of the charming and beautiful Lady Whitmear, who had just arrived in London.

"She has invited us to a tea? Today?" Hathor questioned her mama as she took her seat beside me. "I did not know you were so well acquainted with her, Mother."

"I am not. However, she does not plan to stay in London long so she wishes to meet a few of the ladies of the ton before she leaves," the marchioness said as she stirred her tea, looking over new curtain designs. "I saw no reason to decline the invitation."

"Her connection with Dr. Darrington ought to be reason enough," Hathor argued. "We have openly supported him."

"Their personal affairs are not our concern, my dear. She asked us to tea, so we shall go for tea."

"Do you think she plans to persuade us from his company?"

Hathor turned, looking at me. "He's become quite well known among the ton and highly spoken of. Papa might be right about his future relevance. Maybe she has caught wind of it and has come to put a stop to it."

"Hathor, you need not think so negatively," the marchioness said to her. "It is simply an afternoon tea, not the third act of a Shakespearean tragedy."

"It is just odd, is all, for her to seek us out suddenly without another connection." Once more, she looked at me. "You were with her yesterday, Verity. Did she say anything?"

"Nothing of note," I lied, touching the necklace Theodore had given me.

"Verity, are you feeling all right?" the marchioness asked me.

"I am fine, just a bit tired."

"Well, you should rest. Also, I have not seen you wear this necklace before. Where did you—"

"Your ladyship?" Ingrid arrived at the door. "Mrs. Loquac is here."

No! I sat up, my heart racing. Had she really come to investigate?

"Show her in."

"Your ladyship. Ladies." Mrs. Loquac curtsied upon entering with her assistant.

"Hello, Mrs. Loquac, how are you? Please sit. Ingrid, please pour her some tea."

"Thank you, and I wish I could tell you I was well, but I have heard the most troubling news," she exclaimed, and I cringed, gripping my own hands so tightly they grew numb.

"My goodness. What is it?"

I leaned in, and, of course, the woman thought to take a rather long sip of her tea.

"Oh, good. How refreshing."

"I am glad." The marchioness smiled but was clearly waiting, as was I.

"You shall never believe it, but the most ghastly of affairs has been uncovered. Right beneath our very noses, a trollop, a light skirt!"

The marchioness frowned. "I do not understand."

Closing my eyes, I tried to prepare myself for the horrors about to be unleashed upon me.

"Miss Edwina Charmant was caught in the most undignified manner with her family's coachman yesterday at the park!"

I quietly let out a long breath.

"What? The niece of Mrs. Frinton-Smith?"

"Yes. And they say he and the girl have been lovers for a great many weeks now. There, right in the bushes—"

The marchioness faced us quickly. "Girls, go upstairs and get ready for our outing."

"But, Mama—"

"Upstairs!"

We both stood, Hathor more begrudgingly than I.

"What is the point in coming out if they still treat us as if we were children?" Hathor asked me as we exited. "It is our right to know as much as they."

"I am sure we will hear eventually."

She gasped and gripped my arm. "Exactly! So why bother. But can you believe it? Her coachman? I mean, she is not a lady, but to form an attachment with your servant . . ."

"One cannot help who they come to love, Hathor," I said as I moved to the stairs. While I was glad it was not my scandal, I did pity the girl who would be left open to attack.

"Yes, but—"

"Oh, girls, good, you are here."

We both stopped on the stairs to see the marquess exiting the study, two letters in his hands. "I just received some news."

"Of Edwina? Already? Who is your source? You are neck and neck with Mrs. Loquac." Hathor laughed.

However, her father looked at her in confusion. "Forgive me, sweetheart, but I have not a clue what you are speaking of."

"Mrs. Frinton-Smith's niece Edwina," Hathor said again.

"What of her?"

Hathor sighed. "Never mind. Mother will inform you shortly. What is your news?"

"Ah, right!" he said, lifting the letters in his hands. "I have just been informed that Lord Wyndham's eldest son has finally succumbed to his illness."

"Oh." Hathor's cheerfulness fell. "How tragic for them."

"Yes, but at least the poor man is no longer suffering. I shall speak to your mother about when it is appropriate to send our condolences," he replied and then looked to me. "Ah, Verity, Dr. Darrington has also left town . . ."

"What?" I stepped back down the stairs.

"Yes. Apparently, his father is ill, and he has gone to see him. He writes to apologize for the abruptness of his departure, and he does not know when he shall be able to return. His patients are in the care of—"

I could not hear anything else. It was as if the whole world had gone silent. I could not think, and I found myself unable to breathe.

He'd left me.

Just like that?

With so little care?

With no fight?

"Verity!"

I had not realized I was sinking to the floor until I felt a pair of arms around me. Whom they belonged to, I did not care. Even as they called out to me, as more and more people came to help me, I did not care. The world was spinning. I wished to scream and yet was silent. I wished for nothing more than to . . . to . . . cry. But I could not bring myself to do so.

What was this feeling?

"Quickly! Call for a doctor!" someone called around me.

Closing my eyes, I sought to escape into my dreams, but I found only nightmares there.

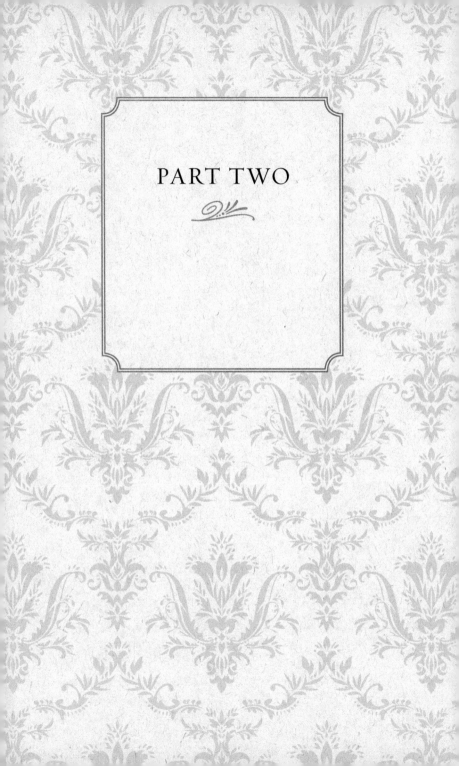

PART TWO

21

Theodore

The estate of the Marquess of Whitmear, my father, was called Wentwood House, and until this very day, I had never seen it with my own eyes. I knew where it was located—the edge of the Peak District in Cheshire—and how grand an estate it was. The grounds encompassed more than fourteen hundred acres but never had I beheld it, despite my father's many attempts. Had I gone all my life without seeing it, I would not have minded. However, now that it was before me, I understood as never before how majestic the name of the man who had sired me truly was, as well as how extensive his property was.

His servants stood in front of the house, clearly expecting to greet Lady Whitmear. When I stepped out of her carriage, which she had insisted I take alone, a short man dressed in black with a balding head of gray hair, clearly the butler from his authority, stepped forward.

"And you are, sir?" he asked me. "Where is her ladyship?"

"My name is Dr. Theodore Darrington. Her ladyship sent me ahead to see Lord Whitmear." I watched as his and the rest of the staff's eyes widened.

"Welcome to Wentwood, Master Theodore. My name is Mr. Ralph Pierce, the head butler here. How was your journey?" He bowed his head, and the rest of the staff followed suit.

"Fine, and I am not master anything, simply a doctor here to see the marquess," I corrected, not sure why he was suddenly so familiar with me.

"Forgive me, Master Theodore. The marquess stated that should you ever come to Wentwood, you were to be addressed as such. As the head butler, I must adhere to his lordship's wishes."

What?

"He said so?"

"Yes, a great many times. All of the staff are aware," he replied and turned back to them. "Gather Master Theodore's things and prepare a room. William, ride out and inform his lordship at once."

"Ride out?" I looked at him. "Do you mean he is not here?"

"Yes, he and young Master Alexander have taken their horses into the fields."

Now I was even further confused. How could he be on horseback? "Is the marquess not greatly ill?"

"Ill? Heaven forbid. As far as I know, his lordship is in fine health. He and Master Alexander ride almost daily."

"That is not what I was told," I whispered to myself as I turned back to look at the rolling hills in the distance. Part of me was looking for my own escape. I had prepared my mind for a man upon his sickbed. I'd been ready to stay and watch over him until he passed and then leave once more. I was not yet sure where to, but . . . now everything was amiss.

"Master Theodore, this way," Mr. Pierce said, gesturing for me to go before him. They had already taken my things, so I had no choice but to follow inside. "I shall lead you to your rooms—"

"I think it is best if I wait for his lordship," I interrupted. I would not feel comfortable until I understood what was going on. No, even then, I doubted I would be able to feel comfortable here. Standing upon the checkered tiles, I felt myself to be a pawn in whatever game Lady Whitmear was playing. Why did she wish me to come here?

"The study then. Do you desire tea?" he questioned, and though he was only doing his job, it felt . . . unnerving.

"Thank you, but no. I will simply wait." I followed him to the engraved double doors. He opened them both before allowing me in.

And the first thing I saw upon entering was a portrait of my father, the Lady Whitmear, and a small boy with shoulder-length curly hair. They looked as a family should—happy. I stared at my father's face—which was similar to mine though his skin was slightly darker, his nose and lips a bit fuller.

How long had it been since I had spoken to him?

Seven years?

He'd briefly come to Oxford, on business he said, and wished to see how I was. I was terribly embarrassed by his presence. All the other students were peering over their books to watch the drama. It was one thing to know I was a bastard, but for him to be there before their eyes was amusement to them and more emotional bullets for their pistols aimed at me. I could not even hear what my father was trying to say to me. I did not wish to hear, so I begged him to leave me be.

And he did.

How foolish I was. No, not foolish but selfish, for I did not ask him to stop paying for my education. I forced myself to turn a blind eye to that fact, convinced myself it was my grandfather who saw to my needs. But anyone with half a brain knew that was not possible. So to ease part of my conscience, I told myself I would not touch more than I needed for my studies. I told myself I would pay all my other expenses

via my own occupation. Still, I was naïve. No one would seek
the services of a young doctor with messy connections. So my
patients were the poor and needy, and while they had much to
offer in the way of medical study, they lacked much in the way
of coin. I had once been paid in eggs. Still, I did not wish to
look to anyone for help. Henry refused to listen, forcing me
more and more into society, and it was through him that I was
able to gain better connections and wealthier patients, not
through my own talent alone.

I was always in need.

I'd rationalized that at least it was a friend and not my father. Now I felt an even greater fool as I thought of my words
to Henry. I would have to write to him and apologize. No, I
had insulted him to his face, so I ought to have the decency to
apologize in the same manner. But I could not return to London, not with her still there.

Verity.

The very thought of her sent waves of emotions through
me. I glanced at my hands, thinking of how it felt when she
had taken hold of them. How, in the briefest of moments, it
felt as if we were free. How I wanted to—

"Theodore?"

I turned toward the door. There my father stood, as in the
painting, though his hair was grayer, his chest rising and falling
heavily, his eyes wide.

"You are truly here? When they told me, I thought it was
some cruel jape." He laughed as he entered. Could servants
jape with their masters? I did not think so. "Well . . . welcome.
I am truly glad you have come, though I am a bit confused.
What has brought you now?"

"Your wife warned me of your impending death," I finally
spoke.

"Death?" He gasped.

"I was told you were gravely ill."

"As you can see, I am not."

"Which is why I am also a bit confused," I replied. However, I was distracted by the boy peeking in at the door.

He hid quickly when our eyes met, though I could still see his curly hair protruding from around the frame.

"Alexander, come and greet your brother, Theodore," our father said, and my eyes widened at the openness of his comment. What was even stranger was that Alexander did not seem surprised by it but, instead, slowly entered and lifted his hand to me.

"Hi."

"Hello," I said in return.

"You must be exhausted from your journey. The maids will draw you a bath, and we shall speak later—"

"I do not wish to impose."

"You are my son. How are you imposing?" he asked, patting the top of Alexander's head before looking down at him. "Is he imposing on you?"

Alexander shook his head no.

"I thank you for your hospitality then. I will not take—"

"Theodore, just go take your bath. You need not be so formal here. Everyone knows who you are to me and that this is your home as well."

"Thank you, sir, but this is not my home." I walked toward the door, where already the butler from earlier stood waiting. I said not one word and allowed him to lead me from them. It was only when I believed myself out of hearing distance that I finally asked for more information.

"Tell me, Mr. Pierce, what have you heard of me?" I asked, as I wished to know what exactly to expect here.

"Only that you are his lordship's son and a great doctor in London."

"Great is an exaggeration," I muttered. "And surely you know what *type* of son I am?"

"What type are you?"

"The one who will not inherit here, despite my age. Is that too vague, or should I be clearer?"

He chuckled. "You need not be. I understood you. However, as I told you earlier, his lordship's wishes supersede your own. And he says you are his son and must be treated with the utmost respect on his estate."

Once more, that did not make sense to me. "Why would he direct you to do so if I have never come here before?"

"I do not know, Master Theodore. You must ask him. We are simply his servants," he replied, leading me down a hall.

"Surely, in all your family's time here, you must have gathered insight into his thoughts?"

"And surely, one as wise as you should also know the answer to what you ask. If not, maybe this shall be enlightening," he replied and opened the door to the guest room. But it was not truly a guest room. Upon entering, I recognized a great many of my favorite things, from the types of books and art that I enjoyed to even the color and style of the furniture. How on earth did he know? However, nothing caught my attention more than the painting above the fireplace. Slowly, I gravitated to it, not believing it could exist here.

"Mother," I whispered, staring at the painting.

"His lordship has been waiting for you for a long time, Master Theodore," Mr. Pierce said gently. "A very long time. To be clear this is not a guest room but yours and yours alone."

"Her ladyship cannot be pleased by that."

"On the contrary," he replied, reaching into his jacket to retrieve a letter. "Her ladyship left this with the coachman to give you once you arrived."

I hesitated but took the letter. "Thank you."

"Of course," he said, and closed the door behind him.

I sought to prepare myself before opening the letter, but there would never be enough preparation, so I began to read.

Dear Theodore,

Yes, this is rather unconventional, and yes, I did lie to you. But I will not ask for forgiveness—it was for the greater good of both you and your father. He has missed you terribly and often inquires after any news of you from anyone who might know. Often, I have told him to simply go see you, but he refuses, locking himself away here at Wentwood instead. He did not wish you to feel further afflicted by his presence, and as you know, a great deal of misfortune occurred in London for him—you as well.

I often wish I could apologize to your mother. Had I known what my family had done, I would not have accepted this marriage or been so intensely jealous of her. The guilt and pain from it all made me wish to avoid you as much as I am sure you wished to avoid me. There is so much history between us, and I doubt it shall ever truly be healed.

So many years have now passed that I find myself wishing for better. But above all I desire joy and happiness for your father. I have tried many times to be a source of comfort, but I do not think it's possible until he has made his peace with you. So, until I return, I leave him and my son in your care.

Lady Whitmear

For the first time since I entered, I finally sat down, completely stunned.

22

Theodore

"Enter," I said, adjusting my shirt as the door opened. I thought it would be a maid or Mr. Pierce, but instead, it was Alexander. For a boy of eleven he was rather small. Though so was I as a child and did not grow taller until much later. He closed the door behind him, staring at me rather intensely. "Yes? Is there something you wish to say?"

"You are my brother."

"Half brother, but yes, I am." I stepped away from the mirror and faced him, noticing his clenched fist. "Does the notion so greatly upset you?"

He crossed his arms. "Yes, for if you are my brother, why have you never written to me? Never sent a card or gift on my birthday? Something—anything?"

"Have you sent one to me?" I questioned, amused.

"You are older."

"And you are legitimate."

He sighed deeply, moving to the bed and falling on it. "I do not really understand what that means. How can a person be illegitimate?"

"He is born out of wedlock."

"So?"

"The church frowns upon it."

"So?" he said again, and this time, I chuckled as I went to the side of the bed.

"You will understand when you are older."

"Since you are older, explain it to me," he demanded.

"Has Father . . . has it not been explained to you?"

He shook his head, which caused all his curls to shake as well. "No—not really. Mama said Papa had another son, that he was older, his name was Theodore, and he could not inherit the estate. But I was not to ask Papa about it because it made him very sad. That is all."

"Yes, that truly is not a good explanation." But due to his age, I could not think of a better one.

"So . . . ?"

I shook my head. "No explanation will make sense till you are older."

He said nothing more, just sat on the edge of the bed, his feet dangling, and once more stared at me.

"Yes?" I asked.

"Shall you be staying here now?"

I did not know what was to happen next in my life. But I was sure I would not be staying here. "No. I am merely here to visit for a day or two."

He frowned, and his shoulders dropped. "Oh."

I was unsure of what I was to say to him, so we dwelled in this awkward silence, so much so that when there was a knock at the door, I all but shouted.

"Yes, come in!"

But still, it was not the butler. Instead, it was my father. His eyes met mine and then shifted to Alexander.

"Did I not tell you not to bother him?"

"I was not a bother, was I, Theo?"

Theo?

"No, he was not," I answered truthfully. I just did not know what to do or say.

"Nevertheless, your tutor is waiting for you, Alexander." Father nodded for him to go.

Alexander sighed heavily and got up from the bed. Before he reached the door, he turned back to me. "Will you go riding with me tomorrow?"

"If you wish."

"I do!" A smile returned to his face as he left. Now I was left with an even more awkward companion.

"If you are ready, follow me" was all he said, exiting as well, and I did as he ordered.

Where we were going, I was not sure, but it did not really matter because the tension would be the same. Though I did grow curious when he led me out to the gardens, where two horses, one brown and the other white, were already waiting beside the stable hand. He walked down the steps to the first horse, leaving the white one free.

"Are you going somewhere?"

"Yes, we are," he stated as he climbed up. "I am sure you would like to rest, but I do not believe this can wait."

The tone in his voice was a bit more serious than when he had first seen me, so I did not argue. Only when I was in the saddle did he kick off quickly.

The man truly was as fit as could be. Most men of his age in London rode but not as he did—as if he were trying to escape the world behind him. In fact, he rode with such vigor that I could barely keep up. The wind that slapped across my face, clothing, and hair was chilling. The land all around me passed in blurs of green. My heart raced to the point that I could feel it in my neck. But once I started to get used to it, I could not help but grin, wishing to go faster, to overtake him. We rode for what seemed like no time at all when, suddenly, we came to a slower trot as we approached a rather large house. It was nowhere near as big as Wentwood, but still, the neoclassical style was quite similar, with a lush path and rose garden in front. But most impressive were its large windows.

"This is Glassden Hall. It sits on one hundred of the fourteen hundred acres here. A good portion of it can be used for farming and boarding. It has approximately fifty-one rooms and three gardens around the property, one of which has a lovely pond, though I think you will find the most magnificent aspect to be its library," he said as I came up beside him.

"It is impressive." I nodded, unsure why he had brought me to see it until I saw him staring at me. Then it hit me, for there could be no other reason. "No . . ."

"It belongs to you, Theodore."

"I did not come for this!" I said quickly, feeling panicked all of a sudden. How could he expect me to accept it?

"Why did you come then?"

"I told you, your wife said you were gravely ill—"

"And you did not even think to question her because you sought to escape the lady you love? Lady Verity Eagleman."

I froze, my eyes wide. Surely, he could not have known. He reached into his coat and pulled out a letter. "My wife also sent me a letter along with you."

"That was highly inappropriate of her. Especially as she reveals Verity's name. What if it had been discovered?"

"All the servants here live by her breath, and such a letter would never have reached anyone but whom she intended it for. And you are aware you do not deny its contents?" he said.

I grabbed the reins so tight the horse protested. Calming it, I tried to think of what to say.

"Lady Verity Eagleman, as the daughter of a duke of Everely, will come with a vast dowry. I shall assume it is at the very least forty thousand pounds, if not much greater—"

"And why would that matter to me?" I snapped.

"I plan to leave you a sum of fifty thousand pounds—"

I laughed. He had gone mad. Perhaps he was ill after all. "Fifty thousand pounds, and this home? What next? A dozen horses? A golden carriage? For what do I need such finery? Am I so pitiful to you that you believe me in need of such great charity? I did not ask for any of this!"

"You did not ask to be a bastard either, yet you accept that as your life!" he hollered at me.

"For that is something that cannot be changed, thanks to you," I countered, and immediately upon seeing his expression, I sought to calm myself. "I do not wish to blame you for things of the past. We are far from that now. I do not hold you in contempt, so you need not seek to make amends in such—"

"You think I do this to earn your forgiveness?" He chuckled. "You believe this to be motivated by guilt?"

"Do you deny it?"

"I do. Theodore, I do this for you because you are my son. Whatever the world wishes to brand you is their concern. Mine is your well-being. I am deeply sorry for the struggles you have had in life, for the struggles you will always have in life due to my failures, but that does not change the care I have for you. As I have sought to bring order to your life, I have also sought to do the same with Alexander. For it is the duty of a man to see to his family, to his children. Did you truly think I would leave you in the world empty-handed?"

I took a deep breath. "Thank you for your care, but I do not need this much—"

"You think it is for you alone?" he interrupted. "Shall you not wed? Have children of your own? Do you think you shall be able to maintain a woman such as Lady Verity in your little inn?"

"I cannot have her! Or any *lady* for that matter."

"You would not have sought to escape here had you not already established some sort of relationship with her."

"I—It . . ." I fumbled over my words. Dammit!

"And so she reciprocates your feelings?"

"What does that matter? I cannot marry her."

"Have you tried?"

"Why are you torturing me in this manner? You know as well as I that no nobleman, most definitely not her brother, would allow me her hand."

"So you did not try," he said softly. "You assumed and accepted defeat and ran, just as your mother and I did."

"What?"

He inhaled through his nose and shook his head. "The mistake your mother and I made was not fighting harder. She feared going up against a great lord, feared what trouble it would cause her family and me, so she ran. And I did not follow. Despite the love we held for each other, we did not dare to fight to the end. And it came at great cost to us all. I regret it. Many times, I have wanted to go back and change my course. But I cannot, so I am now the best man I can be for the family I have. I do not wish you to make the same mistake."

I hung my head. "It was different for you. You were to be a marquess—"

"If you fight despite your situation, what is the worst that will happen? Suitors are free to seek a lady's hand. You commit no crime." He placed his hand on my shoulder. "If her family rejects you, work to change their mind. Show them your worth, of which you have a great deal."

Clearly not. "Is that why you sought to leave me such a fortune and house?"

"I would have left them regardless of whom you chose to

marry." He smiled. "Go inside, look around, and imagine the life you could live here. See it truly, and then go fight for it. I promise you that whatever the outcome, you will not regret it more than never fighting at all."

He left me, and I stared up at the house for several minutes before finally climbing down from the horse and tying it out front. The first thing that filled my nose as I walked up the path was the scent of roses. Bending, I reached out to touch the petals, when I heard her voice.

They will need a great deal of care, but is that not the case for all things? Verity appeared beside me, leaning in to smell them. I knew she was not really there, but I imagined her to be, and it made me smile.

Walking into the house, I saw her everywhere.

This room ought to have the pianoforte, she said, pointing and examining every corner with joy. *And if we move a table here, we can enjoy the view during our meals. Breakfast at sunrise and dinner at sunset.*

"That is far too early to eat," I whispered to myself.

True, but nevertheless, I love the windows! She giggled, and I continued to imagine her here and the type of life we could build.

Walking up the stairs, I looked through one room after another until I found the largest. There, I imagined her sitting in only her nightgown before the vanity, her hair down, bare feet tapping the floor.

My dear—

No, even if we were married, she would not call me that.

Theodore, are you coming to bed? I know your patients mean a great deal, but you should rest. What good is an ill doctor? she demanded, walking over and helping me take off my coat, and I, so grateful she was with me, would kiss her.

I would lift her from her feet, take her to the bed, and make love to her until the sun rose the next morning, and even then, I would not wish to release her naked body from my arms.

"This is insanity," I muttered as I saw the life I wished for clearer than anything else in this world.

In fact, the more I saw, the more I wished it wasn't just my dream.

As I exited the house I could see our life here, but was it really possible? I pondered as I rode back to Wentwood.

"Welcome back, sir," the footman said, taking the horse.

I nodded to him before entering the main house. Just as I was coming into the main foyer, I saw my father step out of his drawing room.

"You have returned . . . have you made your choice?" he asked.

I nodded. "I do not know if it will be possible, but I do not wish to give up without trying . . . I will return to London and speak with her."

"Could you not have had this revelation while still *in* London?" a familiar voice grumbled. My father stepped aside and revealed Henry, hat still in hand. "Now I feel foolish coming all this way to knock some sense into you."

"Henry?" I could not believe it, after our argument. My words to him had not been kind. "You followed me? Even after all I said?"

"Not immediately, as I was greatly aggravated with you, but I left the next morning after thinking over how many punches would placate my anger." He grinned, lifting up a fist. "I have settled on two."

Grinning as well, I nodded. "Reasonable. Shall it be my left or right eye first?"

He chuckled and dropped his arms. "Later, as we have more important things to discuss."

"Is everyone all right?" By everyone, I meant her.

"Before I left, I went to tell . . . *them* I was leaving and heard the Lady Verity was leaving London. She is returning to her brother. She may very well be there already."

"That is a shorter journey," my father said, still watching us both. "Three days on horseback. You can leave tomorrow . . ."

"No, I'll go now—"

"You have not eaten or slept. You cannot go now. Come, young Henry, tell me all about your time in London with my son."

Henry grinned. "Yes, my lord, for there is much to tell."

God help me.

And, Verity, please wait for me.

23

Verity

"Verity?"

Opening my eyes, I looked up at the woman who was said to be the most beautiful in the land, my sister-in-law, Lady Aphrodite Du Bell, now Eagleman. She stood dressed in red before the sun, and the ring of light behind her looked like a halo.

"Forgive me, but you have been out here so long I thought I should come and check on you," she said as she took a seat beside me on the blanket by the stream.

"How long have I been out here?" I asked, still unwilling to get up.

"Well over an hour, nearly two. I thought you may have fallen asleep."

If only. "Do not worry. This is quite normal for me. I can spend all day just lazing about somewhere on the grounds. This is so much better than London." My eyes snapped back open when she was silent, and I sat up quickly, looking to see if I had offended her. "I did not mean your family. I meant not having to worry about balls and such."

She giggled and nodded. "I understand. I, too, spent many years lazing about my family's estate. It is peaceful and allows one to gather one's thoughts."

"Exactly." And I had many thoughts to gather, not that she

knew. It had been a couple of days since my return to Everely. The way my time in London had come to an end was still unbelievably painful to me, and while trying not to dwell on it, I found myself focusing on the drama unfolding here. "Are you enjoying it here, Aphrodite?"

"Firstly, I would appreciate it if you would call me Odite, or Dite is fine."

"But Evander never calls you that."

"He does at times but prefers to . . ." She smiled, shifting her gaze from me to the swans as she shook her head. "Never mind. Um, to answer your question, yes, I am enjoying it. Though I must admit, I am desperately trying to be a good mistress here. As well as a good mother to little Emeline. My mama made it seem so easy to run a house and family, as you may have witnessed."

I could not imagine what it was like to come from her family, which was so rambunctious compared to here. Even my brother's daughter, Emeline, was not one to make much noise.

"Yes, your mother is quite the captain. But she is also very kind to her servants. She thanks them repeatedly for their work. She calls everyone by their first name, which I thought to be strange, but I began to do so too."

"Mama says that once you have good help, they ought to be seen as extended family." Yet another example of the difference between her upbringing and my own.

"My father believed that there needed to be a clear distinction in social status. Servants were servants, not needing to speak unless spoken to." This was also why they avoided me as a child, even when I sought to be friendly. They feared my father would hear of it and punish them.

"With all due respect, I believe your father was a hypocrite," she muttered in clear irritation.

"He was very much the living embodiment of 'do as I say, not as I do.' Look at the trouble he has left with Fitzwilliam." We both sighed. My brother had been rigid and upset of late, but I knew it was not Aphrodite's doing, for she could do no wrong in his eyes. I had only seen this behavior of his when it came to one person and one person alone—our half brother.

"Evander will not speak much of it. But it is clear Fitzwilliam affects him deeply."

"He has affected the whole estate, as I have never seen guards here before." Not footmen but actual guards on the grounds. To prove my point, one walked by on the other side of the stream, and upon noticing us, he bowed before continuing to observe our surroundings.

"Evander insists on them. But in my mind, despite all that I know of this Fitzwilliam, I cannot believe a brother would truly wish to harm his brother."

Yes, because her brothers loved her dearly.

"Was the first murder not between brothers in the Bible?"

Her frown deepened. "Yes. I suppose that makes me very naïve."

"What are you ladies speaking of so intensely without me?"

We both turned to see my brother walking down the hill, and the smile returned to her face as she rose to her feet in a single motion, going to him.

"Were you so jealous, brother, that you sought to interrupt?" I asked, not bothering to rise.

"No. I was rather fearful of what tales you were spinning about me," he said, outstretching his hand for his wife's, giving it a great squeeze.

"Not every conversation is about you, brother. Odite and I were actually talking of my time in London, how I managed to fall wonderfully in love with a handsome young man, only to be jilted and left heartbroken. Oh, the despair. How my heart weeps."

Aphrodite's eyebrows rose in shock. She believed me. However, Evander rolled his eyes at me. "Mind her not. This is what I mean by tales. You would not know it, but she is actually a writer."

"I am not."

"I believe there are several journals to prove otherwise."

"Truly?" Aphrodite smiled. "May I read some?"

"You would have a greater chance of catching clergymen in an alehouse," Evander teased. "She has forbidden any of us from ever looking at her works. She could be another Lady Elizabeth Cary or Aphra Behn, but we would never know."

"Could you not have picked better examples?" Aphrodite grimaced, looking at me. "They did not have the best fates."

He thought for a moment and then said, "Lady Margaret Cavendish then?"

"She married a man thirty years her senior and was barren," I added, only to see the discomfort on his face grow.

"I shall cease speaking before I am buried." His frown caused both Aphrodite and me to laugh.

"We shall free you from the topic. Are you going somewhere?" I asked as I noticed he was finely dressed.

"Yes, I shall take my wife's company now, if you do not mind."

"I mind."

"You shall live," he said, and Aphrodite offered me a small smile before walking arm in arm with him back up the hill. Clearly, she knew where he was going from the way they spoke to each other.

Only when they were mere dots in the distance did I reach into the basket beside me and take out my journal, ink, and quill to write.

June 9, 1813

Swiftly, swiftly the world moved, and
only in my dreams did he kiss me.
The feeling like moonbeams on rippling streams.
'Tis now the day which is crippling.

I paused, as I knew not what else to say. I had wished to come back to Everely in hopes of escaping my heartache in London. How foolish of me to think I could leave parts of myself behind. Here, I was not overrun by questions or looks. However, in this stillness, my mind was filled with him.

Had he truly gone to see his ill father? From our conversations, he never seemed inclined to see the man again. So where had he gone then? Would he ever return to London? Would I see him again?

This was all terribly unfair.

I could not sleep at night, and now I could not enjoy the day because he plagued my thoughts.

How did I even fall in love to begin with? There should have been some clear sign or warning as I began my descent. But it was like I was observing him one moment, and the next I desperately wished to be alongside him.

It happened far too quickly.

But then again, who would ever fall slowly?

Theodore

I was mad.

It was the only explanation as to how I found myself traveling across the country with no plans or thought. The name of this madness was Verity. If someone had come and told me she was to be found in France, I would have been aboard a ship within the hour.

"Do you require lunch, Doctor?" Mrs. Stoneshire, the keeper of the Three Boar Bar & Inn, said to me as I came down the stairs. I had arrived in Allerton, the town closest to Everely House, the night prior. It had been so late I thought I would have to wake the innkeeper to find lodging. However, as if she had been expecting me, she ran out asking if I needed a room and demanded a hefty sum for a small village such as this.

"Yes, that would be nice," I said to her. It would give me some time to strategize. It was not as though I could simply walk up to the duke's home, even if we had been previously acquainted.

She leered like a cat over a mouse. "Right away, Doctor. I shall add the fee to your room."

"Is it not already included?" What inn did not provide food to its guests?

"Maybe in London, but not around here." She cleaned her hands off with her apron and went on her way.

Shaking my head, I took a seat at one of the tables.

"She shall bleed you dry, my friend." A man my age or younger with a freckled face, dark hair, and green eyes laughed at me from the table across from mine, a large cup of what I could only guess was wine in his hand. "Rosemary Stoneshire shows no mercy for those of us who have money to spare."

"And what makes you believe I do?" In fact, he did not look particularly well-off in the slightest either.

"Who do you think you are fooling?" He chuckled, looking me up and down. "Everything about you says well-bred, from the make of your vest and coat to your manner of speaking, on top of that expensive white horse you have outside—the saddle alone must have cost fifty pounds."

Shit.

In order to leave Wentwood quickly, I had agreed to take Etheria, one of my father's most precious horses.

"To what great family do you belong, *my lord*?" he asked, downing the remainder of his cup.

"I am not a lord," I said as he came over and took a seat before me. "I am merely a doctor—which is why, from the coloring of your cheeks, I can say you have drunk enough."

"A doctor?" He hiccupped, looking me over. "If you have a profession, you are the second or third son? No land to inherit but family wealth?"

Despite his drunken state, he was very astute in his reading of people.

"Do you make it a habit of interrogating people upon first meeting them . . . Mr. . . . ."

"Mr. Humphries. I am Simon Humphries." He took in a breath, and I glanced him over to make sure he was not ready to vomit. Luckily, he belched instead. "Believe it or not, I am the local magistrate's s-son. Forgive me. Interrogating is my father's job, but I was curious after seeing the horse. How much for it?"

"It is not for sale, and you are not well," I said, reaching over to feel his wrist.

"Release me!" he yelled as he tried to take his arm back, but he gripped his stomach instead, groaning.

"Ah, for the love of Judas, not again!" Mrs. Stoneshire hollered as she returned with my meal. Angrily, she threw it onto the table and turned back to yell, "John! It's Simon!"

Rising to my feet, I went to his side and caught him before he keeled over. His body was burning up.

"Damn drunk! Comes in here drinking all day, messing with my customers. Can't do nothing about it 'cause of his father. I swear, if he ruins my floors again, I will clobber him," she went on, grumbling, as I checked him over. He had hives around his neck and was struggling to breathe.

"We need to get him home."

"Don't worry about him, Doctor. This ain't nothing new," Mrs. Stoneshire said as a large brawny man, standing a full head taller than me, grabbed him by his arm with ease.

"John, I presume?" I said.

"Yep, he gets all the castaways home if they ain't paying to stay. You enjoy your lunch—"

"I'll follow you. Wait a moment," I said as I moved back up the stairs.

"What of your lunch?"

"Later!"

"That will cost you!"

No sympathy in the slightest, but I did not care at the moment. Instead, I entered my room and took my medical bag. I was sure it was not serious, but it would not hurt to check. When I came back down, the man had completely fainted under the furious gaze of Mrs. Stoneshire.

"It's not far," John said to me, and I nodded for him to lead the way.

"Do you need help with him?"

"It's fine, Doctor. Besides, I don't think he could afford your services and would ruin your clothes." John laughed.

I did not say a word in return, keeping an eye on Simon's condition while also glancing about town. I knew the odds were slim that I would just come across Verity walking about here. But still, I found myself checking.

It took us all of ten minutes until we found ourselves before a white-colored stone house, the finest in town, clearly. And the servants seemed well familiar with John as they just waved him to come in through the back.

"Go inform the magistrate," one maid said to another as we entered the kitchen.

"He has company—"

"Even still, he will wish to know," she said, picking up her skirts. It was then that she noticed me. "Who are you?"

"Dr. Darrington. I met Simon at the inn. We need to get him to bed."

"This way, please," she said, her tone changing after she looked me over.

This was how it often was. Servants always saw me as greater than them, while their employers looked down upon me once they found out my true station in society. Ignoring all of them, I followed them into Simon's room.

"You may go back down, John. Thank you," the maid said sternly after he had put the man to bed.

He did not even blink twice at her tone.

"Dr. Darrington, I do not believe your services are needed—"

"I am aware this is a common occurrence. Nevertheless, I will examine him, as his symptoms are greater than an average drunk," I replied, undoing his clothing. There were bumps on his collarbones as well. "Tell me, does his face often flush like this?"

"Only after drinking."

"And these hives on his chest?" I asked.

"I would not know, Doctor. Why?"

I pressed into his stomach, and he groaned even while sleeping. I pressed into his neck, but there was no bump there, nor were there any under his arms.

"Who are you, and what in the hell are you doing to my son?" questioned a man from the door.

"Mr. Humphries, this is Dr. Darrington. He came with your son—"

"If he is consorting with my son, he cannot be a very good doctor!" he snapped at her.

"I have only met him today, Mr. Humphries, as I am recently arrived from London," I said to him, but the scowl on his face remained as he glared down at his son.

"Regardless, your talents are wasted on this fool. And so is the cost to procure your services, so good day to you—"

"I believe your son is in need of medical assistance."

"What he needs is sense and self-control. Unfortunately, that cannot be bought, for if so, I would have spent a fortune to acquire it for him."

He was quick to respond but was not really listening to me. And I could not force him to accept my aid. So I grabbed my bag. However, before I could say goodbye, I heard a loud crash below us, followed by a thundering voice bellowing—

"You and your mother are exactly the same! Vile, gluttonous pigs, using whomever you please as if they were mere ladders for your lives!"

My eyes widened, as I was sure I knew that voice.

"By God, who is that?" The magistrate rushed back out the door, as did I. The source of the commotion was growing even louder.

"I took what was mine *by right*!"

"I am the first—"

"*You are a bastard!* The son of a butcher's daughter! You have no right to Everely. You have no right to the nobility! We will not have you. The lot you were given was better than you deserved!"

Having reached the stairs, I froze. It was him, Evander Eagleman, Verity's brother, and though his words were not meant for me, they pierced so deeply that my mind went blank. Fear crept into me, as did the urge to run, for he would think me the same, of course.

Only when Evander appeared in the hall and his gaze shifted to me did I regain myself. He also looked stunned.

Not sure what else to say, I noticed his hand and said, "You will need to wrap that hand, Your Grace."

He ignored me and looked at the rest of his company, who urged him to leave, and as he went to do so, I realized *this was my chance.*

I moved to follow him.

"Yes?" he asked.

"You are in need of treatment. Where else were you struck?" I inquired.

"I am quite fine, thank you," he insisted.

"Doctor!" a maid called for me. "Mr. Topwells is in need of your help once you have seen to the duke."

"I am fine. Good day," Evander snapped angrily as he quickly exited and moved into the carriage.

Shit!

"Mr. Topwells, are you all right!" the maid called out.

I turned to see the furious, bloodied man glaring murderously out the door. He, too, was Verity's brother, Fitzwilliam.

"I am perfectly fine." He sneered at her.

"You are bleeding," I said to him, coming closer. He looked me up and down and then waved me off.

"I am fine. I do not need your care—"

"You and your brother share a similar disposition when it comes to doctors, I see," I said, waving my hand for him to sit.

"Do not call him my brother. He is— Why am I even speaking to you?" He scoffed and brushed me out of the way as he, too, left.

I debated returning to the inn, but could not let this chance pass. It would not be so odd for me to go to Everely now—if only to get a glimpse of her.

24

Verity

I could not believe my eyes. I was walking back into the house when I saw him—or saw what I thought to be a figment of my imagination on a white horse arriving at our estate. I nearly threw myself behind a tree to hide. As I watched him approach, panic filled me, and I followed from a distance, unsure of what was happening. The maids were whispering about how my brother looked as though he had gotten into a fight of some sort. But surely, Theodore could not have been here, in Everely, simply for my brother.

"Verity? What are you doing?" Aphrodite asked, coming down the hall.

"Are my eyes deceiving me, or is Dr. Darrington here?" I finally found the voice to ask.

"Yes, he is."

Oh. *Oh.* "Truly, he is here?"

"Yes."

I was unsure what to do or think, so I turned from her and walked back the other way.

"What is he doing here?" I muttered to myself. He had to have come for me, correct? Was thinking that merely my own hubris? There was a possibility that he had come here on business, but so soon after leaving without a word? Was that not cruel of him? Or maybe he did not know I was here?

I turned once more but could not bring myself to walk back

and ask the question to him directly. Instead, I gripped my hands in nervousness. What was I to do? I had no idea what I was to do.

You need not exert any further pressure or effort. That is beneath you. The marchioness's words came to my mind. And since I had no better plan myself, I walked away once more.

It was he who had left me.

If he wished to speak to me, he could seek me out. And if he did not desire to speak to me, I would resign myself to hate him for all of eternity and thank heaven I did not make a greater fool of myself.

"That is that," I said, lifting my head high. Then I thought: What if he wanted to find me but got lost within the house? Everely was rather large. "Ugh, I have lost all my senses."

"Then I am not the only one?"

I jumped, spinning around to find him, his hands behind his back and a soft smile on his lips. Now I had to have been dreaming. Here he was right behind me, in the middle of the hall, while I had been trying to think. It was too soon. I had not yet digested this turn of events, and he had not had to search!

"I know—"

I turned from him as if he were not there and continued down the hall.

"Forgive me!" he all but yelled, and I nearly tripped.

"Will you keep your voice down!" I spun to whisper-yell at him. "The maids will hear."

"I care not who sees or knows. I came here for you. To beg your—"

I ran to him, placing my hand over his mouth, still looking about the hall. Thankfully my brother had caused a commotion, and there was no one here, but that could change at any moment.

"Verity." I felt his lips vibrate against my palm and the feeling of it struck a sensation in me I could not describe.

"Shh!" I grabbed his arm and pulled him into the nearest guest bedroom with me, closing the door quickly. "How can you say such things aloud? What if—"

He wrapped his arms around me and hugged me to him. I wished to close my eyes and hug him in return. But instead, I pushed him away as hard as I could.

"You overstep yourself, Doctor!" I shouted at him. "Have you no decency?"

"Forgive me—"

"No!" Gone were all my thoughts. Now there was only rage. "I will not forgive you. I will not embrace you, and I do not wish to see you. You should not have come!"

He frowned and looked me over, but I moved away, breathing through my nose. "Do you truly mean it?"

"Yes." I did not.

"Very well then," he muttered, walking to the door, and I should have let him go, but instead, the words burst out.

"How could you just leave me so?" My voice cracked, but I swallowed the ache, still unable to look at him. "I was scared, confused, and . . . you vanished without a word."

"Did you not get my letter?"

"What letter?" I turned to him. "The one you wrote to the marquess?"

"No, I wrote to you personally. I knew I could not send it to the Du Bell estate, as Lady Monthermer surely reads them all. So I left it with Lady Whitmear. She said she would invite you all to tea and pass it along discreetly. She did not?" he questioned, his eyebrows furrowed.

My mind went to that day. "We were invited, but . . . I did not feel well and did not go to see her. Then I left hastily with

Damon and Silva, as they wished to return to their country estate."

"Oh." He chuckled and glanced down at his feet.

"What?"

"Nothing . . . it was a rather . . . long letter."

"What did it say?"

"It matters not."

"Then it still would not have been a good enough reason for why you left as you did. I know our connection was brief—"

"What does that mean? Brief in what capacity?"

I opened my mouth to speak, but the words did not come. Again, I did not wish to look at him. It took far too long for me to reply, and he made it worse by waiting. In fact, his stare angered me.

"I am not so naïve that I don't know that . . . gentlemen . . . men sometimes become infatuated and then lose interest—"

"You think my feelings are so fickle?" He was now angry at me.

"I am choosing not to think of your feelings as you chose not to think of mine."

"All that consumes me is you," he declared, his eyes wide. "I left London out of fear of what could become of you—"

"I did not ask you to."

"Verity, the situation was precarious—"

"But you did not even allow the dust to settle before leaving. What if we had been exposed? I waited for that news, waiting for all of the ton to call me a trollop, for Lady Monthermer to break down in horror and shock at my behavior. I did not sleep, nor did I eat. I merely waited, terrified of what was to come. But do you know what never came to mind? Regret. I did not regret taking your hand that day. I only wished we had not gotten caught. I was prepared to say that to anyone. I was prepared to face the punishment for it . . . And you, you had already left me."

"Forgive me," he begged.

"We ought not to get caught once more, Dr. Darrington. Good day," I said, walking past him to the door.

"Verity, I came here for you, and I will not leave until you are my wife."

"Then I suggest you purchase land, as you will need some-place to wait out your days."

"Fine," he said, his voice stopping me from going. "If you wish for me to live here, I will do so. I will do whatever you ask of me except leave again."

I heard his steps behind me. He was so close, and I held my breath.

"Verity, there are a thousand words I could use to describe my feelings for you. I dream of you night and day. You are everything to me," he whispered, his hand upon my waist as he turned me to face him. "I came here because nothing in this world is greater than my desire for you. I am prepared to fight anyone who stands in my way—to my dying breath."

I swallowed hard, unable to look away from his eyes.

"Say the word, tell me you will have me, and I will go to your brother now—"

"My brother would kill you," I whispered.

"I do not care. I do not want us to hide in fear of being dis-covered. I do not wish to be alone in a room with you, strug-gling to control myself. I desire for us to love each other openly."

"And what of my desires?"

"Speak them."

"I cannot."

"Why?"

"I am angry at you."

"Very well, be angry, then," he replied as he stepped away from me. "As I said, I shall do whatever it is you want of me. I will continue to love you and wait. Should you need me, call. I am at the Three Boar Inn."

Quickly, I left the room, and only then could I finally breathe. Had I stayed a moment longer, I would have kissed him.

Oh, how I would have kissed him, and there, in that room, I would have broken all the rules. Again.

Theodore

The moment we were caught, it had felt right to run. It had felt like I was protecting her, but I realized now that I had self-ishly only wished to protect myself. She was right. What if, somehow, people had found out? She would have been left to face them on her own. And who would believe the word of a woman they believed to be tarnished? No one, great lady or not.

"Dr. Darrington." I turned to see Aphrodite walking down the stairs, hand in hand with a young girl.

"Your Grace." I bowed to her.

"I wish to thank you for your care. You always seem to be there when my husband needs you most. We are in your debt," she said with a smile.

"No, Your Grace, there is no debt. I have been paid for my service," I said.

"It was a figure of speech, but I understand." She giggled. "May I ask what brings you so far from London?"

I did not wish to lie to her face, not when one day I hoped to proudly proclaim the truth, but now was not the time.

"Personal affairs" was all I said.

"Oh, well . . . we are grateful to have you, nonetheless." She seemed unsure of what to say next.

"Thank you, Your Grace. I have attended to the duke's wounds, and he is now resting. I shall come back tomorrow to check on him. Good evening to you both." I nodded to her and the duke's young daughter before turning back toward the doors.

A footman had already brought my horse. Climbing upon it, I glanced back at the house, and there in the window, Verity was staring down at me. But I could not read the expression on her face.

Today, I had been given a victory and a defeat.

I had managed to see her, yet she was so profoundly upset with me, which made me more determined to earn back her smile. Pulling on the reins, I left the grounds for now, but I would not leave her, and I truly meant it.

I would not run from this.

The whole way back to the inn, I sought to come up with some plan, but my choices were limited. It was not as though I could go to her with flowers or beseech her daily. This opportunity alone had been a miracle, but I had to wait for her.

25

Verity

With a jolt, I awoke to find the sun nearly blinding and the book I had brought to read lying next to me under my favorite tree, rooted in a field of blue creeping speedwell. They were called weeds, but they were beautiful blue flowers to me. This area was often left abandoned, as it was so far from the house. Even the well nearby was dry, but I had found a sense of peace here. However, I did not think that peace brought with it such dreams. I lifted my hands to touch my neck and face, and they were burning.

"Verity?"

That voice. Why was that voice everywhere?

I glanced up, and walking toward me through the grass, his horse left by a tree, was none other than the man in my dream. Or was I still dreaming?

He knelt before me, his eyes full of concern. "Are you all right?"

"Are you really here?"

"As opposed to where?"

I still could not tell, so I sat up and leaned forward, bringing my face to his, his lips to mine, and just before they touched, he placed his hand on my shoulder and stopped me.

"Does this mean you are no longer angry with me?" he whispered.

"What?" I said softly, looking over his face and then blinking as realization hit me. "I am not dreaming?"

"Do you often dream of me?" He smirked.

I sat back quickly and looked at the bunnies that ran underneath the shrubbery. "Why are you here? I thought you said you would not come unless I called for you."

"I came to check on your brother. Forgive me for intruding," he said, and when I heard him begin to leave, I panicked.

"The house is far from here, and the way back to the inn is in the other direction. Did you really come just for him?" I called out.

"Of course not, and you know it," he replied. "When I arrived, I saw you walking in this direction. I did not hear a word your brother said, as my thoughts were full of you. I thought to return to the inn and wait, but I could not."

"You followed me."

"Yes, and you are a rather fast walker to get this far. Though I did get lost on the way. I nearly thought you had returned to the house."

"What did you wish to happen upon finding me?"

"What were you dreaming of that left you in this state?"

I frowned, and he smiled wide. In the sunlight, he seemed to radiate with pure joy. Once more, he knelt before me.

"Verity, let us not pretend we do not desire each other. I meant what I said yesterday. I wish to marry you, and I will go to your brother and say so. All that stops me now is you."

"I am still angry with you," I muttered.

"What good is it for you to be angry at me and not get to show it? Should you be my wife, you could yell at me to your heart's content."

I snickered. "Would that not make me a disagreeable wife?"

"Nothing could make you disagreeable," he said, taking my hand. "Everything about you is perfection."

"You have clearly forgotten my nightmares—"

"I have not."

"They have not gone away despite all efforts. You wish to have a wife who screams in terror beside you every night?"

"I will take it as a good excuse to hold and comfort you."

"Theodore, I am serious."

"As am I." He kissed the back of my hand. Right there, I could have sunk into the earth. I was supposed to be mad at him, yet I found I missed him. On my trip back to Everely, I wondered why I was fond of him at all. And I realized it was because I did not feel abnormal around him. He was not perfect either. His background was complicated, his demeanor sometimes standoffish or awkward. He was kind at heart, he always went to someone's aid, but in the company of others, he was aloof and a bit disagreeable.

I . . . I loved him, for he, like me, was . . . a mess of raging thoughts and emotions desperately trying to keep calm under the eyes of society. A perfect match for me.

"Verity, you are not saying anything." He rubbed his thumbs over my knuckles. "I made a mistake in leaving you, and I'm genuinely sorry. I know not what to say beyond that. I—"

"Did I not already agree to marry you?" The words fell from my lips before I realized. His eyebrows came together in confusion. I reached to open my journal and took out his mother's pendant. "Did you not ask me with this?"

He stared at it and then me. "I did."

"I accepted then and you—"

"I ran. Now I've returned and you still have it," he whispered, and I nodded.

"It is far too precious to abandon . . . if only you felt the same. Good day." I rose to my feet, not wishing to be so close to him.

"What shall it take for you to forgive me?" he asked.

I frowned. "I do not know. Maybe you will change your mind and run from me again—"

"You do not trust I am sincere." He hung his head and exhaled through his nose before nodding. "Very well, I shall prove it to you then."

"How?"

"How else but to request your hand from your brother?"

My eyes widened as he rushed back to his horse!

"No, wait!" I called out. I ran to him in order to hold him back but I pulled so hard we both slipped and landed in the flowers.

"Are you all right?" he questioned, rolling over to look at me.

"Yes." I winced once.

"Careful, let me help you up—"

I stopped him, holding on to his arm. "You cannot speak to my brother."

"You want a guarantee I shall not go again, and that is the only way—"

"My brother might actually kill you!"

He brushed the leaves from my hair. "You do not believe I was aware of that risk before coming here?"

I frowned. "Theodore—"

"I'd rather die for your hand than live without it, Verity." He kissed my forehead before moving to help me up. "Now come, I must speak with him."

"You are too callous with your life," I snapped. "If it is a matter of believing you, fine, I believe you. Now please—"

"No matter what, I shall need to speak to him, Verity."

"Evander is currently at war with Fitzwilliam." I groaned, as he did not understand. "I fear any other news, this news, will be too much for him."

"When will this war of brothers end?" he asked.

"I do not know."

"Verity, I fear waiting . . . for I cannot stay away from you, and should we be caught, that shall be worse."

He was right, but my brother would not be agreeable no matter how he went about it. "If you wish to do this, maybe it is best I tell him—"

"Absolutely not," he replied as he sat up. "He will not accept me without persuasion."

"Exactly, which is why I will—"

"Verity." He took my hand again and held it to his chest. "I must be the one to fight for you. Your brother will be angry and confused as to how this has happened. That fury will only grow should I leave you to be the one to explain. It would be best, more respectable, if I speak to him. Man to man."

"Theodore, my brother has a deep bias against—"

"Bastards? Yes, I am aware."

"Then you should know that he will not be able to reason well. My brother is not a violent man but, on this issue, I fear . . . I fear—he could very well break his hand beating you!"

"I shall duck." He grinned, and it made me do the same even though this was grave.

"You are ridiculous."

"I am in love with you." He cupped my face. "Allow me to tell the world."

"Fine, but it cannot be now. Maybe . . . maybe during the ball Aphrodite has planned at Everely. Evander will at least contain his anger before guests."

"Fine." He nodded and we rose to our feet. "Then can I beg the pleasure of having your first dance?"

"You may." I beamed and then frowned. "How have you convinced me so quickly? I thought to be cross with you for at least a few more days."

He chuckled. "Is it not because you care for me as well and never wished to part to begin with?"

I wanted to glare at him, but he kissed the side of my face.

"I ought to go. We have put ourselves at enough risk. Write to me at the inn, for I fear I no longer have any excuse to come here for now."

"I will not."

"You will." He smiled as he took a step back. "And I shall eagerly look forward to it."

As he moved to his horse once more, I called after him. "Wait! Oh, how is your father? Did you see him? Or was that just an excuse?"

"No, I truly did go, thinking he was ill, but he was not. Lady Whitmear merely wished me to visit him." He chuckled as he dusted off his shoulder.

"What? All of London thinks you are at his bedside. What shall they think when they hear he is well?"

"Henry has already thought of it."

"Henry? He went with you as well?"

"He followed to condemn me for my actions in leaving you. I am grateful, for it was how I learned you were no longer in London. He said he would return alone and tell all of the ton how I *miraculously* saved my father from death."

I smiled. "I am envious of your friendship."

"Even I do not know how I earned it. Then again, here you are as well, so maybe I am simply blessed."

"Pray you have not used all of that when facing my brother."

"I shall," he said. "Good day, *Lady* Verity."

"And you, Dr. Darrington."

I waited for him to ride off before I collapsed back into the field of flowers. Once again the world had spun so quickly.

One moment I was weeping over him, the next he was before me daring all the world for my hand.

How strange this life was.

I stayed upon the flowers until I could no longer contain my excitement or worry and began to make my way back to the house, my journal and the necklace inside tucked close to my heart. I truly wished for Theodore to ask my brother to allow us to be married but I knew with all certainty how he would react.

"My lady?" I glanced toward the voice of . . . Aphrodite's maid as I entered the house from the back. "Have you been outside? Alone all this time?"

"Yes." I laughed. "I was merely walking the grounds. Why are you so shocked?"

"Forgive me, my lady, I thought you were in your rooms still," she said and then offered me a smile. "Should you wish to walk again please notify me and I shall have one of your maids accompany you."

Oh no. "That's quite all right, thank you," I said to her, quickly going up the stairs. That was the last thing I wanted.

There was a never-ending flow of servants entering the drawing room at the same time as me to find Aphrodite as she looked over the final orders for this ball she had decided to throw out of nowhere. She looked the very picture of a perfect lady, no hair out of place. No wonder Hathor found it unbearable. I chuckled. I actually wished to hear what Hathor would say . . . I had been a bit unfair to her in the days before my departure.

"Verity, good, you are here. What do you think?" She lifted two types of glasses for me to see. "Which, in your opinion, is better for wine?"

I looked between them, eyes wide. "Are they not the same?"

The looks on the faces of all the staff showed I was clearly wrong.

Aphrodite chuckled. "They are not, this is Pacomé glass,

much grander with a beautiful shine in the light. This is a Winston glass, a bit more commonplace but still quite nice and, most importantly, light in the hand."

"Most importantly?"

"Yes, we do not wish our guests to be put off by the strain of carrying their glasses all night," she answered. And even still I could barely see the difference. I was more amazed that she thought of such details.

"I shall leave it to your expertise." I smiled as I took a seat by the window.

"Very well, we shall begin the night with the Pacomé and then afterward bring out the Winston," she informed the servants around her. I watched, wondering if I could ever do the same.

I was not one for parties and I was not sure Theodore was either. But it was expected . . . then again, would we be able to afford it? For the first time I wondered what life would be like off such a grand estate . . . I was sure we would not be destitute but my life would change. It was a nerve-racking thought but neither glassware nor balls would deter my heart.

"Verity, I do not mean to press, but are you all right?" she questioned, gaining my attention. At this moment, she sounded and looked just like her mother. I had not even noticed the servants had gone from the room.

"You know you look very much like your mother." I laughed, partially to deflect.

"Your brother said the same thing only this morning!" She frowned, her eyes plagued with horror. "Really?"

"Your mother is a great lady. Do you not wish to be the same?"

"I love my mama to bits, but I do not wish to become her." She lifted her papers once more, but unlike her mother, who would have let the topic go, she paused and then shifted her gaze to me. "Have you fallen in love?"

"Me?" I panicked. "I—"

Before I could finish, the door opened, and my brother walked in, his face in confusion. "My dear, what exactly did you order that has the maids in such a fit? I just watched them rush toward the kitchen."

She gasped and rose to her feet. "All of the cakes must be finished!"

"All of the cakes?" Evander and I both questioned, but she was already up and running from the room.

Evander looked at me and tried not to laugh. "How many cakes do you think she is speaking about?"

"I cannot guess. My mind is still trying to get used to you saying *my dear*," I teased, rising to my feet.

He was embarrassed. "Yes, I am sometimes shocked too."

"Well, though it gives me jitters to hear, I must say happiness does look good on you, big brother," I replied and wished to tell him of my own.

"Thank you, little sister. However, now I fear you have cursed me." His smile faded a bit. "I have been meaning to speak to you. Forgive me for my neglect."

"I am fine," I lied. I was a mess and plotting my own marriage right under his nose. "Were you not be seen by Th—Dr. Darrington? What of him?"

"I dismissed him. The man frets for nothing. He even forgot his pocket watch. I'll have one of the footmen return it to him at the ball." He walked over and put his hand on my head.

I frowned at the thought of Theodore being *dismissed*, but forced it down as I looked to him. "I am also not your daughter, nor am I a child. This does not work on me any longer."

"Must you be so harsh?"

"Yes, I have been rather soft of late." I grinned.

"Why?"

Theodore. Everything was because of Theodore. "What is it you wish to speak to me about?"

He frowned. "You clearly changed the subject."

"I do not wish to speak to my brother about female issues. What is it you want to say?"

"You must be more careful when walking the grounds," he said, a scowl now on his face. "Fitzwilliam has returned to town."

"I know. Odite and I saw him in town. But what does he wish to accomplish by returning?"

"I fear I know, and as you are not a child, I shall tell you. He hopes that I will die and have no male heir, so that the estate would fall to Gabrien," he reminded me. "If such a thing happens, you know our younger brother will have little power, at sixteen years of age, to stop his mother and Fitzwilliam. They shall once more take hold of Everely."

"Gabrien is not like Fitzwilliam. He is soft-hearted and shy. He rarely ever comes here because he fears causing greater trouble for everyone." I missed him, and it was only via letters that I now knew where he was or what he was doing.

"I know," he said as he placed his hand on my shoulder. "My issue is not with Gabrien, nor do I wish to drag him into this battle. I am simply making you aware. Aphrodite says I should talk more about my feelings. And I fear for you."

"Me? Our half brother is apparently trying to . . . I cannot even say it aloud. And you are worried for me? If worse comes to worst—"

"If I was not here, Datura and Fitzwilliam could very well try to disinherit you or marry you off to some fool."

"I do not like this conversation. You are speaking to me as if you will disappear. Stop it at once."

He chuckled, though nothing was amusing. "I do not plan on going anywhere. I plan to live to a ripe old age."

"Good. Much better."

"Even still, I cannot be foolish and leave anything to chance; these people are cruel." He squeezed my shoulders. "Which is why I have spoken to Mr. Marworth, our family banker, and had a separate account created for your inheritance."

"What?"

"As you are yet unmarried, it could not be put in your name, which is why I have left it in the hands of Lord and Lady Monthermer until it can be transferred to your husband. Your dowry, as well as all of Mama's jewels, are left for you."

"What of Aphrodite and Emeline?"

"I have taken steps to protect them, so you need not worry. Again, I plan to go nowhere. But I believed it only right that you know. Whenever you wish, Mr. Marworth will explain it to you."

This was what he had been doing with his time? Caring for me as always. And I knew, despite how dear Theodore was to me, that it would break Evander's heart to have me be with such a person. The guilt ate away at me.

"Chin up. There shall be a ball at Everely in two days' time. Can you imagine? Never have I seen this place so alive. Aphrodite is very excited. If only Fitzwilliam were not coming."

"He is coming? Here?" I gasped, and he groaned.

"Yes, I know. I did not like the idea either. However, Aphrodite insisted that we must maintain our image to the public after my . . . scuffle with him. He is coming with his wife, Marcella, and, I suspect, Datura. Shall you be all right?"

"That woman no longer affects me as she once did. I promise. I am more concerned about how he aims to kill you, and she is inviting him here?"

"Do not blame her. She truly cannot believe that to be his

intent. You know the Du Bells. They seek to see good in everyone. They cannot help themselves. In Aphrodite's case, she wishes to prove to all the world that I am a good man."

"Who denies it, for you are the best." I smiled, as did he.

"How wise you are, little sister."

"It was you that raised me."

"Now I am concerned . . . What do you plot?" His eyes narrowed.

"Nothing. Go concern yourself with your *dear* wife," I replied and he chuckled, nodding as he moved to leave.

It was only when he was gone that I sat at the desk to write . . . to none other than Theodore.

26

Theodore

I was early.

I did not wish to be so early that I would be the first to arrive at the duchess's ball. But I could not stand the wait any longer. It had been two days since I had seen her. And though she had written to me I was unable to deliver a letter in return out of fear we would be caught. Luckily when I had arrived, there were already more than two dozen people in attendance, walking among the gardens. Eagerly, desperately, I searched high and low for her. She might not have been ready yet. But still I searched.

"I was wondering when you would arrive."

I spun around to see her dressed in white with pearls in her pinned-up hair, a soft, deep-red rouge on her brown cheeks and lips, as if I were not tempted to kiss her enough as it was.

Like always, she had found me.

"I came as quickly as I could, for every passing moment has been excruciating without you," I whispered, trying to fight the smile creeping its way across my face.

"Your words are charming beyond measure, *Dr. Darrington*." She giggled and my heart leapt in my chest.

"Forgive me, *my lady*."

"I shall think on it. In the meantime, tell me, did you get my letter?" she asked. "It cannot be done tonight. Evander is in the worst of moods already."

Would there ever be a good time? I did not wish to push, however, so I just nodded. "I received it. Do not worry. We shall try later."

She let out a deep breath and nodded . . . I was entirely too focused on her chest.

"Theodore, you are staring quite intensely."

"That is how beautiful you are," I whispered. "You make me wish to . . ."

"Shh," she replied gently. "Do you mean to give us away?"

"I fear my patience is slipping," I replied honestly, my heart hammering ever so loudly.

"As is mine," she said softly and I stared back down into her eyes, unable to look any other place. "I wish to kiss you."

My heart leapt for joy just knowing that. "And I you. But we cannot."

"We can."

"Verity, we are surrounded by people!" I panicked, fearful of what she would do.

"Then let us be alone."

"How?"

She glanced to her right and then her left and then stepped up beside me, whispering, "I shall take a turn about the grounds. You ought to go inside. I believe you left your pocket watch behind, ask one of the servants to retrieve it . . . I shall follow."

I was not sure what she was plotting and yet for some reason, I was greatly excited. Swallowing the lump in my throat, I nodded as she moved to greet the rest of the guests.

Walking to one of the doors, I stepped forward to see most of the footmen and the maids rushing about as more guests began to arrive. The place was nothing more than prearranged chaos. It took about five minutes for me to even find a footman not servicing someone.

"May I help you, sir?" one questioned me as I waited in the foyer.

"Her ladyship told me to inquire after my pocket watch?" I asked him. "I left it here when tending to the duke's injuries."

"I am unsure of where it could be, if you would give me—"

"What is the matter here?"

I turned to see Verity had come, and she did not look at me but at the footman, who stood straighter at the sight of her.

"This gentleman is inquiring after his pocket watch. However, I will need to check with Mr.—"

"No need. I know where it is and shall retrieve it. Please see to the guests out back, I believe the staff there are rather overwhelmed."

"Yes, of course, my lady." He nodded to her and without a second thought about leaving the young lady with me, he rushed off.

"This way, Dr. Darrington," she said when I met her eyes . . . oh, I knew now more than ever how dangerous women were.

Silently I followed her up the stairs, and down the hall, casually, with not a single eye upon us, until we entered a bedroom, which would have been in complete darkness had it not been for all the lights overlooking the gardens pouring inside. When she turned back to me . . . I knew this was wrong, I knew this was a sin on every ground and by every account. But the desire I had for her . . . I could not bear it.

"No one shall notice if we are gone for a while with all the—"

Stepping to her, I kissed her lips like a man given food for the first time—hungrily, my tongue in her mouth as she pushed off my coat. It was only meant to be a kiss, I thought to only cross this line, yet soon we both found ourselves upon the bed and my kisses traveled from her lips to her neck . . . down to the mounds of her breasts, her dress rising up as she lifted her thighs to either side, straddling me. It was only when she moved to remove a bit of my clothing that clarity came to my mind.

"Verity, if we do not stop now . . . I will not be able to stop," I whispered to her.

She held on to both sides of my face. "Do you believe it shall be you and me in the end, Theodore?"

I nodded. "I do."

"Then do not stop."

"You do not know what you ask for . . ."

"Show me, please."

Fuck.

She was burning with desire, as was I. Taking hold of her legs, I slowly took down her stockings, exposing the brown of her skin. I did not stop undressing her until all of her chemise was lifted to her waist . . . exposing the very delicate parts of her to me. I tried not to bite my own lip as I felt my manhood harden painfully at the sight. I moved my hand to cup her, and she gasped.

"This is what it means," I whispered as I stroked her up and down, feeling her wetness collect upon my hand. I had meant to tell her more but . . . but fuck all, I could barely speak. This was too much and yet I wanted more. Leaning down, I replaced my hands with my tongue.

"Theodore!" she gasped, and oh, how good it sounded, my name upon her lips.

I wanted her to call out my name more, so . . . so I feasted upon her. My tongue licking circles deep in her.

"Theo . . . Theodore . . . uhhh." She moaned, her hips rising. I stared up at her and watched as she came undone.

She was already so close that when I came up for air and slid two fingers into her she shook in my hands. In and out they slid and each time the tightness in my chest rose . . . the pain of my cock grew worse. She deserved much better than for me to take her in this manner, like a thief in the night, her family and all the guests below unaware of our sin. And yet, I could not bear to stop. Slowly I removed my hands from her only to undo my own clothing until . . . until I was finally set free.

I saw her eyes widen at the sight of me. Leaning over, I kissed her temple and her cheek before moving to help her take off her dress. The sight of her bare breasts, her brown nipples hard in the cool air, made my cock twitch eagerly.

"This may hurt, tell me if I should stop."

Her answer was to wrap her arms around me, burying her face into my neck. Gently I positioned myself and entered her, gritting my teeth to keep from losing myself to excitement, but how she felt upon me left me trembling, so much so I could not help but groan when I was all the way in her. Her grip on my shoulders was tight, and I felt her tense.

"Are you all right?" I whispered.

I waited until she relaxed. It took a few moments before she lifted her head, meeting my eyes. "Is it over?"

I tried not to laugh. "My love, it has only just begun."

Before she could reply, I thrust forward and her mouth parted once more . . . there was no going back now.

Verity

Never in all of my life had I ever experienced such feelings.

It felt as though all of me were being flipped from the inside . . . something that did not sound pleasant and yet the pleasure that crashed over me was never-ending.

"Ohh! OHH!!" Such noises came from me as I held on to him, gasping for air, begging for more . . . and each time I felt him drifting from me he returned seconds later, burying himself within me once more.

I stared up at him and he down at me, his hazel eyes shining, his mouth agape, sweat upon his brow.

"Verity . . . I . . . love you," he said to me but gave me no time to tell him the same, as once more his tongue was upon mine. Our tongues swirled over each other as he slammed harder and harder within me. His hands did not stop there, cupping my breasts and pinching my nipples. Even that did not hurt but only added to my pleasure. How? Why? I did not understand but all of it set me more and more ablaze . . . the fire in my stomach growing.

"Theodore . . . I . . . I . . . what is . . . this?" I felt as though I were going to explode.

"Do not fight it," he said to me as he sat up, holding on to my hips. He pulled back once more before thrusting forward hard and my body rose from the bed, unable to stop the pressure from within me, my toes curled and tingled, my vision blurred. I was so unsure of what was happening but I wished to float this way forever.

"Fuck, Verity," he grumbled and though I could barely see straight I felt him remove himself from me, gripping himself and the bed beside me. He looked to be in so much pain, I reached out to touch his shoulders.

"Are you all right?"

He did not answer, taking a deep breath over and over before gasping, "Forgive me, I could not risk finishing inside you."

I did not understand. "What do you mean?"

His chest rising and falling, he looked at me for a moment before laughing and shaking his head. "Never mind."

"No, tell me."

He was quiet and his eyes were closed as he lay beside me breathing.

"Theodore."

"I'll explain when we are married," he whispered.

"I believe we have gone far beyond that," I replied, lifting the sheet to cover my nakedness.

"True. It is now more imperative than ever that I speak to your brother," he said, opening his eyes, a frown upon his lips. "Though I cannot approach him with a clean conscience any longer . . . not after this."

I tried to shift to lie down as well but winced slightly.

"Are you all right? How is your pain?"

"It is not bad," I said though he did not seem to believe me. "I promise I am well . . . a little . . . scatter-brained but well."

He kissed my forehead. "You should rest. I shall return to the party—"

"I must go back as well or they will wonder at my absence."

"Verity—"

"I am fine, truly."

"You need not push yourself. Besides, how shall you explain the condition of your clothing?"

"I shall say I messed up my dress and was forced to change, if anyone notices at all," I replied, already moving to get out of bed. Which was a mistake as my legs were . . . quite weak. He caught me and gave me a look. Before he could dissuade me again, I said, "Quickly, you must dress also."

"Go slowly," he whispered to me. I nodded, holding on to the bedpost to move to my dresser. I meant to focus but when I turned back to him and saw him standing naked within my room I could not help but feel . . . warm all over again. I was not sure how he noticed but he glanced back at me and smiled.

"Verity, you must dress."

"I am," I whispered, turning from him.

He and I moved to dress to the sounds of the growing party outside. It was so strange, I could hear the music and the laughing but at the same time I could hear the sounds of his moans from earlier in my mind. It made dressing so much harder to focus on, and apparently, he could not bear it, for I felt his hands behind me. At his touch my eyes closed and I leaned back against him.

"You must wear perfume."

"Do I smell bad?" I turned back to him, panicked.

"No, you smell of me . . . of us and what we have done," he whispered as he helped adjust my corset and then dropped to his knees. How his tongue had kissed the private parts of me entered my mind but the thought of that happening again was gone as I felt him touch me softly. I held on to him, allowing him to dress me, trying not to laugh. Finally, when we were done, he looked me over, frowning.

"I do not believe I will be much help with your hair."

I giggled. "I shall fix it myself. You go down first. I shall follow."

"You following is how we got here."

"Do you regret it?"

"I should ask you."

"I do not."

"Then neither do I." He kissed my forehead. "I must go for now."

He sighed before leaving. It was only then that I let out a deep breath. My heart was in knots. What had I done? I did not regret it but . . . that . . . that was more than I ever thought. My mind was reeling as well as my body. But still I managed to get myself together, rearrange the room, and hide the now stained sheets until I could get rid of them.

By the time I finally returned downstairs, I feared all the world would somehow know, that somehow it would be evident something had happened or at the very least that I was missing for God only knew how long. However, once I entered the gardens I was met with only pleasant smiles and loud laughter, as now nearly a hundred people were in attendance. I spotted Aphrodite greeting guests alongside my brother.

Truly no one was the wiser. The only other person who knew of this secret was Theodore . . . and I met his hazel eyes from across the garden as he spoke to some gentlemen. He and I stared longingly at each other . . .

We would have remained staring at each other had it not been for the sound of breaking glass.

We looked over, and there was Fitzwilliam, dressed in a coat so red you would have thought he was enlisted in the regiments. Beside him were a young girl and an older woman with far too much white powder on her face and a string of pearls around her neck. Aphrodite went over to them, speaking of the young girl's stained skirt.

"Something is wrong." I was not sure what but the looks upon their faces and the fact that Fitzwilliam was a part of it told me this would not end well.

As I moved to them, I hoped I was wrong.

But I was sure I was not.

27

Theodore

Days had passed since the ball but there never seemed to be a good time to speak to the duke about the true nature of my stay here. It appeared to be a never-ending onslaught of bad news for him, and I could not bring myself to add to his stress. I had gone back to their home to speak with the duchess about Marcella's condition, telling her I did all I could when I had visited her home without saying more. Marcella's mother-in-law and husband had barely allowed me to treat the poor girl. I was so dejected by the extent of all I had seen and heard that I could barely keep my spirit up to speak to Verity upon leaving. Our meeting was brief, but what could be said between us now that we had been together in such a manner?

I could not delay it any longer.

I did not wish to make Verity worry. For all the strength she had, I knew she was nervous. I was going to speak to the duke without fail today.

"That bastard! Oh, that evil *bastard*! See why I would not have his money." The innkeeper gasped as she came to me, handing me a copy of the pamphlet in her hands. "To think the duke has suffered like this."

I read over it in horror as I reached the section on Verity and her condition. Fuck all! Knowing her, this would be gutting. The one thing she did not want was for people to know her condition. She did not wish to be pitied.

"Where are you going? What about your meal?"

I did not care to eat. I rushed to my horse, needing to see Verity. She was not all right, and I was sure of it.

"Dr. Darrington!"

A horse pulled up before mine with a man I did not recognize but a uniform I did. He was from Everely House.

"Dr. Darrington! The Duke of Everely has requested you come to him immediately."

"On what business?"

"It is dire, sir. Follow quickly," he replied before heading off. Again, I thought of Verity, but I also knew her brother would not have called me if it were not indeed grim. The man hated to be treated for any matter.

I went with him, and no less than five minutes into our ride, I realized we were not headed toward the duke's estate. We rode through the woods until we found ourselves at a small manor covered in vines.

"The duke is inside, quickly!" the man said, taking the reins of my horse.

When I reached the door and stepped inside, the first thing I noticed was blood that was stained on the wooden steps of the foyer, and I knew then that I would not be able to see Verity today.

Verity

Yesterday, I had written to the inn, but he had not come, despite my plea.

I searched for Evander too, but he was nowhere to be found.

My anger prevented me from going to Aphrodite, for it was she who had exposed the secrets of my nightmares and the pain of my childhood to the world with no thought or care. She was far too worried over Marcella to understand the injury she had done to me. No one had been home all day and I had not been able to sleep all night, and now dawn approached once more and still I was unable to reach anyone.

Knock. Knock.

"Enter." I turned to see it was Aphrodite's maid, Eleanor. She was always well put together. However, today, the skin on her face was sallow, her hair was down and messy—not in a bun as was her custom—and the hem of her dress was muddy, even torn. She looked as though she had crossed the county on foot. "What has happened to you, Eleanor?"

"Lady Verity, the duke and duchess have returned and would like to see you in the main drawing room," she said gently, and immediately, I was going to the door.

"Is everything all right?"

The look on her face said that it clearly was not. Picking up my skirt, I rushed out. The only comfort I had, the only thing that kept me calm, was the fact that she had said both my brother and Aphrodite were waiting. Which meant they could not be gravely injured. Nevertheless, to be called like this—something was wrong. The other telltale sign was the servants. It was never good when they stopped whispering and looked away as one walked by.

Was this about me?

Did they know Theodore and I had . . . ? No. Surely, they could not. And yet even still my heart filled with panic.

I was thoroughly unnerved by the time I reached the main drawing room, and the sight of them did not help matters. Aphrodite sat in a chair, her hands clasped together, her tea untouched, staring absent-mindedly at the floor. Evander was no better, as he stared up at the only portrait of our father.

"What has happened?" I asked them, as they did not notice me. Aphrodite stood to attention, and Evander looked at me as though he feared to speak. "You are only frightening me more by not saying whatever it is."

"Verity, sit," Evander said to me.

"I think it best I stand for now," I replied. If they were going to yell at me I needed to have my feet firmly planted.

"I do not know how to say it, but it must be said." He exhaled deeply. "Last night, Fitzwilliam died."

"What?" That could not be right. "Dead? Fitzwilliam? No."

But the looks on their faces said yes. I shook my head and looked at Evander. "You?"

"It was not Evander's doing!" Aphrodite said quickly. "So much has happened, even we cannot grasp the horror of it. It all occurred so quickly."

I listened as they told me the story about Marcella and Fitzwilliam, how they sought to help her escape him, how Mr. Wildingham, her father, had been the one to shoot, and how Theodore had been the one to try to save him. My mind struggled to comprehend how everything could go so wrong. How one moment Fitzwilliam was here, an ever-present thorn, and the next he was gone—murdered. I could not understand my feelings either. None of this made any sense to me.

"Verity?" Blinking, I glanced up to see Evander watching me. "Are you well?"

"I need to clear my head. I shall go for a walk. Excuse me," I said to them. They did not stop me.

Maybe it was a strange sort of grief that had taken over me. Maybe it was not grief at all. But whatever it was, it propelled me into motion, and I wandered about the estate, staring up at the early sun, the air warm and tingling as I walked through the grass. It was a beautiful, clear sunny day, a rarity, and it felt strange.

My brother was dead.

"I knew you would come eventually."

He was sitting at my favorite tree, among my creeping speedwell, his shirt disheveled, stained even, his curly hair a mess of frizz, and his face blanketed in sorrow and exhaustion. When he rose to his feet, I ran directly into his arms, and he held on to me tightly, resting his cheek against my head.

"I am so sorry I could not save him," he whispered.

"He was not a good person."

"He was still your brother. You may grieve for the person he could have been."

That was it. That was it exactly.

Fitzwilliam could have been a great brother. Had we been born of the same mother—no, had our father done right by us, we all could have been happier. If he had been like Theodore, if he had not attempted to fight Evander over property and money, we could have been a happier family.

The tears slipped from my eyes then as he held on to me tightly. I cried there like a child in his arms.

"I am sorry you had to witness all of this," I said, releasing only slightly to look up at him. "Thank you for being there."

"I was coming to you. I saw the paper and wished to see you, but then . . . the world shifted."

"I am tired of it shifting and us not being able to go to each other, to be there for each other."

"As am I." He cupped my cheek.

"Then . . . then let us tell my brother."

"Are you sure now is the time?"

"Time waits for no one. We must tell him."

He exhaled through his nose and then nodded. "After the funeral, I shall come and speak to him."

"I shall be there."

"Verity."

"I. Shall. Be. There." I stretched each word. "You may say whatever it is you please, but I shall be there beside you to face it."

"I love you, Verity Eagleman."

"And I you, Theodore Darrington."

Evander

I felt as though a great weight had been removed from my shoulders, but when I recalled what or who exactly was the cause of that, I was cold. Over the last several days, I sought to free myself entirely of any thought of Fitzwilliam, but I could not.

It was not my fault. I did what I had to do to protect my family, to help another. I knew that. But one's emotions do not always follow one's mind. My solace was her, my beautiful wife, Aphrodite.

She did not even notice me as I entered the drawing room since she was far more concerned with carefully stitching the hem of a gown on the awful-looking doll she had created for Emeline.

"We could simply buy Emeline a new one," I said, gaining her attention.

She frowned as she glanced up at me. "That is not the point. It is meant to be made by a *mama*. Everyone will know if it is bought."

"Then you could have someone more . . . adept make it." I chose my words carefully.

"Are you calling my work ugly?"

"You cannot be skillful in all things, my love, or it would be unfair to the other ladies." I grinned at her while her eyes narrowed at me.

"Emeline now calls me *Mama*, and she wants a doll, so I shall make it, and she shall love it even if it looks like—"

"It was raised from the dead?"

"Evander!"

I laughed, leaning over and kissing her cheek. "I am sure Emeline shall love it."

"Rightly so." She beamed, so happy Emeline had now taken to calling her Mama. There was no going back now. We were a family; how blessed was I?

"Tomorrow, let us all—"

Knock. Knock.

I paused and turned to the door. "Enter."

Wallace, our butler, came in with a rather strange look on his face.

"Yes, what is it, Mr. Wallace?" Aphrodite asked him.

"Dr. Darrington is here to see you, Your Grace," he said, looking at me.

"Were you expecting him?" Aphrodite asked me.

"No." I shook my head, but he had done so much for us that I did not mind the company. "Show him in."

Aphrodite placed the doll beside her and faced the door as well.

"Yes, Your Grace," Wallace replied, opening the door wider. Dr. Darrington entered, dressed in a rather expensive-looking deep-blue coat, his hair cut and fresh, his top hat in his hands. He looked as though he had come for a ball. Just as I opened my mouth to ask what brought him here, Verity entered too.

"Your Graces." He bowed his head to both of us. I looked at Verity, still not sure why she was here or why she remained beside Dr. Darrington. "As you both may have heard, I am the illegitimate son of the Marquess of Whitmear, Lord Francis Theodore Greycliff."

I stared at him, an eerie chill going up my spine as I noticed his nervousness and Verity's attention on him.

"For what reason do you tell us this?" I asked softly, as my heart began to quicken. Surely this could not be what I thought it was.

"I come seeking to marry your sister, Lady Verity Eagleman."

Verity smiled, but I could not grasp what I had heard. I glanced down to Aphrodite, who stared at them, eyes wide and mouth parted.

"My dear, I believe my ears are failing me, or is this some nightmare?" I said to her as all of me went cold.

But she did not speak.

"Evander," Verity called out to me, so my attention returned to her. "Please—"

"Aphrodite, take her from the room," I ordered. "Aphrodite!"

"Stay calm," she said to me when she rose to her feet, giving me a stern look. "Remain calm."

"Get her out."

"Evander, Theodore and I—"

"Theodore?" I repeated as I stepped forward, eyes wide. "You are calling him by his Christian name? Verity, leave this room immediately."

"No, listen—"

"I will not!" I hollered at her.

"Evander, calm!" Aphrodite said, rushing to Verity's side and holding a hand out for me to stop where I was. The man beside them glanced over at my sister and smiled.

"Verity, it is all right to go."

She listened to him—not me, despite the state I was in—and allowed Aphrodite to lead her out of the room, closing the door behind her. Leaving me and this . . . this . . . bastard.

"I understand this comes as a shock to you, and I know my background offends you, but nevertheless, we could not keep it a secret any longer, for we love—"

"It is in your best interest to stop there." I held my hand up, and it was shaking. Closing it into a fist, I swallowed the lump in my throat and forced myself to remain, as my wife repeatedly stated, calm. "I have only one question. What have you done to my sister? Let me be very specific, in fact. How far has this madness gone?"

He did not answer.

"We believed you to be a straightforward, upright man, Dr. Darrington!"

"And I have sought to be—"

Once more, I stepped toward him. "I am well aware that the Du Bells sought your services to aid her health. It is now clear you have used your position to insinuate yourself into her life and cause her current confusion. That is not the behavior of an honest man!"

"I truly did work to help her—"

"You worked to manipulate a fragile, impressionable young lady well above your station. Now you stand before me with no shame asking for her hand?" The audacity of him. "My answer is no. Never! Remove yourself from my property, or I shall have you thrown off it. Do not dare to ever return, and forever keep my sister's name from your lips."

"If you wish to have me thrown out, that is your right, but I shall say what I came to say," he dared snap back at me. "I am madly and deeply in love with your sister, Your Grace. She has made it known to me that her feelings are the same. I came here for her. I shall not leave here without her. I will wait at the boundary of your estate every day for years if need be."

"Wallace!" I shouted, and the doors opened. "See this man removed from my house at once. He is never to return."

Wallace moved to take his arm, but Dr. Darrington stepped through the door of his own accord. I felt a sudden heaviness on my shoulders return.

"Theodore!"

Hearing my sister, I dashed out of the room to see her running to him. "Verity, you will return here this instant!"

She looked back at me, her eyes wide, before turning back to him. "Theodore!"

"Verity!" I marched to her.

"Do not worry. We knew this would be the case. I am prepared to stay here." He nodded to her.

"Did I not say I want him out of my house!" I yelled again, and the footman rushed to show him the door.

When he was gone, Verity spun back to me so furiously and quickly that her dress swirled around her. "You did not listen, did you?"

"Listen to what? Who listens to the words of villains and fiends, Verity?"

"He is neither of those things!" she yelled back at me. "You, of all people, should know, after all he has done. He came to your aid with Fitzwilliam time and time again—"

"Clearly because he plotted to have you. Can you not see? How has he blinded you? Men like him seek rich young girls such as yourself for their own gain. Right before your eyes, not even a week ago, we watched as chaos unfolded all because of a bastard who used a poor girl as his means to elevate his life!"

"Theodore is not Fitzwilliam! If you had listened, you would know. He has his own—"

"My dear sister, he has fed you nothing but lies. That is what such people do. Which is why he sought you out when you were alone. It is my fault for giving you such liberties, allowing you to go about unaccompanied. From now on, that ends. So does your contact with that man. You are forbidden to see him; do you hear me? *Forbidden!*"

"Do you know who you are like at this moment?" she asked suddenly, her shoulders dropped. "Father. You look exactly like Father."

I froze; of all the things I expected to hear from her, that was not one of them, and the disappointment in her eyes as she walked around me, going up the stairs, was wounding.

"Come," Aphrodite spoke suddenly beside me, her hand upon my arm. "You need air."

"Do all my siblings have to torture me? Am I to watch for Gabrien next?" I asked her as she led me out, the air not easing me at all.

"Breathe."

What I needed was peace.

Aphrodite

I was sure something was amiss with her when she returned from London. I thought it must have been the nightmares and sought not to push her. However, there were still times when I saw her look longingly out the window, and it rekindled memories of when I had done the same thing . . . dreaming Evander would appear and come to me. But still, I said nothing and then became so preoccupied with rescuing Marcella and the conflict between Evander and Fitzwilliam that I had not focused on Verity.

Evander was right. She was allowed much more freedom

than a girl of her age and status ought to have, much more than I'd had. But that had been her life since the death of her father, and I did not wish to come now and restrict her.

Over and over again, I saw signs and held my peace. I would not do that any longer. Stepping up to her door, I knocked once, but I heard no reply.

"Verity, it is me," I called, but still, there was no answer.

Quickly, I opened the door, fearful she would not be there. But she was sitting at her desk, writing in her journal.

"Am I now forbidden privacy in my own room?" she asked, not looking at me.

"You did not answer," I said as I stepped in and closed the door behind me.

"I did not wish to speak with you." She continued writing.

"Verity—"

"Evander may have forgiven you for releasing those papers exposing our family, but I have not. You offended me greatly, and now try to speak with me. Why? Does the town require the second edition of my life's story?" Her words were harsh and very much justified. I had exposed her to ridicule without thought for her feelings.

"Once more, I apologize for that and seek your forgiveness—"

"Then help me convince my brother." She closed her journal and looked up at me, hopeful. "He is still hurt and angry over Fitzwilliam, and that is why he will not give Theodore a chance. You, your family, even Evander himself, have met him numerous times, and he is not a devious character."

"People can hide who they truly are, Verity. Evander seeks only to protect you because he cares for you greatly."

She took a deep breath and shook her head. "No, he does not. He has spoken to me several times about the prospects of my marriage. And here comes someone I have accepted, but Evander refuses outright. Why? Because Theodore is illegitimate. Had he been born the legitimate son of the Marquess of Whitmear, Evander and everyone else would cheer. Theodore could have courted me openly before all."

"Do you know what it means to be illegitimate? Do you know what could very well happen to you? There is a woman, Mrs. Marie Loquac, and she—"

"I have met her, and Hathor has already recounted to me the story of her mother's fall from grace. You will not scare me with that," she replied as she stood up to me, fully incensed and strong in character and will. "There will be many who look down upon us. Many will mock me and others will shun me from society, but I care not. I have never been one for society. All of the people who will scoff at Theodore now are the same ones who accepted Father. I *will* marry him; I love him. My only fear is . . . losing another brother in the process."

I was meant to be one of her guardians, yet she had left me unable to respond, for part of me was far too impressed with her and wondered if I had looked as fearsome to my own father when I stood against him to marry Evander.

"All I ask is that you do not do anything rash or regretful. Let us . . . think on the matter," I said to her.

She nodded and took her seat once more.

"I shall see you for lunch," I said as I left her room. And there, outside the door, was Evander, eavesdropping. My eyes widened, and I closed the door quickly before grabbing his arm to pull him away. "What are you doing?"

"I came to see if you had talked some sense into her. But you folded and left," he grumbled at me.

"What would you have me say to her?"

"Verity, this is foolish. Listen to your brother," he said proudly and sternly, which only made him look sillier.

"And in what world do you believe she would have simply agreed to that?"

He sighed and lifted his hands to his head. "I do not understand how this came to be, Aphrodite. Several weeks ago, she scoffed at the mere mention of love and marriage. Now she is beside herself for this . . . this—person. She is not in her right mind. I know it. She is most likely lonely, and he took advantage of my absence. What your mother was doing—"

"Now it is my mama's fault?" I snapped at him. "Do you blame her also for the times I found myself alone with you?"

"Aphrodite, that is not the same."

"It is! There will always be a way for two people to see each other if they really desire—"

"Not on my watch. I will not allow it. Ever," he repeated, nose flared, before he marched away. One thing he and his siblings had in common was resounding stubbornness.

I feared they would damage their relationship beyond repair.

28

Theodore

Her brother had kept to his word as I had kept to mine. He had forbidden me from stepping foot on his grounds and even had his men alerted to look out for me. No more letters had made their way from her to me, either. Nevertheless, I rode up to his boundary for six days and waited from sunup to sundown. I was unsure what it would accomplish, but I continued even still. I had readied myself for this battle and would not surrender. Though I had to admit that the return to Mrs. Stoneshire's inn every night was disappointing. She, on the other hand, was set to build her riches on my head alone.

"Welcome back, Dr. Darrington." She grinned, waiting for me at the door. "You have a guest in your room that will cost you."

I sighed deeply. "Simon again? Can you not bill the magistrate for once?"

"And bring down on me the eyes of the law? I think not. Besides, it is not Simon."

I frowned, not sure who else would meet me there. "Who then?"

She shrugged and then winked, turning away. I had a bad feeling and, thus, rushed up the stairs, two by two, until I reached my door. I paused and took a deep breath before going to open the door. However, I stopped myself, then reached up and knocked.

"You ruin the surprise by having me say 'enter.'"

Quickly, I opened the door, and there she stood in my small room, dressed in a dark cloak and matching gloves, my mother's pendant around her neck, her curly hair down, and her face beautiful as always.

"Verity," I whispered, unsure what to do. She could not be seen here, which meant I could not enter and close the door.

"Theodore." She smiled.

"I am extremely pleased to see you, but you cannot be here," I said from the door, and the smile on her face fell.

"I had to see you. Evander, he has all but trapped me inside. Unfortunately for him, I have long since found methods of escape that he is not aware of."

"By doing so and coming here, he will become even more incensed." I would have to work even longer and harder to wear him down.

She nodded and stepped forward. "I am aware, which is why I propose we run away."

Immediately, I stepped inside and closed the door. "Verity—"

She hugged me, and I inhaled the sweet scent of her for a moment. It had been six days, and I desperately missed her. "Verity, did I not tell you we could not rush? I am prepared to wait him out."

"He will not listen to reason." She frowned, releasing me slightly.

"You knew he would not. What has you so impatient now?" We had spoken intensely on the day I finally went to see her brother. I had repeatedly tried to get her to leave me to speak with him alone, but she would not have it. Ultimately, it did not matter, since, either way, the duke would have thrown me out.

"I do not like being locked inside," she muttered, glancing down. "He knows it and tells me I am free to walk the grounds, but he has two maids and a footman accompany me. You would think I was a princess with a parade behind me. He has gone mad."

"He wishes to protect you—"

"Why are you on his side?" She pouted.

"I am not. I am always on your side, but that does not mean I do not understand him." His words were not wrong. I had used my position to get closer to her, but I could only come as close as she allowed.

"Then let us go to Gretna Green," she proposed with a smile.

"Do you truly wish for that? Fine." I took her hand in mine. "Let us go at once."

"Wait!" She pulled back as I knew she would.

"See, it is not what you want, and I know it. You desire your brother's blessing, and this is not how we shall gain it. You must return home."

She frowned but knew it to be the truth as well. Reaching over, I pulled her hood over her head.

"Where is your horse? I shall ride back with you," I said.

"I walked."

"You what?" I stared at her with my eyes wide, then glanced down at the hem of her dress to see it was stained. "Alone, at night, you—"

"Someone would have noticed or heard the horse," she whispered back. "I have walked here many times in the past."

I could, once more, understand her brother as I fought the urge to tell her never to do so again. She very well could have found herself in the greatest danger.

"I see the worry in your eyes, but I promise you, staying home was often much more dangerous for me."

"Even still, promise me you will not go out alone at night again."

She would not answer.

"Verity."

"Fine, I promise."

I did not trust that, but I said nothing as I led her to the door, then released her hand. Luckily, Mrs. Stoneshire did not have many customers, but there was still the risk of running into a guest or two.

"How did Mrs. Stoneshire allow you in here?" I whispered to her.

"I paid her, of course."

"Of course," I said as she came out into the hall. However, as she did, another person entered the hall. Her brother.

Fuck!

If his eyes could have turned red from fury, they surely would have. He gripped the gloves in his hands so tightly they damn near tore.

"I came back to find her here and was returning her home," I said to him quickly.

He looked only at his sister and moved to the side. "Return to the carriage."

"Evander—"

"Do not test me." He nearly growled. "Return to the carriage at once."

She looked at me fearfully, but I simply stepped aside as well, allowing her space.

"Please, brother, do not hurt him," she whispered, but he would not look at her now. Instead, his menacing glare was upon me. He waited for her to reach the bottom of the stairs before he walked forward. I entered the room, for at least there, he could see nothing was out of order.

"You are to pack your things, Dr. Darrington, and leave here at once," he ordered upon entering.

"You may forbid me from your estate but not from here, Your Grace," I said to him.

His jaw clenched, and he stepped closer to me. Maybe to keep from shouting, maybe to strangle me, I was not yet sure. "What is it you want?"

"I thought I had made it clear: I wish to marry—"

"Do you desire her for her dowry? Is that it? If so, I shall disinherit her."

Now it was I who struggled to contain my anger. "I may be a bastard, Your Grace, but I am not poverty-stricken. Regardless of her dowry, I have more than enough for both of us."

"Not working as a doctor."

"As I told you, my father is—"

"So, it is his money you mean to take for yourself?"

"Is that not your situation as well? Like every other nobleman in this country, are you not simply taking from your fathers before you?"

"You are just like him." He scoffed, shaking his head. "What I have is mine by inheritance—"

"As is mine. Do not think that my brother or my father are similar to yours. The situation of my birth was unfortunate, but he has cared for me and provided what he can all the same."

"You say this now, but one day, your father will be gone, and you shall watch your younger brother—Alexander, I believe—and jealousy—"

"Again, you mistake me for Fitzwilliam!" I shouted in his face. "Can you only see and relate to others based on your own family and experience?"

"Let us say you are correct," he shot back. "Let us say you are provided all you need. You will still never have what *she* needs. A respected title. All the girls she has ever known shall become the lady of somewhere. They shall stand esteemed in society. While you will cause her to live with her head bent in shame. If you truly cared about her, you would see this and leave for her own sake."

"I cannot."

"Then you are—"

"I am in love with her!" I hollered beyond the point of containment. "And as a man who barged into a ball despite being stabbed, as a man who rode into a storm still with fever, you better than anyone else should understand that I simply cannot walk away from her. Do you not think everything you have said has not crossed my mind as well? Do you not think I tried to distance myself? I did. And failed. And in that failure, I realized my love for her was worth risking my life, my sanity, even my reputation, the same as you did." I took a deep breath. "Nothing you say or do has power over me, Your Grace. Only she does now."

He stared at me for a moment and merely turned around, slamming the door behind him.

Once he was gone, I stood back at the edge of my bed, clasping my own hands to calm myself.

But once more I could not help but wish . . . wish marrying her did not cause this much pain and trouble. That, as he said, I could give her all she needed in society along with my heart.

Verity

"Do you know what you have done?" he asked me upon entering the carriage, but I did not look at him. "Verity!"

"Are you worried people shall gossip about me? Thanks to your wife, they already do!" I shouted back to him.

"Do not blame Aphrodite—"

"Why, because she is your wife? Because you love her and wish to protect her? Fine. Then do not blame Theodore. He has done nothing wrong. He never did anything wrong. He tried to stay away, and I went to him time and time again. It was I who used my condition to convince Lady Monthermer to allow us moments to speak." It was even I who led him to my room that night. But I could not say that.

"What has taken over your mind!" he yelled at me.

"How many more times do I have to say I love him before you believe me?"

He exhaled through his nose and closed his eyes. I thought he must have needed to count because of how long it took him to open them again. "Very well, I believe you."

"Now allow me to marry him."

"I will not."

I wished to kick him!

"Very well, I will keep going to see him despite your disapproval—"

"*Verity!*"

"Shall you lock me in my room like—"

"Do not say it," he snapped. "I will not allow you to use the pain of the past to guilt me and keep me from ensuring your future."

"If it is my future, I should be allowed to decide it."

"That is not how society works."

"Damn society then!"

"You have gone mad."

"No, it is you who makes me so." I huffed, turning to look out the window, and as I watched the town go past, I could not help the pain I felt from his refusals. "Why does your love matter more than mine?"

"Because mine is within the acceptable bounds."

"Then extend your bounds!"

"What has happened to you?" He gasped, not understanding, despite all I had said. "I feel as if the sister I have always known has vanished before my very eyes, and in her place is a whole new person who acts without thought or reason."

I turned away from him. As I'd thought, he would never yield.

I feared I would be forced to choose between my most cherished brother and my most beloved. Reaching for my neck, I held on to the pendant Theodore had given me. It hurt deeply, but I knew my choice.

I would not let anyone stop me.

I would go to Theodore once more, and next time, I would not leave.

29

Verity

"Of all the people she could have chosen, she chose him?" said the maid as she entered the kitchen with her bucket. "If I was her, I would look to do much better."

"You ought to be grateful if anyone chooses you, Mary, with a face like that." Another maid giggled as she folded the dough.

"What is wrong with my face? At least my hair is not balding in the back, you—"

"Enough!" the new cook, who happened to be named Mrs. Cook, snapped at them. "Good heaven, geese and goose, you would think we did not have any work left with the way you both chatter on. Mary, go fetch the butter I asked for, and Suzy, go deliver hot water to the footmen at once."

I listened to them grumble, still fighting, before stepping out of the pantry, which had a secret passageway into the kitchen. The older woman turned back to me and gave me a stern look. Mrs. Cook had once been a maid here. However, Aphrodite had given her a promotion upon learning she was much better at preparing meals than the last cook.

"Lady Verity, you are putting me out," she said worriedly.

"No one shall know you were my accomplice. Thank you, Mrs. Cook," I said to her before taking the door out into the servants' yard. During this time of day, there were very few people outside amidst the preparation for dinner.

I promised Theodore I would not go out alone at night, so I chose to sneak from the house before the sun would set. I knew he would try to send me right back or that my brother would immediately come for me. But as I had said to Evander in the carriage yesterday, I would not yield either. He had made sure his new guards were watching most of the paths. However, the route to my creeping speedwells was still not that well known.

"Don't you dare rain!" I said up to the clouds, as the day was rather overcast. I picked up my skirts, climbed over a puddle, and then bent to go through the gap in the fence.

You would have thought I was on the run from the law the way I had to hide behind trees as the guards surveilled. It was ten minutes before I was sure that no one was near. And through all this ridiculousness I had to ask myself again . . . why?

"To have him," I whispered to myself.

"I see you are still muttering to yourself."

I paused. Up ahead, alone, with nothing but a basket of wildflowers in hand, was . . . Datura? I glanced around, but no one else was with her. And we were still very much on the Everely estate grounds.

"What are you doing here?" I asked her sternly.

"I have come to see your brother."

"I am sure he does not wish to see you." I glared at her. Even out in the woods, she still wore her pearls and face powder. "You should return—"

"Why did you not come to Fitzwilliam's funeral?" she asked suddenly.

Once more, I remembered he was gone and nearly pitied her—just nearly. "I did not know him."

"He was your brother!"

"And I did not know him. Just the pain and suffering he left in his wake, which followed him till his death."

"His murder! He was murdered, and no one has sought justice for him. Your brother created the most awful of lies—"

"They were not lies. Fitzwilliam was a bad man, but I do not think he was always so. I think you were the one who made him rotten; both you and Father ruined him. You sought to ruin us all. But neither my brother nor I will allow you such power in our lives any longer," I declared, and with my head held high, I continued to walk past her. "Go home, Datura, and leave us all be. You are not wanted here."

But before I could make it any farther, she grabbed my arm . . . just as she had when I was a child.

"Release me!" I yelled, yanking my arm away from her. "How dare you touch me. I am not the little girl you once tormented, nor are you the Duchess of Everely anymore. Not that anyone ever truly believed you worthy of such a title. You are—"

"I am what?" she sneered, glaring at me.

I stopped as I realized I, too, was about to do what Evander had always done. Shame her for being of low birth. Her sins were many, but her birth was not her fault. However, I could not bring myself to apologize, nor did she give me a chance as she grabbed me again.

"Let go!"

"Say it. I am what?"

"Let go of me!" I screamed again as her nails dug into my skin.

"You all are to blame! The ones who ruined everything. Your brother—"

Kicking her leg as hard as I could with all the force in my body, I pushed her and stumbled back. However, as she fell, so did the basket of flowers, and falling out of it . . . a Queen Anne pistol. She had hidden her pistol, and she was going to my brother. I knew she was capable of anything, and that was why my first thought was to reach for it. But she was closer than I, and grabbed hold of it before I could.

"Datura! What are you going to do?"

"You all are the cruel ones! And yet no one punishes you," she yelled as she lifted the pistol. "This was for your brother, but it is much better he lives to feel as I do!"

I ran.

But I was not fast enough.

Bang!

I felt the bullet whizz past my arm before blasting into a tree, shattering the bark from the trunk, and its force caused me to nearly lose my footing and trip. I stared up at the shattered, missing bits of the tree trunk above me and grabbed my arm. It was bleeding, but I had not been hit by anything but splintered wood. I was so stunned by the blood on my own hands that I did not even feel the pain.

"Be damned, all of you!"

I glanced back at Datura, who had rightly gone mad. But I could not wait, so I ran as fast as I could, sure she would at least need time to reload. I was so concerned with getting away, so panicked, that I did not see the well, the stone wall of it long since broken, and before I could catch myself, I was falling. All I felt was the rush of air passing me before my chest slammed against the earth, knocking the air from my lungs.

"Ah . . ." I groaned in agony, rolling onto my back to breathe. It did not take long before I saw her face high above me.

"Did I not tell you to be good? You never listened to me," Datura said. And once more, I felt myself to be that small child in the darkness, unable to move. "This is your punishment."

She left, and I shook my head clear. I tried to push myself up when I felt pain spread through my foot and arm.

"I am not a child anymore," I whispered to myself as I stared up. It was too high, and there was no place for me to climb, nor could I in this condition. Panic only spread further as the sky darkened.

Someone would come. I was not alone.

"Help!" I screamed.

"Someone help!"

Theodore

It was another day of failure, not that I expected anything different. But as I watched the sun set behind Everely House, I felt an odd dread take me over and could not bring myself to leave.

"When will this form of harassment end?" came a voice from the woods to my right. The duke was upon his own horse, and suddenly, beside him were two huntsmen, one holding his gun and the other his mark—hares. Quite a few of them. That explained the gunfire I thought I had heard.

"That is for you to tell me," I said to him.

He exhaled hard and then pulled the reins of his horse. "Do take care not to trespass on this land. One would not wish to mistake you for a hare."

"I am much larger, so the marksman would either be blind or a murderer," I replied.

He prepared to ride off when we both heard hooves approaching fast from the direction of his estate. Seconds later, we saw her, and she pulled to a stop, her eyes wide at the sight of us.

"Aphrodite, where are you off to in such a rush? Are you all right?" She did not answer him but looked at me.

"She is not with you?" she asked me.

"Who?" I questioned but then realized it could only be one person.

"Verity? Again!" the duke snapped.

"I only just noticed her gone. It was only an hour at most that I had my eyes off her. The maids were told to stay in her hall as well. We searched, but she is not in the house."

Not waiting for either of them, I kicked into my horse and sped toward the town. She was so stubborn! What good did this do? It was as if she sought to actively provoke her brother. I knew yesterday she did not intend to keep her promise—no, I was sure she would insist that she had not broken it, as she had left before dark.

"Verity," I muttered to myself, barely coming to a stop before I jumped down and ran into the inn.

"Good evening, Dr. Darrington—"

"You ought not to keep allowing her into my room," I said to Mrs. Stoneshire as I moved to the stairs.

"Who? I have let no one up."

I froze, turning back to her. "What?"

"What do you mean what? What are you talking about?" Mrs. Stoneshire demanded, but before I could reply, the doors opened once more as the duke also entered, glaring.

"Where is she?"

"Who do you mean?" Mrs. Stoneshire called out, annoyed, her hands on her hips.

"Do not play with me. Where is she?" the duke demanded again.

"Your Grace, the only *she* here today is me, unfortunately."

His gaze shifted to me angrily, and I shook my head, confused. "If she is not here, where could she be?"

It was not that long of a walk, definitely not an hour. But who knew when she had left the estate.

The duke, also realizing, ran from the inn, and I followed.

"This does not concern you!" he yelled at me as he got up on his horse.

"Like hell it doesn't!" I yelled back, getting up on mine.

"I will not have you—"

"Is this really the time for you to be worried about me? First, we find her, and then you can bark at me all you wish," I hollered, taking off.

I tried to tell myself she was out walking, that she was fine. All would be well.

But that eerie feeling from earlier only grew stronger.

Evander

Hours!

It had been hours.

And I could not find my sister anywhere upon the grounds. Even worse, this darkness—I worried how it would affect her. Dammit! Damn him! It was his fault. Had he left as I had demanded, had he never engaged with her, she would never have been lost.

Lost?

No, I would not allow it. My sister could not be lost.

"Verity!" I yelled into the darkness as I searched throughout the grounds with my men. Each one with torches, but still, we could not find her.

"Verity!" I called out once more.

"Your Grace!" One man ran up to me.

"Did you find her?"

He shook his head but pointed behind me. "The doctor is calling for you. I believe he has found something."

I gritted my teeth. Damn him. "Take me to him."

"This way, Your Grace," he said, running as I kicked into my horse and followed him. It took us only two or three minutes before we reached where Darrington was kneeling upon the earth.

"What is it?" I called out to him.

"Your Grace, were you hunting this way?" He rose, his fist clenched upon something.

"What?"

"Were you hunting this way!" he shouted at me.

"No! Why would that matter? I do not have time—"

He unclenched his hand and lifted the object for me to see. It looked to be a necklace of some sort. I believed I had seen it on Verity once before.

"She was here?" I gasped, looking around as if she would suddenly appear.

"She was not alone," he said, regaining my attention. This time, he pointed with his torch to a tree with bark shattered from its side and a ball at the roots. However, only when he brought the fire closer did I see the blood. "Someone fired upon this ground, Your Grace, and if it was not you, then who?"

I heard what he was saying, but I could not come to terms with it, for . . . for these were my grounds, and besides Aphrodite, who did not take to the sport, no one else could have fired. Unless it was poachers, but even they would not risk the sound of gunfire exposing them.

"Your Grace, we must find her, now. Have your men search this area. She frequently visits here."

I could not remove my eyes from the blood. "What if she is . . ."

"It is not enough to be fatal, but still, someone is wounded, and I can only imagine it is her."

I looked at the man beside me. "Call everyone here. Quickly!"

"Yes, Your Grace!" he said as he went.

My eyes now focused on Darrington, who clenched her necklace as though it was his heart and began to walk absent-mindedly forward.

"Your horse!" I reminded him.

But he did not seem to hear me. He just kept walking and searching through the trees. The fool almost tripped in the darkness.

"We will not find her if you break your neck first," I snapped, going after him.

"Shh!" He held his hand up for me.

"What—"

"*Shh!* Get off your horse. It's too much noise," I noticed he was rather comfortable yelling, sneering, and snarling at me. But I said nothing. I carefully got down, making sure not to drop my torch.

Darrington crept again, turned his head, and then walked in the other direction. The look of sheer concentration and worry on his face was evident. Once more, he stepped and then stopped, glancing at me.

"Do you hear that?"

I listened but heard nothing.

"Hear what?"

His eyebrows furrowed together as he spun around, and I was sure he was in so much grief that his mind had broken.

"Verity!" he yelled out, but it was silent.

"Let us wait for the men. We will search—"

"Shh!"

I was ready to hurt him when all of a sudden, I heard it too.

"Theodore!"

I spun, not sure where it had come from.

"*Verity!*" he yelled again, running toward the sound. "Verity, where are you?"

"*Here!* I am here!" The voice was louder, but we could not see her.

"*Verity?*" I called out, my heart racing. Thank God she was alive.

"Verity, we are close. Where?" the doctor yelled again.

"The well!"

"Evander!" Theodore yelled to me, somehow managing to see it and already running toward it. "Verity, are you down there?"

Rushing over, I reached the broken edge, and it was only with the fire's light that I could see her at the bottom. She peeked up at us before coughing.

She mumbled something before closing her eyes.

"*Verity!*" we both yelled at her.

"I need to get down there!" Theodore said, one leg already over the edge, but I grabbed his arm.

"Are you mad? It is at least twenty feet deep! Let us wait for rope—"

"And how do you suppose we get the rope around her if she is unconscious!" he yelled at me, yanking his arm away.

"And how do you suppose you will treat her if you are harmed as well? Think! Someone else will go down."

"I will not allow her to stay in that darkness *alone* a second longer!"

The man began to climb down.

Staring in shock, I watched as he nearly broke his foot as he landed, yet he still crawled over to her. His earlier words came to mind.

Nothing you say or do has power over me, Your Grace. Only she does now.

"Your Grace!" The groundsmen had now found their way to us.

"Quickly! We will need rope," I ordered them and glanced back down at him. "Is she all right?"

"No, she is at the bottom of a damn well!"

I bit my tongue. Oh, how I detested this man.

"But her injuries are not major," he added.

"Hold on! We will get her out and you, too, if we must," I said, grumbling the last part.

30

Theodore

"You are all right," I whispered as I examined her. "Everything is all right."

I could not see clearly, but so far, her injuries consisted of a scraped and bloodied arm, a bruised ankle, and other minor cuts from her fall. Anything more, I would not be able to see until we were out of here.

"Verity, come on, my love, open your eyes for me," I said, touching her face gently. She grimaced in pain. "It is okay. I have you."

"Theodore?"

"Yes! That's right. Open your eyes for me."

"My head hurts." She tried to lift her hand to it but winced. "Everything hurts."

"What hurts the most?" I said, holding her face, but she just groaned, muttering as she fell unconscious again.

"We have the rope!" Evander hollered as they threw it down. "Can you get it around her?"

"She is in and out of consciousness. I will need to tie it around both of us," I called, grabbing it and tugging. "Will the weight hold?"

"Yes!"

I put her uninjured arm around my shoulder and hugged her to me before tying the rope around us both, then wound it around my arm.

"Ready!" I said, holding on tightly to her and the rope.

"*Pull!*" I heard him yell.

"Theodore—" she muttered as our feet rose off the ground.

"You are okay. We are getting out of here," I said to her, gritting my teeth as the rope dug farther and farther into my skin.

"*Pull!*" Evander yelled again.

I could hear them and the horses struggle, and we were only halfway up. My arm burned, but I could not let go.

"*Pull!*"

By the time we reached the mouth of the well, my arm had gone limp.

"Verity!" her brother called as he helped us out and onto the ground. "Verity, wake up."

"Bring the torch close. Let me see her." I rolled onto my side to her, pushing the guards away.

Just as I thought, there was no bleeding or contusions on her head, but still, I could not be sure until she spoke to me properly.

"Verity, open your eyes for me," I said, trying to lift her eyelids to see into her eyes.

"Bright," she grumbled, trying to close them again.

"What happened?" I asked her.

"I was coming to you, and—"

"I knew this was your fault," her brother snapped at me, now of all times.

Suddenly, her eyes opened wide, and she looked at her brother and grabbed his arm. "Datura!"

"What?"

"She . . . she had a gun! She was coming for you! She was going to the house—"

His eyes widened as he lifted his head to look back toward his home.

"Aphrodite." He gasped in horror.

"Go! I shall be with her! If everyone is out searching, the house will not be as well guarded."

After witnessing what her son had done and how unhinged Datura already was, who knew how much further she had descended into her insanity.

"Evander, go!" Verity said, trying to get up. "I am fine."

"You three, with me!" Evander yelled to his men as he ran to his horse.

"You are not fine," I snapped at her as I helped her sit up.

"I am since you are here. I knew you would find me." She smiled, and even with the dim light from above, I could see how wide it was. She was smiling. In this condition!

"This is why I asked you to promise not to walk alone. Verity—"

"Please, do not yell at me, I feel bad enough," she whispered, and I stopped, as she was right. Now was not the time. Having her before me took away my panic. Now, in its place, came anger: at her, at her stepmother, and at myself. Bending down, I took her hand and kissed the back of it.

"You had me genuinely petrified."

"Me too." She took a deep breath.

Thank heavens the well was not any deeper. I was not sure of the condition of her mind, but at the very least, she was alert and speaking.

"Datura—she took aim to kill me. She looked as if she wished to burn the world down. We have to return to the house. Who knows what she is doing," she said, trying to stand but falling into my bruised arms.

"You are in no condition to be getting up right now."

"Theodore, they are my family!" She once more tried to stand, holding on to me. "Please, I need to get back and see what is happening. I—I was not there with Fitzwilliam. But—"

"Calm yourself! We will go. We will go," I said, steadying her before wrapping my arms around her waist. She held on to me, limping toward my horse. I tried to take hold of the reins but winced.

"You are hurt!" She reached for my arm.

"I am fine."

"You are not fine!" she said, parroting me with a stern look.

"My hand is a little bruised but nothing more." I ignored the pain and got onto the horse first to prove my point, then pulled her up into my arms to sit in front of me.

"Are you all right?"

She nodded, and only then did I kick into the horse, the wind blowing the scent of her all around me. I was sure she could feel my heart racing at her back.

Oh, how I never wanted to let go of her, and I prayed that I was not riding her into more danger.

"I fear I shall never have a dull moment with you," I said.

"Who wishes for a dull life?" she replied.

We arrived to find the duchess standing outside the house along with a few maids. In the duchess's arms was the young Miss Emeline.

"Aphrodite!" Verity called out to her as we came closer. "What is happening?"

"She was in the house. I do not know how she entered, but now, she refuses to leave. Evander said she is threatening to hurt herself!"

Immediately, I got off the horse.

"Stay here," I yelled to Verity as I ran into the house.

It was simple to see where I should go from where all the servants were looking—up the stairs. I went up, two by two, nearly slipping when I reached the top. I checked to the right and left for where to go before I noticed the crowd in the hall. Evander stood at the door with his butler before him.

"Make way! Make way!" I pushed them and finally saw the

woman herself. She sat in a chair crying and muttering to herself, a pistol pointed at her head.

"How long has she been so?" I whispered to Evander as he glared at her.

"Since I arrived. She threatens to shoot if we enter," he grumbled, shaking his head. "I have half a mind to let her."

"That is not recommended," I said, then looked back at her. She was just as Verity said, not in her right mind. "Dowager—"

"Stay back!"

"I am!" I said with my hands raised. "See, I am back."

"They are the cruel ones!" she hollered, her entire body trembling. "All of them took everything. They took my son, my baby—"

Evander scoffed beside me and opened his mouth to speak, but I grabbed his arm. This was not the time to take account of who was right or wrong. His words would only provoke her madness.

"Do you not have another son, Dowager?" I asked her gently, remembering my conversations with Verity. "Gabrien. I have heard of him. I was told he is very kind and sweet and wishes to travel the seas one day as a naval officer. What shall become of him? Do you not care for him?"

"Of course I do!" she snapped, finally making eye contact with me.

"Then why would you do this? In his family home? Do you wish to haunt him forever?"

"No, I—they are the ones that haunt us!" She pointed to Evander. "He and his mother! All of them! They will not leave us be! They mock us! Always—"

"And Gabrien will be left to further mockery," I said, taking one step in now. "My mother, she, too, was mocked and insulted. She, too, was hurt deeply by this world, by those with great status," I continued, taking another step. "And she . . . did as you wish to do now. Do you know whom she hurt in the process? Me. The rest of the world moved on, and only I was left to remember. It was me the others insulted in her stead. I do not believe she wanted that for me. Do you wish that for Gabrien?"

"They shall already mock him for Fitzwilliam's transgressions."

"And you believe that twice the mockery is better?"

"I just . . . I just want . . ." She stopped. "I wanted what they had. Why was that wrong?"

"The answer you seek cannot be found with a gun," I replied, stepping toward her. I outstretched my hand. "Please give it to me."

She looked up at me and placed the gun in my hand.

"Get her out of my house now!"

Within moments, she was in the hands of the footmen and dragged from her seat.

"You will make her worse—"

"I do not care!" Evander shouted at me when I sought to stop them. She screamed as they took her from the room.

"She is clearly experiencing—"

"She shot at my sister! The woman you claim to love? And you wish to show her compassion because she is mad? She inflicts pain on others, and now we must comfort her? I do not endorse that type of treatment!" he snapped before following them out of the room.

He was not wrong. She could have killed someone, and not just anyone—Verity. The thought made me furious, but as I stared at the gun in my hands, my left bruised badly, I thought of my mother and felt relieved I had at least saved another young man from that same horror.

It very well may have cost me my chance for Verity's hand, though.

What a horrid day.

Verity

Datura screamed in fury as she was dragged from our estate by the footmen. Evander stood with Aphrodite and Emeline at the entrance, comforting them. He kissed both of their heads before sending them back inside. He tried to send me, but I could not take my eyes away from her.

"You killed your brother! All of you. It is all your fault—"

"When will you take responsibility for your own actions?" I asked her in anger and pity. "Everything that has happened is by your own hand."

"That look." She nearly shook in rage. "How I have hated your face . . . From the first time I saw you, I knew that you would grow up and have the same look she did. She died, yet it was as though she had returned once more with you."

"Remove her this instant!" Evander ordered, shaking as I was.

"Let go!" Datura screamed as they pulled her away. "All of you are the murderers! You are the cruel ones! *You!*"

"We must get you inside." Theodore left me no room to argue as he picked me up despite his own injury.

All the footmen and even my brother stepped aside to let him, so I knew everyone was rightfully shaken.

"Verity, your injuries." Aphrodite came to me, still holding Emeline.

"I am fine—"

"She is not, Your Grace," Theodore interrupted. "She needs

to go to her rooms. I will need fresh bandages, clean water, towels, and a bandage for the wound on her arm. Also, she will need food, she has been out for hours—"

"Everything shall be brought to her room. Eleanor, please show Dr. Darrington the way. I shall put Emeline to bed and call the maids."

I glanced up at him, but he would not put me down, so I rested my head against his shoulder. When I was down in the well, I kept calling out for him until my throat grew sore and my body numb. I knew if I kept calling, he would come, and finally, when I heard him call back, it was as if all of me re-laxed, and a sense of peace came over me.

I closed my eyes for what I thought was only a minute. However, when he called my name, and I opened them, I real-ized I was already on my bed.

"Verity?"

"Hmm?" I looked up to see that he was staring down at me. I tried to sit up, but he pushed me back down gently.

"Stop," he ordered, holding my head so I could sip spoon-fuls of soup. Each time I tried to speak or move, he stopped me until I had finished at least half of it.

"How bad are my injuries?" I asked, licking my lips.

"No matter how bad they are, I shall heal them."

"And what of yours?"

"I shall heal them after I am done with you. Close your eyes. I can tell you are tired," he whispered.

I nodded and then remembered my brother. I grabbed him and shook my head. "Evander will throw you out again."

"He will not," said Aphrodite, who was on the other side of the bed. "I promise Theodore will be here when you wake. Rest."

I was unsure if I could believe her, but Theodore nodded when I looked at him. Exhaling, I closed my eyes again.

What a long day. Evander would surely never let me leave the house again.

Aphrodite

He sat silently in our room with his head in his hands. Slowly, I walked over and knelt before him, placing my hands on his knees.

"Once more, it is clear to me why your father refused me your hand," he whispered tiredly, and when I brought his hands down and looked into his eyes, they were red, not from anger but sorrow. "What order of madness is this? First Fitz-william, and now Datura? How did she even manage to enter?"

"Verity says there is a secret passageway from the kitchen. It is how she escapes."

He threw his hands up and shook his head.

"I wished to fill our lives with joy," he muttered defeatedly. "I wished all of our days together to be filled with laughter, long walks among the flowers, and the most dazzling of amusements. I wished Everely to be a haven for my family as I'd always dreamed it could be. Instead, we have faced all kinds of deviancy. Had this been your family—"

"This is my family," I finally spoke, taking his hand. "I am an Eagleman. You are my family, this is my home, and no matter what has transpired, I have not lost faith that we shall make this place a wonder of bliss."

He lifted my hands and kissed the backs of them. "Forgive me for starting our marriage like this."

"There is nothing to forgive." I smiled, kissing his hands in turn, but I knew I could not hold back any longer. "Evander, something must be done for Verity."

"Oh, when she wakes up, I shall lecture her till she is deaf—"

"Not about that." I believed she had already learned that lesson the hard way, traveling alone and getting hurt. "I mean her reputation."

"What of it?"

"Evander, all the town, if not the county, is talking about her and Dr. Darrington. Do you think they are fools? First, he was welcomed here, then he was banned, next Verity is at his inn, and now add to the story that he carries her into the estate bloodied?"

"She was injured—"

"Even still, I fear what will be said of a young lady who has gone through all she has with a man she's not wedded to. It is all a massive scandal that shall last throughout her life."

He frowned. "What are you saying?"

"I am asking if Dr. Darrington's birth is so pernicious that you would rather leave your sister open to ridicule."

"She will be the subject of ridicule for being with him."

"But at the very least, she will be with the man she loves and who loves her. Even you must admit that." I squeezed his hand. "She looks at him as I look at you, and he looks at her as you look at me. Is that not what you want for her? To be loved?"

He closed his eyes and hung his head. "I see it, but I struggle to accept it. What if we are only seeing the good side of him? What if I accept this, and he is like Fitzwilliam?"

"You must let go of Fitzwilliam, my love. He is gone. You must look at Dr. Darrington as he is. There is nothing similar between them in my eyes. You must set aside his position and question him as you would have any other suitor who came for her hand."

"I know him to be soft-hearted, since he requested we be gentle with Datura even after all she has done, all he had personally witnessed."

"Compassion toward one's enemies is a godly trait, so you must not fault him for it."

"We are not in heaven. In reality, women are to be protected, and I do not believe he can do so."

"Did he not jump into a well after her? I believe he will manage to take care of her admirably."

He frowned and nearly pouted. "Must you advocate for them?"

"How ill-suited it would be for me to be named Aphrodite and not champion love."

"Of course, it would be now that you seek to adhere to your name." He scoffed and laughed as he pulled me into his arms.

31

Theodore

When I entered her room, she quickly shut her journal again.

"Double, double, toil and trouble; fire burn and cauldron bubble?" I said to her, making her mouth drop open and her eyes widen.

"*Macbeth?*" The duchess's eyebrows furrowed as she looked at me from her seat at Verity's bedside. She glanced between us. "What is the reason for quoting that?"

"Nothing. He is merely teasing me," Verity replied, and I hung my head to hide my smile.

"I see. I shall step aside and allow you to work, Dr. Darrington," the duchess said, rising.

"Thank you, Your Grace, and thank you for the room as well. Forgive me for putting you out."

"There are far too many rooms for me to be put out. If anyone has suffered, it is poor Mrs. Stoneshire." She giggled and moved to the window. "When I sent for your things, she nearly wept."

"You sent for his things?" Verity asked, sitting up, hopefully. "So, does that mean—"

"He was injured in the process of saving you, Verity. It would be most impolite of us to send him back to an inn," she said, and I watched Verity slowly sink back into the bed dejectedly. Walking forward, I sat on the side of the bed.

"How is your arm?"

"Fine. How is yours?"

"Sore," I replied, taking her arm to examine it myself. It had been only a few hours since everything had unfolded, but I was glad to see the wound did not look infected even after being left exposed for so long.

"Is it wise for you to treat yourself?" she asked me as I redid the dressing for her.

"Is it wise for you to walk alone into town at any hour of the day?" I replied, causing her to frown.

"Evander already lectured me. I believe my ears are still ringing, and now you come here to join him."

"Whatever he said was correct—"

"You are not to be on his side."

"Why?"

"Because he is against us."

"He is against me, not you. But whoever is for you is ultimately for me."

"And whoever is against you is against me. So ultimately he is against us."

I stared at her, and she stared back. Again, I found myself seeking not to smile. Instead, I focused on her ankle, which rested on a pillow. I pressed the side of it with my good hand, and she winced. "It is not broken, but it is sprained, as I thought. We will need to wrap cold towels around it for twenty minutes every two to three hours for another day or two."

"Eleanor shall see to it," the duchess said.

"Next, I shall rescue you," Verity said rather sternly. "I have been the damsel in distress twice now."

"Twice?" The duchess gasped, not aware.

"Yes. I fell from a horse in London, and he came to my aid then too. Any more accidents, and I shall seem as though I belong in a medieval folktale." Her brown eyes shifted to me. "Next time, I shall be your heroine, I promise."

"Can we not avoid a 'next time' altogether?" I asked, genuinely afraid of any further dramas unfolding. Reaching into my pocket, I pulled out the necklace for her once more. "I fear this piece of jewelry has seen far too much in this life as it is."

She gasped and sat up. "I worried I lost it!"

"It led me to you," I said, wishing to put it on her myself, but instead I put it in her hand carefully.

Knock. Knock.

"Enter," the duchess said.

"Your Grace, the duke would like to see Dr. Darrington in his study," the butler said.

"Why?" Verity sat up once more. I tapped her leg to get her attention, and when she looked at me, I shook my head.

"I shall be back. Your Grace, will you please see to it that the towel is as cold as possible?"

"Yes, of course," the duchess said to me.

Rising from the bed, I moved to the door, where the older man stood with no emotion on his face. We walked in silence and it was far too fast for me to gather my thoughts before we arrived at the door. He knocked once, then waited.

"Enter."

"Your Grace, Dr. Darrington is here."

"Show him in."

The butler stepped aside, gesturing for me to proceed, and when I entered the room, the door closed behind me. The duke sat behind his desk, leaning back into the chair, his eyes closed. He said not a word, so I spoke first.

"If you wish to throw me out all I ask is that you do so after she is well again," I said. He still did not open his eyes, so I stood in silence.

It felt as though minutes had passed before he finally spoke. "How much is your inheritance?"

"Fifty thousand pounds."

"Is it guaranteed in your name?"

"Yes, and already transferred."

His eyes opened, and he sat up, looking at me. "How much land do you own?"

"One hundred acres, including a manor house called Glass-den Hall—also guaranteed—as well as a farm, which brings in further income."

"Where is it?"

"Cheshire."

"Is that not where Wentwood House is located?"

I nodded. "Yes, it is."

"Then it is safe to assume the one hundred acres given to you were taken from that estate."

"Yes, it was."

"Do you own any other land or property? In London?"

"No."

"But have you not lived there all this time?"

"My grandfather and uncle own a home. But after my uncle married and had children, it became rather cramped, so I sought long-term lodgings in an inn."

"You did not think to purchase a home there?"

"It made little sense for me to have one only for myself, and I spent much of my time visiting patients."

He took a deep breath and held his hands together. "One hundred acres was taken from your brother's future inheritance; he did not care?"

"He is but a boy. I'm not sure he knows."

"And when he grows to be a man?"

"I do not believe he will mind, but I won't know until he is older."

"What of his mother? Does she mind? What is your relationship with her?"

"There is no relationship—no, that is untrue. I believe there to be no bad feeling between her and me. She has done much for me already," I answered.

"How so?"

I did not wish to lie to him any more than I had to. So, I told him the truth, of how we were caught in London and why I had left there before coming to Everely. He rose to his feet and moved around his desk.

"How could you be so reckless?" He gasped. "You risked her reputation time and time again. Both of you have gone beyond the realm of decency and propriety."

"I will not deny it." And if he knew how much more beyond the realm of decency he would have shot me.

"Was this all to force my hand? To make it so difficult to salvage the name of my sister that I would be compelled to accept you?"

"With all due respect, Your Grace, you did not come to mind in those moments." Nothing and no one else did.

He inhaled through his nose, and dropped his hand once more. "My sister is too precious to me, Dr. Darrington. Long before I cared for anyone else, it was merely the two of us seeking to survive in this house, in this family. As you may have noticed, we have had our share of . . . tragedy. I am unsure if she remembers, but long ago, I promised her that I would ensure her happiness. She tells me she is in love with you and believes you to love her as well. Should I accept you, I am not sure she will have that happiness, for love is important, but so is acceptance, especially in society."

"I may overstep, Your Grace, but your first wife, was she not accepted into society? Were you not accepted? Was this home happy then? What about your mother and father? Were they too not accepted?" He did not answer, so I continued, "I believe love to be more important than your society."

"I do not wish her to enter another family of complications."

"All families have complications, but I assure you, mine could never eclipse or even match yours," I replied, causing him to frown.

"What of your work?"

"What of it?"

"Do you intend to keep seeing patients?"

"Yes."

"You do not worry about bringing some sort of disease or deadly ailment to your family in the future?"

"I take many precautions to refrain from doing so. And should I ever believe myself in danger of that, I would separate and seek treatment for myself."

"Is it really worth such a risk if you have land and wealth?"

"Yes, as it is who I am," I said to him. "And so far, that has led me here."

"I wish to say no," he grumbled as he outstretched his hand to me. "However, my sister's future now lies with you, *Theodore*."

It was as if I had finally gotten a miracle, seen an angel. My chest hurt, my eyes burned, and all of me shook as I took his hand. How shameful it would be to weep. I hung my head and gripped his hand tightly. "Th-Thank you." I even struggled to get the words out.

"I leave you to tell her."

"No need!"

We both paused at the voice coming through the door behind me. Quickly, I let go of his hand and opened my eyes to see her standing on one leg, holding on to the door.

"Verity!" we both yelled out.

"Forgive me. I grew nervous." She smiled widely. "He said yes! Truly, he said yes!"

I reached out to her, and she hugged me tightly. "I said you were to stay off your feet."

"Where is Aphrodite? She was to wait with you while I spoke to him," Evander asked, going to her other side to help me. I wished to lift her but feared it would push her brother beyond his limit for the day.

"She was, but then Eleanor rushed to her, and she went running out of the room as if the house were on fire without even looking at me," she explained, still smiling as she now turned to Evander and hugged him. "Thank you, brother. Thank you for accepting him."

"Your Grace!" Once more, the butler came in, but this time, in a rush.

"Wallace, what is going on?" Evander asked him. "Where is my wife?"

"Your Grace, the Marchioness of Monthermer has just arrived and wishes to see . . . Lady Verity," the butler replied, and we all froze.

"Well, good luck to you, sister." Evander stepped away from her.

"Evander!" She gasped out loud, and he shrugged.

"I have given my blessing, and you believe yourself ready to face society, so go face the brunt of it."

Just when I thought we had made it to the end, a sinkhole appeared.

Verity

I tried not to feel like a little girl when I entered the drawing room. However, I did not feel like a grown woman either, as I had to limp inside, holding on to Theodore. She sat by the fire like a work of art, dressed in deep violet, a jeweled cap on her head, and diamonds around her brown neck. Opposite her sat Aphrodite, who also looked incredibly nervous despite this being her home now and not her mama's.

"Godmother, welcome. I was not told we were expecting you," Evander said as he followed me in. He looked at Aphrodite, probably wondering why she had not told us, but she stared back, shaking her head to indicate she had not expected her mother either. When the marchioness looked at her daughter, Aphrodite immediately lifted her teacup.

"I received a letter from your brother saying he had transferred your inheritance to our guardianship should anything happen to him," the marchioness said, looking at me. "It left me most worried, and that worry grew as further talk reached the ton. Imagine my surprise when I arrived in town today and heard that not only had my goddaughter nearly been killed and left to die in a well but she was said to be attached to one Dr. Theodore Darrington."

I glared at Evander, whose eyes widened as he realized he was to blame for this.

"Well, someone speak." No one did. "Aphrodite, there is not enough tea in this world to stop you and me from this conversation."

"Your ladyship, I will answer all you require, but may Lady Verity sit?" It was Theodore who dared address her.

"Of course, she may sit, for this is her home," she said, and he helped me to a seat before them, but to make it more evident that he was tending to me as a doctor, he took a pillow from the chair and set it on the ground for me to rest my injured foot upon.

"Now, someone, tell me the truth of what has occurred." She waited.

"Godmother, it is so much—"

"That is why I am already sitting, Evander. Out with it," she demanded. You would think she were the duchess here.

Then again, the power of a mama was greater than any other. Quickly, Evander and Aphrodite began to explain what had occurred over the past few weeks. I thought she would panic, shriek, or, at the very least, show some emotion, but she took it all calmly.

"Where is that—where is Datura now?" she asked Evander.

"In prison, awaiting her trial. I am to speak to the magistrate later on the matter. However, she will be brought to justice."

"Finally, now that is settled." She sighed, then her hawkish gaze shifted to Theodore and me.

"Now, Dr. Darrington, my question to you is, what is your relationship to my goddaughter?"

"We are to be married, Godmother," I answered for him.

She stared at him, then me, and then my brother. "You have accepted this?"

"As you said, talk of them has spread, Godmother, and they clearly love each other. It is better they marry—"

"Well, *I* do not accept this," she replied sternly. "And as her dowry is formally in my family's care, she shall not see a glimpse of it."

"Godmother!" I pleaded, sitting on the edge of the chair, but Theodore stepped forward.

"The duke already threatened us with disinheritance, your ladyship," he said to her. "And I will tell you, as I told him, I have enough of my own to take care of—"

"I will not let Luella's daughter be known as the lady who married the bastard of Whitmear." She did not speak the words angrily. "I promised her upon her deathbed that I would see to it that both her children were happy and respected in society. This match, as it is, cannot stand."

I felt myself growing angry. "I will—"

"What do you mean *as it is?*" asked Theodore, interrupting me. "Are you implying our match could be made another way?"

"Could? It must."

"I do not understand." I frowned. "How else could we be matched?"

"Theodore— Do you mind me calling you Theodore?" she asked politely.

"No, your ladyship."

"Good. Theodore, as I said, my goddaughter cannot be married to a man with the title of a bastard."

"I am a doctor."

"How nice for you, but that means nothing for us," she shot back, her head high. "Your position in society is all that matters, and in our world, you are a bastard. We must change that."

"How do you propose to do that?" Theodore asked her.

"By making you respectable—having you knighted."

"What?" Everyone in the room spoke at once.

"Mama, such a thing is not easily done, especially for one so young," Aphrodite said to her.

"You are correct. For most, it is nearly impossible. However, with the right support, even the impossible can be done with ease." Her eyes shifted to Evander. "Did your mother not leave you with one other mighty benefactor?"

I glanced at my brother, unsure of what she was talking about, to see him shaking his head. "Godmother, you cannot be serious? I cannot go to her with a request like this. All the world will know it was so obviously done to bolster his reputation, which could very well diminish the crown."

"The crown?" I gasped.

"The queen?" Aphrodite said. "You wish to take this to the queen?"

"Lady Monthermer, I thank you for your efforts—" Theodore began to speak, but she interrupted.

"I have not even begun to apply my efforts."

We all stared at her as if she had grown two heads and horns.

"Such youth and yet such lack of imagination." She shook her head at us. "How do you believe any great family achieves their standing?"

"War?" Theodore replied.

"Notoriety. And you, Theodore Darrington, are well on your way. None of you seem to see it. This girl you all sought to help, Marcella, should the truth be known, it would be a great embarrassment to the Wildingham family, correct?" she asked.

"Yes." Evander nodded.

"And the Wildinghams are relations to whom?"

It was then that I saw what she meant. "Sir Zachary Dennison-Whit, the county's MP, who happens to be the rumored right hand of the prime minister."

"Very good, my dear." She grinned, nodding. "And here comes the legend of Theodore Darrington. The great doctor has saved countless members of the nobility, such as Lady Clementina Rowley and Lord Benjamin Hardinge, along with tending to the sick in East London, before coming to Everely to seek the hand of Lady Verity Eagleman. In doing so, he came also to the aid of Mr. Wildingham in his deep grief over his poor daughter, was there for him till his end, and then Dr. Darrington rescued his beloved from a well. All of the ton will be abuzz with the news, and the queen shall suggest he be knighted. Who would object to such a fine young man?"

I glanced up at Theodore, who was just staring at her.

"Do you truly believe that will work, Mama? Why would the queen, of all people, be inclined to help?"

"My mama told me once that should I ever be in real trouble I was to seek an audience with the queen. That she would come to my aid, that she was our family's greatest benefactor," said Evander softly but the look on his face was still unsure. "But I never truly thought to ever go to her."

"Yes, I have noticed, as you did not even seek her aid for yourself." The marchioness frowned. "But your mama was truthful, as the queen owes a small debt of gratitude to her."

"What?" both Aphrodite and I said in shock.

"It is a long story I shall not reveal that leaves me confident in her aid now. Thus, this plan shall work. Besides, everyone loves a good hero," she said. "So, let us give them one."

"If so . . . once it is done, who would dare speak on his birth?" Evander said as he nodded in agreement with her.

"Godmother, is this your only disagreement with this match?" I asked, somewhat amazed. I expected her to be . . . harsher. When I was in London she made it quite clear Dr. Darrington was not a suitable match.

"You believed I would not accept this match on account of what I have said in the past?" she asked me.

"Yes," I replied.

"Even I believed you would not accept this, Godmother," Evander added.

Her eyes shifted between us all before she sighed. "I must admit I would have preferred things not be so . . . complicated for you, Verity. That said, my greatest desire is to see you truly happy. And as I have not been able to do much to that end, I shall at least see to this."

"Thank you, Godmother," I said softly, not wishing to lose my composure.

They all went back and forth in their scheming for this knighthood. However, when I glanced up at Theodore, I noticed his demeanor had changed and his head had lowered.

He was not happy.

I could tell.

"Theodore, what do you think?" I said loudly so they could all speak *with* him and not around him.

They paused, looking at him, and he forced a smile. "I shall do whatever it takes for your blessing, your ladyship."

He meant it, but at the same time, I knew something was not right. Seeing me watching him, he smiled, and I was sure I would have to seek him out privately.

"Mama!"

I jumped at the voice and turned to see the door open as none other than Abena ran into the room, dressed in yellow, her hat falling from her head.

"Mama, look! Is this not the most horrid thing?" She lifted the doll Aphrodite had made with a massive grin on her face. "Emeline said Odite made it."

Aphrodite gasped and grabbed it from her. "Do not make fun of my daughter's doll, Abena!"

The marchioness's eyebrow rose at the word *daughter*, but she focused her attention on Abena.

"You are to go out and return as a lady would before greeting the duke and duchess and then everyone else in the room," her mother ordered.

"Mama—" She was stopped by the look on her mama's face.

Abena sighed, then picked up her hat before exiting the room. A moment later, there was a knock.

Everyone looked to the marchioness, who looked to Aphrodite.

"Enter," Aphrodite said gently.

Abena, with a puckered face, came in, then curtsied. "Hello, Evander, Odite, *Mama*, Verity . . . Dr. Darrington? You are here too? Who is ill? Why is everyone always ill?"

The marchioness inhaled slowly, staring at her daughter. Finally, she said, "Please tell me your Emeline is not so difficult to manage."

"Not at all." Aphrodite grinned.

"Good. I wished to leave her in London, but I feared your father would not fare well with her and Hathor alone."

"Papa said I am to give this look to the duke." She turned and made a very strange face at Evander, who stared down at her and laughed.

They continued laughing, and when Emeline entered, all the conversation shifted, allowing me to whisper to Theodore.

"What is troubling you? And do not tell me it is nothing."

He glanced down at me and said softly in return, "For a moment, I was frustrated that I was still not good enough in her eyes to have your hand. I would never be good enough despite all my efforts unless there was some title attached to me."

"I will tell her you do not wish for it. I do not care if you are knighted or not. Forgive me for entertaining the prospect."

"There is nothing to forgive. I know your feelings clearly. I wanted to say to the world, 'My background does not matter. See, even as I am, I am permitted the hand of the most beautiful Lady Verity Eagleman.' It was a moment of my own selfish pride."

"You are not selfish."

"Then I am ungrateful for not considering the family before me, people who shall become my relations. A man died seeking a life akin to what I have been so open-handedly given. I will not sulk but accept and be thankful."

I was still not sure he was all right. "Say the word at any time, and I—"

"Theodore," the marchioness called once more, and he stood straighter, looking to her.

"Yes, your ladyship?"

"You shall return with us to London?" I was not sure if she was asking him or telling him.

"You wish to take him back to London?" I asked.

"He cannot possibly be knighted here," she stated and then looked at him. "Three days' time to depart should be adequate, should it not?"

"Yes, your ladyship." He nodded.

"Then I shall come too," I said quickly.

"You are injured," both Evander and Theodore said at the same time.

"It is but a scratch," I lied, trying to put my foot back down off the pillow only to wince.

"See how she has become?" Evander exhaled, looking to our godmother. "Even Hathor is likely more reasonable than Verity at this moment."

Aphrodite giggled while I glared at him from the corner of my eye before focusing on the marchioness.

"Godmother, it shall be weeks, maybe months, if at all, for a knighthood to be granted—"

"Theodore." The way she called his name was beginning to feel like a reprimand.

"Yes, your ladyship?"

"Shall distance or time cause you to forget the Lady Verity?"

"Never, your ladyship."

I stared down at my hands to keep from grinning so obviously.

"Then, as I said, three days' time."

"I shall be ready. Now Lady Verity ought to return to her rooms for rest."

I lifted my head to look at him as he dared tell her what was to be done. But he simply faced her.

"Very well. Aphrodite, summon Eleanor to *help* them." By *help*, it was clear she meant *chaperone*, but I would not fight, for at least now we were together.

Finally.

32

Verity

"Oh, how I wish to be rescued by the hands of a handsome gentleman," two maids whispered, giggling to themselves as I passed by them and entered my private sitting room. All the town spoke of Dr. Theodore Darrington as though he were some poetic hero. I could only imagine what the gossip was about him in London. I had just sat down at the window with my book when I heard someone at the door.

"Enter," I said, hoping for a letter from Theodore. Instead, it was Evander.

"Do not look so disappointed. It is a bit hurtful," he said.

"I am never disappointed to see you, big brother," I said, sitting up from my chair. "How are you?"

"That is a question for you, not me." He sat beside me. "I know you hate to be kept inside, even if it is for your own good at times."

"Should I not be the one to determine my own good?"

"When your senses are working, yes," he teased me.

"You have come to fight?"

"No." He smiled. "I have come to tell you that you were right."

Now I set the book down completely. "Truly? On what matter?"

"How many matters do you believe there to be?"

"Far too many to count."

He laughed and shook his head. "The one I speak of is marriage."

"Oh, no, you are not permitted to change your mind."

"I am not, but I recalled when you told me in London, before you lost your mind, how you worried I would take the loss of you. I realized I am not going to take it well." He frowned.

"It is not as though I am to marry tomorrow."

"Yes, but it is much sooner than I thought. Just as I had sought to create a haven here, you flee," he replied and stretched out his hand for me. When I gave mine to him, he squeezed it tightly. "But at the same time, to know you are happy makes me happy."

I squeezed tightly back. "Let us not have these words until I am actually out the door. It still does not feel real to me. Besides, I fear our godmother greatly underestimates the task before us. Their whole family always believes everything shall turn out as they plan."

"Yes, the Du Bells are like that." He chuckled, then shrugged. "But then again, why would they be any different when, in fact, they do get what they wish. I am confident Lady Monthermer would not propose something that was beyond her power."

I truly hoped not. But still, I was not sure when Theodore would return. "Have you heard any news of Theodore? I have not gotten a letter."

"Are letters to move so quickly? I saw you had one sent out again today," he teased me.

"It is just . . . Well, have you?" I sought to hide my embarrassment.

"No. I am sure one is on the way, for I doubt he can withhold himself either."

"You talk as if you were any better. I saw how you yourself waited for any news of Aphrodite."

"Touché." He chuckled, but the smile on his face faded. "I did wish to speak to you on another matter."

"What?"

"Datura."

The joy in me faded as well. "Has it happened?"

She had been tried and sentenced with a capital punishment. However, it had not been carried out yet.

"No, I interceded."

"You what?" I gasped. He, of all people, advocating for Datura? "Clearly, you are the one not in your right mind."

"Maybe." He chuckled and took a deep breath. "Gabrien wrote to me."

My shoulders dropped at the reminder that while she was a nightmare for us, she was his mother.

"She is still Gabrien's mother, and how could there be any semblance of peace between us if I wrote to tell him of the death of his mother not even a month after his brother's passing? He begged me to have her spared that punishment at least, and seeing as how your Theodore worked to spare her as well, I believed that not doing so would brand me cruel."

He was right.

"So, what is to happen to her?"

"Theodore will provide a statement to the court attesting to her state of mind. They dismissed that before, as her crime was just too great. However, they shall listen to me. She will be punished for her crimes with confinement one town over."

"Gabrien will still be able to see her," I replied, and a strange feeling filled me when I thought of the position he was in.

"I will go see her moved to another prison today."

"Can I not come as well?"

"Verity, let me handle this, and you think no more of it or

her. It is over. She shall never be able to disturb our peace again. I heard you are even sleeping through the night once more." He beamed, though it was not altogether true. I had new medicine given to me. While my nightmares were no longer as bad, they had not simply vanished as I wished them to.

Before I could answer, the door opened, and in walked Aphrodite. "Evander? Do you not have things to attend to in town?"

"I was telling Verity the truth of it. And now I shall go." He rose to his feet and went to his wife. "Show me out?"

"Have you lost your way?" She giggled.

"Yes." He outstretched his arm to her and turned to me. "Verity, I will—"

"Evander," I said as I, too, rose to my feet. My injury was still rather sore but not so much I could not stand. "I understand you mean to protect me, but I truly believe I will not be able to rest until I see her punished with my own two eyes. Right now, she is just somewhere in my mind. I must go. Please allow me."

He said nothing, just stared at me for a long time before nodding. "Very well, but you shall wait in the carriage until I say otherwise."

"Thank you."

Theodore

The marchioness said she had not yet begun to apply pressure; I did not realize at the time what exactly she meant. However, my first week back in London gave a clear indication of her power and influence.

"Hello, Dr. Darrington," a lord greeted me on the street.

"Good morning, Dr. Darrington!" Two ladies giggled as I passed.

"How are you, Dr. Darrington?" The shopkeeper waved.

"Good lord, it is as though I am not even here," Henry said from beside me as he watched them all with the same bewilderment as I did. "Not even a nod to me. Me!"

"How on earth did word spread like this? Was there a paper?" I asked him, nodding again to another man who greeted me. I feared I would strain my neck at this rate.

"I do not know about others, but my mother called the modiste a few days ago—I believe her name to be Mrs. Marie Loquac. Anyway, she went on and on about your time in Everely and all your heroics as though you were part of some epic. She told of how you were given extensive property by your father and thousands upon thousands of pounds. Said you were dripping in gold and silver but were still *so* kind-hearted that you dedicated your life to aiding those in need. She even said you saved the magistrate's son, Simon Humphries, from a deadly disease."

"A what?"

"Apparently, he was covered in boils bigger than rocks from head to toe, blind in one eye, and deaf in one ear, and everyone was at a loss for why until you came and cured him completely."

"There were no boils, no blindness or deafness, nor was he deadly ill from anything other than stubbornness and too much drink. I told the man to refrain from port and brandy. Advice he did not listen to, by the way."

"Nevertheless, the story has been set," he added as we turned the corner. "And that is not even the half of it."

"There is more?"

"Yes, it is said you are one of the secret doctors to the royal family, which is why there is talk of a knighthood."

"What?" I nearly tripped on the side of the road. "The royal family? Who? When? How?"

"No one has cared to explain or clarify. The talk just grows and grows like a beast. Do you know what my mother has been saying lately?" He paused to look at me, full of amusement and shock. "How much of a waste it is that we did not engage you to my sister, Amity, before the marchioness stole you away for Lady Verity. She is cross with my father for making the connection between you all."

I stared back and then laughed. Lady Fancot, his mother, wishing I had married her precious daughter? "The ton has gone mad."

"Mad for you, Dr. Darrington." He laughed, shaking his head as we walked on. "You are the prize of the ton."

"I feel myself to be the fraud of the ton," I muttered, nodding to yet another gentleman who passed by me.

"Well, you must continue the farce as we go into the heart of the lion's den," he said when we finally reached Black's Gentlemen's Club. I had left Everely only a week ago and spent time with my grandfather, waiting for the marchioness to send word for me. After several days staying out of sight, I was finally sent an invitation by the marquess to come here today.

They had not been hostile the previous time I had come here, as they knew the marquess to be my benefactor. I did not expect to notice a change in the way they looked at me when I entered, but it was undeniable.

"Theodore!"

That was another change—the marquess calling me by name from his gaming table as though I were his son or a close friend. Even Henry's eyebrows rose.

I said nothing as I walked up to the table of Lord Bolen, Lord Hardinge, and Henry's father, Lord Fancot.

"My lords," I greeted them all.

"Bring up a chair. Do know I shall not go easy on you," the marquess said to me, and before I could remind him that I did not partake in gaming, a footman had already brought another chair for me to sit at the table. The fact that one had not yet been offered to Henry was not lost on me. And the marquess himself gave me a look as if to say this offer was not to be rejected. So I took my seat as they dealt out a new hand of cards.

"I hear you have been granted a new estate," Lord Hardinge said as he looked over his cards. "What is its production? Wheat or barley?"

"Cheese," I answered, looking at the cards in my hand.

"Cheese is good, and the value of it grows. However, cows are fickle and take too much effort to keep," Lord Bolen stated, folding his hand.

"Cows are not fickle. You are merely impatient." The marquess snickered, then looked at me as he tossed a note into the center. "How many tenants?"

"About half a dozen or so," I said, taking a card.

"Much too small. You should seek to improve those numbers. A good estate needs good tenants, and I tell that to Henry all the time, do I not?" Lord Fancot asked, looking to Henry right behind me before Lord Fancot threw a note into the center.

"I do not recall," Henry replied, causing the man to glare.

"Well, you ought to recall. The running of an estate is just like a good game—if you are not paying attention or leave it all to luck, you very well might find yourself at a loss," Lord Hardinge said, tossing his note in before revealing his hand. A grin spread across his lips as he looked at the marquess. "You cannot always win, my friend."

"True, but today I shall." The marquess revealed his hand as well, and his cards were much greater.

"Damn you." They all chuckled before glancing at me.

"Do not feel bad. Somehow, he is blessed in both life and cards." Lord Bolen rolled his eyes. "You shall lose to him often."

"I do not believe I have lost," I said, showing my own cards.

"What?" The marquess sat up and looked at the cards before me.

I tried not to smile. "I do not game, my lord, because I nearly gave my grandfather a heart attack after beating him and all his friends once as a child. He said I have an unnaturally blessed drawing hand."

There was silence for a moment before the marquess broke out in laughter. Once more, he glanced back at me and shrugged.

"It seems that today is the day I take the loss," he replied, his jaw clenching before his attention was taken by another man. He sat up and called out louder, "Sir Grisham, where are you going? And with no greeting. Have I offended you?"

I turned to see the man in question pause mid-escape. Was he escaping us—no, me?

Slowly, he turned around, and once more silence prevailed as everyone turned to watch this drama unfold. When Sir Grisham finally reached the table, he bowed his head.

"Offend me, your lordship? Why would you ever?"

"Well, last we spoke, you seemed disgruntled by my choice of guests. I wished to ask if you still felt this way and if there was anything that could be done to accommodate you better?" the marquess questioned.

Sir Grisham's grip on his cane tightened, and he would not look at me. "No, my lord, I believe everything to be fine."

"Brilliant," the marquess replied, lifting his cards again.

I watched Sir Grisham go. But the silence continued. The crowd parted for another who walked into the room, with three others behind him, dressed nearly as finely as the dukes already present.

"Is that not the prime minister?" Henry whispered behind me.

I did not know the prime minister from Adam, so I could not answer, but as he walked up to the table, greeting a few men on his way, I had a strange feeling this was the whole purpose of my visit.

"Do not stand," the marquess whispered to me just before the man reached us.

"Lord Monthermer, I see you are still robbing men blind."

"On the contrary. It is I who have been robbed, Prime Minister," the marquess replied, which made the rest of them laugh.

"You? By whom? I dare say I wish to shake that man's hand."

"That would be the famed Dr. Darrington, sir." Lord Hardinge nodded to him. "He apparently wishes to be known throughout England."

"I merely wish to keep my bank accounts healthy," I said and nodded to the man before me. "Prime Minister."

"Ah, Dr. Theodore Darrington, it seems I cannot escape your name of late. I thought you to be some grand figure, but you are about the same age as my son, if not younger. How does one garner such a reputation so quickly? I wish to know for the next election." There were a few chuckles as they waited for my answer, but I knew not what to say in reply.

"Modistes," I finally said, lifting the cards. "I hear they are quite the storytellers. I believe that next, they shall say I slew a dragon in Derbyshire."

There was silence, and I was sure I had made a mistake until the prime minister laughed, which caused the others to laugh as well.

"I shall leave you to your game, gentlemen. Lord Monthermer."

"Prime Minister." The marquess nodded in return, and the prime minister went on his way.

I glanced at Lord Monthermer, confused. I leaned in and whispered, "Did I pass that test or fail it?"

"Passed," he muttered back. "He detests those who put on airs."

"So what now?"

"Now you wait."

I tried not to be discouraged but waiting and not seeing Verity made me rather on edge.

"Patience is a virtue needed the most in marriage," the marquess said aloud for the rest of the table.

"And marriage is needed the most for a gentleman, is that not what I always tell you, Henry?" Lord Fancot pressed.

"Is that what you are always saying? Strange, it seems I always miss it. Theodore, I do believe I might need my ears checked later. Until then, excuse me, gentlemen." Henry quickly made his escape.

Lord Fancot sighed so heavily that his gut shook the table, causing the rest of them to laugh.

"Theodore, as his friend you ought to advise him, as he clearly shall not listen to me," Lord Fancot said to me.

"I believe that wise men ought to advise from a position of safety, my lord, and I have yet to arrive there, so I shall remain silent for now." Though one day, I would hope to find out the identity of the woman who held his heart in such a bind. I wished for him to find the happiness I had discovered with Verity.

Even now, I wished to write to her.

I prayed she was not doing anything dangerous.

Verity

"Did I not tell you to stay in the carriage?" Evander snapped at me when he noticed I had entered the jailhouse. The smell was horrid, and the darkness far worse, as it made every cry, cough, and scream seem much more haunting.

"I could not wait," I whispered, staying close to him.

"I have noticed this to be a new trait of yours." He sighed and then looked at the cell behind him, which was all stone but for the small door of iron bars.

"Is she in there?"

"Yes, she is to be kept here and not farther inside."

"Is it worse farther inside?"

"There are—it does not matter. You shall see her, and we will leave immediately," he said as he took my hand to help guide me so that I did not step into any of the pools of water gathered.

When I entered and reached the bars, I saw that she did not have a bed, only straw to lie on. Gone were her jewels and lace, and gone was the white powder upon her face. For the first time, I saw her stripped of all finery and left in a dingy brown dress, no shoes, only socks in which there were holes. Her gray-gold hair was matted with straw, and I dared not guess what else. When she glanced up at me, she stared as if she did not know who I was.

"Say your piece now," Evander instructed.

"I have nothing to say."

"What?"

"I have nothing to say to her," I replied and turned to head back out. She was the one who was locked up and had to behave, while I was the one who would go on and live happily.

I was finally free of her.

Finally.

33

Theodore

S ometimes no matter how we try, it is impossible to gain all we wish for in life. Nevertheless, as I stood before my grandfather, I still desired to push my luck.

"I shall be getting married tomorrow, Grandfather," I said to him but he did not look up from his table of medicine. "I wish for you to be there . . . I wish for our whole family to be there."

"Is that so, *SIR* Theodore?" I turned to face my uncle as he glared from the doorframe. "Are you sure those lordly folks will want to share a table with us?"

"I do not wish to fight, Uncle, I merely come to extend the invitation—"

He chuffed. "We do not need your invitation, *sir*. They are far too grand for us."

"Uncle . . ."

"I knew it," he replied, glaring at me. "You never wished to be us, you've always wished to be them. How does it feel? Betraying your family, your mother, and crawling back to that man, begging him to accept you, give you an estate, money . . . your soul so easily bought."

The reason I had waited so long to talk to them was because of this. How I knew he and my grandfather would react to me coming to good terms with my father. Nothing could change how they felt about him, and they had good reason to hate him. For me to stand up now, going on about the lands he had given me, of course it seemed like a betrayal. I glanced back at my grandfather, who had not looked away from his boiling pot.

"I have grieved my mother all my life and I will always think of her. But, Grandfather, this woman I love—"

"You must provide for her." He nodded and finally glanced up to me. "I wish you both peace, Theodore, truly. But we shall not be coming. And it is best for you not to return often to Langley Cross . . . a man of your position now—"

"Grandfather."

"Theodore, go without regret, my boy."

I knew not what to say to him, and when I looked back at the stern expression upon my uncle's face I knew there was nothing I could say. I had gained much over the weeks: a new connection with my father and brother, respect in society, as I had now been knighted and given a title, but most importantly I had gained Verity. In so doing, however, I had lost my grandfather and uncle. For now. I knew, or at the very least hoped, it would not be forever.

As I walked out of the house, I glanced around Langley Cross. Nothing had changed here. I had changed no one's circumstances but my own.

"Dr. Darrington!" a tiny voice called out to me as I took the reins of my horse. When I peered over the gate there stood a freckle-faced girl with pigtails along with another boy in a slightly tattered jacket, both of them with oranges in their palms.

"Amanda and John . . ." I said, remembering their names. They grinned up at me.

"Yes, sir." The boy nodded to me. "We saw you come and wanted to say hello!"

"Well, hello back, how are you both feeling?" I asked as I

brought my horse through the gates. "Have you been eating well?"

"Good! We eat lots of fruits now. Mama says you are the one that keeps sending them to us. Is it true?" the little girl questioned.

"Absolutely not! As a doctor I only prescribe the nastiest-tasting medicines," I lied, glaring down at them, and they narrowed their eyes at me.

"Are you sure it's not you?" the girl asked again.

"Very sure. Now run home for supper."

They sighed and nodded.

"Bye, Dr. Darrington!"

I watched them go off and a small smile crept onto my face. I wasn't able to help all of London, but at least I could assist them with this newfound wealth of mine. Taking the reins of my horse, I rode back to my father's London home . . . where I had waited out the rest of my bachelor days. It was not at all as big as the Du Bells' as he did not often stay in London. It was made of sand-colored stone and the outside was covered in hundreds of roses. The moment I stepped before the gates, the footmen and my younger brother ran toward me.

"Theo! Where have you been?" he exclaimed rather pensively. Apparently, I would be overrun by children today. "You promised we would go out riding."

"Forgive me! I forgot. Can we go later?" I replied, messing up his hair to his annoyance.

"There is no time later. You have a letter and soon you will be busy," he grumbled.

And just as I prepared to argue, other footmen came forward with a letter. Alexander exhaled deeply, his point proven.

"It shall take only a moment!" I assured him before lifting

it. Sure enough it was from Verity. Quickly I opened it as we entered.

September 19, 1813

Dear Sir Theodore Darrington,
I congratulate you on your knighthood, may it fit nicely with your bachelorhood! As you have displayed not a care for my welfare in the past days, I shall not care for yours.
Lady Verity Eagleman.

I tried not to laugh. You would have thought it had been months since we had spoken to each other and not merely three days.

"Would you like tea, sir?" the maid asked as I moved to the drawing room.

"I am fine," I replied.

"I want tea!" Alexander said, following me.

Taking a seat at the desk, I grabbed the paper and ink to begin my response.

"Who are you writing to so joyfully?" asked my father as he entered.

"Lady Verity," Alexander grumped as he sat upon the chair drinking his tea. "It is always Lady Verity he writes to. Now she's going to write back. And he will wait so he can write back and we will never go riding."

My father tried not to laugh as he glanced at me. "Would it not be much easier to go see her?"

"Yes, it would be. However, I have been forbidden." I sulked.

"Forbidden?"

"Yes, her family says she must focus on the wedding planning and I am a distraction." Why such plans took so long was beyond me. They had chosen to have the wedding here in London while everyone had gone back to their country estates for the fall so it would not be such a big society affair, and because I had hoped to convince my uncle and grandfather to attend.

"Surely there is not much to prepare, as the wedding is tomorrow," he said, moving to my brother. "There is no reason you cannot go see her now, should your brother allow you to miss today's ride."

I looked to Alexander and he shook his head no.

"We'll ride twice later, and I'll get you the cake you like."

He grinned and nodded.

And I was bolting to the doors.

Verity

Hearing giggling from behind me, I turned to see Aphrodite sitting with her book by the window.

"You are laughing at me!"

"You merely remind me of Hathor right now," she said, as if that was not harsh.

"In what way?"

"Your impatience and overreaction."

"He has barely been able to see me, for you all keep him away with threats of postponing the wedding. In public gatherings, we are not able to speak freely. All I have are letters," I replied.

"Yes and the poor footmen are fatigued by how often you both send these letters back and forth down the street. How many letters have you sent today? A dozen?" she teased.

"I have sent only one so far." I frowned. "I thought it fitting, as he has not replied to me for three days."

"Was that not because he was out of London to see a patient?"

I glared at her. "You are no better than Hathor, the way you pick on me now."

"What has Hathor done to pick on you?"

"Each time I see her now she calls me a liar and traitor."

"Liar and traitor? Why? Because you shall wed before her?"

"That is exactly the reason. She also blames Abena for cursing her."

She laughed outright and shook her head at me. "Hathor shall get over it in time. Now, is it not best for you to get some sleep? Tomorrow is a rather big day."

When she said it, my stomach began to quake once more.

Tomorrow I was to wed. I could hardly believe such a day had finally come. It had taken months but just as my godmother said, Theodore had been given a title, and thus she along with everyone else could no longer turn up their noses at him.

"Your Grace?" Eleanor said as she entered the room.

"Yes?" Aphrodite replied.

"Sir Theodore Darrington has arrived in hopes of speaking to Lady Verity."

I rose so quickly I nearly knocked over my chair.

"He is here?" I gasped out, quickly moving to adjust my clothing and hair. And Aphrodite giggled at my expense once more. I found myself feeling rather silly.

"Send him please," I said, trying to be calm.

"I think not," Aphrodite stated, drawing my attention. "I believe he was instructed to wait until the appointed hour—"

"Aphrodite!" I snapped.

"Very well, send him in."

I moved to see him standing at the door with a bouquet of red roses. He did not look to me but instead focused on Aphrodite, bowing his head to her.

"I know I come without appointment, Your Grace, but I received the most concerning letter and I thought the matter could only be addressed in person," he said seriously.

"I see. Well, whom do you wish to address?" Aphrodite questioned.

"My fiancée."

I tried not to smile so wide but I could not help it. My lips moved of their own accord. Aphrodite gave me a glance.

"Very well, I shall go see to my daughter for the moment. Verity, do please see to our guest."

I nodded to her, neither Theodore nor I moving until she stepped out of the room. When she was gone, the expression on Theodore's face changed, the look in his eyes taking my breath away.

"So, I have not cared for your welfare?" he asked, his eyebrow risen.

I sought to stand my ground but as he stepped closer and closer, each part of me began to tremble. I bit my lip, nodding as he placed the roses upon my writing desk. He stepped so close to me I could feel the warmth of him.

"Forgive me, my dear lady, I promise, from tomorrow you shall never be left alone again. I fear you may even grow tired of me," he whispered down to me.

"Is such a thing possible?" I asked in return.

"I do believe we will have a lifetime to find out," he said, reaching up and cupping my face.

"I am both nervous and excited."

"What unnerves you?" he leaned near to whisper. "We have already shared a bed, have we not? Or is that what excites you?"

There was that sensation once more. That desire to reach out and . . . return to bed. Ever since that night, we had been unable to find another moment to do so again. But the desire was always there when he and I stared into each other's eyes for long enough.

"You wish to seduce me, sir? I shall not allow it." I lifted my head up to look at him defiantly.

"Indefinitely or until tomorrow?"

I shrugged. "We shall see tomorrow."

He opened his mouth to speak when there was a cough at the door. We both turned to see my brother glaring at him intensely.

"Do you not have patients you ought to be seeing?" Evander snapped at him.

"No, Your Grace, I have cleared my schedule, as I am to be wed soon," Theodore replied.

"Soon, as in not currently. As such you are a bit close to my sister."

"Evander!" I called out to him as Theodore took a step away from me. "Must you still be difficult?"

"Yes, I must, and you ought not complain, as you have had it quite easy."

"Easy? In what capacity has anything been easy for us?" I frowned.

"Do you think knighthoods are so simply given and over mere months?" Evander scoffed as he took a seat, still glaring at Theodore. "Would you not agree, sir?"

"You do not have to agree with him," I said, quickly moving to touch his arm when once again Evander cleared his throat.

"I dare not anger His Grace . . . at least until tomorrow." Theodore snickered.

"Well, let that be our truce for the evening," Aphrodite said as she came in holding Emeline's hand. "At least until we have had supper?"

"I will not be able to avoid his company after tomorrow. Can I not be given a reprieve tonight?" Evander frowned.

"Think of it as a way to soften the blow," Theodore said to him, causing both of them to exchange glances. I looked to Aphrodite, pleading for her to help me. Why Evander had gotten more childish as this day approached was beyond me, and I had no method to stop him.

"Emeline, grab Papa's hand so we may go to supper," Aphrodite said, and the little girl rushed to Evander's arm, grabbing on tightly.

"Come, Papa, there is pie!" she exclaimed, causing the tenseness in his jaw to relax as she drew him away.

"Hurry, you two, before he finds another reason to storm in here," Aphrodite said to us.

"Thank you, Your Grace." Theodore smiled.

"You may call me Dite or Odite, Theodore, we are basically related now, whether my husband can stand it or not." She giggled before walking out the door.

I glanced to him and I saw that the look in his eyes was somewhat somber. "Theodore?"

"Hmm?"

"Is everything all right?"

"Yes. How could it not be?" he answered, but still I felt his expression was off.

"How did you fare with your grandfather and uncle? Shall they be in attendance tomorrow?" I had wished to meet them before but he had discouraged me from doing so. I did not push. I, more than anyone else, knew family was often . . . complicated.

"They refused," he replied softly. "I knew they would. It is a lot to take in for them. They believe I have abandoned them and they are not altogether wrong."

I reached for his hand. "You have not abandoned anyone, Theodore. Maybe in time, with persistence, they shall come to change their minds."

"I can only hope," he said, placing his hand over mine and offering me a smile. "In the meantime I will not allow it to dampen our occasion, for we have fought quite hard for this victory no matter what your brother says."

"Now you have the courage to speak against him." I rolled my eyes.

"I will not risk his temper till I am sure we are wed."

"Let us risk it just once more," I replied and leaned in closer to him.

He smiled, leaning in as well before kissing my lips, and all of me tingled once more. I was sure we would have stayed there if not for the sound of heavy footsteps. Quickly we separated.

"We shall continue . . . tomorrow," he replied, squeezing my hands tightly.

I nodded, too happy to speak as he led me out and toward the dining room.

Only when we were seated, eating and talking, did I notice for the first time: We were all happy. Evander picked on Theodore, Theodore did his best to defend himself while throwing light jabs back, only for Aphrodite and me to giggle at their silliness. Even Emeline happily hummed as she ate. I never thought . . . it could be us. That in this house, the place where my mother had passed, in this place where I was born without her, there would be so much joy.

I could not wait for this to be our forever.

Epilogue

Theodore

"NO!" The sound of her scream caused me to bolt up from bed. I was still not altogether used to it, seeing her suffer so terribly at night like this. Her bonnet falling off her head, her curls every which way as she twisted and bent into a ball, clinging to herself. Shifting in bed, I turned and wrapped my arms around her, hugging her gently.

"You are all right," I whispered into her ear. "My love, you are all right."

I said it over and over, holding on to her tighter and tighter, until she finally relaxed and her breathing evened. It was only a few moments until she was completely calm. I let go of her and sat up in the bed, reaching for where her bonnet had fallen. The last thing either she or I needed was for her to wake up mortified at the state of her hair. Though I feared, since the sun was just beginning to rise, there was little she could do to save it. However, just as I had reached for the headpiece, I heard her voice whisper to me.

"What are you doing?"

Withdrawing my hands, I glanced down at her, smiling. How could I not when she was the very first thing I saw every day now? "Your bonnet fell off. I wished to retrieve it."

Her hands went up to her hair and I shifted, allowing her to sit up in bed.

"Did I have a nightmare again?" She frowned, her shoulders falling. "I thought I was getting better."

"You are," I said, brushing a few curls from her face, though they bounced back intently. "You made it through the whole night and it has been a while since your last one."

She was still not pleased with herself. "I do not mean to keep disturbing you—"

"You are not disturbing me . . ."

"Theodore—"

"What have I told you to call me?"

She tilted her head to the side, giving me a look. "Theo—"

"That is not correct . . . *wife*."

"How long am I to simply address you as 'husband'?" She giggled, staring at me.

"For as long as we are married, and so forever." I grinned.

"It is cumbersome to say always. At least 'dearest'?"

"I have no problem with 'dearest,' it is you who cannot say 'dearest.'"

"I can say it!"

"Very well, go on." I nodded to her.

"Dearest."

"In a sentence."

She opened her mouth but looked away from me. "Dearest, will you—"

"To my face!"

"Theodore!"

"See!" I laughed.

"I can do it!" she proclaimed, once more turning to me, her eyes directly pairing with mine. She took a deep breath before speaking again. "Dearest, will you please . . . I cannot say it when you look at me like that!"

"How am I looking at you?"

"As though you wish to devour me."

I grinned. "That is how I am always looking at you. So, go on."

She glared and I waited. We went on and on with our staring competition before she spoke again. "*Dearest*, I am tempted to hit you."

"Very good, know I shall accept only 'my dearest,' 'husband,' or 'my love.'"

"How did we get on this topic?"

I shrugged, reaching over and pulling her closer to me. "I do not recall, my love, but let us not dwell on it, as we have more pressing matters to attend to."

"Such as— Theodore!" She gasped when I flipped her onto her back.

"'My dearest,' 'husband,' or 'my love,'" I repeated as I kissed her neck. "How many times am I meant to teach you this lesson?"

"I am unsure, as I am quite stubborn . . ." She giggled as I began to lift up her gown.

"Yes, I have noticed. No matter. I have a great deal of methods to explore."

"Is that so—" I silenced any further argument with my lips.

From now until my dying day, I would always change her screams of fear to pleasure. I would spend my life chasing away her nightmares, for she was my dream turned reality.

She was my most beloved wife, Lady Verity Darrington.

Acknowledgments

I wish I could say something more than thank you to all of the people who helped me create this book. Because without Natanya, Shauna, Mae, Jordan, Molly, Sarah, Taylor, Colleen, Rogena, my parents, my friends who feel like sisters, my actual brothers who honestly did very little but made me laugh once during this process, and, of course, all the fans who reached out to me, encouraged me, *Verity and the Forbidden Suitor* would not exist. They say it takes a village to raise a child. I believe it takes a village to do almost anything so I am truly grateful for the people around me.

I can't say more than thank you. I can only hope to never disappoint the faith you all have in me.

J. J. McAvoy has written numerous independently published novels that have been translated into six languages and are bestsellers in Turkey, Israel, and France. McAvoy's historical romance series featuring the Du Bells includes *Aphrodite and the Duke* and *Verity and the Forbidden Suitor*. She is active and delightful on social media.

jjmcavoy.com
Twitter: @JJMcAvoy
Instagram: @jjmcavoy